Dana Dances
on
Paper

Darcel Turner

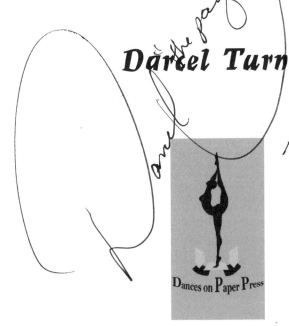

Dances on Paper Press

New York

Dances on Paper Press
P. O. Box 340734
Brooklyn, New York 11234
www.darcelturner.com
www.geocities.com/darcelturner

Turner, Darcel
Dana Dances on Paper
I. Fiction

ISBN: 0-9747347-0-5
Library of Congress Control Number: 2002115185

Cover Art: Marilynn Page
Photography: Lou Roole
Cover and text design: Jonathan Gullery

Note: Any means of actual living or non-living persons mentioned in this book are for the express use of entertainment, education, gratitude and artistic expression from the author.

Soft cover-$15.00 Hard cover-$23.00

Acknowledgments

Only God is the one my eyes are toward. I breathe only for you. My best friend, the most high, my heavenly, divine Mother and Father. Thank you for the piggyback rides.

Mommy you have taught me so much in your life. Your love, patience, artistry, dance and humor are memories I still feel and treasure. I thank you for showing me unconditional love and letting me know that I have always made you proud. May your soul rest in peace, Queen Defrager. I love you forever. Dad, Roosevelt Coleman, I thank God that you are still here for me and my family. I know your love is true, I love you. Donell Rudy Turner. I will always love you. Roosevelt and Rashika Coleman, I love you. Let's keep building.

Geneva "Nawnie" Turner, the backbone of the Turner family. You gave me femininity; strength, pure love and you have saved my life numerous times. You have healed me, supported me and molded me into being the special person you reaffirmed for thirty years. Your love keeps me afloat. Thank you for generously sharing your wisdom, your strength and your powerful love. Nawnie, I love you so much. God bless you.

Amani Fela Greene and Diani Eshe Greene, my beautiful children. You two bring joy to my life. Everyday, I'm falling deeper and deeper in love with you two. If it weren't for you, I would not be this happy. You are my greatest supporters, my best friends, my students and my teachers. Q: What would life be like without you? A: Complex. I love you eternally.

The father of my beautiful children: Talib, I thank you for your support. I love you, eternally.

Thank you DuEwa M. Frazier for everything and much success for Lit Noire Publishing.

Thank you Angeli R. Rasbury for your editorial services for D.D.O.P. Marilynn Page, God blessed your hands with designing beauty. Danny Simmons, thank you forever. Dr. Brenda M. Greene and Dr. Perry Greene, I love you and I thank you for being a positive example for the community. Thank you to the Turners, Swintons, Jestines, Colemans, Greenes, and Mooreheads.

Beautiful children: Cinnamon Turner, Master Sharleek & Sweet Essence, Marcel Coleman, Marlon and Marquis Moorehead, Kwesi and Nigel Phillips, Kamau Keller Hamilton, Rakim, Tyonka, Zyanna Washington, Divine's Damali, Kai Mullings, Tafari, Rasheed and Rasheeda, Jihad Wilder, Elijah, Chandani, Jihada Smith, Tony Cottrell Jr., Akosua's Awesiri. From St. Marks Avenue: Miles, Omar, Shihada, Harith, Jeffrey, Dorel Gopal, Miles Cordoza, Bilal and Princess Mayt, Christopher Tracey, Tyler Enrique Turner, Chuma, Chi-Chi and Kai Osse, Christian, Ariel & Brandon, Courtney, Sade, and Andre', Ahmair Cooper, Emmanuel, Ashley, Alyssa, and Sylvia's Jasmine. I love you.

Special thanks to Rodney Cochrane, thank you for everything. I love you.

Friends: Felicia Marie McLaughlin, Marsha "Milan" Gopal, Kendra Phillips Griffin, Nicole Creary, Karimu Hamilton, and Cheryl Long, Lynell Rennis, Prince Holman, Greg Stevenson. I love you.

Photographers: Howard T. Cash, you have a beautiful book, "Nudes and Romantic Poetry," Ptah Hotep, Jeannie Smith, Terrence Jennings, Lou Roole, thank you. Cey Adams, Ali, Radway McClaren, Kyle, James McFadden, Karen Tyson, Wadline "Stonnie" Cooper, Tahirihana, Osagyefo & Kassim, Jose' Santos (my first customer you believed in me), Jerome Wright, Erykah, Bazz, Sanchez Stanfield, Ascari, Rodney Joseph, jessica Care moore and Dante Smith. I love you so much Queen Sister James and I thank you for your support. Darmone and Sister Judith, thank you.

And thank you to the Johnson's Prepatory.

I dedicate this book to
Mommy, Amani & Diani

The beautiful ones (R.I.P.)

Dora Cain Robinson, Aunt Blaus, Defrager Turner, Ammar
Simmons, Dell (from 680), Marcus Coleman, Javotte Greene,
Meklit, Brenda; Sheila, Aaliyah Dana Haughton, "Miss Strong"
Marjorie Lops, Marilyn Monroe, Minnie Riperton,
Josephine Baker, Nina Simone & Fela Kuti.

Notes from the Author

I've been writing ever since I was eight-years-old. After a while writing became a part of me, like breathing. Growing up as a child, I was very shy and it didn't help that I was brought up around the mentality of "a child should been seen and not heard." Through this, I embraced writing, vented half of my frustrations in my journals and the other half into my dancing. When I was happy or upset, I wrote to keep myself sane and centered.

All throughout middle school and high school, teachers asked me, "Darcel what do you want to be when you grow up? Are you interested in enrolling in college?" I did not know what I wanted to be at the time. School became discouraging for me because all of my peers already knew what they wanted to be. Many wanted to be accountants, paralegals, doctors, nurses, engineers and architects. I would ask them why they chose those professions? Their response was, "Because that's where the money is."

Well, I observed and learned, early on in life, that money doesn't make a person happy, it only temporarily satisfies your wants and needs. That was when I sat down and really thought about what I wanted to be in my life. I needed to know what my purpose here on earth was. I didn't want to use up my valuable energy for the sake of "paper" - money. I wanted to work at something I loved doing and something that would keep me happy . After I consistently questioned the Creator in my journal entries asking, "Lord, what am I going to be in life? What am I here for? What is my purpose here?"

One day the answer whispered back and said, *Darcel, it's right there.*

"Where?" I looked around.

It's right there in your hand. You're purpose is in the pen and paper."

"Writing! All this time, it was right in my face. I am a writer!" I exclaimed.

It took me years to actually learn how to listen to my inner voice, again. Had I not asked for guidance, I probably would've been working a job that had nothing to do with me living out my purpose.

It took me a long while to complete this novel. Writing in first person was quite difficult because of it's limitations. I had to stay inside of Dana's mind, thoughts and feelings. It was good that I got a chance to write in third person through Dana, writing her first chapter, "Seeing Through the Wool." Throughout Dana's experiences she began to transcribe her life on paper, which is why I titled the book, "*Dana Dances On Paper*." One can look at the title in two ways, *Dana Dancing on Paper* (meaning money). Which is clearly understood in the later chapters but I prefer to use it in a much broader sense as Dana uses her *Dancing* energy to write *on Paper*. *Dana Dances on Paper* is a novel loosely based on my life and many of you will probably identify with Dana's journey and experiences. This novel is like a river: taking you on a journey, flowing over rocky roads (of the ghetto), clashing with the birth of hip hop, seeping and weeping through the crack drug eras, through Dana's trials & errors, and then dropping you down the Jamie waterfalls into the sea of self-discovery, self-recovery and self-love.

Dana Dances on Paper is written from the heart and soul, from my past and present experiences combined with my imagination. Writing this story was very therapeutic for me. There were some parts in the story that made me cry, laugh and fall in love again. What an experience it was to create DDOP! I encourage anybody who has something they love to do, to just do it! Do what you love. Don't listen to the "dream-slayers" or naysayers. They speak only out of fear. Fear is not healthy. Adrenaline is. Love yourself and once you build up the courage to do what you love to do, then that is when the beauty of life will find you.

Darcel "the page Turner"
Brooklyn, New York
2003

Contents

1
faith

That was it. That was the first time I felt we traveled together emotionally as a family. Mommy finally saw through the wool Daddy-James pulled over her eyes. It took six years for her to finally accept certain truths about him. Mommy told me and Donell, she was tired of him, his paranoia and his insecurity bullshit. When she finalized that she was ready to leave him for good, I couldn't help but have my stack of doubts. This wasn't the first time she left him. After a while, Mommy's running away started to lose its affect on Daddy-James. Then came the bits and pieces of respect Daddy-James lacked for her. Over time Daddy-James lost the healthy fear he once had for her. Mommy on the other hand gained toxic fear of Daddy-James to the point that she felt helpless when he whipped our asses. After the fourth run-away, Daddy-James felt it was unnecessary to call the cops because he knew that in a couple of days Mommy would return. Shit became monotonous after a while. The last time we all ran away from him, and returned, we found Daddy-James knocked out on the bed, the house smelling like reefer with Earth, Wind and Fire harmonizing in the background.

The more Mommy talked, the more I started to believe in her. Why did I believe Mommy this time around? Perhaps it was the lightness in her voice or that twinkle of light that beamed from out her eyes that made me give her the benefit 'without a doubt'. This time around, judging from the tones in her voice, I could tell she was centered in her deepest truth. She wasn't venting or popping junk about leaving him based on anger. I believe she seemed *pretty* clear this time around. The more she talked, the more truths spilled like tears from her eyes. She shared her feelings with us in our private sector, the bathroom. Canary yellow was painted on the walls with stamps of orange daisies on top. On top of the sink laid a row of rainbow colored seashells Mommy and I picked on the beach nearby. The faucet sang a high soprano pitch dripping a stream down the drain. A warped red bucket sat underneath the sink swallowing drops of hot water that leaked from the pipe. Donell and I stood still listening to Mommy whisper.

"The straw that broke the camel's back was looking at these six, big ass whelps on my baby's thighs. I can't take it no more." Daddy-James sneakers squeaked pass us. We all froze. After he passed, Mommy continued, "We gotta get outta this damned house. Look at us." Donell and I looked at each other. "We're losing our spirit. If we don't leave, shit, we're just as good as dead."

Sundays was the day of the week most of the people in the building enjoyed their free time. Some family's went fishing, others go and praise the Lord and the few like me and Donell, who loathed Sundays, had to be up at six-forty-five to do chores. Our rooms had to look immaculate or else Daddy-James would whip our asses. We never went to church unless we spent the weekends over his mother's, Pastor Grandma Jimmy. She was the only one who took me and Donell to church. Every chance we got to being away from Daddy-James was heaven.

I lost count of the times I looked over my room to make sure it was to Daddy-James's liking. All sixteen of my Barbie dolls sat with legs crossed on top of my windowsill to dry. I bathed and shampooed the eight black-curly haired dolls, the three long blonde-haired and the three shoulder-length red heads. There wasn't enough room to fit my two Ken dolls, so I sat them in the blue convertible. All of their outfits were hand-washed clean and laid on top of the radiator to dry. My Holly Hobby oven and my pink dishes and china teapots were all put away on top of the shelf. All of my markers, colored pencils, paint bottles and Crayola crayons were stacked neatly in rainbow order on top of my drawing table. My shirts, slips and pants were all ironed and folded in my dresser. All dresses and skirts had been pressed and hung in my closet. Shoes and sneakers, shined and cleaned, lined in the closet and all of my homework and textbooks were laid open across my bed, in *his* order. I quietly placed the empty bottle of Mr. Clean into the wastebasket, then sat on the edge of my bed and waited for the floor to dry. Once the floor dried to a soft shine finish, I tiptoed over to see if my Barbie dolls hair had dried. It was still damp so I tiptoed into Donell's room to see what he was up to. I noticed Daddy-James and Mommy were still knocked out in the bed. Donell was sweeping the inside of his closet. I went back to my room and swept the inside of my closet too. I looked at my Pacman watch. It was almost noon. Everybody on the block should be coming back from Sunday service and changing into their play clothes. I sat at my desktop where I practiced my artwork and waited. I did a little scribbling while listening to Daddy-James talk to Mommy. I listened to their every move. Hopefully they will tell me and Donell to eat breakfast and go outside.

I didn't want anyone to see me looking out the window so I stood on top of my chair and saw a few of my friends outside.

"Eh yo, Donell!" Shouted Michael wearing his shredded Yankee hat and dingy uniform. Donell went to ask Daddy-James and Mommy if he could go outside and play baseball. Donell had to disappoint his team. Michael and his teammates walked away, dragging their bats across the street to the park.

A few minutes later, I heard Charmane, Sherika, India, and Sherice simultaneously sing my name from under my first floor window. Charmane and Sherika wore the same colors. They were halfway over the fence. India chewed gum like a cow and drew planets in the dirt. Sherice's mousy voice kept asking me what time was I coming out because everybody was ready to play freeze tag and steal the bacon. I knew if Donell couldn't go out, then I had no chance.

The powerful sun beamed through my pink curtains and high-lighted my lavender walls. I saw Mommy walking toward the kitchen listening to Daddy-James talk her ears to deaf. Then he asked her for the third time if she heard him.

"Yes Boobie, I heard you." She said in a patient, annoying tone.

I took my chances again and dashed into Donell's room. The sun shone directly into Donell's water blue room. Both of his shades were pulled to the top. I noticed his aloe plant had grown three inches higher from the day before yesterday. His room felt safe for some reason. I spun around in his room. It looked immaculate. He had three more shirts to fold and he would be finished. All of his GI-Joe men stood side by side in his shoe box ready for attack. Some of his match box cars were lined in traffic on top of his two windowsills, the remainders were all parked against his wall. His collection of two hundred and seventy Marvel Comic books was wrapped in plastic and stacked on top of the shelves that Mommy sawed and mounted. All four of his transit maps covered one whole section of his wall. Three thousand and four baseball cards were stocked proudly on top of his shelf.

"Donell," I whispered. He looked up from sweeping the debris in the dustpan. "Could you please take a look at my room before Daddy-James does?"

"You're finished?"

"I don't know. Please, help me out and check it for me. I don't want to get in trouble if I didn't do it right."

"C'mon Dana, you should know how your room's supposed to look."

"Please, Donell. Could you just show me one last time?"

"Hold on." He swept the rest of the dust mixed with torn apart soldier abdomens and plastic cars without wheels, onto the dustpan and poured it into the waste basket. "Ok, come on."

Daddy-James and Mommy were still talking in the kitchen about how the dudes on the basketball courts played. It smelled like they were cooking turkey bacon and pancakes. Donell and I scurried into my room and I closed the door. I watched my big brother look around my room. He pointed to the plastic bag of toys behind the radiator on the floor.

"It looks good in here. Put this under here." I put the bag under my bed. "What's this?" He refolded the blanket and tucked my sheets in between the mattress.

"Dana, if Daddy-James see this paint still on the floor, he's gonna give you a beating."

"Help me get it up." I was about to cry.

"Dana," he moaned, "I gotta hurry up and finish putting my shirts away before Daddy- James come and whip *my* ass. Just go in the kitchen and get a knife so you could scrape it up."

"No! I'm scared. I can't go in the kitchen."

"Why, Dana? You're being ridiculous, just go Da..." We heard sneakers squeak. I prayed, 'Please, God let him make a detour to the bathroom.' The light in me and Donell's eyes collided and caused an explosion of adrenaline mixed with fright. The squeak of his sneakers stopped short at Donell's room.

Daddy-James called out, "Donell!" We jumped.

"Yes!" He hurried out of my room.

"Boy! Stay in here until your room is finished. Got the nerve to ask me if you could go outside and play baseball! Matter of fact let me see your homework."

I heard his book bag zipper open and close and then pages flipped.

"Number one, your homework is supposed to be laid out on your bed." He opened my door and looked at my bed. Then he went back to my brother,

"You was just in Dana's room. You saw her homework laid out on her bed, didn't you? Now why didn't it strike a cord in your dome to lay your homework out too?"

Donell couldn't answer that difficult question.

"Boy, speak up! You want me to make you speak up?"

"No."

"Uhha. Now tell me why didn't you have your homework out on your bed, but had enough audacity to ask me if you could go outside?" As soon as Donell was about to explain, I heard Daddy-James smack Donell. And that was only the beginning. The buckle of Daddy-James belt jingled. Donell screamed in pain. Every scream he cried out, I cried too. My body shook up and down like I was electrocuted. I stood in the corner at the end of my room. I heard mumbled voices so I stepped back on top of the chair and saw everybody sitting on benches. Some were leaning against fences looking up at Donell's open window. Dudes covered their mouths with fists laughing at Donell's screams. I could've fainted from hunger and nervousness.

The doorknob turned and his beady eyes pierced through his brown-tinted, thick glasses. Whites dotted the sides of his eyes and the corners of his dry lips. Half of his head of thick braids were taken out. His head look like a half-blown away Dandelion. Those small, intense eyes scanned my room. Sweat was gliding down his sideburns. I stood half way in the closet like a statue.

He nodded his head calmly, "Okay," he said approvingly. "Let me see your closet."

I leaped out of the way of his hands. He frowned.

"How the fuck! The hook is supposed to be inward not outward. In a uniform fashion! Each hanger should be three-fingers apart. Three fingers apart! What are you backwards?" I shook my head intensely and backed away from him. He followed me and demanded I put my shoulders down.

"See your ass don't listen neither. You want an ass whipping like I just gave your brother?" I frantically shook my head no. His shark grip devoured the back of my neck and pushed me into Donell's room.

"Look at Donell's closet. How many times have I told you to hang your clothes inward?!" I couldn't remember. Donell was sitting on his bed with his underwear on. His eyes were just like a rabbit's. Our eyes connected and Daddy-James broke it.

"Huh? How many times, Dana? Take off all your clothes. I'll be right back, you wait till I get back for your ass whippin'!"

I stripped away each garment. I quickly ran over to my bed and pulled out my diary from between my mattress.

May 23, 1982/ Sunday
Dear Diary,
This letter is for you God. God, please don't let Daddy-James beat me.
Please. Please. If you don't let him beat me, I will always believe in you
but if you let him beat me, I will never believe you exist, I will never
believe in you. I won't say prayers, I won't say grace, I will never believe
in you.

Dana Strong

I heard the jingle of his buckle. That alone cut my faith in half. Daddy-James and Mommy were talking about going to the store or something. I must've stood in the middle of the floor shaking my behind off like a vibrator. The front door slammed and seconds later my doorknob turned. I backed up against the wall.

"Dana, what are you doing standing there naked?"

My voice was hoarse, "Daddy-James told me he was going to give me a beating."

"For what?" She picked my folded clothes off my bed and told me to get dressed.

"Go and eat. There's some French toast and turkey bacon on the table. When you're finished, wash your plate and come in the bathroom." I went into the kitchen and saw Donell standing over the sink washing out his fork. My heart broke into painful pieces when I saw what looked like giant, burgundy veins on the back of his thighs. I tapped him on the shoulder and said,

"Donell, I'm sorry." He nodded his head to me and told me he loved me too. I said a long grace to God because now I am a believer. My faith in God will never cease, only increase. That was a true miracle. A Sunday miracle. I couldn't finish my cold French toast, I was too shaken up to eat.

After I washed out my plate, I went to the bathroom where I found Mommy rubbing cocoa butter on Donell's whelps. It looked bad. She repeatedly said that this was unnecessary. I wasn't physically scarred like Donell but very much on the inside. I was still shaken up and Mommy looked so sad. She stared at the rainbow-assorted seashells on top of the sink.

"I'm tired of this shit. This is gonna be the last time I'm ever going to be rubbing cocoa butter on my children." She focused on Donell's brown and red legs. "The straw that broke the camel's back was looking at these six, big ass whelps on my baby's thighs. I can't take it no more." The front door slammed. Daddy-James sneakers squeaked pass us. We all froze. After he passed, Mommy continued, "We gotta get outta this damned house. Look at us." Donell and I looked at each other. "We're losing our spirit. If we don't leave, shit, we're just as good as dead."

"Boobie? I'm back." He shouted.

She cracked the door and yelled back, "Okay, Boobie. I'll be out. Could you start making the dinner?"

"Okay, and then we can do *that*, right?" He hinted to her.

"Yeah." She closed the door and ran the tub water so that he wouldn't hear our conversation. She sprinkled some chamomile flowers in the tub water.

"Don't worry, Mommy has a plan for us. Y'all don't deserve to go through this. Mommy love y'all. I'm so sorry that I put us through this." She reached to hug us and we hugged her back.

Donell and I stood in the bathroom and waited for Mommy to finish rubbing the cocoa butter on his belt marks. I didn't want to go outside nor show my face to anybody but the pillow. I looked forward to sleeping activity. I just wanted to sleep this hell away.

Mommy whispered something to us in confidence. If only my jaws could stop chattering and gushing water would be quiet, I wouldn't have to strain my ears to hear what she was telling us.

Donell asked, "Are you planning to leave Daddy-James again? For good?" She nodded.

"Where will we be going?"

"We might have to stay at Nawnie's house for a little while until I get myself together."

She closed the cocoa butter jar and pulled us toward her with Donell on her right lap and me on her left lap. We all hugged and kissed. We told her we loved her too.

"Listen y'all. I know I got good kids. Can't nobody tell me I don't. All this beatin' has gotsta stop. Look at Dana." Nothing on Donell's stiffen body moved except for his red eyes.

"My baby is all shaken up. I can't let him keep doing this to us. We're going to my mother's. Y'all don't say nothin' to nobody about this. Y'all hear me?"

"Yes, Mommy." We whispered.

"I'm not saying what day we're leaving, but when the day come, I want y'all to be ready. C'mon. Give me your homeworks. Donell go in your room and Dana you get in the tub. Dinner is almost ready." Donell sorely eased off of her lap and we gave Mommy our homework. He closed his room door and Mommy came into the bathroom with me.

The moment my teeth paused on chatter, I asked, "Mommy, how long are we going to be staying over at Nawnie's house?"

"I don't know. 'Till I get myself together, find a job and us an apartment. We'll talk about that later okay?"

She turned the water off and I stripped off my clothes and sat in the tub. The sweet, scent of chamomile relaxed me. Mommy bent down on the floor and we hugged. When she opened the door, the hallway smelled like he was cooking green peppers and steak. After I dressed myself in my pajamas, I hit the pillow. Didn't want Daddy-James to see my face for it might remind him of giving me that ass whipping.

As I lay on my bed I stared at the window listening to the older kids talk, rap and laugh. The sky had turned royal blue and the giant beanstalk swayed randomly with the wind. A ray of blue light coming from the hallway flashed in my eye and woke me. The silhouette was Mommy. She came in and sat on my bed and caressed my hairline. We hugged for a long time and I didn't want her to let me go.

"I promise, I will never put you and Donell through this again."

"Mommy, I miss Nawnie." Mommy blinked her long lashes fast.

"I miss her too." She continued. "It's been weeks since we've spoken to her."

"Dana, Mommy's saving up money so we could find another place to stay, God willing."

"God willing." I repeated.

"Baby, did you say your prayers?" Deeply and sincerely, we prayed together. In my own mind, I prayed to God and asked that he put Daddy-James to death in his own sweet way (no disrespect).

I asked Mommy to lie down with me. She held me in her arms. Every time my body trembled, she rubbed my back. The front door slammed and it startled us. Mommy jumped up and sat up. Sneakers squeaked toward the kitchen. The clicking of our new stove indicated to me that he had to light his cigarette. Mommy forced her tired eyes open. She sat up. The devil walked toward my bedroom. I pretended

I was asleep. He called Mommy into the bathroom. I tightened my grip on her finger. After they closed and locked the bathroom door, I stared at the ceiling and thought about our future.

As happy as I was to hear the news about us leaving "the devil" Daddy-James, in the same breath, I thought about the nine people already living in Nawnie's four bedroom apartment. Where are we going to sleep? I'll be happy to be closer to my cousins and family but what about my privacy? Hey, for my sanity, anywhere is better than here.

2
the next level

DANA. *The softest voice called on me.*
"Hmm?"
CHANGE IS HERE.
"It is?"
YES AND DEATH IS SURE TO FOLLOW.
"I'm scared."
I WILL NEVER LEAVE YOUR SIDE. I WILL GUIDE YOU, AS LONG AS YOU DO NOT STRAY FROM ME.
"Yes, Father. When will death come?"
LESS THAN SEVEN YEARS.
"Hmm."
WAKE UP MY LOVE. KNOW AND BELIEVE THAT YOU WILL BE WELL TAKEN CARE OF. BECAUSE I HAVE CHOSEN YOU.... DO NOT TAKE HUMAN CONTACT FOR GRANTED. HUG HUMANS AS MUCH AS POSSIBLE, FOR THERE WILL COME A TIME WHEN TECHNOLOGY WILL BE THE MIDDLEMAN.
"You mean like robots?"
SOMEWHAT. CLOSER TO A STAR TREK'S REALITY.
"Cool!"
DANA, THE WORD IS COLD. COLDNESS. MAN WILL LOSE TOUCH WITH THE HUMAN FORCE. HUMAN CONTACT WILL LOSE ITS IMPORTANCE. COMPUTERS, WALKIE TALKIES, REMOTE TELEPHONES...
"Remote telephones?"
YES... THERE WILL BE NO BOUNDARIES, NO TIME TO MEDITATE ON MANMADE INVENTIONS. THERE WILL BE NO RESPECT FOR THE LAWS OF THE LAND. OUR PEOPLE WILL WALK AROUND DELUSIONAL. KEEP ME CLOSE TO YOU AND YOU WILL NOT LOSE YOUR WAY, WAY ,WAY. WAAAAAAKKE.
"Up, Dana."

"Hmm?"

"Good morning, it's time to get up, Baby." Mommy greeted me with her hair standing straight up on top of her head.

"Good morning, Mommy. I had a weird but beautiful dream." My voice cracked bad. I stretched.

"About what?"

"I don't remember. All I know is that I was scared of dying but God told me not to worry and that no matter what, I will be alright in His care."

"That was a beautiful dream, baby." She rubbed my back. "But what were you dying from?"

"I don't remember. I don't even know if it was me who was dying. Maybe it was someone close to me. All I remember was I got scared."

"Well, I'm glad it turned out positive. I want you to go to the bathroom and then come in Donell's room. I wanna talk to y'all about something."

I stretched again and ran to pee.

"Dana." Mommy called me softly. She didn't want to wake Daddy-James.

I stepped into Donell's room. She was standing over Donell picking his hair. He was fully dressed. Everything looked nice except for his pants. They were way too baggy but that's how he liked them. He said that wearing tight corduroys were for punks. I beg to differ.

"I was just asking Donell was he ready for this."

"Ready for what?" I asked.

I looked at Donell and he managed to raise his eyebrows to show me his excitement.

"We're leavin' Daddy-James."

"Today?"

Donell and Mommy shook their heads. Mommy looked at the both of us.

"Y'all remember when I told y'all there's gonna come a time when we'll have to leave him, right? Remember what I told y'all in the bathroom a couple of weeks ago?"

"Yup," we simultaneously said.

"Well, today is the day. Your mother can't take it no more. I'm sick n' tired of his abuse so it's time for us to move on. Again, I'm sorry okay for letting this go on for so long. I just thought things would get better once he got himself a job."

We found it difficult to tell Mommy that it was okay. 'Cause it wasn't okay. Getting whipped damn near everyday was not okay. Mommy should've left him after the second time he started beating on us for stupid, irrelevant reasons.

"Are we still going to Nawnie's house, Mommy?" I asked.

"Yeah." She confirmed. Mommy removed some lint from Donell's hair. I couldn't stop smiling. Neither could Donell.

"Now listen. Do y'all still wanna go to school today or go straight to Nawnie's house?"

Donell said, "We could go straight...."

"Noooo! I have to say good-bye to Charmane and Sherika."

Donell backflipped, "Yeah, I wanna see Michael and Anthony and Joe before we leave."

"Okay, so y'all leave school after second period. Don't tell nobody we're leaving, just say we're going on a vacation. Donell, you remember how to get to Nawnie's house, right?"

"Yes. Take the A train to Broadway Nassau, go upstairs to Fulton Street, take the 5 or the 2 to Jackson Avenue, then get off."

"That's right. My baby's smart." Mommy smiled. "I want y'all to stay close to each other and hold each other's hand. Okay? I'll meet y'all at Nawnie's house this afternoon."

"Mommy," I asked, "does Daddy-James know about this?"

She whispered strong. "Dana, what do you think?" Donell tried to hold in his laugh but couldn't. Mommy turned around and looked at him and he busted out laughing.

"Donell, put this in your pocket." He stuffed the $5 bill into his beige corduroy pockets.

"I want you to buy two tokens with it. Whatever change is left over is for emergencies. If y'all get hungry, y'all can buy something with it, but try to hold on to something just in case if you have to make a phone call."

Donell and I struggled to keep a straight face. I couldn't stop visualizing the Whatchumacallit candy and super bubbles and Linden chocolate chip cookies we were going to buy.

"Now listen," Mommy said, "all of your clothes n' stuff is already packed up in bags. Dana, your clothes are hanging up behind the bathroom door. Go and wash up."

I left while Mommy was still talking to Donell. I stood outside the door for a minute.

"This is a big responsibility that I'm trustin' you with, Donell. I want you to watch and protect your sister and yourself. Don't talk to no…"

The water gushing out from the faucet in the bathroom, drowned Mommy's rules. I stood on my tippy-toes to look myself in the mirror for the last time in this house (of horror).

"Thank you, God, for answering my prayers. Thank you for letting us leave him finally. Thank you. Amen." I smiled a big one at myself.

Donell and I always held hands when we walked to school.

"Dana, we're doin' it!"

"I didn't think it would happen this fast."

"I know." We both looked both ways before crossing the street.

"Let's go buy some candy." I said.

"After second period."

"Ahh, man! Why not now?"

"'Cause Mommy said we have to leave school after second period. Patience, sis patience. Wait for me at the gym's exit door and then we'll go to the store."

In class I did a lot of scribbling, sketching and bullcrapping in Mrs. Goldstein's Social Studies class. Today, I was the class clown. I made everybody turn heads and laugh at me or my jokes, whichever, I didn't care. I sat and leaned on the two legs of my wooden chair and then balanced myself on the one leg. Mrs. Goldstein shouted, "Dana, sit properly!"

Out of the two years I've seen Shane, I never thought he was cute up 'til today. I had the courage to tell him just that. My best friend Charmane sat in the front. She always sat in the front. It helped her to stay focused. Charmane is a good girl. I looked at my watch. It was 9:26. Class will be over in four minutes. I began to write Charmane a letter, when Mrs. Goldstein walked past my desk to the boys snapping on each other.

September 16, 1982

Dear Charmane,
I can't tell nobody else, only you and Sherika. I'm moving today. My
mother, brother and I are moving to the Bronx. I'm going to miss y'all.
When your phone gets turned back on, give your number to Sherika. I
already got Sherika's number. I'm going to miss you, Charmane.

Your best friend,
Dana

"Trina." She didn't turn her big head around. I whispered louder, "Trina." She turned around and Mrs. Goldstein looked up from her text. I played it off. "What page are we on?" Mrs. Goldstein annoyingly said, "The page is 41, Dana."

"Oh, okay. Thank you, Mrs. Goldstein." She continued to read about the Spaniards conquering the Aztec Indians' civilization.

"Trina," I whispered again, "please pass this to Charmane."

My note passed from hand to hand until it arrived on Charmane's lap.

I liked the way Charmane's hair looked. It was in a soft, puffy mushroom style with all of her baby hair laying all around her small hairline. Charmane's mother doesn't believe in using the hot comb on her hair. She puts grease in it and sets her hair in rollers. Charmane got that good hair because of her mother being half-black and half Cherokee Indian.

I sat up and took a long look at everybody's face because I may never see them again. I looked at Sherika joking with Parish as usual. I looked at Parish wearing his plaid shirt soaked with heavy perspiration under his arms. I looked at Desmond and his peasy head and ashy elbows, Melinda with her stuttering self and beautiful teeth, Mrs. Goldstein's reading glasses and burgundy lipstick, the two quiet ones (Latasha -n- Jermaine), Desiree the witch, Carol and April the troublemakers, Sheila, the bully; the one who never forgets at the end of the day that she's going to "beat you up", Nancy Colon, the tattletaler, and Elizabeth, the Mona Lisa-pancake face.

Then I looked at Charmane and her eyes had tears in them. She put her head on the desk. My note was passed down to Shane. He handed me the note along with a wink of an eye.

Dear Dana,

What!!! So fast? I'm going to miss you too. Here's my address, so we can write each other. I'm sad. I love you.

Charmane Cute
454 Beach Channel Drive #5B
Far Rockaway, N.Y. 11693

Your best friend,
Charmane Cute
P.S. Tell me why you're moving after class.

After the bell rang, me and Charmane met up in the girls' bathroom.
"Wait a minute, where did Sherika go?" I asked.
"She's still talking to Mrs. Goldstein about her grade. So Dana, why are you leavin'?"
"You don't remember? My stepfather beats the shit out of us."
"Oh." She frowned. "That's right. You are so lucky. I wish my mother had your mother's courage."
"I'm sorry, Charmane, I wish she did too. I wish I could take you with us."
"Dana, we have to write each other. Okay?"
"Okay."
"I'm running late for Mr. Schwartz's class."
"I hate his class," I said.
"Lucky you." She embraced me and ran off.
"Bye, Charmane!"
"Bye, Dana!"

It was sunny outside. The sun's warmth brought balance to the coldness. Yellow, red and brown leaves were all over the place. Donell and I dived in the gigantic pile on the side of the schoolyard and pretended we were swimming.
"Let's race!" He challenged me, "on your mark, get set, go!" We raced to Beach 60th train station and didn't look back at J.H.S 198. Whatever we were running to couldn't be worse than what we were running from. We fled. Donell and I were the fastest runners on the block. But now we have to pass down the crown to Che' and Lisa. We relay-raced up to the candy truck and bought two bags of potato chips, one Linden chocolate chip cookies and one Whatchumacallit candy

bar and stuffed them into our book bags. We raced upstairs. Donell won. (That's only because he's taller than me). We slowed down the pace before reaching the token booth. A serious, calm face made me look older and standing on my tippy toes made me look taller. The clerk looked at us with suspicion because we were under age to be riding the train by ourselves. She hesitantly gave us our tokens. *I can't believe she gave us the tokens.* Pushing through the turnstile felt great. Donell and I held our heads high, when we saw the expressions on the adults faces. I felt the respect. It felt wonderful to receive recognition from people when we were accustomed to "going under" the turnstile.

Donell and I held hands again as we walked the long Straiton Avenue platform.

"See, you couldn't tell me I didn't know what I was doing when I was studying those subway maps."

"Boy, oh boy." I sighed. "I didn't think we were going to leave him this soon."

"Mommy was dead serious, man. I'll never forget what Mommy told me. She said, 'Always be prepared for the best and the worst.'"

We boarded the A train and sat down. We pulled out our candies, composition books and pencils from our book bags, grubbed and started sketching. Adults were watching me and Donell's pieces. Some people smiled and told us they were nice drawings. Donell likes to draw cartoon figures. I like to draw realistic faces. He drew Heath Cliff fighting Thor and The Thing. I drew faces of passengers sitting on the train. We didn't speak to any strangers and tried not to look at the panhandlers. Throughout the ride in Manhattan, we sang our school's songs. I changed up songs and sang a tune Nawnie enjoyed singing to me ever since I was in nursery:

"I'm Miss Special, I'm Miss Special
If you look, you will see
Someone very special, someone very special
Yes, it's me, yes it's me."

Donell always tried to out-sing me. He wasn't confusing nobody over here.

"Don't... push... me, cause... I'm... close to the...edge."

"Donell! Donell! Stop it. People are starting to stare at us."

"So? *I'm try-yin not to lose my head.*"

"Well, I'm saying good-bye to those Sunday beatings, washing all those dishes." I raised my head from the notebook and looked at my brother.

"Yeah. And no more homework checks, no more Daddy-James borrowing our allowance money and not paying us back."

I hit my head against the train window, remembering something. "I forgot my diary!"

"Mommy'll bring it."

"She doesn't know where it is. It's between the mattresses."

"So call her at work and tell her where it is."

"Hell no!"

"C'mon, Dana, you really think Mommy would read your diary?"

"I don't know."

"You have to trust in Mommy. She's trusting in us."

"Trusting in us with what?"

"With this! We're takin' the train all by ourselves to Nawnie's house."

"Yeah. But dag if she reads it, she'll put me on punishment for the rest of my life."

"No she won't and she ain't gonna read your little diary. Just tell Mommy where it is."

On the walk to Nawnie's building, we passed the Spanish bakery, the Senior Citizen's center, four tenement apartments, and a few burned down empty lots. We stepped over newspapers and broken pieces of glass broken from bottles, held hands as we crossed the street and hopped over dog do-do. We passed stray alley cats meowing in heat, filthy garage dogs barking at cars and Mr. Lopez throwing bread to the pigeons. His hair has gotten whiter. I noticed on the side of an abandoned building facing Nawnie's building was a poem written in graffiti style:

The Bronx is the place to be.
The land of the creatively free.
The boro of lovers practicing lovemaking
In abandon buildings, in the staircase, or on top of roofs
Graffiti's popularity will be stained on the backs of buildings and on the
waists of trains.

A few friends we hadn't since last summer, were in the hallway, looking fly as ever. In the Bronx, style and growth are rapid!

Queens was sterile and too quiet for me. Although I will miss my friends Charmane and Sherika, I know I am going to enjoy this whole new world over here in the boogie down Bronx! Where it is live! Where the girls jump double-dutch faster, they act freer and sexier too. The Bronx, where the real creativity lives, like the graffiti! It surprised me to see the girlfriends I remember playing hopscotch with, doing cheers with, or walking the monkey bars with last summer are now wearing tan and black sheepskins, like they are grown already. Little Linaya, Rose and Olympia used to stamp their feet into tin soda cans and walk around in them, pretending the soda cans were high-heel shoes. Well, now they're wearing high-heel shoes with Lee jeans.

The time was a quarter to twelve. Donell and I made a detour to Gompers school. We sat on the school's playground and observed the Bronx's kids. Some were wearing their Lee jeans high water style with tube socks and a funky pair of Adidas. Others wore the navy suede Pumas with Jordache jeans and short, maroon leather jackets. What made the Bronx so def is the Playboy sweatshirts and the funky Kangols everyone was rockin'. Some girls were dressed like Madonna with the big bow in their hair, twelve black, neon orange and yellow rubber bracelets around their wrists. There was a crew of seniors who brought their boom-boom boxes in the yard and played freestyle and hip-hop music until the assistant principal told them to turn it off.

A lot of Black and some Spanish girls were sporting big gold Pisces earrings and hair extensions. Around their necks herring bone and gold rope chains and on their fingers were two and four-finger gold-nugget rings. It was a surprise to see the twins; Shana and Wanda. They were fraternal twins. If Wanda's head weren't so wide and Shana's head weren't so square, they would look identical. We walked over to them. I tapped Shana on the shoulder and her crew turned around. Shana and Wanda's eyes widen at us.

"Oh my God! Dana and Donell what's up?" Their smiles were amazingly identical. I noticed Wanda checking Donell out. "What cha'll doin' here?" Asked Wanda.

Donell said, "Chillin'. We're at 815."

"Word?" We nodded. "This is Coco and Sahidah." They waved at us. I reached to shake their hand. Sahidah put her blow pop back in her mouth and shook my hand. Her ponytail held four-flavored blow pops in them. Two green apples, one cherry, and a grape.

"She's acts all proper." Wanda laughed. I observed the twins. They didn't rock their nappy ponytails any more. They adopted mushroom hairstyles with the big cabanger earrings. Their mushrooms looked very different from Charmane's. They relaxed their hair. It was all bouncy and shiny like those Dark 'n Lovely models. Their hair laid and rested on their necks and over their shoulders. They told me they get their "Wash 'n Set" at their auntie Thelma's salon in Harlem. It was refreshing to see they were still cool and not conceited. They informed Donell and I about Chucky's Poolroom on the corner of 151 Street. They said you had to be 18 and over. Shana said she had a hook-up with getting us fake ID's. Shana said,

"Trust me, Chucky's is the place to be. All the fly-guys and fly-girls, MC's, D.J's and breakers be partying up in there. It's fun y'all. Come on Friday's."

"Friday's are the freshest!" Smiled Sahidah with red teeth. The bell rang and the teachers started gathering their students. As Shana walked away, she repeated, "Whenever y'all want to get that hook-up, let me know."

As Donell and I walked out the schoolyard, I asked him is he going to get a fake ID, he said he wasn't interested. Neither was I. I'm not that eager to turn 18 or to fake 18 to find out what's happening in Chucky's Poolroom. I'm just happy to be able to be myself for once. I'm safe and I'm here with my family and away from that monster, Daddy-James.

3
overexcitement drains

Today is October the thirtieth and I'm tired from a long day's work. When I say work, I mean school. It's been a little over a month we've been living in the Bronx. I'm proud of Mommy for staying away from James this long, I just hope we can hurry up outta here. I wonder what is Charmane and Sherika up to. I wrote them two letters already and they have not corresponded. I also wrote Michael Jackson a three-page letter. Mommy told me not to have any expectations, that way I won't get my feelings hurt. Easier said than done.

Today in school, everybody in my class was acting careless and crazy 'cause tomorrow's Halloween. Tight security didn't even prevent the Blacks from bombing the 'Ricans with eggs and the 'Ricans didn't stop bombing back in the cafeteria. After lunch period, our teacher Mr. Cruz had us all calm down to watch a movie called "West Side Story," a beautiful musical drama. My close friend Sahidah could not stop talking about the love scenes in the movie on the walk home. It reminded her of what she and D.J. do during lunch period. Only difference is, they have taken it a little further. Every time she tells me of their sex episodes, I find it so hard to believe she can really get down like that. Not me, I'm too scared.

Sahidah's body is developed like a woman's. Her hips are shaped like kissing parentheses. Maybe she was developed like a woman because she got her period early. She could even fit into a woman's size bra. She proudly revealed to me that she was a size 36D! I'm nowhere near that, not even close. I'm only in training. And the guys in school are always talking about how much ass she carry. Why must they always lust at a girl's body? What about what's in her head or her personality or her spirit? I don't understand these Bronx guys. I don't understand how Sahidah does it either. How can she not notice or not even look at a man but still capture him? Get their mouths hanging wide open. It can't be just her body. It has to be something more than just her body. It's ridiculous how I can't bring Sahidah home without my cousins and my brother losing their power over her. I don't know why. I mean Sahidah is alright, but she ain't no Vanessa Williams. Her hair is never done but still guys chase her. Maybe guys just don't notice big things like that. She could even run the same clothes for three days straight and still hook a guy. No matter how pressed my clothes are, how clean I am or how neat my hair is, the guys I want to notice me never do. I'm always attracting the geeky ones. It's okay, 'cause one day I'm going to grow up and fill out and be as beautiful as ever and as strong as a lioness and I will surpass all these guys who can't see me now.

My school is having a talent show next month. I'm going to dance off of two songs; one is Whitney Houston's "How Will I Know?" and the other is Janet Jackson's "What Have You Done for Me Lately?" I would do "Billie Jean" but Sherman got that. He's a better Michael Jackson impersonator than I am. At rehearsals, every body caught the vapors after Sherman freaked the Michael Jackson Motown 25 move. I was inspired to write a secret poem about him. I shared it with my girl, Sahidah. :

Sherman.

Whenever I say or hear your name, I smile.
Milky caramel skin,
Probably feels softer than getting 8 paraffins
smooth like the texture of the back of a Hershey bar
Thick, shiny, black baby hairs,
You're brilliant like a north star.
Teeth with a slight overbite, confident in ev'ry way
Especially when you freak Michael's moves,
Make me wanna sing "Say, say, say".
Smells so fresh, like fresh curl activator mixed
with baby powder.
Sherman...Sherman...I wanna call out your name louder.

After reading it, she laughed and said she really liked it. She excitedly wanted me and Sherman to go out with each other so that we could all double date. I told her to be patient and he'll come. At the end of the day, Sahidah met up with me and we walked home as usual. She handed me back my poem that I forgot to take back from her and confessed that she showed it to Sherman and his reaction wasn't very positive. I screamed on her for exposing my business and bringing me bad news. He told her 'I wasn't his type and I was too nice of a girl for him.

"Why'd you have to go back and show him my poem, Sah?"

" 'Cause Dana, I thought it was nice and I thought he'd like it."

"I confided in you, Sah. Now he's thinking I'm on his shit. He's going to be telling his friends that I'm sweatin' him."

"No, he won't. I'm sorry but I couldn't take it Dana. I couldn't take seeing you run around being Sherman's secret admirer. You're bigger than that."

"So what, that's your opinion. You shouldn't have done that, man." She sucked her teeth,

"Well, I felt like if you like somebody, take the risk and tell them. Don't be a punk about it and hide behind a smokescreen."

"Ain't nobody being a punk or hidin', Sah. I'm angry at the fact that you disrespected my wishes. You out of all people."

"Well damn, Dana! You blowin' up like it's the fuckin' end of the world."

"It's my face I'm tryin' to save dummy. You put me out there prematurely!"

Sahidah looked up at the sky, "Okay, I don't know what she's talking about." She said in a matter-of-fact tone. We caught the attention of passersby. I didn't care who was looking, what I had to say was more important than what others were probably thinking.

"No, but seriously, Dana, you can't be goin' around likin' Sherman wastin' time while homeboy don't have the slightest clue of you likin' him."

"And you know what, that's why there is a word called 'Secret Admirer'. Don't you know what that means? It means to secretly admire someone. Sahidah, I'm not mad at the fact that you showed him my poem, I just wish you could have respected my wishes instead of getting all excited and running off with your mouth to him."

She followed me into the handball courts. I walked around to the other side of the wall to check and see if anyone tagged over my graffiti. "Crack is Wack", sprayed in red was still there, untainted. That's whats up. My piece had been up there for three weeks now.

I sat down and she did not follow.

"Look, I wasn't running off with my mouth..." She defensively waited for me to say something. I said nothing, I was too tired to continue arguing. She rolled her eyes, "Like I was sayin', I figured if I asked you, you would've said no anyway."

"That's what made you wrong in the first place."

"You think you're so grown like you know it all. Aren't you glad you're not in dreamland anymore over him, Dana? At least now, you know how he feels."

"That I'm too nice for him? Too nice of a girl? I really wish I was back in dreamland."

"Dana I just wanted to see you happy. I wanted all of us to go on our first double date."

She sat down on the ledge next to my silence. I did not look up from the ground. She opened her book bag and pulled out a paper bag. She pulled out the Hostess Twinkies.

"You want one?"

"No, thank you." I said.

"Come on, Dana. I know you want one. Stop frontin' like you don't love you some Twinkies."

"I don't want any."

"Okay, alright I'm sorry." Still silence. "Okay. Pretty sorry? Sincerely sorry? Could you forgive me?"

"I'll forgive you if you promise to never open your (big) mouth about my business again without my consent."

"Okay. I promise." She blushed.

"Raise your right hand and say, I Sahidah." She rose her right hand.

"I Sahidah."

"Swear to never spread Dana's business around without her consent."

"I Sahidah, swear to never spread Dana's business around without her consent."

"Okay, shake hands in trust." We shook.

"Here." She shared the other Twinkie with me. The creme filling hit the spot as we resumed our walk home.

"So Sah. What did you ask him?"

"Girl, you're crazy." She laughed loudly. "After all that chastisin', now you want to know how it all happened." Men in cars hissed like cats.

"Inquiring minds want to know, Sah." Laughter was a positive release for the both of us. "Tell me Sah, did you ask Sherman what he meant by me being too nice for him?"

"I was about to get the scoop but his crew started to come around. I don't know, I just assumed he likes bad girls." She lowered her head as if embarrassed,

"Did you ever hear him talk?"

"No." I replied then she shook her head in shame.

"What's wrong? His teeth are messed up?"

"What? Girl! No." She laughed. "Honey child! When he opens up his mouth and speak, he's definitely no Michael Jackson." My heart crumbled at hearing this.

"No Dana. Dude is straight up hoodlum."

"I don't believe you. He looks too soft and beautiful to be a hoodlum."

"Believe what 'chu wanna. I spoke to him, myself. He can dance like Michael very well but he ain't nowhere nearly as reserved and modest as Michael Jackson. Michael's a sweetie pie with a beautiful voice, Sherman is a hoodlum who can dance. He ain't no different from those muthafuckas in McKinley projects. Girl, I kid you not, He the type a nigga that be likin' the girls who wear tight Lee's and shell-top Adidas with big bamboo earrings. Dana give him up...he's way too fast for you."

"So, you're saying..." Urging her to bring out her point.

"I'm sayin', he's not a virgin, Dana."

"How you know?"

"I know guys like him. I can tell when a guy is already knocking boots."

"So..." I thought, "He like those home girls who wear those big name earrings and extensions too?"

"Yup. Don't you go changin' now." I sucked my teeth like 'you better not even go there'. She continued.

"I dealt with guys just like him. I know Sherman's type. He's not for you. You won't like him."

"Well, I wish I had the opportunity to make that judgment for myself, Sah."

"I said I was sorry, already."

The weather was pretty warm outside. People were saying that we had to be careful, 'cause it's "Indian Summer." If you're not careful, you can get sick and catch "ammonia." It was too warm outside for Sahidah and I to resist tying our jackets around our waists. We stopped by the store so she could buy her three Blow-Pops to put in her ponytail. Her nipples pointed out from her Ms. Pacman t-shirt. We walked by men who licked their lips at her.

We kissed each other on the cheek before she crossed the street to St. Mary's Projects to see her Boo, D-Jay. I felt like a grown-up when we kissed each other on the cheek to say good-bye. I glanced across the street and she cheerfully waved. I waved back and three grown men interrupted our vibe by trying to rap to her.

My brother accuses me of being jealous of her. I'm not jealous. I just don't feel comfortable walking down the streets with her sometimes. I love to hang out with Sahidah at her house but not in public. We can't even share a joke without her being interrupted by a stranger, while I am left looking silly finishing the laughter all by myself.

I wouldn't mind getting that kind of attention one day. I don't see how some of the pretty ladies around here could get angry and be ungrateful when men on the street pay them a compliment. Maybe it's because they get *the wrong kind* of compliments. One thing I promise myself, is the day *the right* kind of compliments come my way, I'm going to thank God with a smile.

$3^1/_2$
gallons of tears

A whole bunch of guys and girls from school were standing in front of Perez's Record Store, pointing past his dull, glass window. "We Are The World" was playing in the speakers. We all sang and shouted Cyndi Lauper's verse.

Oooh! The new Michael Jackson posters and the "Thriller" and "Beat it" jackets! I can't believe it! Everyone bragged and made bets on who was going to be the first to wear the Michael Jackson jacket for school next week. I have to get it. Mr. Perez, the record store-owner, shouted the price to everybody.

"The jackets are $59.99!"

$59.99! Damn! I hope Mommy can afford it. Before I walked away, I inspected what Michael Jackson was wearing on the "Human Nature" poster. I finger-combed my bangs and then looked past my reflection in the display window. Okay, a white button down shirt, a yellow knit-ted vest, white khakis, and of course, his black penny loafers (although they're not visible on the poster). If Mommy can't get the jacket, then I'll be wearing that outfit for school next week. Michael Jackson is my hero. The best dancer, singer and entertainer breathing on this planet and I have yet to meet him.

As I approached John Adams' 21st story project building, I noticed the lobby was crowded with Catholic school students and their parents. Melissa was standing quietly with her father, who is now a widower. Melissa and I were friends until her mother passed away. Her mother and Mommy was real tight. All string 'n ties were cut when Melissa's father tried to come on to Mommy, I guess because of his loneliness. After that, Mommy didn't feel comfortable about me going over to hang out at her house. Rumor has it that Melissa is her father's new wife. I don't like to believe every thing I hear. That's one thing about the projects that scares me. Everybody believes what they hear. In the ghetto, people love gossip like they love money.

While everyone waited for the elevator, the lobby's back door made beats with the breeze. And every few minutes you'd hear feet patting down the staircase. To my left, there were three six graders pressed against the wall with one foot planted on the wall. They thought they looked cool bopping their heads beat-boxin' with their Jan Sport book bags on their backs. The fifth graders, in front of me, kneeled on the lobby floor, killed time playing the foot game, "Doug-e, Doug-e, diamond step right out," and that game turned into their making comparisons about whose patent leather shoes were real or fake. They argued that the real patent leather shoes didn't have cracks in the crease.

The adults started complaining about the elevators and housing authority.

"Please, Lord, don't let the elevator be broken," I said to myself. Twenty seconds later, the 'elevator up' red indicator lit up and the elevator door rattled itself opened. The people who were waiting made way for those who came out of the elevator. I had just made it in and so did Troy, my older cousin. He has me by two years. Troy always keep a smirk on his face. He so lucky to always keep a fresh pair of sneakers on his feet and fresh gear on his back. There's one thing that I find sad about Troy and that is he never got to know his father. His father passed away from kidney failure when Troy was only a year old. Family always said Troy was a happy and bright baby, always smiling.

I said, "What's up?" He pressed the 13th button. I pressed it again (force of habit.)

Musk cologne mixed with floral perfume floated in my face. Some people were listening to the scraping elevator window or watching the lights go down. Others stared at the floor or jiggled their keys, but no adults bothered to look at each other. I wondered why? Only the preschoolers made eye contact with each other.

I raced Troy down the hallway toward the door. He won because his legs were longer. Donell opened the door for us. Troy ran toward the kitchen yelling,

"Last one's a rotten egg, rotten eggs lock the door!" Donell ran behind him. I locked the crummy door. Troy dropped his Jan Sport book bag on the washing machine in the kitchen and participated in the topic of the afternoon. Donell was in the kitchen with our other cousins cracking jokes and telling sex stories. I think Donell inherited our sense of humor from Mommy. Some true, some exaggerated, mostly fiction. Like how could Donell, who is only 13 and a half years old, squeeze Miss Vanessa's butt at the community center party last weekend and then why would she try to have sex with him in the stair-case? That's bogus! Miss Vanessa was in her mid-thirties, she has too much class to be stooping to Donell's level.

Everyone in the kitchen was cracking up laughing, with textbooks and notebooks open. Someone had a Mickey Mouse T-shirt drying in front of the oven, supported by a broom. There was aluminum foil covered over pots and pans that was sitting on top of the stove. Whatever it was, it smelled good like Salmon Crochet or fried fish. Lamonte's radio sat in the window sill. DJ Red Alert was spinning my jam, Whodini's "One love" on 98.7 Kiss FM. I turned up the volume and started dancing as usual.

Nine-year-old DeShawn began to make Kool-Aid, which wasn't going to last a good 15 minutes in this house. He sloppily stirred the fruit punch and poured himself a cup, then placed the silver pitcher into the refrigerator. Seconds later, three teenage roaches cleaned up the spilled Kool-Aid for him. As everyone in the kitchen went for grabs on the new flavor, Fruit Punch Kool-Aid, I pulled my brother aside.

"Donell, is auntie Bitch here?"

"Nope."

"Where's Mommy?"

"In the bathroom." His facial expression looked blank, careless and callous-like. Donell's eyes looked through my eyes intensely. And I felt it. That was our private hint. So he resumed to hiding behind his jokes and I placed my heavy book bag on the floor near Auntie Berlinda's living room. No one is allowed in her immaculate living room because she said, 'We always fuck it up and didn't clean behind our messes.' The house felt stuffy from the oven being open. I went into her living room and opened the windows. The breeze felt so good against my neck and stomach. She had the illest view of New York City's skyline. I can never tell which building was taller the Empire State building or the Twin Towers.

Mommy and Berlinda weren't speaking because Mommy felt Berlinda had a bad habit of gossiping about us to her friends. Mommy said, 'Berlinda had disrespected their friendship and our privacy. I agree. Just because Mommy was temporarily out of work, doesn't make her an idle person. Jeez, give her the benefit of the doubt. Okay, Mommy fell down but she didn't fall off. I know she's going to get back up. She always does. Mommy is an artist, and a damn good one too. I believe in her. She told me, "Berlinda uses displacement on us. Her livelihood is recycled." Maybe one day that'll make sense to me.

After waiting for about thirty minutes for Mommy to come out the bathroom, I closed the window and knocked on the bathroom door.

"Hmm?" Her voice was full of fuzz.

"Mommy?"

She cleared her voice a few times. "Hi, Baby."

I quickly prayed to myself, "Please, Lord, not today. Please, let my ears deceive me." I waited and waited and sat on the floor with my head against the standard colored walls. I had a de ' je vous. I thought about the past.

I knew Mommy more than she probably knew herself. I remember two years ago, I was crying my eyes out for her. I begged and pleaded with her to stop it or try and get some help.

"OK, Baby. Mommy's gonna stop. This is the last time."

"Mommy, my teacher said that people who smoke can get lung cancer. Mrs. Lawson said doing drugs is also a way for people to contract AIDS. Mommy? Mommy?" I repeated myself, "The teacher…My teacher said if you do dr…"

"Mm Hmm, I heard you Baby." Mommy's eyes were still closed.

I hugged her, hoping my love would sober her up a little bit.

"Mommy, please, I don't want to lose you. Please, Mommy, take care of yourself."

"I will, Baby. Mommy's going to get her act together real soon. Stop cryin' ok?"

I didn't want to okay her. Why? So she could turn around and do it again? I wanted to cry until my eyes teared blood and then maybe she would see how serious I am.

"I love you, Mommy."

"I love you too, Baby." She wrapped her arms around me and lost her grip. She was too engulfed in her high. The more I looked at her, the more I cried. She didn't look alive. In fact, she looked like she was floating or dancing underwater somewhere down on her own planet.

I heard the toilet flush and the door knob turned. Mommy came out looking like a sleepwalker. She dragged herself into Berlinda's living room. No one was supposed to be in her living room when she was not at home.

"Mommy…Mommy, do you want to lie down on the bed?" I figure maybe if she took one look at me, she could see how she was hurting me. Although I am not strong or courageous enough to open my mouth and speak my mind to her 'cause I was brought up, *children are to be seen and not heard*, instead I used my eyes. I'm God's transmitter. I talked through my eyes. Everything I wanted to say, I said it through my eyes, and God conveyed it to Mommy's spirit. The silence of God deep down inside me nudged Mommy's high and vulnerable spirit.

"Dana!" Her swollen eyes opened slightly. "Get outta my face, ya fuckin' up my high! Matter uh-uh-uh fact, go to the store and get me a pack of…" Mommy faded out.

"Newport in a box?" I finished. "Mommy…Mommy!" I shouted.

"Hmm?" She faded back in. Then lifted her head and with her slacked finger, she scratched the end of her drooping mouth and the secret wound underneath the Band-Aid on her inner arm.

"Newport in the box, right?" I struggled with patience for her. I'm trying, I was really trying to swallow this anger and frustration I had for Mommy. Tears, don't start! She ain't worth it. Tears, don't come! Maybe if I look up at the ceiling, it might help my tears go back to where they came from. Sahidah successfully held back her tears whenever she told me of the breakups she and D.J. went through. But I realized my tears carried more weight. They just waterfall.

Mommy was dragging her words along, speaking in raspy whispers. I hated to strain to hear her sentences. She was this short from losing my respect, word up!

"Go to the store and gimme a p-packa Newports in a box and a sixteen……. ounce of Pepsi." Her eyes were still closed. I guess she didn't have enough strength to look at me. I took the five dollars from the tips of her fingers. Her sedate body jerked from my cutting eyes. At this point, I wish Mommy would come home at six like everybody else's Mom and dress in business suits. I detest this part of her being an artist. Mommy always told me, she is not a 9-5 robot, she's an artist. I believe you can be an artist without getting high like this. I don't mind weed but all that chemical stuff got to go.

I slammed the door and stormed down thirteen flights of staircases sprayed with chrome. The time was 4:50 and I was glad to be out of her frowning face. I flew down to the 9th floor and looked outside the window to see who was in the back park. It had to have been almost

70 degrees 'cause everybody and their momma were sitting on the benches. I spotted Auntie Berlinda sitting on the bench with her groupie friends. They all were smoking cigarettes. '*I hope she stays outside until tonight, man. That is all I need is for her and Mommy to get into it. Especially while Mommy's high.*' Berlinda is such a big show off. She had everybody in awe of her new red, JVC/TV radio. In my opinion, her crew is weak, lookin' like a bunch of monkeys. Everything they see Berlinda do, they did.

But still it felt good to open the back door and hear the outside air clog my ears. The planes roar east and west and the trains clack uptown and downtown. The girls stomp and clap their cheers while playing double-dutch. Boys on bending knees, playing skelly. The St. Ann's Catholic church bells ringing, five times. The crispy red and orange leaves swaying back and forth from tree limbs. Leaves diving to landing. Freedom! Babies laughing in swings, kids riding down slides and running up slides, others on see-saws and rowing big wheels. Rhaheem, Kelby, Chubby, and Sahidah were playing freeze tag.

"What up, Dana! Time out." Sahidah ran out of the park to speak to me.

"Tag, you're it!"

"No that ain't fair, Kelby! You heard me say time out!"

"That don't count, you have to make the T sign with your hands. You're it." Kelby said

"No! That ain't fair. I already said time out. I needed ta ask Dana somethin'!" She shouted.

"You know you was about to be it! Don't try to escape and Dana's no excuse."

"I ain't tryna escape. Stop, Kelby! You play too much! Dana, didn't I say time out?"

"Yeah, she did." I witnessed.

"Go ahead and talk to that weirdo, Michael Jackson-wannabe-freak!"

Sahidah tried hard to hold in her laugh. "Shut up, Kelby! Dana, you wanna play tag wit us?"

Before I could say I couldn't, she said, "Please, I don't wanna be the only girl playing against three boys." I showed Sahidah the cigarette and soda money. She understood.

"What she showin' you. More Michael Jackson stickers?" Kelby sarcastically assumed.

"Kelby, nobody's tawkin' to you. This is a A, B conversation so C yo' way out!" Sahidah rolled her neck and eyes around. Her forehead glistened.

"Ahh, that wuz wack." Kelby said. But that was Kelby's wack opinion.

"Yo', what's the hold up?" Shouted Rhaheem from inside the park. "Come on, let's finish the game!"

"Ok!" Shouted Sahidah. She turned to me and said, "So Dana, I'll see you in school tomorrow?"

"Yeah."

Kelby sang Annie's theme song, "To-morrow, To-morrow. I love ya, tomorrow."

Rhaheem in his holey jeans, joined in, "It's a hard knock life for you!" This went on as they critiqued how I spoke, snapped on my love for Michael Jackson and dissed my new Olympic sneakers. They laughed at them and said they were the fake Reeboks. I didn't waste my time with Kelby and Rhaheem's trivia. They wasn't worth it. I just wanted to enjoy this beautiful day. I didn't care what the hell they had to say. They're jealous. They're not really my friends anyway. Well, Sahidah is cool but the rest of them can kiss my grits. I don't hear people on TV talking like them. Every successful person I know do not speak illiterate like Kelby and Rhaheem, even if they did use slang. So therefore I'm going to train myself not to speak like them.

Around here, people are so dag on backwards. The dumber you are, the cooler you are. I wish Mommy surrounded me with decent kids who spoke well. That way I could learn and exchange thoughts with them. I'm trying to better myself as a person and it doesn't help when my friends (or foes) tease me about the way I choose to speak.

I took the long route to the store to see what cuties were on the basketball courts, not that they would stop playing their game for me. Those who noticed me would wave and I would manage to wave with a smile. I skipped across the street, leaped over a turned over metal garbage bin and did the Indiana Jones jump over the river flowing into the sewer. I know it was Tito and his boys who turned the hydrant on. It ain't that hot out here. Anyway, I purchased her sixteen ounce of Pepsi and Newports in the box from Lisa's. On the skip home, I slowed down and didn't see auntie Berlinda sitting on the benches. Her whole crew was there except for her. Ah sugar-honey-ice-tea!

I wish Mommy would get her act together real soon, so we could get away from all of this. Ever since she gathered up the strength to leave Daddy-James, she lost the strength on sticking to the plan of taking us to the next level. Moving. Daddy-James has been asking Mommy to come back. Why? So he can get hand-n-belt-happy on us again? Hell no! He doesn't appreciate us. There has to be a way out of this. I look forward to Mommy getting her act together so we can get out of this cramped, roach infested, little ass apartment. She need to get "the monkey off her back", clean herself up, so I can at least have a decent talk with her. I want my own room. It's heart-wrenching that I can't have company here and what's worse I can't even talk to Mommy about my day. To keep my spirits up, I try to keep in mind what Mommy always drills in my head,

"Be thankful that we got family to come back home to. Thank God we don't have to sleep in the streets, or on the trains. Thank God we got Nawnie's backing in this, 'cause if we didn't we would still be over in Queens dealing with James' shit." So I still have to be thankful and grateful for what little we do have. And that is having a tight-knit family, even though there are some members who are loose stitches.

On the way back, I walked over to Pat. She was smoking her cigarette watching the Soaps on Berlinda's portable TV.

"Hi Pat."

"How you doin' Dana?" She smiled with cream colored teeth and chocolate gums.

"Fine. Have you seen Berlinda?"

"Yeah, she just went upstairs. She said 'she'll be right back."

My fingers were still crossed when I knocked on the door. Behind the door I heard Berlinda yelling,

"Defrager, you know better not to be in my living room! You better get your shit together and pay attention to your damn kids. They need you. Look at you. Look at you, you're fucking up your life and that shit is affecting everything and everybody around you. As your sister, I'm telling you, your shit ain't together. Get it together."

I couldn't hear Mommy's strained and hoarse voice but I definitely heard Uncle Jerry's roar. He intervened and it sounded like he was trying to defend Mommy.

"No! Everybody knows this Jerry!" Berlinda cried out. "Nobody's supposed to be in *my* damn living room!"

"Be easy Berlind. She's gettin' out." His voice carried down the hallway. "All of y'all go in your rooms. Donell! Troy! Jason! and DeShawn, go in your rooms!"

I knocked on the door again, this time in three sets of five's. Auntie Geneva's weird boyfriend who everybody in the house accuses of being a thief and a freeloader welcomed me in. He wore a played out J-five afro. Personally, I think he would look cuter if he cut his hair into a flat-top. He grunted and said,

"Hello, Dana. You see what's going on?" I nodded. His eyes were red and he grunted a few times. I figured he must've been smoking reefer again. But hey, that's his business. Mommy is mine. I found Mommy sitting in the kitchen still nodding with distress fixed over her eyebrows. Auntie Berlinda walked out and slammed the door. I peeked at the living room and Troy was sitting on the linen chair enjoying 48 hours on HBO. She rearranged her peach couch so that it was blocking the entrance to the living room.

I really want to lose my composure when I see people, especially Mommy looking like a dope fiend. Like those fiends, I see nodding off on Southern Boulevard. I want to lose my immaturity when I see people, especially Auntie Berlinda behaving like a spoiled brat. Nawnie always told me,

'Life is bigger than our problems.' That's the truth. I don't care, Mommy might feel good but this drug doesn't make her look good or smell good. Her pores emitted not her Egyptian musk oil but sour chemicals. She told me that the people we see nodding off in the streets, especially on Southern Boulevard are junkies. She takes care of her business in the privacy of her home. *Yeah, yeah go ahead and justify your addictions! I'd rather you not do it at all, Mommy! I'd rather you just continue to play basketball, paint your colorful pictures, work on your silk screen and jam to music while we choreograph some new steps...*I wish I could have told her this. But I'm not strong enough yet. As a pre-teen, I try to be strong and sometimes I feel like I'm grown but as always Mommy's force brings me to fall on my butt like a ten-month-old baby trying to walk. I figure now is the perfect time to show her my other side. Her force is nothing but a fizzle.

"Mommy!" I called her again. "Mommy!" Auntie Geneva's weird boyfriend stood near just in case anything should go down. He should be minding his own business.

"Hmm?" She raised her eyebrows with eyes closed. I removed the paper bag and placed the cold bottle of Pepsi in Mommy's hand, hoping the coldness would awaken her reflexes. It didn't. She whispered,

"Thank you." (Well at least she thanked me). Mommy heard me suck my teeth, which made her lift her eyelids revealing diluted pupils.

"Why must you do this?"

"What?" Her voice was hoarse, she cleared it some more, "Why must I do what?"

"Get high." I couldn't help my eyes from squinting with anger. "I hate it! I hate it so much!" My face shook the tears out my eyes.

"Imm, imm, imm" She said, shaking her head in disbelief. She barely kept her eyes open. "Let me tell you something. I am a grown woman and you're a young lady. I am your mother and you are my daughter. I brought you into this world, I was the one who pushed you out. Don't you ever come at me like that! You hear me girl? I might be high 'n all but you stay in your place." She sank back under. "Imm, imm, imm." Her mouth frowned and she lifted her heavy lids with strained pupils. She continued,

"Don't you evah, evah as long as you got teeth in your fuckin' mouth suck them shits at me." She relaxed her eyes. "I am worth more than that Dana." Her conscience brought out the polluted tear that fell onto her breast and seeped into her heart to purify. I walked away toward Nawnie's room. She's probably playing solitaire, trying to keep her mind off of her arthritis.

4
give

So I squeezed past the coats and pocketbooks that hung over her squeaky, door. Is she asleep? Nawnie was lying down with her back facing the television. She was awake watching M*A*S*H through her hand mirror. I guess her arthritis is bothering her right arm now. *Mental Note: Pray for Nawnie tonight.*

"Hi Nawnie."

"Hi, Baby. How was school?" She asked turning her body around slowly.

"It was okay. I watched a movie called "West Side Story.""

"I remember watching that movie years ago. Did you like it?"

"Yeah, I liked the way the story was written. One day I'm going to write stories like that."

"I can see you writing stories *greater* than that."

"Yeah…I liked the dancing scenes too, but I didn't like the fighting scenes. It was sad that Maria's boyfriend… how could I forget his name?" I snapped my fingers.

"Tony?"

"Yes, Tony. I thought it was sad how Tony died."

"Yeah Baby, it happens. Happens all the time. That's what happened to your Auntie Geneva's first boyfriend. You remember her first love, Marvin? Someone stabbed him to death. God bless his soul."

I lowered my eyes in prayer.

"Baby? Are you okay?"

"Yeah."

"Did you eat?"

"No."

She seductively advertised her fish and dinner items.

"Nawnie made collard greens, corn on the cob, macaroni 'n cheese and I fried some Porgies. Go and make yourself a plate."

"I'm not hungry." I sighed.

"You're not hungry? I even made some banana puddin' for dessert."

"You did?"

"Mmhmm. You can have some puddin' after you eat your dinner."
Nawnie looked at me a third time,
"What's the matter with my Miss Special?"
"Nawnie…" I whined.
"What's the matter Baby?"
"My mother's not looking right again and I told her how I felt about it."

My throat felt like a knot was blocking my swallow and when the block allowed me to, the pain was all down in my chest. I think she understood my pain.

"Let me tell you a little story about when your mother was pregnant with you?"

"I remember. I was going to be an abortion but you begged her to keep me so she did." I said with boredom, tears welling up in my eyes. Nawnie smiled with patience and slowly sat herself up.

"Come here. Sit next to Nawnie. Good, good. Now Nawnie don't wanna see her Miss Special crying like that. Baby so sensitive." She pulled two tissues from the box and dotted my cheeks.

" 'Cause if I see you crying, then I'm gonna to start crying. And you don't wanna see your Nawnie crying, do you?" She asked softly.

"No." I sniffed.

"Okay. So you're gonna relax and listen to Nawnie's story?"

"Yes."

"Okay. Now let me see." She looked up at the wall through her big Chanel glasses. "When your mother was carryin' you, somewhere in here," she pointed toward her heart, "I felt this baby she was carrying would be a special baby. I just knew in my heart and in my gut that she was carrying a special girl. See Nawnie had all boys. Lamonte was the first, then Troy, then Donell and then Jason. I had four grandsons, all these boys! But, no girl. For some reason, I don't know, maybe it was God telling me that Defrager was carrying a special little girl in her tummy."

"And that's when you begged her to reconsider," I stilled frowned.

"Ahh-huh," she smiled.

"Were my mother and father still together at the time?"

"Oh yeah," she laughed. "They shared their episodes of fightin'. Breakin' up and makin' up. That's expected in teenage relationships. You think your mother is stubborn now. She used to tell her sisters and brothers to tell Rudy she wasn't home when he'd visit."

"Why?"

"Just to punish him for whatever he did to her. She used to make your father cry like a baby. I don't know any man that loved and put up with a woman like your father did with your mother."

"Then why aren't they still together if he loved her so much? Why did he leave her?"

"That's a long story. I'll tell you when you get a little older."

As I listened, she felt inclined to say more.

"She was his first love, and he was hers."

"He fell in love with her first?" I asked.

"No Baby, they surrendered their chastity, their innocence to each other. That's how your brother was made."

"They lost their virginity together? At the same time?"

"Ahh-huh. But Sweetheart, when you was made, you was stitched with certainty and knotted in special."

"Really? What happened to them? How did she end up with Daddy-James?"

"Family issues. Your father's mother and Defrager were like odd and even, night and day. You know how your mother likes to dress."

"Yup. Cute and sporty."

"She's a free-spirited woman, and you know your grandmother's a conformist."

"Nawnie what is a conformist?"

"Conventional and conservative. She's the very opposite of your mother's lifestyle. But your father *did* come back around the time your mother started dating James."

"Oh yeah, I remember! The living room was dark and my father had me and Donell sitting on his lap. I was about five and Donell was six, and we were trying not to laugh at him. I remember my father kept crying and kissing us. But we didn't know why he was crying. He just kept telling us over and over no matter what happens that he will always love us."

"Mmmhmm. Everybody was mad at your mother for not taking him back."

"Why didn't she take my father back?"

"I'll tell you when you get a little older OK?"

"OK."

"I can't believe you were only five and you remembered that far back?" I nodded. "See how special you are?"

"What made me so special, Nawnie?"

"I think it was more so the timing. Let me tell you a little family history. See, I was the only child from my mother but I was the fifth cousin in my family. I had seven children and your mother was my fifth child and you my Miss Special, is Nawnie's fifth grandchild, 7 lbs. 5oz., born at 5:00 in the morning on the fifth day of the week. But I think it's more than just the mathematics Sweetheart, it's just somethin' that God blessed you with."

"How do you know this to be true? If I was so special, wouldn't I be a princess of a rich land somewhere in England or Africa?"

"Baby, never question God. Wherever God places you in this life, it's for a good reason. You be grateful for where you are in this moment. And Sweetheart, you don't have to be a princess to be special. That's just what you are, take it or believe it."

"I'll do both."

"I know some of the things she does hurts you. It hurts me too, but your mother is your mother. And that doesn't stop her from loving you. She's a grown woman and Nawnie can't always interfere in her life like that. Your mother went through too much in her life, Sweetheart. A whole lot of disappointments with your father and his mother. I stop questioning why Defrager does the things she does," she sighed, "but she's my daughter and I love her and accept her. That was the hardest thing for me was accepting certain flaws about my daughter. I'm just glad y'all left James."

"Me too. I hated those beatings. All my friends used to tease me and Donell about our beatings 'cause he would have us stalk naked with the windows and curtains wide open when he whipped us. Everybody would see us! I don't ever want to go through that *ever* in my life again."

"Mm, Mm, Mm. And you won't. I promise you that. Not as long as Nawnie's livin'." Her eyes reassured me.

"Baby, I prayed every night for your mother to leave that crazy man. Hittin' on my babies like that. I don't wanna talk about that right now, Nawnie's nerves ah bad. I just thank God, y'all are here with me." She rocked back and forth. "Safe...Safe. Thank ya Jesus." We hugged. Nawnie always had her way with bandaging the open cut on my heart that Mommy sliced.

"Nawnie?"

"Yes, baby?" She sighed a relief after the embrace.

"Is your arthritis still bothering you?"

"I almost forgot about that." She softly chuckled. "It comes and goes, ya know?"

"What does it feel like?"

"Oh, you don't wanna know."

"I do. Please tell me."

"Okay, like tiny little pins sticking you. Like if you stand in front of a fire hose or a fire hydrant. Have you ever had a sample of what that feels like?"

"That hurts?"

"A lot. When I was a little girl living in the south, a farmer hosed me down."

"He did? Why?"

"Because I walked on his grass and picked a Dandelion. He was a wealthy, lonely and mean-spirited old man." She rubbed her arm and wrist, "this arm's feelin' cold and numb. I have to call housin' tomorrow to get this window fixed."

"I'm going to knit you something, Nawnie, to keep your arm warm at night, okay? Instead of a leg-warmer, I'ma call it an arm-warmer."

She laughed with her mouth closed.

"Okay, Baby. Nobody's as sweet as you are. Nobody's as sweet as my Miss Special. Did you do your homework?"

"Not yet."

"Then you'd better get to it before you go to bed."

"Okay."

I started with the math problems, subtracting how much I said I hated Mommy for getting high and added more understanding.

5
lumps of shuga

One of the things I love about Nawnie is her thick 'n creamy, healthy red undertone, butterscotch mix complexion, topped with a Cherokee glisten. While she was enjoying her conversation with cousin Dora from California on the phone, I must've counted over a hundred beauty marks on her arms, back, neck and legs. I love her skin. I love the temperature of her skin, especially on those hot summer days when I press my hand on her meaty and cool arms while sucking my thumb. I don't know any grandmother that is as sweet and as special as Nawnie. Her calmness is The Way. She's always calm but don't push it. Her light side is just as powerful as her dark side. And I think Nawnie is aware of this.

Nawnie is the mother of seven, and grandmother of eleven. She told me she lost her mother when she was only two months into her life. Two months after her mother, Dora Cain Robinson, gave birth to Nawnie in New Jersey. Dora hemorrhaged to death at the age of 18 (God bless her soul). Nawnie said people used to tell her that her mother, Dora was the sweetest person they could have ever known. In the early spring of 1927 Nawnie still an infant, was taken into the custody of her maternal grandparents and they moved her down to South Carolina. When Nawnie became a teenager, she dropped out of school and moved up to New York to find a better life. She tolerated and lived with her difficult aunt. Nawnie was very much admired for her creative style of dressing. At seventeen she dressed like she was a star from Hollywood. It wasn't long before she landed a job coordinating and styling Broadway performance artists. She knew how to put anything together and make it work. She could wrap a model in a towel and make it a fashion trend. She made enough money and moved out of her auntie's house. Living alone gave her a chance to experience solitude and Self. After two years of living alone, she told the universe she was ready to have her own family and be a wife and a mother. If she wanted to she could have married, rich and well off men. But see, she didn't care to marry money for that would take away her substance and sweet purity. Patience was a plus for her personality, her character. She waited for quality love instead of falling for anything that flattered her fancy. She was falling in love with herself and she patiently waited for the man who loved himself as well. Nawnie fell in love and married my grandfather, Larry Strong. She had all seven of his children and became an early widow at the age of 35, when the baby; Auntie Geneva, was only 5. Having to raise all seven children by herself, it surprised many that she retained her sweetness.

Nawnie has a wonderful way with how she expresses her love to us. Her expression was always wholesome like organic, apricot-honey mixed with vanilla extract, salted butter, sprinkled with some fresh cinnamon, and pure nutmeg in cooked oatmeal on an early Saturday morning. A warm, sweet and nutritious love. The recipe is called *Nawnie's love.*

I remember when I was five, the devil Daddy-James moved Mommy, Donell and I away to D.C. so we could be away from Nawnie. He told us, 'her love was spoiling us.' Love is love. *Nawnie's love* was fresh to me and strong because Mommy found a way to get away from Daddy-James and telephone Nawnie.

That following day, Nawnie was knocking on our door in D.C. I will never forget that visit. She bought Donell a Batman costume and a Batman Mobil with the doll and she bought me a Raggedy Ann doll. She asked,

"What is my Miss Special going to be?"

"A cheerleader!"

"A cheerleader? Let's see what Nawnie has in the bag for her cheerleader." She pulled out two red and white pom-poms and a mini skirt. She'd "Oh" and "Oh" at my cute little dance moves. She'd shake her shimmy and I'd follow her. Nawnie would nod her head smiling watching me dance until I got tired. I used to love all of the attention she gave me. When Nawnie came around, I felt safe and free. Because she reiterated to me,

"When you're with your Nawnie baby, you are free. Free to be what ever you wanna be. My Miss Special." Daddy-James would smile forced and fake smiles at us. She loved to keep me happy by drawing a bubble bath for me. She taught me how to blow bubbles from my fingers. We sang our favorite Billie Holiday and Nina Simone songs. While I sat in the bathtub and observed the rainbow in the bubbles, she hand-washed my panties.

After she helped me put on my favorite "Wonder Woman" pajamas, she sat me down on her lap and painted my nails Christmas red.

When it was time for us to escort Nawnie back to Amtrak, my heart ached so bad I wanted to die. We cried together, kissed each other, hugged and waved 'see you soon.' We didn't like good-byes. As soon as she was out of sight, Daddy-James snatched me from my vacation of un-inhibitions, interrupted my high of loving myself to reminding me of going back. Going back, like a beautiful, hot-curled hairstyle that gets caught in a sun shower. Going back, like feeling like I'm the most special somebody until Daddy-James comes along and wrongfully reminds me that 'I am not special and don't let whatever Nawnie said get to my head.' I believed in Nawnie's words for they carried truth in them. Nawnie's words were like magic. Whenever Daddy-James pissed confusion in my ears, Nawnie was there to detoxify my thoughts and break his curse. She would unscramble my puzzled mentality and pour tender love into my subconscious with prayer.

As sweet as Nawnie is, she is also a hard worker who made a conscious decision to decline welfare. Her Broadway days were over. A lot of the performance artists either passed away or retired. Nawnie in her late fifties would rather work for some Jewish rich woman and care for her fresh, bratty daughter, Kelly, than to sit at home and watch soap operas, collect government handouts and become meddlesome like her bitter neighbors. Besides, Nawnie has always been a private person. She's different from all of the other scorned grandmothers who habitually park themselves on the bench in front of the senior citizen's office and gossip about other peoples' lives and kinfolk.

I don't think they had anything much to say about us because we, "the Strong's", kept ourselves tight, physically, materialistically and personality.

When it came to our clothes, Mommy never had to worry about me. She only bought me undergarments. She only had to buy clothes for Donell. Nawnie didn't have any clothes for men because her employer was a woman. A mother of one daughter who was along with me in age. Nawnie used to bring home stylish, expensive, designer gear. I mean clothes that were bought from all walks of life handed down from the rich. What those rich folks considered damaged goods were two-time worn mink coats that had a little rip or snag on the collar. They would dispose a fresh pair of "Joan & David" shoes in a heartbeat if it had a spill of red nail polish on it. That's what I call wonderful nonsense!

I remember early spring like on a Saturday morning, all of my aunts would gather in Nawnie's room and sort and pick out the clothes they liked from 7 big shopping bags. Billie Holiday, my favorite, sometimes sang softly in the background. Billie's voice set a calm and cool mood to the house. Berlinda snatched the dress that I laid on the chair to try on. The black, silk Kenneth Cole dress. Berlinda believed the dress was made for her size and her height only. I'm really supposed to believe that I was too short for the dress. She believed the dress was supposed to fall just above the knees. I thought the dress fell real nice around my hips.

"Whatever," Mommy said, "it's a petty issue, anyway. Breathe that shit out and breathe in 4giveness, Dana."

Expensive and quality clothes can never go out of style, especially when you take good care of them. Well, I've been sportin' "the *run-way* look" for sometime now since Nawnie stopped working. My black sweaters are *run way* down to a charcoal gray and my white button downs are *run way* down to off-whites. Bleach ain't helping none, it ripped two pairs of my *runway* white jeans. On the serious tip, I'm starting to wear Mommy's clothes and I'm sneaking clothes out of Auntie Geneva's closet without her consent.

Nawnie had to stop working because everyday she complained about her corns, her calluses, her gout, her arthritis, her asthma, and, let me not forget, her sore eyes. She complained so much, to the point where I started ignoring her. When she would call on me, I tried to act like I didn't hear her so maybe she might call on Lamonte, Jason or Troy to cook her a cheeseburger or softly scramble her some eggs. Or maybe she could ask Donell to make her some tea or DeShawn to go to the bathroom to fill up her used Welch's jar with water so she could take her pills. Or put medicated eye-drops in her eyes or adjust the TV antennae. Why couldn't I have been a boy so that I wouldn't have to wash the dishes, clean the bathroom, cover my chest, be in the house before dark, or sit with my legs closed?

I truly love Nawnie, even though she gets on my last nerves with her complaints. Deep in my heart I still love her and I always will. If it weren't for her, I wouldn't be here. She's one of my closest friends and Mommy's my best friend. That's why I find it so hard to maintain friendships with girls my age on my block because one, they're too fast and two, I don't like to fight over what he said/she said. I like to take things slow. I haven't kissed a guy yet though. If or when I do decide to, the only guy I'd kiss right now is Michael Jackson and if I don't get the opportunity to kiss him then maybe Sherman Smith, in my school.

6
helfare

That annoying reporter on 1010 WINS awakened Nawnie. Then Nawnie awakened me. She called me softly and sweetly.

"Baby?" I heard her the first time. Could you make me invisible, God?

"Baby, it's time to get up. It's 7:30."

Ah man! "Please Nawnie, could you please wake me up at a quarter to?"

"You'll be late for school. Come on. After you take your shower you'll feel better. You better hurry up before Auntie Geneva gets in there. You know her hour-long shower ritual. Trust me, she'll have no problem making you late."

I peeled the ever-so-warm-like-being-in-the-womb electric comforter off of me and was reawakened by the cold naked floor.

"Dag!" I stamped my foot hard on the floor, Nawnie acted like she didn't hear me. I thought to myself, *I should've played sick!* As I passed Uncle Jerry's room, he quickly closed his door. A different girl again?

I locked the back bathroom door and sat on the toilet with my hands covering my face. A warm fog mixed with Uncle Jerry's Carrington cologne helped me to relax. I looked through the slits of my fingers. Baby roaches trailed lines along the dewed, yellow wall. I dropped my straps and waited for my gown to slide down to the floor. I protected my feet by standing on top of my gown while brushing my teeth. Stepped up on top of the bathtub ledge, turned the medicine cabinet mirror toward me and inscribed my tag up name Destiny across the foggy mirror. Then I wiped it out and began to stare at what looked like little jelly mountains. I'm not pleased with how my body's developing. They look confused! One of my breasts was larger than the other! I recited my mantra with eyes closed and visualized big and balanced breasts. As if pumping iron, I started with:

"I must,
I must,
I must increase my bust. Balance..."

Twenty one times in the morning and twenty one times at night should do the job. I wondered what was Sahidah's formula for having such perfectly developed breasts? I lathered, rinsed, scrubbed then rinsed again. Thank God it's Friday! I patted my face dry with my towel. Lotioned and oiled my skin. Where's the Secret? Damn, I hate to use Tussy deodorant! While adjusting my training bra, I heard Nawnie limping down the hall to wake the boys up for school. I hurried and slipped on my pink Perry Ellis jeans, stuck some toilet tissue in my right bra cup, and buttoned two buttons on my white LeTigre shirt and ran out. I watched them plead for five more minutes of sleep. Nawnie is firmer with the boys.

"No, ya shouldn't've been up all night playing those video games. Get up! Time for school!" I stood behind Nawnie, trying to keep a straight face. They all moved as if they were swimming in quicksand. Their room looked like a dry swamp.

Cobwebs in corners,
Coats and school clothes hung over door shoulders,
blankets half-way covered the floors,
Bad breath mixed with Troy's snores,
Fogged up windows,
Jason's sweat and slob flattens his polyester pillows.
The room smelled like stale pretzels from DeShawn's peeing problems
A pair of size 8 pampers will help solve them.

Troy turned around on his knees and stretched his butt in the air. Donell rotated his head around and tighten his thighs while he stretched on the bottom bunk. Jason pushed his pillow away and it landed over DeShawn's face. Boy was I tempted to play "roach" on them ears. I wanted to grab a thin thread and glide it all over Jason's face and ears but he was wrapped tight like a burrito in his linty, green covers with toilet tissue stuffed in his ears.

I went back into the bathroom and carefully laced my white shell top Adidas with florescent pink laces. I styled my hair in a ponytail with a bang on my forehead and a bang on my neck. Someone's dingy toothbrush was used to hold down my sideburns with soap and water. Then I glossed my perfectly heart-shaped lips with Vaseline. All I needed to complete my fashion statement was Troy's baby blue LeTigre jacket.

As soon as Nawnie opened her squeaky door to her room, Troy's butt sank right back under the covers. Donell couldn't go back to sleep so he sat up with eyes transfixed on Jason's open eyes. He was probably wondering how does Jason sleep with his eyes open.

"What's goin' on back there?" Nawnie shouted from her bed, "Are you boys up?"

"Yeeeahssss," the morphine choir sang.

I went back into the bathroom as soon as I heard Uncle Jerry yelling like thunder heading toward their room,

"Don't y'all give Nawnie a hard time!" I closed the bathroom door and peeked through the crack.

"Didn't y'all hear Nawnie call you?" He barked, "Y'all get y'all asses up right now! It should only take Nawnie one time to wake y'all up for school. Donell!" Donell stood up like a soldier. "You go in the bathroom first!"

Donell walked quickly into Nawnie's bathroom to brush his teeth. I waited for Uncle Jerry to disappear before I decided to knock on the boys' open door.

Everybody was sitting up with red eyes and frosted mouths. All eyes were on me.

"What do you want?" Jason sneered.

"Must we use displacement?"

"Shut up." DeShawn hates my sarcasm.

"No…" I turned to Troy. By judging from his attitude, I could see he was going to diss me, but it wouldn't hurt to try. " Troy, can I wear your blue LeTigre jacket?"

"Is you crazy!? That's my breakin' jacket!" Jason's eyes smiled. He loved to see me and Troy go at it.

"Come on, Troy? I'll wash it if it gets dirty."

"Girl, you don't even know how to wash your own clothes. No, no, no! I'll be retarded if I let you fade out my clothes."

"Come on Troy, please? Don't nobody wanna fade out your clothes. Do you see any of my clothes faded?"

"They need to be faded wit all them do-do stains in your panties." Jason laughed so hard, it sounded like a scream.

"N-O, now solve it. Look at what I'm wearing," he pointed to his freshly pressed clothes hanging over the closet door.

"I'm not tryin' to get fresh. Don't you know today's Halloween, stupid?"

"I'm not stupid."

"If wearing my Le'Tigre jacket on Halloween isn't stupid, then what is?"

He got me so pissed off, but what could I have said? I had to defend myself. I'm not going to let him or anybody call me stupid. One day, I will be a wealthy woman so I would never have to ask anyone for jack. I must come to my senses, I must've forgotten today is Halloween. I couldn't get upset with Troy over his dumb jacket. He was right, it didn't make any sense to go to school all dressed up anyway since kids are going to be bombin' today.

Before leaving for school, each of us went into Nawnie's room to say goodbye. Clutter and dimness was the signature of Nawnie's bedroom. She kept her thick violet floral drapes closed to protect her arm from letting the cold draft come in, through the broken window. Her cozy, violet, floral drapes protected her skin from the burning hot sun.

"Okay Nawnie, we're ready to go," I said for all of us.

"Okay Baby." She turned her TV Guide downside, slid on her Chanel reading glasses and adjusted her rainbow arm-warmer that I knitted for her. She's been wearing it every night. *Note: Knit Nawnie a brand new one.*

"Sweetheart, turn on the lamp for Nawnie." Donell turned on her reading lamp.

"Thank ya Baby." I heard Nawnie wheezing. She took a moment to use her asthma spray. A few moments after her breathing quieted, she pulled out her purse from under her pillow. That was her new hiding spot. She gave us all a dollar a piece to buy snacks. I always bought my favorite sunny doodles, a tonic water, sunflower seeds and a quarter to play a two-hour game of Ms. Pacman. We thanked and kissed Nawnie goodbye. I kissed Mommy too. She was sleeping next to Nawnie, and I told her I loved her too.

Although I may not have the same amount of responsibilities that grown-ups have, I do carry burdens. My definition of a burden is: unnecessary problems that we carry around inside us. My burdens are heavy. They're heavy like my eight textbooks. The difference is burdens are invisible. They hide inside my head and heart. Nawnie's illnesses and her pains are burdens I carry around in me. I carry Mommy's escalating drug addiction, my father Rudy and Daddy-James' broken-hearts. My abnormal puberty is also a burden that's getting too heavy for me to be carrying around. Maybe that could be the reason why I go to church every Sunday. Not to pray for only myself, but for my friends and family.

It is 12:30 and I thank God school is over. My class had a half-a-day today and I don't know if any other schools had a half-a-day too. I won't take any chances; I'm running my butt home. I saw a Freddy Kruger mask that scared me and I almost got hit with an egg. It was probably Rhaheem and his bad ass brothers from their 18th floor window. Thank God it wasn't a bullet. Sha-heem wasn't lucky enough to die from the 9mm that confined him to an electric wheelchair. Homeboy is paralyzed from the neck on down. Sad, sad, sad, I'm telling you.

I hoped Mommy was home so that I could ask her to buy me that Michael Jackson poster and "Beat It" jacket. Speaking of the jacket, Jose was stupid enough to wear his Michael Jackson "Beat It" jacket today. Wrong move dude. His "Beat It" jacket is now "Beaten Up."

As the elevator door rattled behind me, I heard Netti, Olympia and Jackie gossiping in the staircase about which guy in the projects they wanted to bone, who just had an abortion and what superstar they wanted to meet and have babies for.

"What about marriage, y'all?" I shouted.

"What about it?" They came back at me.

"Y'all want babies so bad, why don't y'all just own pets?"

"Dana, mind your B-I," Netti's voice echoed from behind the staircase.

As I turned the corner of the hallway, Mommy's back was facing me as she closed the door and locked it. She sported her white biker shades, her blue 501 Levi's and her Ever last sweatshirt. Mommy's S-curls shone nicely. My senses were greeted with her sweetest and softest Egyptian musk oils.

"Hi, Mommy," (Thank God she was sober.) "You look *nice*. Where you going?" Mommy's make-up sat pretty.

"Thank you Baby, come with me to take care some business."

I'd rather go anywhere than to be up in that crowded house. Anywhere except for *taking care of business*. Taking care of business sounded like the Human Resource Office, the public assistance office, the damn welfare building! Damn it! I had no other choice but to go, 'cause Donell wasn't around. He had baseball practice.

As we neared the dingy, dusty, gray building on Third Avenue, I lowered my head and shifted my eyes hoping no one from school or the neighborhood would spot me going in. I'll die if George sees me. I skipped in front of Mommy and opened the door for safety. Mommy held open the other hard plastic door that had been sliced with tag-ups. That door looked like a blizzard of signatures and love poems. All types of green, pink and white papers were posted all over the walls. Notes of rules and regulations on neon green and orange papers were positioned on filthy parts of the dented walls. Decades of dust on metal fences protected the dull windows. Some of the windows were broken. What cheapened this whole place were the fake gold trimmings on the tiled floors.

Impatient, overly frustrated recipients stood on long, unnecessarily boring lines. Wow, I was surprised to see a few familiar faces up in there. Sahidah's mother was there and Melissa's dad, a few parents from Cynthia's crew and I'm not calling anymore names but they were in there. Let's just say there was a handful of familiar faces I would've never thought would be in a place like this. We sat and waited for Mommy's name to be called. The social workers called a lot of foreign names.

A tall, big-boned, dark-chocolate woman stood on the line with her twin baby boys crying in a double stroller. She stood behind a few Latinos. She kept moving her stroller back and forth harshly to calm them down. I don't think those movements would calm babies down. Well, anyway, this woman huffed and puffed, and rolled her tired and puffy eyes around and around in her head. She licked her ashy lips over and over again. The more she licked them, the ashier they became. She sucked her teeth and her mumbling grew louder with patience already expired.

"They think we got all fuckin' day for this shit!" Her babies began to cry. She gave one a blow pop and poured Shasta soda into a nursing bottle for the other. She stabbed the bottle into her son's screaming mouth. Someone voiced on the speaker,

"Does anyone here speak Spanish? I need a translator in window #2." The line waited for about five minutes.

"What the fuck is this shit?" She blurted out. "Move this mutha-fuckin' line! If the old lady can't speak our language, then ship her ass back to Puerto Rico or wherever the fuck she came from! That's the problem with America, this country got too many damn foreigners comin' in and outta here! Like they fuckin' sumthin'! It's y'all. Y'all muthafuckas," she pointed to the social workers, "are letting these for-eigners rape y'all, this whole system! They rapin' this muthafuckin' country and you know what they do? These muthafuckas go right back home to their wives, their countries. America's a fuckin' mistress."

People started laughing. The social workers ignored her. Ignoring her encouraged her to say more. The angrier she got, the more spit flew from her dry mouth.

"Look we ain't got all day ta be waitin' for this old lady, damn it! Shit! Ain't there a muthafuckin' social security section in this building? It's one fuckin' 30 and I been waitin' here since 10 fuckin' o'clock this mornin'! If she can't speak English then that's her fuckin' prob-lem. Move this muthafuckin' line damn it!!! I need some food stamps, my damn kids is hongry!"

"Shit, I've been here since they opened up these doors." Lil' Tina just had to put her two cents in, trying to befriend the upset woman.

"Hold my spot," the woman was out of breath. "I need to smoke a fuckin' cigarette before I fuck somebody up in here!"

Four, middle-aged Latina women stood on the line, talking amongst themselves in Spanish. They wore sacks under their eyes, Filippo Totti jeans and confusion all over their faces but their tongues spoke certainty with harsh truths. Right in front of Miss Loud Mouth's face, just as she took away the empty bottle from her son's snoring mouth, the group of women began gossiping. They gossiped in their native language about her snotty-nosed-ashy-legged *ninos*, her *sucio* stroller, her bad atti-tude and this damned *loco* welfare system. Their eyes and their body language told it all to me.

I definitely didn't belong in a place like this. These social workers smiled showing tartar mixed with their clients' torn apart hearts between their teeth. Floss!

"Mommy? Why do these social workers look and act like they're the ones on welfare?"

"Hmmph, you're right about that. They sure do. Tacky right?

They got no fashion sense. Let me tell you something. When you're around garbage all day, after a while it doesn't stink anymore. Some of these people just don't care and some of them are just stuck in their own limitations. You think these people in here are crazy? You think that woman who was talking over there is crazy?"

I shook my head yes. She directed her eyes to the social workers,

"It's them who are crazy. They get off on hurting your self-esteem 'cause theirs are suffering. They will break you down, down, down until you believe in nothing. This system is one big trap. A year goes by, then five, then ten years go by and you're still on welfare, stuck in stagnation. Only a few people with purpose and determination can escape this shit. Never get on this shit. Get your education, Dana. They are worse than vultures. At least vultures wait until you die, shit these people here will eat you up alive along with your ambition, hopes, your spirit and then break your heart." We shook our heads together like damn that's a crying shame.

"Always, Dana, always seek in knowing yourself. You know how the famous saying goes, 'Know Thyself?'"

"Yup."

"And always love yourself. *Know Thyself* and *Love Thyself*. Even if you feel like no one loves you, love yourself more. Don't you ever forget that. Know that you always got me and God. You hear me?"

"Yes, Mommy."

"But ultimately, you got yourself."

That's something to think about.

"But why, Mommy? Why is it so important for me to know myself?"

"Why?...Dana, *you* are all *you* got," she said pointing to my heart. "If you don't study yourself and know yourself, there are evil people out there who will test you and use you and take advantage of you."

"And what happens if I get tested and I fail?"

"See, that's why you have to *Know Thyself* so you would know how to deal with contention. It's not for me to tell you what's gonna happen to you, only *you* would know. Overstand?"

"Yes. But what steps do I take to get to know myself, Mommy?"

"Girl, you're just like I was, when I was a little girl. Askin' so many questions but that's good...Study yourself. Know your weaknesses and your strengths. Find out what ticks you off and what makes you blush. What rubs you the wrong way, and learn how to control it, work on it and work on not taking everything to heart. Find out what and who is good for you and what and who is not good for you. Balance it, develop it, develop you. Do you. Loving yourself unconditionally will get you through life a whole lot easier. Spend time by yourself like you've been doin' and you'll be fine. When the time comes for God to show you the way, you better be ready, willing and open to it. Put it short, Dana, pay attention to what's happening around you. You always got to be conscious of what is happening around you."

"Okay. Mommy it seems like its so much work. How would I prevent myself from getting heartbroken?"

"We all go through heart breaks but there are different degrees and many levels of it. For instance some people cry, some kill, and some lose their minds but then you have those who pick themselves up, dust themselves off and keep it movin'."

"I want to be like that."

"Then you have to 'Love Thyself'. It's really simple, baby. I have to get this book for you. It's called The *Tao Teh Ching*."

"Dow De Ching. Who wrote it?"

"I think a Chinese man name Lao Tzu."

I whispered, "Did you hear what that lady was saying about the old Spanish lady about going back to Puerto Rico?"

"Yeah and she acts like *this* is her country."

"Yeah...It's the white peoples' country."

"Where'd you hear that?"

"Guys in the park be saying stuff like that."

"No, Baby. That's not true. Do you know whose country this is?"

"Umm, the Indians?"

"The Native American Indians," she corrected.

"Dana, What do they teach you in history class?"

"Boring stuff about Christopher Columbus's travels and how the Spaniards stole everybody's land. Nothing about us, just about their history."

"I swear if I had more money, you and Donell would be up in an all private black school. I have to take you and Donell to the museum and the library. Y'all need more exposure to the truth."

Mommy paused for a moment. "But you know what? Even lies are buried in the library. Get it lie-bury? Well, you can never hide the truth for long."

Mommy looked in her pocket book, "Oh, I forgot to give this to you." She pulled out an envelope.

My heart skipped beats. I took it. There was no name but an address. It wasn't from Charmane or Darwin because neither lives in Encino, California. Mommy smiled at me. I carefully opened the envelope and found myself breathing heavy with anticipation, so I relaxed. It was a one-page, typed letter. Addressed to not Dana but to a Dear friend. After reading the letter, I recognized his signature. With my tongue, I licked my finger and glazed it across Michael's signature. No smudge.

"What's the matter Dana? Aren't you happy he wrote you back?"

"It's just a printed copy. He didn't read my letter."

"Dana, you really think that?" I showed her the letter and I pointed to his signature.

"Well baby, at least you got a response. A lot of his fans send him letters and a lot of them aren't as lucky as you. Be grateful that you got something back."

I sighed, "Yes, I am. Mommy, when we get home, could we frame it?"

"Definitely."

I smelled the letter, there was not a scent of his cologne, his jerry curl juice, his body scent, nothing on it. I examined the texture of the paper, the font, the color of ink and his famous signature. I slid the letter carefully back into its envelope and held it in my hands with care.

Mommy detested this ugly, dismal, and dirty place. Angry by the all day bullshit of sitting and waiting for her name to be called. The welfare system felt like a topsy-turvy, "Twilight Zone" coupled with "The Price is Right" kind of luck. Mommy said it fucked with her nerves to have to tell her coke-headed, social worker all of her business, plus she said, "Places like these are very draining, dehumanizing and demeaning."

"Mommy a lot of mothers take their baby's father to court for child support. How come you never took my father to court?"

" 'Cause, I'm not a lot of mothers baby. I wouldn't want him to do it to me, so I'm not doing it to him. I believe in Karma. It doesn't feel right in my heart to do it. I believe in karmic debts and karmic rewards. I want the rewards."

I think this place is Lil' Tina's hangout spot. Lil' Tina knows all of the social workers by their first name and seems proud of it. She stood around bumming people for cigarettes. I caught her pick-pocketing an elderly man. But see, she knows not to mess with my mother 'cause Mommy could see straight through Lil' Tina's game. Mommy's reputation is timeless. The most Lil' Tina has ever said to Mommy was, "You still lookin' good Pepsi."

"Hey, Manny what's up? Yeah, Hector is giving me the fuckin' run arounds again. Yeah, I've bin waitin' all mornin' for my muthafuckin' money!" Lil' Tina's voice scratched like static. "Yeah, uh huh…Hey Mish Parish, How you doin'? Yeah, ha-ha, I'm here again, okay, I'll see you next week."

Then under her breath to Manny she coldly uttered, "Can't stand that phony ass bitch…" Lil' Tina rolled her eyes as she simultaneously lit up her broken-in-half cigarette, facing the 'No Smoking' sign. Lil' Tina's eyes were bloodshot and a comb was parked in the back of her damaged hair and I noticed she lost two more of her teeth. Somebody must've beaten her up.

Lil' Tina exclaimed,

"What? Manny I didn't know they cut off your checks! Why didn't you keep your face-to-face appointments?"

Mommy looked up from her New York Times paper.

"Damn, she just blew up his spot." Mommy chuckled privately.

A masculine social worker, named Mrs. Williams interrupted Lil' Tina and told her to shut up her big mouth. It only made matters worse. Tiny, Lil' Tina began shouting this time not yelling. She started bragging,

"That's right, I'm a be a second grandmutha!" She stood with legs wide apart in a proud stance beside her pregnant daughter, Tanisha. Tanisha has me by a year or two. Wow, I wonder if she is scared about having another baby. She wobbled to snatch her two-year-old son's wrist.

"Come here!" She yelled. Her son's soiled pamper dangled between his legs. He laughed and ran around chairs with his legs wide apart to prevent his pamper from slipping down. She caught him.

"Now stay right here and don't move! Or I'ma punch you in your face!"

I turned to Mommy,

"Mommy, why did Lil' Tina call you Pepsi?"

"That used to be my nickname when I was a teenager."

"Where did you get the nickname from?"

"I used to drink a lot of Pepsi soda. I used to love me some Pepsi."

She continued to read and I looked around at everybody. Tanisha smacked her little boys' hand. He cried very loud. I looked at her big, basketball belly.

"Mommy, when the baby comes out, does it hurt?" She looked up from her paper.

"What made you ask that question? You pregnant?"

"No, Mommy!" I reassured her. She exhaled,

"Thank God! Dana please wait until I turn 80 before you have a baby. I don't want to be no early grandmother."

I laughed. "Okay…Mommy look," I directed my eyes at Lil' Tina's daughter, trying not to use my finger, "Tanisha's pregnant."

"Again? Baby, I know I told you how painful labor is for many women. What's that word I'm looking for?….Excruciating! It's so painful that you will lose all of your strength, even your life, if you cried tears."

Wow, I can't imagine a pain like that. I don't know about having kids. I'm scared to have sex much less have a baby.

7
times of showtime

I despise drug dealers! All these losers are trying to make that fast money. The new drug out is called "Crack." I tag up "Crack Kills" and "Crack is Wack" everywhere. I tagged up in staircases, on elevators, on the trains, on my bike, even on the handball courts. I got so mad one day, I tagged all over the new crack building near Woodstock Co-ops. I hope my message sank into everybody's dome. It's only the weak and foolish-curious who turned to drugs like crack. I swear if Mommy ever thought of doing that stuff, I would send her away. Besides, she's too strong for that stupidity.

I really am not liking the way this world is turning out. The way the government is pouring trash into my community onto my street heroes. Too many shoot-outs started happening around the block, which was the primary reason why I didn't like going outside. It wasn't safe anymore. One by one, crack started recruiting the soldiers on the block. Crack broke the trust and love that kept black families together. Breathing wasn't easy anymore. I could exhale through my own world of music. In my world, I found a gift God hid inside of me. It was dancing. I always knew I could dance but now I've realized it's power and potential. I realized that I could take my gift to the highest of heights and heal with inspiration.

Ever since Mommy bought me that lavender stereo with a recording tape deck, I have not stopped. Talking about happy? I don't have to depend on Troy for his walkman anymore. Now I have the freedom to dance and listen to Michael Jackson and Janet Jackson, Five Star, Debarge, New Edition, Whodini, Run DMC, the Jets and Guy anytime I want. I can now save my money instead of giving Troy my money for batteries. Mommy said she's going to manage me and take me to the Apollo Theater as soon as my dance steps get tighter.

Dancing is my love. I dance everyday and I won't stop until I work up a sweat. I'll dance anywhere. I'll dance in the kitchen, in the bathroom, I don't care as long as I have music. I've improved on impersonating celebrities from Whitney Houston's easy two-foot dance step to New Edition's dance routine to Michael Jackson's "Billie Jean", "Beat It," and "Thriller" videos. I even know The Jets choreography to "Crush on You." See right now, Mommy can't afford to put me in dance school. It's okay though. I just taught myself new steps to DeBarge's "Stay With Me". I work hard to stay on top of the latest dances by watching Troy dance and Friday night videos. Troy pissed in my ear and told me that I was wasting my time with dancing. He told me that Mommy is only taking me to the Apollo Theatre in my dreams.

I'm fighting to keep hope and optimism in my mind. It has been hard to get a hold of my Aries mom and I'm bothered by her third absence this past Sunday. I know she's been hanging tough with Shirley and Shirley's cousin. I don't mind Mommy doing whatever she likes, but let it be constructive. She hangs out with Shirley and I know they be gettin' high. Donell told me that I shouldn't let Mommy stress me out with her drug habits. She has her life and I should concentrate on building a better life of my own. But I can't help it, Mommy is a part of me. I want to share my 'better' life with her. She's my backbone and my foundation towards my solid future. If she falls, then where will I be?

It's been three months now that Mommy hasn't taken me to the Apollo. So I've decided to go by myself. Auditions were held every Monday at the National Black Theatre. I asked a woman to sign the contract for me because I was underage. She claimed me as her daughter so I could audition. I gave the producer my tape and I danced off of "Nasty Boys." By the look on the producer's face, I knew I earned some fans. Then that Wednesday, I was to enter the backstage of the Apollo Theatre. Security was tight because it was said there were celebrities there. I looked on the program and saw my name. Right then and there I felt like a star. Ralph Cooper Junior met me in the dressing room. The I.O.U dancers and Aaron Hall were the special guests. Mostly everyone backstage were drinking lemon tea and being extra cordial toward each other. People were nervous about losing out to the Sandman. Some of the contestants put themselves down so they could receive comfort and confidence from the others. While they were constantly putting themselves down, I was keeping my head up. I wanted to win, so I acted as if I won already. I was poised and humble. I know my dancing is that good that I won't be getting kicked off by no

Sandman. I'm going to remain neutral either way, whether I win or lose. Anyways, my dancing is bigger than winning. It's an exclusive gift that people can enjoy watching and feeling.

Mr. Cooper opened the door to the dressing room and solemnly said, "Break a leg everybody." He must've been doing this stuff for years. I looked at the schedule and saw that I was to go on after the singer Charlie Cottrell. My adrenaline was so strong that my body quivered from head to toe. My hair was styled like Janet Jackson on her "Control" album. I was dressed exactly like Janet, down to the silver hoop earrings with a small, silver key in one hoop. People treated me differently, like a celebrity. I almost felt like Janet Jackson.

Being on the Apollo's stage can be very addictive when you're used to getting a certain love from your audience that you don't get at home. Even though I couldn't see my audience because of the blinding stage lights, I loved the attention the Apollo gave me. My turn came to break a leg (figuratively speaking) and all I had was five minutes to put my all into my performance. Five minutes was not enough for me. If only I could dance on stage for an hour! Boy, do I envy Michael Jackson's audience.

It was time for the audience to judge. I stood there calm even though I wanted to win. A man standing beside me was breathing heavy and fast. He looked so nervous, begging the Apollo to pick on him. Thirty performers on the Apollo's stage had been narrowed down to five. The Apollo seemed to favor singers over dancers. Kiki Sheppard placed her hand over my head for the second time, and the audience's roars weren't as loud as the first time she came to me. Someone up on the balcony called out my name. I couldn't see their face but I definitely recognized the voice. My beautiful Mother.

So, I was the one subtraction of the four who was left on stage. Charlie Cottrell won. I didn't take it hard. In fact I think I did a great job for someone who didn't have to bring her whole posse to the Apollo to root for her and at the same time the Sandman didn't take me out, either. So I think I did pretty good. But damn, I was this close to winning, this close. If I could sing as good as I can dance, no doubt I would be the winner. But I'll try again. Next time I'll dance off of "Control."

Mommy met me backstage in the dressing room. She smiled. She looked good and vibrant. The eyeliner drawn around her eyes enhanced the shape and made looking into them a stimulant for bored eyes. We started to walk toward Sylvia's restaurant holding hands when two

guys and a girl gave Mommy a Polaroid of me dancing on stage looking into my zone. They asked for my autograph in advance before I
made it to the next level. That felt good!

Mommy reserved seats for us. I looked at the menu and Mommy
told me to order whatever I wanted. That's the good thing I love
about Mommy. When she gets money, she's not afraid to spend generously.

"Mommy, how did you know I was performing tonight?"

"Troy and Nawnie told me."

"Where's Donell?"

"He caught DeShawn's cold."

"Is he sleepin' in Nawnie's bed tonight?"

"I think so. Nawnie wants to keep a close eye on him so she could
remedy the cold. He'll be fine, though."

The food was off the hook and fulfilling. I couldn't stop myself
from picking the meat off the chicken bone.

"Danaaaa." Mommy sang in a tone like 'girl you just don't know.'

"What?"

"Danaaaa. Danaaa, girl you just don't know." I laughed at the
expression on Mommy's face. She closed her eyes, curled her lips and
shook her head from side to side,

"Giiirrl, you should've heard what the people in the audience were
sayin' about you."

"What did they say?" My ego was hungry.

"They said you should've won. This girl told me she brought her
whole posse for one of the singers and she said, 'she couldn't help but
to root for you too'."

"Really?"

"She was the friend of the winner."

"Charlie Cottrell."

"Yeah, that was the name she told me. You didn't hear them
calling you "Janet?"

"Oh, that's what they were sayin'?"

"You know there was people out there who was upset that you
didn't win. Isn't that something?"

"I'm going to win next time. Next time, I'ma dance off of
"Control."

"And I'll be right there." She forked her macaroni and cheese and
collard greens together. "Mmm, this is good. Wanna try some?" Even

though I was full, I tasted her combination.

"It is good. Mommy, do you think I should've won?"

"Definitely. If I had known how people do at the Apollo, I would've brought everybody on the block there. But, Baby, you did an excellent job without bringing a posse. At least you know that your talent is honest and not fraudulent. One thing you must keep in mind about the Apollo Baby, is they're more audio than they are visual."

"Yeah." I sighed.

"And, Dana, don't you feel bad."

"No, no I'm okay. I'm kind of used to it."

"Used to it? This wasn't your first performance?" I shook my head no.

"This is like my seventh performance at the Apollo. I even made it to being special guest once."

"Dana, why didn't you tell me all this? Why didn't you tell me you were performing tonight?"

"I don't know. Sometimes I can't keep up with you, Mommy. I don't know where you are most of the time."

"Listen to you! Now, c'mon Dana you tryin' to diss me?"

I laughed, "No."

"Yeah, you tryin' to diss your mother. You know if I'm not at Aida's house, I'm at Shirley's. Next time you perform, I don't care where I am or what I'm doing, you let me know when you're performing so I can be there. I know I told you I would manage you and I didn't forget. I'm just trying to get my shit together, business wise. Don't let me slow you down now, you keep going. I'll catch up."

"Okay Mommy."

"I need to get a beeper, just in case you need to get in touch with me."

"Yeah, that's a good idea."

"Want some dessert?"

I looked at the menu and was attracted to the picture of the apple cobbler. I thought to myself, *'Damn, I should've joined the church choir at Karron Baptist then I would've been a great singer by now. Oh well. I'll just be the best in whatever I love doing'*. My thoughts must've been written all over my face 'cause Mommy paused on her food and smiled at me,

"Dana, I'm proud of you."

8
the magic age

The good news is, I'm gaining popularity around the block and in school because of my dancing skills. Sherman refuses to acknowledge my talent. I don't know what's his problem, maybe he's still mad at me for having a crush on him. It's okay 'cause my classmate George is acknowledging my talent. George teases me whenever he sees me and say, 'There goes that famous girl.' to his best friend Tray. He always makes me blush. It seems like the more I look at him the cuter he gets.

I have fallen in love with this game I call flirtation. I have grown with practice to become a very skillful flirter. I see no harm in flirting, it's a harmless activity. I am thirteen and a half, and Mommy and I have grown much closer in the last few months. Last year, I was a slim 120-pound girl. This year I'm a thick 135-pound lady. All credit due to Nawnie's down south home cookin'. Humph, on the block, I am treated with a different kind of respect and recognition from everybody. I've been waiting forever for mother nature to bloom me.

I'm loving my toned thighs, my curvaceous figure and my new-found sex appeal. I thank God that my breasts are balanced and two sizes larger. God blessed Nawnie's nourishing food. It's bugging me out that I'm getting the same kind of attention Sahidah used to get. All of the guys on the block are now checkin' for me, (finally). Girls are threatened by me, and I'm hearing through word of mouth that these chicks are plottin' on me. Still they better recognize that I come from a huge family. Dudes I don't give play to, who sells on the corner started nicknaming me "D.T.D," whatever the hell that means.

On the train, I pocket at the least, four numbers a ride. Around the way, you can forget about it! I got all the cuties velcroed to my bra strap. I ain't even gonna front, I'm loving this attention and I'm ready to let loose, but it would have to be with somebody special who I love and he has to be in love with me. But more importantly, he has to respect God. 'Cause if he doesn't respect God, then he wouldn't respect himself and as for me, I'm out the question.

A majority of the girls on this block are not virgins. They think it's uncool to be a virgin. I'm not giving up my virginity to just anybody who wants me. He has to be special and beautiful. I wouldn't mind George. If Sherman wasn't so mean, it would be him. Hmm, if a genie granted me one person to give my virginity to besides God it would be, my future husband Michael Jackson. I'm glad Mommy gives me the freedom to love Michael Jackson for she sees no harm in it. There are too many girls my age and even younger who are falling in love with local cats and having their babies. Mommy feels blessed to know that I am breaking those patterns. Mommy always reminds me,

"Life is broader than the streets. You want to see life? Walk through Central Park, look at the birds, look at life in motion, go to the beach and watch the ocean. You want to see life? Look beneath your feet and watch how the ants do their work or look up at the moving sky better yet look in the mirror and appreciate God's magnificent design."

I started a new diary. Well, now that I am no longer a little girl anymore, I will word "journal" instead. I can't mourn over the journal I left behind in Far Rockaway anymore. I have to keep my fingers crossed that Daddy-James doesn't throw away my bed and find the fallen journal on the floor and pick it up and read it and then in his desperate attempt to reconnect with Mommy, tell her all the fresh things I did. God forbid he doesn't do that.

9
he was so a black man

I lost my purpose with two hobbies of mine. I've stopped going to church and I've stopped playing with my Barbie and Ken dolls. It doesn't make sense anymore. Why should Barbie and Ken have sex every time I play with them? It's been two years since I've stopped going to church but I still maintain my relationship with God in my heart and mind. I stopped going to Karron Baptist church because I realized I was going for the wrong reasons. I went to church for entertainment purposes. I didn't care too much about reading the "good book", I just liked watching and listening to the sweating preacher with the damp handkerchief, the responding organ player, the Holy Ghost and all the dancing feet.

But my favorite part in church was The Carolina Choir. I fell in love with a woman in The Carolina Choir. When I first saw her, I thought her face was hideous. Her cheekbones stuck out of her cheeks, her teeth stuck out of her mouth but when this middle-aged woman opened her gigantic mouth to sing, the only thing that stuck out was her pure, angelic voice. The more I watched her sing her true heart out, the more she blossomed in my eyes. When she sang, she didn't care how awkward she looked or how big her mouth appeared or how imperfect her bone structure was, it was about the message she delivered to us how joyous she felt and how her voice fulfilled our ears. After a while I didn't care anymore about her beautiful imperfections. In fact I fell in love with them. She turned into the most beautiful creature I've ever seen in all of my thirteen and a half years. Her second soprano voice brought chills running around my crown.

If the congregation hadn't bothered me with so much questioning, I would still be a silent member. Maybe they didn't appreciate my sleeping through prayer sessions and scripture readings. Well, I didn't appreciate some of the lies and hypocrisy that went around in there, either. Like when it was time to go up to the altar to receive my blessings from young Pastor Thomas Junior, the line would go past the back of the church. There stood about 27 finely dressed women to about five handsome men. I felt they all were being too dramatic when Pastor Thomas Junior, placed his magical olive oily palms over their foreheads. It looked like they were illustrating how they had orgasms. They would jump around, flapping their wings like chickens, crying out, "Thank ya Jesus! Gloorrray, Hallelu-ooojah!" It wasn't hard to decipher the real Holy Ghost from the imitators. I thank God for blessing me with the power of discernment. After a few months, too many predictable things started happening in the church. Mostly everyone in there conformed and copied each other, 'cept for the retarded kids, me and Melissa.

Just recently, I started to feel different about worshipping. The sisters would call out the Lord Jesus over and over again giving him praise. Melissa was the only girl I felt real comfortable talking to about the things I didn't like what I saw in Karron Baptist church. Our friendship did not exceed the church. Even though she lives in the same building with me, Melissa is a loner. She keeps to herself. I remember she whispered to me one morning during worship at the alter and she said, "Don't it seem like they all are trying to compete with each other just to get closer to God? Like they all are trying to be God's favorite or something?" I just shrugged my shoulders.

"What angle are you coming from with that?" I asked

"My angle. Look around." We paused and observed and I almost laughed. One by one, each person developed loads of foam sliding out of their mouths. They lost self-control by saying Jesus a hundred times. *Were they supposed to surrender?*

Melissa whispered quickly, "Sister Gain." We both closed our eyes pretending.

Throughout the rest of the service, I could not stop thinking about all of the hypocrisies in the church. One thing that didn't make any sense to me either was when everyone is calling out Jesus' name a hundred times over and over until foam comes out of their mouths, it makes me wonder if Jesus called out his own name a hundred times or did he call out to God a hundred times until foam came out of his mouth. I believe all Jesus had to do was believe, 100%. Who made up these rules? I don't know. I hope when I get older I find the truth in all of this.

I can't be like them, I could only be Dana. Yes, we make mistakes. I know we are imperfect human beings but damn, strive to be better! Strive to be perfect in your own way! Isn't it possible? If Jesus was able to do it and he breathed the same air I'm inhaling right now, then why can't I? I think a lot of times adults are just too lazy to clean up their irresponsible and carnal ways and they leave it up to kids like me to suffer for their sins. I think they'd rather wait until something bad happens to them or until they get too old to be bad before they decide to walk in the straight and narrow path of righteousness. Shoot, if Jesus as a child could do it, then we all can do it too. Aren't we all God's children? Aren't we all special? I know Jesus was and Jesus knew he was too and Nawnie knew I was that's why I know I am too.

Mommy said to me, "Know Thyself" and I found out one thing about myself. I detest being obligated to things. I don't like to go to just one church every Sunday. I like to roam different ones. I hate monotony. Too many churches want me to become a member and conform to their stale traditional ways and then expect me to not question or analyze their belief system. I'm not going to eat what they feed me in the dark. I need light to eat, to see what I am feeding myself.

I found myself going to Karron Baptist Church more often than the other churches in the neighborhood. Karron's felt like I was inside of a smaller Carnegie Hall. They had a balcony with an oval roof. Lemon walls, stained glass windows and not one seat was left empty. And when The Carolina Choir sang, holiness filled my ears.

The straw that broke the camel's back was when the congregation started inquiring about my personal business and pressuring me to become a member since I've been coming to the church for a year. What more did they want? I paid my tithes. Then they suggested I join their Sunday School program with the rest of the children who were around the same age as me. I didn't socialize too well with all the children who were in my age group. Maybe it was because I wasn't like them. I never came with a parent so there was no way they're parents could bond with mine and they could bond with me. I don't know. I guess I just like to deal with God all by myself.

Just to shut them up, I attended Sunday school, and as soon as I headed upstairs to the class, Pastor Thomas Junior started asking me all these personal questions about my parents and why they never came to church with me and this, that and the other. Right then and there was when I questioned myself as to why was I really going to church. What was I trying to prove? Who was I trying to be? And does God really care about my appearance and punctuality and whether I brought a parent with me or not or was it really what was in my heart that mattered? *Did I always have to go to church to praise God?*

The Sunday School teacher, Sister Gilmore was very excited about finally educating me on the teachings of Jesus the Christ and his disciples. She wanted me to sit right next to her. She read some paragraphs from the children's bible but I was distracted by the exalted paintings of Karron Baptist's version of Jesus, Noah and Moses on the wall. She snatched my attention and pointed to the picture of Jesus dying on the cross in the Bible.

"Um, Sister Gilmore? Why did Jesus look that way?"

"Like what, sweetie?"

"Like that," I said pointing to his crucifixion in her book.

"Can anyone help answer Sister Dana's question as to why Jesus Christ looked the way he did? We're on page 77?" Some pages turned. Many 'Me's' cried out with hands waving and shaking in eagerness. She picked on a child much younger than I.

"Because he was in pain being crucified," said the snotty nosed, seven-year-old.

"Very good, Tiffany." Then she turned to me and smirked, "Does that answer your question, Sister Dana?"

"I guess. I never knew your hair could turn bone straight and blonde and your skin could turn white when you're getting crucified," I spoke in a respectful tone. From the expression on her face, I think she took it as I was being sarcastic. I think I disrespected her Jesus Christ. All of the kids started laughing at my comment or probably at Sister Gilmore's twisted facial expression.

"What? What do you mean?" My question confused her. She probably feared it.

"My mother read me a scripture in the adult Bible about what Jesus looked like. It said his hair was woolly, his skin was black as coal and his eyes were fiery red."

"Oh really. Where at?" When she spoke, her words were short and fast and her body became as stiff as a crack head. She was ready to prove me wrong and I was not prepared to prove Mommy right.

"I don't remember. But I know it's in there somewhere."

"In their somewhere," she murmured. "Sister Dana, you need to get your facts together before you speak in the name Lord Jesus Christ. Maybe your mother should join you next week during service."

"Yes, Ma'am." My chin aimed for my chest.

"You sayin' Jesus was black? Jesus was no black man!" A dark-skinned, bald-headed, husky voice, sharply dressed, boy shouted.

"He was so a black man!" I defended what I knew was the truth. Mommy would never lie to me. Then Sister Gilmore broke us up. The rest of the group began talking amongst themselves about what they thought of my opinion.

"Everyone quiet! I mean quiet. Timothy, stop it this minute! Stand up and read these two paragraphs on page 79 starting with 'The Resurrection.'"

After I told Miss Gilmore that little piece of info, her personality shifted to someone far off somewhere. She wasn't warm anymore towards me. I felt uncomfortable because she treated me as if I had a disease or somethin'. I wonder was she on the devil's side or God's side? Was she in the dark or in the light? One thing I smelled on her, what I sensed, was a lot of fear. I don't know why, I wasn't trying to hurt her. I can smell fear miles away because I've experienced being in the core of it, dealing with Daddy-James.

Once the morning session was over, intermission began. Half the congregation went down stairs to get a plate of food. Miss Loula from my building was serving fried chicken, candied yams, collard greens, chitterlings, corn, mash potatoes and my favorite corn bread. I was too hurt to eat. Their ignorance just slashed my appetite to pieces. One of the pastors standing with the deacons and reverends approached me with a soft smile and lightly placed his hand on my shoulder and said,

"Sister, it would be better if you come to church with a parent or guardian." I told the pastor, "A guardian accompanies me every Sunday. A guardian angel." They all laughed at me and said 'I was cute.' What happened to *their* belief system? The pastors told me to bring a parent to church with me on Sunday.

While heads were in their bibles, I was writing in my journal.

May 5, 1984
Dear Journal,
Does Jesus really look like the man hanging on their walls? Then why would the Bible lie? Hmm, his hair was woolly and his skin was like coal. Coal is supposed to be black, right? Okay, okay, stop doubting yourself. Dana, remember when Mommy got on you about doubting yourself? Nearly put me on punishment for hanging onto doubts. Shouldn't they know the truth? It's sad that, sister Gilmore fought to defend a lie.

I left twenty minutes before service was over. I put the Bible in my book bag, and rode my bike through the handball courts. Got off and did a quick hopscotch game and resumed to ride back home. As soon as I walked in the door, I told Mommy what happened to me. She explained 'that not everybody could see the truth. And sometimes when you present the truth to some people, it is hard for them to accept it.

"It's sad that when you start asking serious questions, people back away and call you crazy or evil for attempting to even think differently. Don't start thinking clearly, they'll throw you into a loony house." She sort of laughed but I knew she was not joking, "I know one thing, it's hard, but I'm trying to unlearn a lot of my negative ways, Dana." And with that, Mommy lit up her cigarette. "I need to arrest a lot of my toxic desires too. Dana, I really hope you use my shortcomings as lessons you could learn from and not follow."

"I'm not going to follow your mistakes, Mommy. Trust me, I'm learning."

"I know I ain't the most perfect person in the world, but the parts of me that you find that are good, use them to help develop yourself. 'Cause Baby, I ain't gonna be here forever." She continued, "And don't be upset with them people at church. They don't know any better. They conformed and programmed in the darkest and saddest way." She thought again, "Well, not all of 'em, most of 'em. They don't wanna grow. They are comfortable where they are. The light is too bright for them to see. You understand what-I'm-sayin?"

"What light?"

"Follow me, Dana. Stay with me." She flapped her two fingers back and forth at our foreheads. She continued, "Subliminally speaking, when you are being lied to, you are in the dark, right?"

"Right. And when…" I interrupted. "When you find the truth, you're in the light!"

"Exactly Baby. You know me. That's one thing I despise is a liar. I love the truth. I don't play that shit…and Dana?"

"Yes, Mommy?"

"I don't want you going back to that church. There's plenty of churches around here you could go to besides Karron Baptist Church."

"Yeah, I wanted to get a rest from church for a while anyway."

"Mmm." She turned her attention to me.

"I want to get inside my own head and heart. And like you said before, get to know myself, you know? In church, they want to dismiss your questions with hand-me-down answers and then smear Jesus all over your emotions."

"Nicely put." She listened totally.

"Thank you and Mommy, I know from the bottom of my heart that Jesus was a black man. And I know all the prophets were black too. That's just common sense."

"Yeah, yeah. But understand this too. Dana, you're going to find little, white flies everywhere but…"

"Huh? There is such a fly as little, white flies?"

"No!" She laughed, "I meant to say little, white lies. I always get those two confused. I guess somewhere in my subconscious flies and lies are similar. All they do is buzz and irritate me."

"That's true."

"Dana, what I'm saying is don't try so hard to focus so much on the pictures and images, you see. That stuff can throw you off your path and point. Those little white lies caused a whole lot of confusion and fear in peoples' hearts. Okay, we know the truth about what color Jesus was. It clearly states it in the Bible but then, you have to move on to the bigger picture. Don't focus too much on the details of skin color. Let's look at deeds."

"Yeah, but Mommy why do the people in the church accept those drawings? Why can't they have an artist draw a picture of the real Jesus?"

"I'ma say it again. It balls down to what I taught you last week about fear and the slave mentality. And while we're on the subject of race. Do you remember the note I told you to always keep in your head?"

"Yup. All black people are not good and all white people are not bad. I think I want to start getting into either the Kingdom Hall or the Mosque."

"What?! Girl, you're too much." Mommy laughed, "Why do you want to be a J.W.? Because of Michael Jackson?"

"No!"

"Yeah."

"No! Exploration. But really I want to start relaxing on Sundays for a while."

"I hear you, Baby."

When Sunday came back around, I tried to relax but my body was accustomed to getting up early for church. Mommy and I decided to utilize those wee hours into choreography. We created dance steps to Guy's "Groove Me," and studied the choreography Janet Jackson's "Pleasure Principle" video. I'm going to be a star some day, I promise. And later on when I'm in my late twenties, I'm going to write books and put all of my dancing energy into my books. Then when I'm almost forty, I will write a play out of my journals and build a stage that looks like an open book, have a band, and dance on the unique stage. And when I'm fifty, the special number five, I will buy an island of my own and name it *God's playground*. Yeah, that sounds nice and if Mommy's alive, she will help me grow herbs and plantations and keep the land as organic and natural as possible. My whole family will live on this island of mine, a free country. Uncle Jerry will spin the sounds in the field with my band while celebrities and tourists enjoy the sounds.

On some sunny Sundays, Mommy and I would take long walks down to the Village and we'd talk and build on the meaning of life. If she had money, she would take me and Donell out to fancy restaurants. Sometimes we would go out of spontaneity. Funny thing about Mommy is she never placed great importance on appearances. Of course, our clothes were always neat and clean. Mommy would always say,

"Having character, self-respect and dignity is what matters. You have some people who dress down and they're the wealthiest people in the damn country. It's the way they carry themselves. The contentment in their eyes, their etiquette and their character says a lot. And then you have some folk who dress up in the finest clothing but their minds are still in the gutter or they're spiritually and morally bankrupt. That shit is tacky as hell. They'll spit on the ground and not think nothing of it. What's that saying? You can take the man out the gutter but you can't take the gutter out the man." So when we went out to fancy restaurants, Mommy, Donell and I did not let our surroundings affect us, we controlled our surroundings. The key was to always remain centered and not for a minute let any body sway you. We stayed centered and relaxed in character. With that attitude, waiters and waitresses always treated us with great respect.

It wasn't long before I began to see that God's extension wasn't only in a church or on a picture frame or on a cross or in a Bible. I found that God was everywhere! In, out, up, down, over, under and around everything! I saw bits and pieces of goodness of God in everyone. Even in me. Nawnie told me the more I am good, the more God will shine through me. Sometimes I see God's design in someone's beautiful eyes, a beautiful voice, a personality, or even hidden beauty like that sister in The Carolina Choir at Karron Baptist Church. I don't think Heaven resides only in the skies but Heaven is in humble, peaceful and beautiful places and Hell is in painful, confused and ugly things. Confusion is the darkness of Hell. Some church people are confused when they say things like, "I'm getting dressed up for the Lord!" I look at them like they're crazy. God was there helping you purchase those clothes on your back. Maybe their God might be impressed with your gear or your pretty Sunday hat. But I believe our God's concern lies within the content of our heart. The lightness, the innocence, its purity.

10
jam

Today is my birthday! I'm floating. Mommy hot-pressed and curled my hair early this morning. I can't stop myself from going into the bathroom and fluffing and playing in my beautiful, silky hair. I look like a beautiful, black Barbie doll. My hair looks like a loose Jerry curl except I don't have all that juice. I can't wait to go outside to show off how pretty I look to everyone.

My hair is bouncing like a slinky and resting perfectly around my neck. I pull it to see how long it is and it reaches to the bone of my shoulder blade. My bangs are so long, they are touching my chin now. I let go of my bangs and they bounce back just above my eyebrows.

"Dana, come here! I'm in the back bathroom!" Mommy shouted.

I stood at the doorway. Mommy didn't look at me.

"Sit down." Her eyes were focused on her reflection in the mirror. She squinted her eyebrows together to line them.

"Since today's your birthday, you ready to start wearing eyeliner?"

"Really, Mommy? I've been waiting my whole life for this day."

"Look up and try not to blink." I sat up poised. My eyes fluttered tears while she sketched my eyes beautifully like hers.

"What about my eyebrows?"

"You don't need pencil, your eyebrows are thick enough. You got your fathers' eyebrows." She dipped her brownie in the Vaseline jar and smoothed out my eyebrows and then glossed my lips. If only Sherman could see me now, he would be *on it like a hornet.* "My baby is beautiful!" She exclaimed.

Nawnie doesn't sing the "Miss Special" song as often to me as she used to. I guess I'm getting too big for that kind of stuff. Nawnie's been mad at me 'cause of the way I've been dressing lately. I love my new body and I'm going to flaunt it to the whole wide world. Nawnie said her fingers have been itching lately. We all know what that means. It means someone in the family is either pregnant or is going to get pregnant. I know it ain't me. I hope it's Auntie Geneva. She needs to have a child of her own so she could quit bossing us around.

Mommy and I have been waiting for the elevator, which seemed like forever. The butterflies in my stomach are just as anxious to get outside as I am. Some of the losers in the building like to skip floors by pressing the red stop button. Sometimes they hit the stop button lightly so that it doesn't ring while they skip floors. Mommy and I peeked through the two elevator windows and watched the elevator car slow down to the fifteenth floor. Without stopping to open, it proceeded to go down. Mommy quickly walked toward the staircase and shouted,

"Y'all better not do it! Let it stop on the thirteenth floor, y'all!" She ran back to look through the elevator door window. The elevator slowed down to our floor but, instead of the doors opening, it jerked up and down and then proceeded to the lobby. They sho' nuff disrespected us. Mommy knew the secret to forcing the elevator to open back up. She shook the elevator door in a sideways rocking motion. It made the elevator jerk back upwards. Whoever was in the elevator started screaming, "Hey stop it! Eh Yo! Stop it, Yo!" The voice sounded familiar. Mommy shook the hell out of that elevator door until it opened. She's fresh!

It was Rhaheem, 'Lil Cynthia, and Melissa standing with stiff and nervous smiles.

"Now y'all should be ashamed of yourselves. I asked y'all nicely and y'all still skipped our floor." They apologized. I smirked at Rhaheem the way Troy smirks at me. On our way to the train station, Mommy and I picked up the pace. My hair bounced and Mommy's leg muscles flexed. As we walked pass two other project buildings, we drew mad attention. There were too many evil eyes around here. Well, I ain't gonna let them bother me because Mommy and I are protected by a thousand angels. We stopped by the store and Mommy bought her favorite, a tall can of Old English beer.

"Baby, we have to hurry up before the train comes." We ran up the stairs by two's. We checked for undercover cops. After two guys hopped the turnstile, we followed. Nobody paid at Jackson Avenue train station. We ran for the open doors of the 2 train and rode her to 149th street Grand Concourse. We transferred for the 4 train, sat down and all eyes were on us. We stayed centered and relaxed and blocked them out.

"Dana listen, what we just did wasn't cool. If I had more money,

I would pay the fare. Mommy didn't get her check yet so I had to borrow some money from Nawnie. I promise you as soon as I start this job at the cleaners, I'm gonna make it up to you for your birthday, okay?"

"It's okay, Mommy."

"Dana, I don't think we're going to make the 2 o'clock movie. If you want to kill time, we could hang out in the Village."

"Ooh yes, the Village! Forget the movies. Let's go to the Village. Let's just have fun! I love hanging out with you Mommy, I love you! You're my best friend!"

"You're my best friend too and I love you too, Dana." Passengers were drawn to her smile.

Everyone got off at 42nd street. An old Indian lady stayed. Mommy loves her Old English beer, but why drink beer when you know it's gonna make you pee? We walked through the trains' car. Nobody was in the last two cars. Mommy had to go. She peed in between the cars. I guarded her while she peed. Hey things happen. Thank God she didn't make an accident on herself. The train was swaying and I held on for dear life.

We got off at Union Square and walked from 14th Street to Washington Square Park. I like the way the people from the Village dress. They seem to be freer than folks in the Boogie Down Bronx. People around my way dress alike, like clones. The people in the Village dressed like models from magazines and actors from movies. Even the black people from Manhattan looked different. Punk rock is a fly style, it shows a carefreeness about the person. I like the style of faded old jeans with holes in the knees, the black police shoes, and the Blues Brothers' sunglasses.

Their stores were much nicer than ours too. Their buildings had nice spacious terraces with chairs and plants in them and not that storage junk or graffiti I see around the way. Where's Dr. Jay's? The village had exotic stores that we didn't have in our communities like Sun Glass Hut, The Vitamin Shop, The Gap, Benetton, Banana Republic and even supermarkets with fancy names that I can't even pronounce. Fordham Road has nothing on the village! People around the way don't even know there's a whole 'nother world out here. They think it's all about them and their local reputations.

The fumes from the buses blew in my face. The birds' songs sounded louder and people around me walked slower. That is a sure sign that winter is over.

For my birthday, comedians, jugglers, musicians and dancers entertained me in the circle of Washington Square Park. Then we walked to 34th Street to visit the Empire State Building. We walked around Macy's and took mental notes of how the dummies were dressed. I noticed wealthy white women going in and coming out of stretch limos. 'One day I will be wealthy.' I thought. Across the street there stood a nice boutique store. We went in. Mommy had to go to the bathroom again. While she used the restroom, I saw the most prettiest, daintiest, unique pair of yellow and white crystal stub earrings cut in the shape of a daisy.

"You want those?" Mommy startled me from behind.

"Yeah, but they're forty-five dollars." I know Mommy can't afford these earrings.

"Do you mind if Mommy puts it on layaway?"

"I don't. When will you be able to get them out?

She took her change from the cashier and smiled at me,

"Soon."

Mommy, let's do something else. Let's go somewhere. Let's head back down to the Village." We made a detour and headed toward Washington Square Park.

Mommy sounded apologetic,

"Dana, all I got is $4 left."

"Mommy, I don't care about the money. I'm happy!" I exclaimed. "I'm happy winter's over, I'm happy to be hanging out with you on *my* birthday and please, please no movies Mommy and..."

"Girl, slow down. You get too excited just like yo' mammy giiirrrl." She joked around.

"Ooh, I have an idea!" I said.

"What?"

"We could go back around the way. I think Uncle Jerry's supposed to be DJ-ing this weekend in the courts or is it next weekend?"

"That's right, I think it is this weekend. We could do whatever you want. Okay? Today's your day, Baby." She landed a triple kiss on my, what she calls "chunky, chink cheeks." She smiled and shouted with glowing pride,

"My Baby's 14 years old!"

I couldn't stop blushing and batting my eyelashes.

"Mommy!" I whined. A few passersby smiled with Mommy.

"Okay, okay, I didn't mean to embarrass my Baby like that. But, Dana I'm proud of you. Look at you. You're growing nicely and you're taking your time. You're not fast like a lot of these girls running around here getting' pregnant early and shit." We stopped to hug and my arm did not leave her waist. It didn't matter who was looking because we were in the village. In a place where nothing you do surprises these non-conformist, open-minded people. Mommy looked at her red "Public Enemy" digital clock that hung around her neck.

"It's still early. Even if Jerry is jamming today, it won't be until later on this evening." We chilled for a few more minutes, looked around. Sammy the corniest comedian was talking in a circle of a small crowd of people. Mommy got up and fixed her shorts.

"Ain't nothing happening. Let's go sit at the pier and kill some time." She suggested.

"Sounds good to me."

Mommy and I wore the same colors, blue and white. We showed off our legs. I wore my white dungaree skirt and my blue t-shirt. Mommy wore her white Liz Claiborne buttoned down shirt and her dungaree Lee shorts. Mommy received lots of attention from all types of men. I heard a few men utter to Mommy as we walked by,

"You better work!"

Our legs are strong but I can see that Mommy's legs had more of a story to tell than mine. Mommy's legs showed depth and definition of true womanhood. As we walked down the hill of Christopher Street toward the pier, I felt so high in the clouds that I didn't want to let Mommy's hand go. I felt so proud of Mommy for being my mother and my friend.

We sat on the ledge of the pier staring at the sparkling water that separated New York from New Jersey. She sat with one leg prompt up on the ledge, like a Virginia Slims model, with eyes looking far away.

"Something about water calms me." She took out her cigarette pack from her shirt pocket and fulfilled her habit.

"Mommy, I'm so proud of you."

"Why you say that Dana?"

"Because you take care of yourself. All of my friends in school say you look like a teenager."

"Oh, Baby. Maybe it's because I do everything in moderation."

"What do you mean by that?"

"I mean when I work out, I don't overdo it, when I get high..." I giggled because of her frankness.

"I get high maybe once a month and when I smoke, it's almost a pack a week. I'm tryin' to slow down though. I need to quit."

I love it when we talk. Our conversations are very expensive and quality like diamonds. Shoot, we are worth more than *diamonds*, because we are naturally eachother's *best friend*. What I like about Mommy is her straight-forwardness. I like the fact that she hides nothing from me. She always told me,

"Why hide? For what? Why should I hide from my children? Life is too short to be hidin'. What? You gonna wait till you on your death bed to spit up the truth? Always tell the truth that way your conscious and heart is free and as light as a feather. I like to keep it real with my kids, word up because y'all are a direct extension of me. I don't play that shit. I don't keep secrets from y'all and I won't. Shit, secrets are too heavy to be carryin' around. I treat y'all the way I want to be treated. Everything I know, you'll know. I don't want you to make the same mistakes I've made, I want y'all to learn from them."

We stayed for about an hour and it started to get crowded with a lot of women that looked and dressed like men and lots of men that looked and dressed like women. Mommy straight up told me, 'they're dressed in drag.' She said, 'not to be afraid of them. Never judge them. Keep my mind and heart open to everybody because I'll never know what message God sent them to give to me.' She continued, "They might look different and act different but we must remember that we all are one. We all are part of God."

We saw a Muslim brother selling incense, oils, Qurans and chew sticks. Mommy bought a $2 bottle of Egyptian Musk. We put some on and it made us feel spiritually powerful and ultra feminine.

On our way back home, we shared her token and went through the turnstile together. I did something today that I never did with anyone in my entire life. I rode in between the train cars with Mommy. The noisy clack and screech of the train, the flashing lights going by, the art of graffiti on the walls, the smell of smoke in the tunnel, all of it was dangerous to me and it was the most wonderful feeling! Mommy and I kept a tight grip on the bars, as the train swerved from station to station. Mommy transformed into a teenager. Instantly, she became my number one best friend.

As soon as the doors opened at Jackson Avenue station, we felt the thunderous bass vibrate through our bones. The bass made me want to kick my feet up and run a fifty-mile marathon. I wanted to scream! The jam is tonight! This is the best birthday in my world! Mommy had two dollars to her name. While the man prepared the sandwich, I had to ask Mommy, "Mommy, what was that about on the train?"

"What do you mean, Dana?"

"Us riding in-between the train cars. That was what I call 'exhilarating'. We never did that before."

"Exhilarating? Good word. Well today is your birthday, right? Now, what we did was what I call 'spontaneity'. I think it's nice to do things just out the spur of the moment. You are 14 years old, boy I remember when I turned fourteen. You know what me and my friends did on my birthday? We jumped the back of the 61 bus and rode it to Third Avenue."

"Weren't y'all scared?"

"Hell no. That was the last thing on our minds. Close your eyes and open your hands."

"Mommy, you didn't. I thought you didn't have enough money to buy them?"

"Right now I don't."

"Thank you so much Mommy. I love you. Why you play so much?"

"Because it's in my nature and I love you. Here, let me put them in." I stood still, inside the congested grocery store. Dudes were buying forties. Chicks were buying Calvin Coolers and I felt so brand new and beautiful in my beautiful daisy, crystal earrings.

We shared a spiced ham and cheese hero and followed the music. On our way toward the basketball courts, we passed crews of people sitting on top of cars and chains that were connected to the 2-foot poles that protected the uneven grass. As soon as Uncle Jerry turned up the volume, people began filling the basketball court. The music played on but no one danced, because the attention was still on the basketball players. The game should be over soon. Uncle Jerry and his boys carried more crates of records to his table.

While I was eating my half of the hero, Mommy placed her tall can of Old English on top of the cemented chess table and got up to help Uncle Jerry wrap a rope around his table and speakers. The court lights flickered and glowed on the basketball players and their squeaky sneakers. Ponies, Pumas, Adidas, Nikes, Converses ran across the faded court grounds. Sweat, spit, blood mixed with adrenaline pulsated through headbands and wristbands. A Band-Aid wrapped around a man's athletic thigh jumps high and score.

I looked toward the fluffy indigo clouds gliding across the light blue sky. The birds played their game of tag above the trees. A crew of about nine funky fresh guys came bopping into the park, taking the short cut through the torn, metal fence. Four of the guys wore red sweat suits with "The Break-Dancer Crew" written across the front in white letters and their tag-up names written across the back in black letters. They wore their suede white Pumas and their clear white Cazals. The waves in their hair made them look drop dead fine. Uncle Jerry spun my jam, "Something Like a phenomenon." A short dude from The Break-Dancer Crew did the wave, spun like a whirlpool to the shore of a pose with one leg over the other and one hand on his hip and one behind his head. He attracted competition. Then another crew came walking through. They all had their hair in cornrows going back. These guys wore baby blue satin Adidas suits and Adidas sneakers with baby blue thick laces. I couldn't tell which crew looked cuter.

A little boy brought over an extra open cardboard box for them to break dance on. A couple of the Adidas crew dancers warmed up for their new routines. Three pretty girls accompanied them. The guys with the braids took off their jackets for their girls to hold. One of the wavy-hair-Puma guy spun on his head like a top without dropping his Cazals and magnetized the crowd. Everyone looked at him with awe.

Big clouds of smoke covered the street across from us. It was the Hispanic's grilling pork in front of their tenement building. It smelled buena! The children and their mothers were sitting on their fire escapes looking down, enjoying the music and entertainment. Mommy sat back down next to me and took a sip from her beer. All of the young children were playing on the monkey bars and slides while singing and dancing to the hip hop and R&B songs. Some little girls were dancing with each other, shaking their colorful barrettes on ponytails, nodding yes or no as they were teaching each other the "Cabbage Patch." Uncle Jerry spun Run DMC's "My Adidas" and a few girls began dancing with each other doing the "Cabbage Patch." Ho! Ho! Ho! Run DMC is the freshest rap group! The Adidas crew did the freshest dance routine. They did some new dance steps I had never seen before.

Miss Loula from the next building came at the right time. She and her three daughters held aluminum pans of food! She never failed us when it came to her catering. I can proudly say that in my neighborhood, amongst my people, love came before money…occasionally.

Melissa and Amina needed one more person to play double-dutch with them. They asked me and I said no. I didn't need to hide behind a game of double-dutch. I wanted to see what was going on. Fly guys and fly girls from Forest projects, McKinley projects, Woodstock and St. Mary's projects came strolling into the jam. Mommy and I started the "Bus Stop" together and then DJ Darryl and his three sisters joined in. I felt very special doing the "Bus Stop." I was the youngest dancer amongst the adults. All the kids watched us. We definitely got our share of attention from everybody.

Then people got up and started doing their own dances. Some people competed and others danced together to the bass music. The music brought about a beautiful vibration amongst everyone on the basketball court, like Hasaan and a bunch of his friends were out there poppin'. Donell and his friends weren't dancing. They rapped to girls and collected phone numbers, competing to see who's going to score the highest amount. Troy and his boys were competing with each other, doing the electric boogie dance combined with the robot and the moonwalk. Whenever Uncle Jerry changed the music, I saw hands raised in the air of approval. Mommy and I did the snake and the wop. Sir Charles came through with his Polaroid and snapped a picture of me and Mommy doing the snake. Mommy took the picture and sat back down to drink her beer. I freaked the snake. I attracted a lot of attention with my flexibility and rhythm. I shuttered my body and then slowed it down and then jumped back into the rhythm of the music.

"Go Da-na! Go Da-na! Go! Go! Go Da-na! " The girls cheered me on. It turned into a battle between the boys and the girls. One of Hasaan's friends started popping around me. Rhaheem and Kelby walked into the circle with arms crossed. Their expressions looked at me like, 'I know you ain't gonna attempt to take him out. You ain't nothin' but a Michael Jackson freak!' I became nervous 'cause I didn't know how to pop like Hasaan's friend but I knew how to do the wave. One real cute guy shouted while staring me into my eyes. "Oooh, that girl got skills!" He wore a nice, black tanktop. The muscles in his arms looked delicious and tight. He wore a silver name belt that read **MOET**. As I got a closer look, he looked just like Sherman. His compliment gave me confidence and I forgot all about my nervousness. I rolled my eyes at Rhaheem and Kelby after I came up doing the snake and then popped my chest up and down, in and in and out and out and in and out. By the crowd's reaction, I knew I was doing it right.

All the little 8 and 9-year-old girls shouted,

"Go, Dana! Go Dana!" I felt like a star. People were pulling out their hands so I could give them a pound. I even gave Kelby a pound. Rhaheem held himself back from letting me give him a pound. I didn't want to give his pissy hands a pound anyway.

I sat back down next to Mommy and she had to admit that Moet was a fine, young man.

"Mommy I swear, I think he's Sherman."

"Sherman?"

"Remember the guy I had a crush on in JHS? He had jerry curls and he knew how to dance like Michael Jackson?"

"Oh yeah. That's him?"

"It looks like him. If it is him, boy he got nice muscles."

"Well, he's fine but not finer than your father was." She said, "He looks good but he has roving eyes. How old is he?"

"I don't know. Sherman has me by a year."

"No, he gotta be older than that. He looks about seventeen."

I didn't care. Besides, age ain't nothing but a number.

"How could you tell, Mommy?"

"Mother's intuition. Maybe because I've been around the block a few times."

I watched Mommy sip her beer and check Moet out.

"He looks too fine. That spells trouble for me. Look at all these girls trying to get at him." She said.

"I know!" I whined.

She looked at me.

"Well you better be careful dealing with a guy like him." She stopped herself. "Enjoy your birthday, Baby. Be upstairs at 10:30."

"Oh! Thank you, thank you, thank you, Mommy. I love you!" I triple kissed her cute cheeks.

"Love you too. I'll be right back." She took another look into my eyes, "And Dana, don't court him, let him court you."

"Okay." Mommy moved around ungracefully. "You have to go to the bathroom?" I asked.

"Yeah. It's getting cool out here. I'm a bring down a jacket for you. It ain't summer yet." And she strutted her sexy, purposeful walk fast, damn near running out the park. Many admired her attractive legs. I felt so proud of her.

The girls on my right knew they were lookin' cute, rockin' their new shell top Adidas with yellow laces that their working mothers bought for them. On the front of their yellow t-shirts printed in orange letters was SHUGA SWEET CREW. When the SHUGA SWEET CREW laughed and talked, they all exaggerated their head movements to show the bounce in their freshly done mushroom hairstyles. Their double golden bamboo name earrings made a hallow clacking sound to show everybody that it was made out of real gold.

Moet was leaning on the fence with his boys reciting Doug E. Fresh's and Slick Rick's "La-di-da-di." He flirted with the fly girls, but his attention was more on his music and his boys. The girls sang Slick Rick's song toward Moet and his boys sang back toward them. It kind of turned into a singing game.

"He is soooo cute. I wanna drink some Moet!" they shouted. 'Lil Cynthia and her crew made sure they was heard. The fly girl Elaine shouted, "No. Just give me a shot of Moet! I'm fine with just that." The SHUGA SWEET CREW laughed and passed down cigarettes and Double Mints. They exhaled Kool "O's" from their mouths. Them girls knew how to smoke their lungs off. 'Lil Cynthia and her crew of ten girls built chemistry with Moet and his crew of eight boys.

I peeked over at Moet and his eyes met mine. Maybe because I was a new face to him? I pulled away eye contact and at the same time pulling him in. Shyly, I looked down and then I returned to him. He was right there with me, interested and amused. I think he liked my stylish way of flirting (Thank you Mommy.) His eyelashes were unbelievably thick and long like my old "Hug Me, Mommy" baby-doll. A complexion like the color of deep wet sand. Braids neat 'n clean. Medium size cornrows going back with a curl at the end of each braid. A silky, smooth, hairline, highlighted with soft black baby hairs. He could electrocute me with that luminous smile. Moet's dimples posed close to his nose when he smiled, which made his eyes smile as well.

I tried to hold on to what little patience I had when he signaled for me to come over. I told him he had to meet me half way.

Mommy always warned me to never 'waste my face', meaning never let people grow tired of seeing your face all the time. That's the fastest way to lose your magnetism. No matter how hungry and desperate I get for a man, never let him know that I'm hungry for him. 'Cause once he does, his respect for me goes down the tubes. Men love to respect a strong and full woman. It turns them off to be around a needy and empty woman.

Lord knows I wanted to run over and jump on top of him like a kid to a carousel but I'm strong and I'ma be in control. Those hungry girls liked to foam at the mouth when they saw us. If their eyes were arrows, I know I would've been dead already. I know they wish they were me. They wish they were in my shoes, in my skirt, and in my humble body. They probably wish they had the courage to jump me and scratch up my face to make me look ugly and stomp my bones out so that I could no longer dance. They better not try to 'cause my mother is from the streets and she would fight anybody for her children. They know Mommy's reputation. She never lost a fight.

When we connected, it felt so special. He smelled different from George. He smelled like a pleasant, soft cologne. He smelled so clean and his teeth were shaped perfectly like Mario Van Peebles. He lost his overbite. Is he really the same person?

"How you doin'?"

"Fine."

"What's your name?"

"Dana."

"Dana? My name is Sherman but everybody calls me Moet."

"I knew it was you?"

"What do you mean?"

"You don't remember me? I'm the girl that used to hang out with Sahidah."

"Oh shit. Uh, pardon me. You're Dana?" I laughed, "Yes."

"Yes. You definitely don't sound the way Sahidah described." I commented.

"How did she describe me?"

"I'm not going to rat on my girl." I said.

"Well you don't smell the way "your girl" described."

"Excuse me? What are you talking about?"

"She told me you had…" He paused and laughed. "I don't mean to laugh but she said you had a bowel problem."

"No she didn't. Never! She said you spoke like a hoodlum and I was too nice of a girl for you."

"Oh!" His muscles were more pronounce the harder he laughed, "She's a crazy story-teller. I never said that. I always thought you were a cutie." His mellow voice sounded beautiful and sincere.

"We got a birthday in tha house, y'all," Uncle Jerry announced on the mic. His right hand man, DJ Darryl, started scratching and cuttin' up Stevie Wonder's version of Happy Birthday.

"I have to say happy birthday to my niece, Dana! Come to the tables!"

"Ha.Ha.Happy B-B-Birth-day to ya." Everybody sang and clapped together.

Uncle Jerry shouted me out on the mic. I felt everybody's eyes pointing at me. I walked carefully to the tables, hoping I wouldn't trip on anything.

"See ya later, Dana!" Sherman said. I liked the way he said name. As I sat down I thought about what Sahidah told me three years ago. What the hell was she talking about? Sherman doesn't sound ghetto. 'Lil Cynthia's crew looked like they rejoiced at my absence. Uncle Jerry made me sit behind the tables until my curfew was over.

"You sit here and wait for your mother to come back! What time she said you had to go upstairs?"

"10:30."

"That's too late. You sit here and wait until she comes back. That boy is too old for you. You made 14 not 17." I sat down. If only there were a desk in front of me to hide my face on. I sat there and watched everybody enjoy my 14th birthday. Jerry was never a failure at embarrassing me. I guess he felt responsible for me since he was the only male role model in my life right now. My father has not been around since I was five, so Uncle Jerry felt responsible for me. Lil' Tina walked up to Uncle Jerry.

"Hey, Jerry man! Why do that to her? Today's her birthday! Don't let her look all sad and shit! Let the girl dance and have fun!"

"Not wit none of these boys around here! She's stayin' right there until her mother gets back."

"Come on, Jerry!" He blocked Tina out and put his headphones on halfway while he mixed in another record. Lil' Tina just shrugged her powerless shoulders and walked away. Everybody went crazy when he played KRS-ONE's "The J-the I-the M- the M-the Y, the J-the I the M, it's Jimmy! It's Jimmy!"

Mommy hadn't come back yet! Melissa and Amina were still nice enough to ask me if I wanted to play tag with them. I wish I would've said yes when they asked me the first time to play double-dutch. I answered for Uncle Jerry.

"No, I can't!" I shouted over the music.

"Why can't chu' play wit us!?" Melissa asked loud enough for Uncle Jerry to hear.

"Because I have to wait for my mother to come back!"

We couldn't grab Uncle Jerry's attention. Maybe he was blocking us out like he did with Lil' Tina too. My eyes did not meet theirs, my eyes searched to find Sherman. I found him near the entrance of the park chasing Elaine. Sahidah must've just came. She was sitting with Cynthia wearing her SHUGA SWEET CREW t-shirt. Elaine's hair was bouncing all over the place. She is like the flyest girl out of 'Lil Cynthia's pack next to 'Lil Cynthia. She has a nice hazelnut complexion with glassy dark-brown almond shaped eyes. Her hair is thick and black with shiny waves that stretches to the middle of her back. Elaine's figure is thick and compact. I spotted Elaine pointing her fingers all in Sherman's face, provoking him while Sahidah joined her. It looked like he liked it and he liked chasing them. I couldn't take my eyes off of him and his beautiful physique, his beautiful smile, his beautiful everything. I have to say the only advantage this girl has over me is her age (she's about seventeen) and her dad is still in her life. Her dad and mom are still together. That's about it, though. I got teen spirit, talent and personality to take me to the many levels I need to go in my life.

I asked Uncle Jerry for permission to go to the bathroom. Maybe if I walk pass them, I could see if Sherman genuinely digs me. I wonder how many girlfriends he must have now. Uncle Jerry told me to hurry up and don't be slick 'cause he got his eye on me. I walked toward the bathroom and I could not find them. I even walked around the bathroom before going in and I did not see them. The bathroom was packed with Puerto Ricans and black girls. Girls were in there smoking cigarettes and weed. Migdalia was tying up her t-shirt to show her navel. The skinny girls stood to the side envying the thick girls' figure. Thick is in. Curves are in. The skinny girls coveted thick hips and big breasts. They carried Loula's plate in their hands and ate high caloric cupcakes and drank sodas. What they need to do is get into Nawnie's food.

Elaine walked in the bathroom and breathing stopped. My jealous heart jumped. Migdalia didn't kiss her ass, she licked it. I said hi but she looked at me with no recognition. It was a very chilling vibra-

tion. I felt lower than a comma. Maybe it's my own insecurities or perhaps, it could be my sensitivities that is feeling her masked insecurities.

All the girls who were prepping themselves up in the mirror, fishing for attention from each other, couldn't hook a compliment once
Elaine stepped in. Two by two, girls started to leave the bathroom.
Shortly, the SHUG SWEET CREW filled up the bathroom with laughter, gum popping, cigarettes and gossip. Sahidah didn't look my way.
Something inside me prevented me from approaching her. She showed
me shade in her silence. Then Migdalia and I left the entire bathroom
to Elaine and the SHUGA SWEET CREW.

"Dana," Uncle Jerry commanded, "I don't know where your
mother is, but you betta go upstairs. It's too late for you to be out
here anyway. Birthday or not, you still have a curfew."

"But my mother said I could stay out until t.."

"Look, you go upstairs girl!" Uncle Jerry barked, "It's too late for
you to be out here." It was hard to hold in my tears but I did. And I
kept a calm face. Everybody sang Frankie Beverly's, "Before I Let Go!"
I was too embarrassed to look at Sherman who stood near by the
entrance with his boys. I walked out the courts toward my fucking
building! I can't wait until I grow up and have my damn freedom!
Freedom to come and go as I please! Where's Mommy? Damn it!

"Where you stepping off to?" Someone asked me from behind.

I turned around and it was (Scream!) Sherman! No, he can't be talking to me. Me? Out of all those fly home girls in the park?

"Home." I tried to be nonchalant. I pretended as if guys chase
after me all the time.

"Why? It's still early. Shouldn't you be enjoying your birthday?" His
lips looked so juicy and mouth so clean.

"Yeah, but my uncle doesn't like to see me talking to any guys.
He's very protective of me."

"Oh. He saw us hookin' up?"

"Yeah."

"Where he at? I'ma talk Money into letting you stay."

"I don't think you'd want to. He's the tall one over there," I
pointed. He looked over at Uncle Jerry and I saw his eyes shutter at
his great height and confident aura. Uncle Jerry's chest and back were
stronger than gravity. His body stood upright while he was spinning
the turntables. The Johnson & Johnson's baby oil brought out the

cherry brown in his complexion. The shine brought out the definition in his arms. I know one thing for sure, Uncle Jerry should be
called DJ Sheppard. 'Cause he kept colorful herds of women flocking
around him. They may say that they're in love with my uncle but I
believe it's just lust. That's my family's trademark. We, the Strongs are
a symbol of power, popularity, sensuality and respect. The curse of the
Strongs is our trademark can sometimes work for us and other times
work against us.

"Oh he got that," Sherman said, "but he can't walk you home
now can he?" I blushed. We talked and flirted up 13 flights of stairs until
we reached 10:30. We made our time quality. In our conversation we
came to know the truth about Sahidah. She befriended him and twisted
stories around, telling him falsehoods about me, to keep us from getting acquainted. But see we were destined to meet.
    "Thank you Sherman for walking me home."
    "Nah, don't sweat it. So what sup, birthday girl? How old are you
now?"
    "I don't want to tell you."
    "Why? You ashamed?"
    "I ain't ashamed."
    "You look about seventeen."
    "I'm close to that. If we get to see each other again, then maybe
I'll tell you."
    "I like that. I like you." His eyes provoked my heart to believe his
every word. He has a lot of potential, too. But I don't know if I want
to invest my life and time into him since he's planning on leaving for
college this September.
    Both of Sherman's beautiful hands held my hands and swung them
in his as if we were already boyfriend and girlfriend. I felt overwhelmed
by his beauty and body scent. His muscles glistened as he stood strong
like a lion. Somebody in apartment E turned their radio up. "Beautiful
Ones" played on the radio. We slowed danced against the brick wall.
Intimacy with Sherman frightens me because I hardly know him, but
damn! This is a once-in-a-life-time opportunity. Home girls would
love to kiss a guy like him. They would dream all day and fantasize in
the staircase about a guy like Sherman. It curls me up inside to think
of all the girls who're sweating and looking for him right now in this
very moment. Wondering where did that fine guy go? Humph, he is

spending his time with me y'all!

He made me feel so special! Shoot, Nawnie was right. I am special and if you're nasty call me Miss Special. Nah, let me stop. The Force MD's "Tender Love" played behind apartment E's door. He tried to kiss me but I weaved my way out of it.

"So we gonna keep in touch, right?" He asked.

"Yeah, I guess."

"What chu' mean, you guess?" He went to steal another kiss from me. I turned my face around and he missed my lips. He laughed right in my face,

"What chu' doin'?" I felt embarrassed.

"I'm not ready to kiss you, yet."

"Come here." Sherman gently touched my chin and exhaled through his nose. His nose touched my nose. His determination turned me on. He tried again and this time he succeeded because I surrendered to the warmest and softest peck. He disconnected and smiled,

"Happy Birthday, Dana." He wrote his math on a small piece of paper and placed it in my palm.

"Thank you, Sherman." I watched him fly down the stairs by two's reciting Big Daddy Kane's lyrics while I held my hand over my heart so that cupid wouldn't shoot it.

11
i.c.u.

Mommy can be so unpredictable at times. She hasn't been home for the past four days and Nawnie started to get worried until Dr. Goldsmith at Mt. Sinai Hospital called and said that they had to admit her in for pneumonia. Pneumonia?! How?!

Auntie Leniece, the eldest aunt, took me with her to see Mommy. She shared her life with me on the way there. We talked about cousin Lamonte's singing career. She said, "Tonka baby, I'm so proud of my son. You know he's about to get a deal with Arista?"

"Arista Records? Whitney Houston is on Arista!"

"Yup. See what happens when you stay focused and work hard on your craft?"

"Yeah, it pays off. You get your rewards. I remember he practiced everyday on his Casio singing his own songs."

"Just remember this Tonka and I tell Lamonte this all the time. Just because you got there and you got your record deal, honey it don't stop there. There is more work to follow. So there is this old saying, it goes, 'it's not about what you reap all the time but it's about the seeds you sow. Never stop sowing those seeds and don't stop once you start receiving all those accolades. I tell him, you gotta keep working toward perfection. Whatever that is." I soaked it in for a moment.

"Auntie Leniece, can I hear you sing?" When she smiled, the gap in her teeth made her look even prettier.

"What song do you want me to sing?"

"Billie Holiday."

"Not 'God Bless The Child' again?"

"Please."

She closed her eyes.

"Close your eyes...and rest your tired body next to mine..."

"That's not how it starts." She put her finger to her mouth to hush me while she continued.

"Nobody knows more than you...these hard times that we're livin' through. So ba-by we'll go on and on. Lord knows we got each other…"

A beautiful second soprano voice looped with a soothing melody relaxed my ears, my mind and my spirit. I know for sure if Leniece was in any kind of trouble, she could probably sing her way out of it. What my ears and heart heard made other people on the train stop talking and listen to her beautiful voice. We could not stop smiling. Maybe it was because she couldn't stop smiling either. She made me proud to have her as my blood. Next thing I knew, she tapped me on my lap and we walked off while finishing her song. Heads followed our direction.

"That was Savannah Band."

"Savannah Band? When did they come out?"

"They came out in the mid seventies. One girl and a band."

"Do you think Uncle Jerry has it?"

"Yeah. I know your Uncle Junior definitely has it. He was the one who introduced me to it."

We stopped by the gift store and picked up some Haagen Daz vanilla ice cream, two Get Well balloons and cards. Writing a check out to the gift store, made my aunt look so important. I filled in the card and signed it, 'Love Always, your loving daughter, Dana.' We also bought some Spanish food, Mommy's favorite, yellow rice, black beans, plantains and roasted garlic rotisserie chicken. Auntie Leniece paid for it with a check too. What does that mean? Why doesn't she like to use money?

They placed Mommy in the Intensive Care Unit. Before Auntie Leniece opened the door she looked through the square window then held her face. I did not let her crying dissuade me. Mommy couldn't have looked that bad. I knocked, then entered. Mommy's pretty round eyes looked away from the television and brightened up when she saw me. She smiled,

"Dana!"

"Hi, Mommy." We hugged and kissed. I love her so much.

"Leniece, stop it. Come in!" She said in her-trying-to-be patient tone.

"Defrager? Are you okay, honey? I'm so sorry babe. I don't…"

"I'm fine. I don't feel as bad as I might look."

"Mommy, you don't look bad." I pressed the top of her hair down. Dag! Auntie Leniece need to control her emotions sometimes. Mommy thanked us for the gifts and food. She sat up in her craftmatic bed with the oxygen tube wrapped across her face. Auntie Leniece couldn't hold it in any longer. She bursted out crying, again. She went into the bathroom to gather herself. Mommy was very calm. She just looked at Auntie Leniece in a pathetic way. Like maybe my sister need to admit her own self in the hospital. Mommy told me about Auntie Leniece and her dramatic personality. She said she's been that way ever since she was born. Mommy was so annoyed with her sister's maudlin behavior, she rolled her eyes and turned the channel on the TV set.

"Dana, I'll be home tomorrow. OK?"

"OK. But Mommy, what happened?"

"We'll talk about it when I come home."

"Are you feeling okay?"

"I feel a little weak but the doctor said I should be feeling alright by tomorrow. Where's Donell?"

"I think he, Jason and Jamel went to the after school center at the HUB."

"Well, when Donell gets back tell him to call me. They turn the phones off at ten."

"Mommy, I don't like to see you looking like this."

"I know, Baby, and I don't like feeling like this either. Come with me to the TV room."

"Aren't you going to eat the food we bought you?"

"I'm not that hungry. I'll eat it later."

Mommy walked slowly to the TV room. I double tied her blue hospital gown. She weakly knocked on the bathroom door.

"Yeah?"

"Leniece." She called, "Me and Dana are going in the TV room. It's three doors down."

We all hung out in the TV room with Mommy's new friends. Some were visitors and others were patients. They really enjoyed Mommy's down-to-earth sense of humor. She makes friends quickly like a gregarious kindergarten child. Auntie Leniece walked in with make-up in tact wearing her forced smile. She ain't foolin' nobody over here. A few minutes later she relaxed after we all kept laughing at the "Richard Bey" show.

12
watch yo' back

I hate this block! Gigi "The Instigator" came knocking on my
door with Sahidah and two other girls from Lil' Cynthia's crew, telling
me that Elaine's crew is going to jump me for trying to get at Sherman.
What did I do?

"He was the one who wanted to talk to me." I defended.

"Well, I don't know about all lat, all I know is people is mad at chu'
for talkin' ta Moet. Ya better watch yo' back, girl." said Gigi pressing
her finger on my temple and rolling her evil beady eyes at me. I swear
if she didn't have back up, I would've swung on that fuckin' bitch!

"And you know better than nat, Dana! You know not ta mess wit
Elaine. Her peoples is from the 'Shuga Sweet Crew'! They will jump
anybody in a heartbeat, especially if you tryta play them or they man
out!

My tone went soft. "Well, I wasn't trying to play her and I didn't
know Moet was her…"

"What?" She interrupted. "We're not in church, Dana, you can
speak up." She turned to her girls, and they smirked.

"I said I wasn't tryin' to play her. And you know that, Sahidah. You
know me. She's taking things too personal. If I knew that Moet was
her man, I would've told him to step off."

"Yeah right." Gigi licked her lips hard and said, "Well now you
know. All I-know is ya bet ta step offah Moet. One, he's down with
"The Forest Crew." Two, muthafucka was probably drunk rappin' to
yo ass anyways."

"Oh shit!" They all said.

I tucked in my top lip and bit down hard. Felt no pain. "So why
didn't Elaine stop him from talking to me?" I asked.

Some short girl walked up on me and said, "Girl, you just don't
know!" She shook her head, "She was about ta slice up your pretty face
until me and Sahidah held her back in the bathroom." A tall big boned
girl caught my attention by making a loud sucking sound and opened
her mouth to reveal a razorblade underneath her tongue. I turned to

look at Sahidah but she looked away.

I muttered, "Thank you."

"Look, Dana, I know you ta be a real nice girl," Gigi said, "You don't belong wit a nigga like Moet. Okay? He's too wild for you." She turned to her girls, "He from Forest Projects?" Heads nodded. "Them Forest niggas will fuck a girl like her, whip her out, get that ass pregnant and be out and on with the next chick? See girl, don't set yo'-self up, step offah his big dick. You might hurt yourself."

"Gigi," Shorty called, "How you know he got a big dick?"

"Bitch, don't try that with me. Word gets around. Moet's a hoe, okay." My heart ached. Gigi turned to her friends and pointed at me, "She be trynta talk all white 'n shit, Dana needs to be wit them white boys in the suburbs. You-know-what-I'm-sayin'?" I swallowed nervous spit. One of the girls put her 2 cents in, getting her thrills off of riding my fear.

"Dana, we just warning you, watch yo' muthafuckin' back. You hear? You hear? Word um up! Watch yo' back."

They warned me alright, but it felt more like a threat. Punks! I can't believe Sahidah didn't utter one word in my defense. Her silence showed me that she was down with them all along. What a punk! And how could I have been so niave. Even though we stopped hanging out, I still considered Sahidah to be a decent person. She's nothing but a feeble coward. I don't trust any of them jealous bitches now!

My eyebrows rose toward my forehead as the elevator door closed in our faces. I wandered through the house looking for privacy to think and pray. Everyone was in their quarters so I went into Nawnie's bathroom. I can't tell Nawnie what just happened, it'll give her an asthma attack. No bandage can soothe this broken heart of mine. I need to speak to Sherman about this. I don't want to fight. God would you fight my battles for me? Mommy needs to move us outta here. I miss having my own room.

13
limited lifelines

It's been about a week since Mommy has been home from the hospital and I noticed she's not being herself. She's been quite quiet. That's not Mommy. I should've heard her infectious laugh echoing throughout the house by now. Or I should've heard her twinkling melodies of her silver bracelets. Saturday mornings meant playing handball for Mommy. But why is she still here? I didn't even hear her smoker's cough lingering through the hallways. Where was she hiding? Auntie Berlinda has been down south for a good week now and, boy, are we enjoying her absence. She locked her VCR, JVC/TV radio, all of her video tapes and her TV inside her wall unit cabinet. Only Troy and Nawnie had the key.

It's funny how around the time Auntie Berlinda left, Uncle Junior came not to visit but to stay for a few weeks. He bought his music equipment and 3 suitcases with him. Nawnie said that Uncle Junior could sleep in Berlinda's room while she was away but when she gets back he would have to sleep in the room with the boys. 'Uncle Junior is going through a lot of stuff,' Nawnie told me. She said, 'his boyfriend and roommate Jack passed away. Uncle Junior and Jack were together for 13 years.' Now that's a long time. I'm not sure if Uncle Junior left his managerial job at Dime bank. I asked Nawnie how come Uncle Junior is the only one in the family who speaks proper English. And why does he put so much emphasis on his T's when he speaks? She told me he had a talking problem when he was a child. He didn't speak clearly and he was a stutterer due to his being a very quiet and non-social child. So she sent Uncle Junior to a tutor who specialized in people who had speaking problems. I think his tutor did a very good job with him.

Uncle Junior played classical music all morning. All that time he used in playing his classical music, I could've been practicing my dance steps in Berlinda's living room. Where's Mommy? He changed the music. Ooh! Barry Manilow. I love his voice. I peeked in the living room entrance.

"Can I come in?"

"Sure." He said.

Albums, movie soundtracks, "Close Encounters of the third kind", "E.T.", Frank Sinatra, Nat King Cole, "Raiders of the Lost Ark", Sammy Davis Jr., Minnie Riperton, "The King and I", and Liza Minelli. All of the Motown albums were spread faced up in chronological order across Berlinda's peach leather couch.

"Dana, do you know who this is?"

"Barry Manilow."

"ExcellenT. ExcellenT musician." He changed the music and entertained me with his favorite, Diana Ross and the Supremes. He did a fantastic impersonation of her. His lean, very tall body moved just like hers. He hunched his shoulders and swayed his head from side to side, and smiled like Diana.

"That was nice!" I clapped. "Uncle Junior do you have Savannah Band?"

"Whoa, how do you know about Savannah Band?"

"Auntie Leniece told me. She even sang the song to me."

"You know I introduced her to them?"

"Yeah, she told me."

"They're still one of my favoriTe bands. UnfortunaTely they did noT grow Together. They broke up before they could come ouT with their second album."

"Oh that's too bad."

I moved the albums to the side and sat on Berlinda's comfortable, peach leather couch while he played Savannah Band for me. I loved them! The lady's voice sounded so sweet and sensual. If I could sing like her. Auntie Leniece had that singer down pact to a T! To an Uncle Junior T!

"Uncle Junior, would you let me borrow this album? I love it. I promise I won't scratch it up. I'll be responsible with it."

"Noooo." He thought about it for a moment and looked at my face then squeezed my cheeks, "Okay, I'll make a deal with you. I will leT you hold iT for a week buT you must return iT unscratched when you're finished listening To iT."

I enjoyed all of the musical education Uncle Junior fed me. Out the blue she called my name. I followed the echo of Mommy's voice into the back bathroom.

"Close the door," she said.

I obeyed, pulled the toilet lid down and sat on top of it. Mommy was sitting in the tub, squeezing water from her washcloth onto her even brown back and arms. Her pretty eyes. Her round and pretty eyes looked up to me for strength and understanding. They looked sorry and hopeless. Her eyes glanced at the floor, then to my eyes and back to the washcloth. She told me what the doctor said.

"Mommy, does that mean we can't eat from the same plate? Can I still wear your clothes?"

"Yeah, you can still wear my clothes," She smirked, "I just have the virus. You can't get it through eating. You don't have to worry about me hurting you, Dana."

"No! I wasn't thinking like that, Mommy. I know you won't hurt me."

"The doctor gave me some things to read regarding the virus. When I come out the tub, I'll let you look at it."

"Okay."

We were silent for a long minute. Then I took the chance to ask her,

"Do you know who gave it to you?"

"I don't know. Probably James. But I'm not sure." She began to weep.

"Come on, Mommy. It's okay." I got up and circled my hand on her moist back.

"I'm sorry, Dana."

"Sorry about what?"

"For not listening to you. I should've stopped while I was ahead." Pauses...sniffles...I knew she was scared.

"Did you tell Donell or Nawnie about this?" I handed her tissue for her nose.

"Uh-uh, I'm not ready to tell them yet."

"Nawnie said her fingers have been itching her so much that she know one of her babies is with child." I said.

"Well don't worry, it ain't me."

"Okay." I kneeled on the damp towel that was on the floor beside the tub ledge and hugged her.

"I'm gonna miss you," I said. *I knew this shit would happen! I knew it!* And she lightly hugged me back trying not to get my t-shirt wet.

"I'm gonna miss you too, Baby. I'm gonna miss all of y'all. The doctor said if I take my medication and everything, then I got a good ten years to live."

We held each other tighter and then she kissed my forehead. I'll savor every bit of it, hold on to every piece of this moment so that I never in my life forget about it. I did the mathematics in my head. I'm 14 now, if Mommy stays healthy, she will live till I am 24. God willing.

"Dana, have I been a good mother to y'all?"

"Why do you always ask me that?"

"I don't know. Sometimes I feel like I should have given you and Donell more, you know?"

"You cool, Mommy."

She slightly smiled. I continued,

"I thank God that we can talk to each other openly like this. A lot of my friends don't even get a chance to express anything to their mothers." I love to see her smile.

"Mommy, I'm gonna pray for you. And if you need me to, I'll help you take your medication, okay?"

"Okay, Baby. Listen, I want you and Donell to stop fighting and start taking care of each other."

"Okay."

"Really. 'Cause I'm not going to have the strength I have now. When I'm gone, y'all will have to look after eachother."

"Mommy, please don't talk like that."

"Like what? It's the truth...Baby, give me some time alone to think..."

"Will you be okay?"

"Yes, I just need to just think and pray."

"I love you Mommy."

"I love you too, Baby."

And I carefully closed the door, skidded my left shoulder against the hallway wall, didn't care if roaches were in my way or not. I dragged my body into Nawnie's room and began writing. Venting my feelings down all over the paper.

Dear Tonka,
I lay on my back and stare beyond the ceiling
Letting tears quickly drip down in my ears
Clogging in the sounds I no longer want to hear
I counted two

Three coming from my right eye
And four streams of tears came rolling down from my left.
They rolled too fast that after a while I lost count.

By Dana Strong

Why! Why me! Why Mommy! Oh God, help me. Help us. Troy and Donell were laughing at something on TV. Ain't nothing funny, this world is crazy! I can't sit here anymore. Where's my radio, I have to dance through this or I'll go crazy.

14
lilac kisses

Dear George a.k.a Wize,

I love you very much. I want you to meet me after school so we could walk home together.
Love always,

Dana

Dear Dana

That's fine with me. I love you too.

Love
Wize

I love George. We're both sophomores in high school now. We've known each other since junior high but we just started getting serious last semester. George is a simple guy with hidden beauty. Like, the more I look at him, the more he turns out to be cuter and cuter each day. His skin resembles the color of a roasted turkey. I like his eyes too. He has cute bags underneath them. I'm not talking about those mean bags like Hasaan and his brothers but something like George Jefferson's bags. He got those eyes with the bags under them that make him look like he's smiling all the time. And when he smiles, his eyes flash at me. He also has nice, big, straight and white teeth that I love to stare at. He doesn't dress as fly as Sherman and he doesn't dance as good as Sherman but George is natural and sweet and respectful. He has a very interesting body scent too. I don't know what it is but he has this scent that smells like iron and ivory soap at the same time. I'm feeling his thick little afro too and his tag-up name "Wize."

We talk on the phone every weekend. We've been going out for 6 months nows. Nawnie likes George. She said she likes the conversations we have over the phone. I don't know what she's talking about. Most of the things we usually talk about is homework assignments, what we're going to do tomorrow or what TV shows we like best. For instance he likes "The Odd Couple." I like "The Honeymooners." He likes "The Three Stoogers." I like "The Little Rascals." He likes " What's happenin'?" "I like " Good Times. He likes "Sanford and Son" and I like "The Jeffersons." Most of all he like "Carol Burnett & Friends but I think "The Benny Hill show" is way, way better.

We sometimes talk about what we want to be when we grow up. George wants to be either a geologist or anything that deals with the earth and its history, and he also wants to be a politician. I want to be a dancer, a writer, and maybe a gynecologist.

I don't consider myself a sophomore because I don't carry myself like one. I'm very mature for my age and it's funny how the seniors think that I'm in the same grade with them. That's because when I was a freshman, I used to hang out with the juniors. This year the juniors are now seniors. And they think I am along with them. That's cool but I'm feeling the downside to hanging out with the seniors. They all are graduating next semester and I will be stuck here with my peers. Bor-r-ing! What I've learned about this school is that it is getting to be more and more boring. I feel I could be learning so much more interesting things outside the classroom than to be sitting in this old, unattractive building reading three decade-old textbooks and sitting and listening to corny teachers who can't even relate to me as a *student* much less as a person.

I lost interest in school once I made it to the 8th grade. My mind began to wander outside the classroom and daydream into foreign lands. I could have cared less what the teachers told me, I wanted them to show me. I held on to school because I didn't want to disappoint Mommy. Everybody, especially Uncle Junior kept drilling in my head

"Get an education. Get your education. Finish school."

So I did and I was accepted to Wilton HS for dance. Once I made it to school, at first it felt like one big afternoon party. Cuties all over the place, fly gear, conversations, flirtations, new teachers, new programs and the freedom to come in and out of school as much as I pleased. If I was late, I didn't have to worry about getting scolded or my privileges taken away. All I had to do was fill out a late pass and go to class. Too much freedom is not good sometimes.

I believe high school ruined the relationship George and I had.

Our program cards weren't the same anymore. The only class we had together was homeroom. We still kept up our routine with taking the train home together.

Today, was very unique and unusual. I wondered why today he preferred to stand up with his boys. He was acting very distant toward me, detached like. I don't know if he heard the rumors yet but hey I don't care anymore.

Wilton High is popular for having fine cuties but after seeing their faces five days a week for over a year, you kind of get tired of them. I know there is so much more to life in this small world, than being in this big, boring school. These cuties are becoming monotonous with their game. They're predictable with standing around hallways between classes, flirting, conversing or modeling their new clothes and sneakers. Me, personally, I'm ready to move on to bigger and better things like cut a record or write a book someday.

I'm beginning to see that school is not holding me down like it used to. Most of the time I cut classes. I consider Mondays and Fridays part of the weekend. If I need to pick up my train pass on those days, then yeah I'll come to school but any other day, you can forget it.

There are only two subjects I love. They are Science (human biology) and Aerobics. I received awards for both classes. I love my aerobics teacher, Ms. Rockefeller. I never miss her classes, which are on Wednesdays and Thursdays. I love Ms. Rockefeller because she gives me the freedom to help choreograph dance steps for the class. Aside from Aerobics and Science, school is boring as hell! It seems like the only thing these public school teachers care about is my attendance and their next paychecks. I can count on one hand, all the teachers who really cared about their students overall education.

I try to psyche myself into making school more interesting by dressing unique. I love versatility and I believe the world worships originality. Unlike everybody else, people in school wear the newest kicks, the same jeans, same hats and identical coats by the same designers. Levi, Cross Colors, the Gap, Karl Kani, Guess, Patrick Ewings, Tree-Torn, Reeboks, K-Swiss, Timberland and the list goes on. Forget about Jordache, Sergio Valente and Lees. Why do these nerds still wear their Lees jeans when they should know that they'll be walking home with a snatched off Lee patch.

I like playing around with my hair. Like on Tuesday I might wear my hair down in a doobie looking like Janet Jackson's "Pleasure Principle" video wearing all black, or Wednesday I may fluff it out to the Whitney Houston look, wearing my tight jeans and white ribbed turtleneck, or on Thursday I might pull my hair back in a ponytail like Sade. With every hairstyle I wear, my clothes must fit the look.

It tickles me to see the reactions on my bathroom friends' faces whenever I enter. Kenisha, Pamela and Samantha are always gossiping, smoking, fixing their make-up or questioning and interviewing me on how I hook myself up to look like celebrities.

"I get my artistic flavor from my mother. If I want to look like a model, I can. If I want to look like a homegirl, I can too." I tell them.

Today something hurt me so bad that I began to doubt my self-confidence. When I went into the bathroom, Kenisha pulled me to the side and told me that people in school are spreading rumors about me being a "wanna be" and that guys are saying I'm a "bi-sexual D.T.D." She said the acronym for D.T.D. was Dick-Teaser-Dana. So that's what the guys from around the way was talking about. Talking about humiliation! I know I'm different! I know! I'm different because I'm not no ordinary chick. I just wish I knew who started those rumors. It was probably some jealous punk who didn't understand the meaning of life and didn't have a bit of knowledge of self. The person who is spreading these rumors about me, has to be any one of those people sitting in the lunchroom.

Shit, I could care less if I don't sit with the popular crew. All they do anyway is sit like statues and play spades throughout their whole lunch period. I don't fit in with nobody's crew but my own. Can't nobody understand my level of maturity and I refuse to stoop to their level of ignorance. You got the "5 Per Centers" standing on the side of the building, acting all serious like that attitude is gonna take them to higher heights of well roundedness. Beating up a brother who forgot his lessons or "today's mathematics" is not going to make him any smarter. I hate hanging around them because everything I wear or eat to them is made out of pork! If it's not my lipstick, it's the Ivory soap I use. If not the Ivory soap, then the quarter water I drink. That nit-picking makes me wanna pull out my hair!

Then you got the "MC's" sitting on top of the lunch tables banging beats with their fists and beat boxing with their mouths. I'll bust a rhyme every now and then. They know me as Darcel. I'm not MC Darcel or Darcel the MC. I'm simply Darcel. Darcel means "God's beautiful masterpiece." I think Kool X is one of the nicest rappers in this whole school. He stood up on top of the lunch table and started battling random MC's. I think he's even nicer since he didn't spark me from out of the crowd. Respect! 'Cause my strength is not free-styling but if I had to, no doubt I would hold my own. Everybody ciphered and started showcasing their rhymes and unique styles. I enjoy it when the guys let me spit my tight verses. Last week, I came up with an ill verse that made heads bug out! I think it was how I flowed and used my smooth voice on them. That shit intoxicated their ears! I said:

Darcel Sells! You can bet your sweet ass
Rolling funky beats with the mega blast!
None of y'all heads can fuck with this
Take no shit from a powerful chick like me
T-H-E Iron Dee
I got mad energy
Somewhat like a battery
The name is Duracell
Or shall I say Darcel?
Muscles is what you lack, in fact that spot I'll attack
I, am a woman who wastes no time
You fuck me over, I'll rush you like wine.
Fighting me when a girl is inviting me in her ring
    I do my thing
Hit you with 2 blows in 1 swing
Self-defense is only common sense
Intelligence, benevolence,
Enough of that, let me get back on track.
Seldom I do fight but when I fight
I'm like the once defeated Iron Mike.
Virgo the critic creates the dope lyrics.
Think before you blink
An eye for an eye
A tooth for a tooth
The Gemini side
All I speak is truth

They bugged out over me. I gave everybody pounds and took their compliments with grace. I don't rhyme too much with them anymore. We all grew in different directions. They're testosterone levels reached the boiling point of intolerance on my part. They need to open up their ciphers to the sisters, maybe we could teach them a thing or two. What would be even better is if the sisters opened up their own ciphers, like what MC Lyte and Queen Latifah are doing. I don't know, girls can be catty at times.

Then there's the "Cool Crew", you know? The girls with the doobies and fly sneakers sitting on their boyfriends' laps profiling, wearing his chunk jewelry around their necks. They wear their beepers on the outside of their gap and Calvin Klein jeans and they never rock the same Troop jacket twice in a week. The cool guys wear Vaseline around their lips and keep a diamond earring in their ear. Their girlfriends steady poppin' gum while giggling from their highs. I don't think they have the time to spread rumors about me.

The remainders are the "Nerds and the Foreigners". They sit with people who can only understand their language and culture. If I could speak in their native tongue and eat the "welfare" school lunch with them, then maybe I could be a part of their genius circle. Well, I don't need to be around anyone to make me feel smart. It's something I have to feel within myself. I know me and all I need is me.

But you know what, to get back to my feelings, whoever made up that rumor can kiss my smooth, pretty brown ass. It was probably one of those jealous MC's. But I can't make assumptions, the truth will eventually come out.

After school George and I walked home not holding hands. We weren't too far from his building before it began to snow lightly, like flurries. He rang his intercom and his twin sister buzzed us in. George lives on the 1st floor in St. Mary's projects. He lives two blocks closer to Jackson Avenue train station than I do. I'm about six blocks away. He went inside to drop off his books.

"I'll be right back," he said in his deep voice. George is very short with his words, straight to the point. I don't mind, I like his conciseness. He came back out and stood in the front of his door. Each time we tried to make out, his younger sister kept opening and closing the door, so we went into the staircase. I let him kiss my neck and nibble on it. He started sucking. If he gives me a hickie, I will definitely get in trouble but I feel the need to prove those rumors untrue. His sister and her friends kept peeking at us through the staircase window, giggling. George took my hand and said,

"I know where we could go." He opened the staircase door and quickly said to his sister, "Get back in the house, Tisha!" He startled her.

Her eyes very soft and droopy on the sides as she looked up at him. Tisha spoke slow, "Where you goin'?"

"NOYB. Get back inside the house before Miss Madison sees you. I'll be back in twenty minutes." We watched her skinny legged, wearin' catholic school stockings with runs in 'em, run back inside. She locked the door.

"Where we goin'?"

"I'ma take you to this hideout spot, I found."

"Where?"

"It's outside in the back of this building."

"Wait George. Isn't it snowing?"

"Good, the more snow the better."

"You buggin'."

"I'm sure everybody's stayin' inside. Ain't nobody tryin' to come outside in the snow. Don't you see that's good for us?" He smiled at me, standing behind me while opening the back door. The snowflakes grew thick before our eyes.

"Ooooh look! It's beautiful out here!" I spun around and made a pizza pie print on the ground.

"Look at the sky! It's dark but then again it's not dark!" He started laughing. "What? What's so funny?" I questioned.

He laughed some more. "You Dee. You." He mimicked my spin.

"Stop George."

"Nah, you're cute." Then he looked up at the sky too. "Yeah, the sky looks fresh. I think it's the snow that's lighting everything up," he said.

I slid my arm through his arm and walked up a grass hill freckled with freshly fallen snow until we were up against the window of the laundry room. My back leaned against the warm window as he grabbed my waist and gently brushed his pelvis against mine. I love George's five o'clock shadow. He's looking so mature now. I looked at the sky,

"George, what color do you think the sky is?"

"It looks like a light lilac." He looked at me, "Come here. Are you cold?"

"No."

"Give me your hands." His hand felt extremely warm wrapped around mine.

"Damn, girl, they're freezin'!" He tucked my wet 'n cold hands inside of his goose leather jacket pockets. "You need some gloves." He turned his black leather hat to the side and tilted his head down. I jerked my head back. "Come here." He tenderly demanded.

I shared my first kiss with George. His breath was very pleasant to my senses. I let his moist and juicy lips suck in mine. If heaven is like what I feel right now, then I am not afraid of dying. He digressed for a moment to kiss my numb, red nose.

"Rudolf. I'ma call you Rudolf," He teased.

"Shut up." I laughed. I was less hesitant this time in receiving his lips. George was bolder than I thought. He stuck his tongue in my mouth, and I caught a head rush probably from the sweet nectar of his tongue. When George tightened his grip around my waist, the way I was feeling, he could be the one to take my virginity. We kissed for about a good half an hour, nonstop. Something about the scent that breathed out of his nose made me want to kiss him forever. Gently, I stroked his smooth jaw-line.

"George, I wish I could stay." He softly pecked my forehead, "My aunt knows the schedule to my after-school program. I have no after-school classes today."

"Damn." He sighed deeply. He walked me down the block. The corner guys gave him pounds and showed me love. We slowed down to a stop at the end of the block and we kissed again. I can't believe I was bold enough to kiss him out in the open.

"I wish I could walk you home but my sisters are in the house by themselves. I'll walk you home tomorrow."

"It's okay, George."

"Okay, I'll see you tomorrow, my Dana." Those words are glued to my heart. As I walked away, he teased me with his favorite line, "There goes that famous girl!" I blushed.

My lips were sore and numb. It hurt when I licked them. Each time George appeared in my mind, I would get a rush up my spine and through my heart causing me to take in an extra breath. Walking those few blocks home was a skate. I caught every snowflake God sprinkled on my tongue. My toes were numb from standing for so long in the snow, but it was all worth it. My sweet George. The mystery in that song is gone forever:

Me 'n George
Sittin' in a tree
K-i-s-s-i-n-g

DeShawn answered the door. I was preoccupied with humming my favorite song by the Force MD's "Tender Love."
"What's up, 'De? Who's here?"
"Auntie Berlinda and Uncle Jerry's not here."
"Yes!" I could smell franks boiling on the stove.
"You're funny. Nawnie went food shopping. We have to meet her at Pioneer with the big shopping cart."
"How much time do we have?"
"I don't know, about a half of an hour."
"Is my mother here?"
"Yeah, but she's in the bathroom."
Shit! "Okay. Anybody called for me?"
"A crazy girl called and said she was Moet's girlfriend."
My heart jumped, my underarms itched. "What did she say?"
"She said it better had been a rumor that it was you who called for him."
Who the hell she thinks she is? My mother? "What?!"
"Yup."
"What did she sound like?"
"I think she was a black girl."
Bitch making demands on me?!
I realize that if I continue to deal with Sherman, yes it would be a challenge but I would also be gambling with my heart and risking getting my face sliced up. George's touch flashed back into my mind. *Take in a deep breath Dana.* Chills went in and out, tingling my spine.

I'm beginning to feel good again, now let me see how Mommy's doing. I knocked on the bathroom door, hoping for the best.

"Mommy? You okay?"

"Yeah, Baby, you can come in." I hesitated.

"Dana please, I'm not shittin'."

"Oh."

She was sitting on top of the toilet seat blowing her nose. Before she threw the tissue into the wastebasket, she posed like a basketball player. "Mommy, you're funny." She made the perfect shot.

"I'm tired of these fucking buggas in my nose." She was steady pickin', "When will they end?" Then she glanced at me blankly. "Dana, what's so funny?" She sucked in her teeth. "Shit, everything I say or do right now is funny to you."

"No, I'm sorry, Mommy."

"Mmmhmm." She rolled her eyes and continued to blow and pull out and blow it all out.

"No, seriously." I gathered my serious expression. "Is this part of your symptoms?"

"Mmmhmm." She stared at me keeping her serious expression. I know Mommy was provoking me to laugh. "I don't see nothing funny, Dana. How was school?"

I said nothing.

"Uhha, shit ain't funny now," she teased.

"Mommy," I whined, "school was the worst..." She cocked her head to the side, pressed her finger down on her left nostril and blew with her eyes nearly popping out of her head. The bugga missed the toilet paper and flew over my shoulder and landed on top of Nawnie's damp bed sheet that hung over the door to dry. Oh my goodness! I couldn't stop tears from rolling out my eyes. And my stomach hurt so bad. Mommy couldn't front she had to laugh too. My day was made.

15
rubicon

Today, DeShawn fucked everything up for everybody! DeShawn can remember my drama with Sherman but forget to tell me what Auntie Geneva said about her new homework check policy. It's stricter. We all didn't do so well on our report cards last term. She raised the bar on us. The new rule in the house was we were not allowed to go outside or to receive phone calls on weekdays. Mommy consented to Auntie Geneva checking our homework again. The highest grade I received was a 95 and that was for aerobic class. All of my cousins closed their texts and went off to bed. She couldn't stop herself when it came to me. Maybe she hates girls. I had to write and rewrite my homework until it was neat enough to meet *her* standards. What has gotten into her?! PMS!?

"Would you give God a paper like this?" She asked.

"No." I wanted to say God doesn't care about my penmanship, he cares about what's in my heart. But that would've been a vacation to hell up in here. When she saw that my homework wasn't good enough for her, she started saying things like, "Do you think Michael Jackson would want to read a paper like this?" After I rewrote my paper, it brought her satisfaction to have found one of my weaknesses. Michael Joseph Jackson. Now if I didn't complete my chores or if my homework was not neat enough to suit her, she'll say things like, "You think Michael Jackson would want to marry a dirty woman? Get in that shower, girl!" If I had a choice to choose between Daddy-James beatings or taking Auntie Geneva's verbal abuse...I'd rather be dead. If I had to choose what kind of heaven. It would be a mixture of Nawnie and I in D.C., Me and Sherman dancing in the hallway, George and I kissing against the laundry window and our music would be the beautiful singer from Karron Baptist Church in "The Carolina Choir".

Auntie Geneva finished checking my homework around twoish. As I was getting ready for bed, Nawnie's lamp was still on. She was up nursing Mommy's fever and cold sweats. Mommy was under the quilt shivering and coughing. I patted and rubbed her back all night. We overslept. I got to school late and Tray put a stupid smirk on his monkey looking face when I walked into class.

"D-D-Dana's, not a virgin no more. W-Well it's about t-time, y-y'all k-k-kissed." Everybody started laughing and joking around with me and George. I couldn't believe George was laughing along with them!

Dear George,
Did you tell Tray, what we did? Yes or No. If yes, why?
Love,
Dana

Dear George,
Did you tell Tray, what we did? Yes or   No.   If yes, why?
Love,
Dana

Mrs. Colleen is looking. We'll talk later.
Love,
Wize

"George, why were you laughing with everybody at me?"
Still laughing! "No, I wasn't laughing at you. Tray's stupid."
"Yeah, right."
"Dana, repeat what Tray said."
My memory raced, "He said, I wasn't a virgin n-no more and it was about t-time we k-k-kissed. How did he know, George? I didn't tell him. And what's so funny?"
"You're funny. You know that ain't right to be mocking him like that. Dana. Kissing is not the same as doin' it."
"Doin' what?"
"You know? The nasty? Sex."
"Oh." I wanted to shrink and disappear. "Well how did Tray even know we kissed? Who told him, George?"
"Tray doesn't even know what he's talking about." He whispered, "He's the one who's a virgin. He never kissed a girl before."
"Stop lying."
"Word to mother." We both laughed and stood by his apartment door. He looked into my eyes and said, "Dana, I've got some news."

"Good or bad."

"Sad."

I moaned, "Oh. What is it?" My heart pounded over.

"I'm moving next week."

"You what? You're movin'? To where ?"

"We're moving down south. South Carolina."

"Why didn't you tell me this earlier? Why wait just before…"

"I know where you're taking this. Dana I didn't know up until last week we were moving. And it was definite once my mom's bought the trailer home." He turned his mouth up and said, "Can't wait to get away from these projects."

I was silent for a moment. He's my boyfriend and I'm going to miss him. He made the projects sound like as if it were a shameful place to live in. I don't think he will even miss me.

"What's wrong with the projects?" I questioned.

"Dana, don't you see it?"

"See what?"

"The intercoms, the drugs, the drug dealers, the way we're livin' on top of each other. How we don't even own this piece of land but working real hard, breaking our backs to pay rent every month to live on it. Look at how all the brothers are going in and out of jail and everybody around here thinking it's hype to be tough. It's a set-up, a trap. But it's also in the choices we make. And these girls out here thinkin' it's cute to have babies. Getting pregnant like it's going out of style, man! Like they'll instantly become women. Marriage ain't even in the equation. Look at Lil' Tina's daughter."

"Yeah, Tanisha?"

"Yeah man, she's going on her third kid from some other dude in McKinley projects. I think that shit is sad. You mean to tell me you don't see it, Dana? Our generation is going down."

"Wow, I never looked at everything like that. I mean, I do want to move but into a bigger apartment, you know? I'm lovin' these cook-outs, the jams and the block parties."

"True, but Dee, all jokes aside, you have to start looking at things from a more political and economical perspective. Things ain't right around here and we have to put a stop to it. We have to make changes. My uncle tells me, 'we need to make mental changes first."

"So you think moving away is saving our community?"

"Not really, I'm trying to save myself first and then I can save my community."

I felt ashamed for not knowing this, for not being aware. They never taught me this in school. This was so hard to see. So these are the things Mommy's been trying to tell me all along to 'stay awake and be aware.'

Most of us from the projects believed people who lived in houses were so corny and square. People who lived in houses lacked that edge in style. They were the ones who followed and tried to keep up with our trends and dance steps. Yes, us project folk. I hope George doesn't lose himself in his new environment. But it shocked me to hear George spit this much knowledge in my ear. He was definitely saying some heavy stuff. I never took my life or my surroundings seriously, the way George did with his. He sounded like those college students I watch on the TV show "Fame." They talked about how they want to give back to their communities and make a big difference in the world. And I felt like I was Leroy, the one who was being difficult, and couldn't see the light. Well, I haven't seen anybody from my neighborhood touch on the things George talked about.

"Shoot, the people over here never did anything for me so why should I do for them? That's what politicians and mayors are here for, right?"

"Wrong. Time to wake up Dana. We can't keep relying and depending on strangers to take care of our needs. We have to start taking responsibility for our own problems."

"You're right."

"My uncle, Born, told me that by us living in the projects, one family on top of another, is like the same experiments the scientists used on laboratory mice. A project? Get it?"

"Yeah."

"They need to tear down these projects! 'Cause don't nobody deserve to live this way. Look at the way we eat and drink. We eat the worst batch of food, they ship the lowest grade of food to our communities. And nobody is doing shit about it. Just because we think we're the lower class, we eat whatever *they* feed us. But yo', have you been to Manhattan, where the middle class and the over class live?"

"Yeah. It's nice. I'd like to live over there one day."

"Dana, look at the way those people eat. They eat fucking well! *Their* food and produce are no later than yesterdays. Their shit is picked from independent farms. Shit, I've never seen half the fruit they carry in their supermarkets over here. Yo', we'll be lucky if our supermarkets carried pineapples. In *their* neighborhoods they have all kinds of exotic fruits 'n shit."

I got hyped on the truths he was bringing to me.

"Let me ask you a question, Dana. Have you ever eaten fresh red raspberries or mangos?"

"Yeah."

"Besides the ones in your favorite Now-and-Laters candy." I didn't have an answer.

"They got D'Agostino's and some other crazy foreign names like Gristedes 'n shit."

"Yeah, that's true! I remember walking through Manhattan with my mother and seeing a D'Agostino's. Around here, we got some ol', cheap old Pioneer or Bravo or Fine Fare supermarkets."

"Now you see?"

"Yup, You remember there used to be a nice Met Food on the corner? But they closed it down for Sanchez's video store?" I recollected.

"Sanchez's video store? Sanchez's video store? That shit ain't even a real video store. They be sellin' up in that piece. You think mayor Koch would even think of building a Block Buster on our block. Hell no! Just think, all these abandoned buildings and empty lots could be used for homes and businesses."

I just stood there thinking, soaking it all up and surprised to hear knowledge and cuss words fly out of my George. 'Life is serious now,' I thought.

"George, I didn't know you had this much knowledge in you."

"Dana, that's only a quarter of what I let everybody see. I'm telling you this because I'm leaving and I can't leave you without you being aware of what's going on."

"George Smith, I'm gonna miss you."

"Dana Strong, I'm gonna miss you more, mi amour."

He finally said it! Well I'm glad to know that my sweet George will be missing me. We made out. I'll deal with all that knowledge and information later. Right now the mood is here.

We made our kiss and hug meaningful. I isolated my every thought and feeling and put it into the kiss. We grinded against each other. George still didn't move his hands from my waist. His bulge behind his zipper swept my pleasing point. Our kiss tasted salty.

"I love you, George."

"I love you too, Dana." He kissed my tears.

When I got home, Mommy was sitting at the kitchen table, sketching out some pictures of women dressed in fashionable clothes. That was one of Mommy's talents. She can design her behind off. She had her colorful pencils lined across the dining table in rainbow order. It looked so pretty. Red, orange, yellow, green, blue, indigo, and violet, in that order are my favorite colors. She filled her models' face with the color brown then she took a pull from her cigarette. We spoke briefly. Mommy was very focused on what she was doing. I looked into the refrigerator to see if anything special was in it. *Ooh my favorite, cherry cheesecake*! I pulled it out and read the note on the container, "DON'T TOUCH!!! AUNTIE GENEVA'S." I smoothed out the frosting with my finger and quickly licked it off, then placed it back into the refrigerator. I slumped down next to Mommy. She held me with her left arm and continued to sketch with her right hand.

"What's up?"

I sighed, "Nothin'."

"Come on, Dana, you act like I don't know you. I wasn't born today. I'm gonna ask you one last time. What's the matter?"

"Mommy," I whined, "George is moving down south."

"Down south, where?"

"South Carolina."

"When is he leaving?"

"Next week."

"Oh damn, I know you're gonna miss him."

"Yeah."

"Hold on." She finished coloring the woman's dress in black and red. Then she paid me the respect of looking up from her paper. "Did you do your homework?"

"No."

"Do your homework and we'll talk about it later. Listen, from now on I'm going to start checking you and Donell's homework, okay?"

"Yes!"

"'Cause I don't like the way Geneva's been having you up all night."

"Thank you, Mommy."

I went into the front bathroom. The boys were listening to the radio and blasted the volume to D-nice's "The 808". I couldn't understand this weird dampness in my panties. I peed and wiped myself. I kept wiping this sticky aloe-like gel from my privacy. *What in the world do they call this stuff?* Jason shouted something to Donell.

"Yo', you nasty man!" And the both of them started cracking up laughing. What was so funny? I knocked on the door but no answer. I walked in. Donell aimed his McDonald's straw at me and hit me on the forehead with his toilet paper spit balls. He can be so disgusting, I swear! I turned my eyes up to peel the toilet paper spitball off of my forehead.

I nearly screamed, "Y'all are nasty!" A whole colony of toilet paper spitballs was mashed all over the ceiling.

They laughed and I left. Boys!

I only had to write an essay for my English class and read pages 116-120 of my social studies textbook. Mommy met me in the hallway and we went into our office to talk.

"Lock the door." I locked the back bathroom door.

"Dana, before we get into your boyfriend, I have to tell you something." I sat down on the toilet seat.

"You know we don't like being here, right? You know we're accustomed to having our own, right?" I nodded. "You and Donell always had your own room. I know you're getting tired of this. Y'all are not the only ones. Housin' is taking forever to get us this damn apartment. James said that he didn't take my name off the lease. He still want us to come back…"

"No, Mommy. I'd rather stay in Nawnie's funky bed than to go back to Daddy-James. Please, we can't…"

"We won't and don't talk about my mother like that. Listen. How do you feel about us staying at a shelter?"

"I don't know."

"It's temporary but they would help us find an apartment a whole lot quicker than us staying here being on the waiting list. There won't be any privacy for us but it ain't too much of a difference from here."

I didn't care, since George was leaving anyway. Besides I need a change, especially from this living situation, this block and my school.

"I don't care about privacy at this point. But what about my school? Am I going to get a transfer?" I asked crossing my toes.

"No, we'll still be in New York. Whether it be the Bronx or Manhattan, as long as there's a transit system, you'll still be going to the same school, my dear. Don't try ta out slick this slicker, darling." *Damn! She's too smart.*

"Mommy, I really want us to get outta here, too. If the shelter is going to get us our apartment quicker, then let's go. Not only that but I'm sick 'n tired of Berlinda's mouth and Geneva's stinkin' attitude. And I hate it when Berlinda lets Troy and everybody else go in her living room to watch HBO 'cept for us. I wish we could have a VCR and a TV bigger and better than hers."

"We will. Dana. Please be careful not to covet her things. That is not cool. You know what's more important though?"

"What?"

"You, me and Donell. We got each other. That's what she doesn't have with her son. He's always hanging out in the streets. Did you ever hear Berlinda and Troy tell each other they love each other?"

"Nope."

"See, what we got is worth more than everything she owns. Nobody can take our love away from us."

"But, Mommy, I hate it when she embarrasses me in front of her company. And I love Nawnie with all my heart, but I need my own bed. I want to smell like me, not like her." As I went on talking, Mommy did not disagree with anything I had to say. It was my truth and she respected how I felt.

"I feel the same way, Baby. We're gettin' outta here. I didn't know it affected you like this."

"Yeah, and Donell, that's why he's always outside or downstairs at Jamel's house 'cause it's too crowded in the backroom. Now that Uncle Junior's sleeping back there that makes five of them in that one room. Mommy, we really have to leave. I'm sick of everybody gossiping to their friends about your business and how we're on welfare and how you be getting' high 'n stuff." (Hint, hint).

"They need to stop that shit! Like they don't be sniffin' all that coke in the back room. I don't ask them for any of they shit and they sure as hell won't offer me any. I can't believe them! I do my shit in the house by myself and I mind my own fuckin' business! I don't bother nobody."

"Mommy calm down."

"No! I can't believe that bitch Berlinda is so quick to point fingers and piss in people's ears about me and my children and what I do.

There has been plenty of times I gave her my last cigarette or loaned her money, and when she didn't pay me back I ain't stress her. I said nothin'! Nothing! That's wrong, that shit is wrong, Dana, and that shit hurts. We're getting outta here. See, God don't like ugly. Go in the living room, get me a cigarette. Light it for me."

I'm so happy we're leaving. I didn't hesitate going into Berlinda's living room. I lit her cigarette on the stove and gave her a half burnt cigarette.

"Thank you, Baby." She didn't notice, "That shit hurts." She took a long pull. "She's my sister and all, but there's a sayin', 'blood is thicker than water.' Shit, you know my friends, Shirley and her family, they love us. Remember this Dana, sometimes Love is thicker than blood." She stared at the floor thinking and pulling in her cigarette, blowing out stress. Her eyes studied the white-tiled bathroom floor with sneaker prints all over it. Mommy is so beautiful.

"Dana, I want you to start gettin' your things together. When Donell come in, tell him we're leaving this weekend. I have to go out and take care of some business."

"Okay. Mommy, I'm so proud of you." Her eyebrows relaxed.

"Thank you, Baby. Listen, don't tell Nawnie we're leaving, I'll tell her."

George and I have been hanging tough within the past couple of days. Today, he called me to come over. Mommy was preoccupied with packing. She said it was fine since he was leaving the next day. I left my homework on top of the kitchen table for Mommy to check.

When I arrived at George's house, I couldn't believe he invited me in. His mother's apartment was nearly empty. There were boxes in the living room and nails remained in the walls.

George's bedroom carried his unique scent of iron and ivory soap. On the floor near his bed were 10 and 20 pound iron weights. A four-pack of ivory soap, his school textbooks, and Brut cologne sat on top of his wooden dresser.

All of his sneakers and shoes were all paired neatly in crates. A green towel was laid over his radiator. New Edition, Kool Moe Dee, L.L. Cool J. and Eric B and Rakim posters were taped to his walls.

"So this is your room."

"It was my room."

"I like it. Are you taking down these posters?"

"Nah."

"Where's the fam?"

"My sisters are down south and Ma-dukes stepped out."

"Is she coming back?"

"In about an hour."

"If you're leaving tomorrow, why isn't the rest of your furniture packed in boxes?"

"My moms' is subletting this apartment. We're leaving some things here for the tenant."

"I wish I could go with you, George."

"I wish you could come too. But we could write each other, and maybe when I start working I could save up some money to send for you."

"Okay."

George got up and closed his bedroom door. A half-naked Jane Kennedy was taped onto the back of his door. He looked at me weird but I knew what that meant. I'm so scared of the pain but I'm ready to cross over. I love George and I know he wouldn't do anything to hurt me. It is time and it has to happen. I wanted it to happen. I want this to be a special experience for the both of us.

The sweat on our foreheads did not run across our temples. It sat like dew on petals. George sucked me so well. The more he sucked my neck, the more the humidity rose in the room. I grew weaker from his hickey. He then fondled with my sensitive breasts, rubbing his fingers back and forth over my rock hard nipples.

"Stop," I sang his name. George stopped and rose up to crack open his window. He resumed to rubbing his diamond against my hooded pearl. Time skipped and flipped on us. I couldn't stop George from sucking my 36C's. His head swirled around and around. His tongue jabbed my nipples as if he were a lizard. That was the most powerful feeling in the world to me. I felt helpless. He pulled his key out and tried to find my door. I was too slippery so he guided my hand to touch it. Warm, hard and moist. Medium, I think.

"Put it in." He said.

My shiny red spandex leggings stayed locked around my ankles, just in case. I stared at his dingy white ceiling with peeled paint in the corners. His right ear heard my 'hahs and hmmms and uhhs'. It hurt like a bite. Because I love him so, I let him pump in hopes that the sex would hurt less. I tried not to 'ow' because my cousins said, "owing turned guys off." George was too excited to think clearly. I tried to slow him down by squeezing my thighs around his hips. My head and neck arched back with each inch George put inside me.

"Open your legs more." He selfishly demanded. Then he stopped for a moment to ask me if it hurt.

Hell yeah nigga!

"Yeah." I calmly said. He couldn't even pause himself. It seemed as if his dick controlled him. I took in the pain, he enjoyed himself being wrapped inside of me, up on top of his own planet. He didn't stop until he made it inside my main frame. Just when I was getting comfortable with how he was beginning to feel, the scaredy cat jumped out of me! This is it? This was all? I've been robbed! This is what every-body made such a big fuckin' deal about? We kissed again and the kiss wasn't the same. His kiss was tired, wet and sloppy. He didn't have to do me any favors with his wack afterplay. Shoot, I wanted to leave.

Defrager had a woman-to-woman talk with me one evening after the first day of my period. I was twelve. She told me once that she hope I would wait until I go married to cross the bridge to the other side. She said it would be first priority that I reach my orgasms before my partner. If he isn't considerate or discipline enough to control himself then he is not wor-thy of me.

"How do you feel?" George pulled up his Hanes underwear and Silver Tab jeans. I followed by pulling up my panties and red spandex.

"George, I didn't come."

"Huh?"

"If you can huh, you can hear."

"What do you mean you didn't come?"

"Just what I said. I didn't come. I didn't reach my orgasm." I said.

"Dana, wait."

George ran after me. "Dana! Why you tryna diss me?"

"I have to get back." We struggled and he pulled on my clothes. We tugged back and forth but I stuck to my guns and got in the ele-vator before his mother came back. I felt different. Well, I should be happy now that I'm not the last virgin in school, but I'm not. I feel so foolish. I wish I could have rewind everything that just happened and stayed my behind home. Then I would've still been the old me and not have to worry about this new person I'm becoming.

Sorely I eased on home. I couldn't stop thinking about what had just happened to us. I don't feel like speaking to anyone. I've changed. I'm a young lady trapped in a woman's body. I crossed the fifth street and forgot to look both ways. Luckily the driver saw me and honked her horn.

Once I made it across the street my eyes did not look up from the pavement. I was not looking for money or jewelry or crack. I was just looking for an answer, asking the same questions in my mind, '*How can I reverse what just happened?*' and '*Can I be a virgin again?*' I know one thing's for sure, George's hugs and kisses will not be missed. He showed me a side to him that was not human. He lost control when we did it in the saddest way and he lost my admiration for his being a gentleman. All the self-control I admired him for is now out the door. I gave my virginity up to an ordinary dick.

Before I went into the building, I finger combed my hair to cover the hickey that he put on my neck. I'm so scared. Everybody went into the first elevator. I waited for the second one to come for my privacy. I dipped my finger down there and smelled lust.

Donell opened the door for me. I didn't feel like talking to anybody so I went into the bathroom, peed fire, took Nawnie's hand mirror and did my own gynecological self-examination. My labia majora was swollen and my labia minora was reddish-pink. George messed up my tight, little hole. When I observed my hole yesterday, it looked like a perfectly round glazed donut. Now as I looked at it, it looked like an open mouth, saying, "Ho, ho, ho." Not like Santa Claus's "Ho, ho, ho," or Grandmaster Flash's, "Ho!, ho!, ho!" but an unclean Ho, ho, ho…whore.

The hallway toward the kitchen was very smoky. It smelled like Nawnie was frying lamb chops but then again it could have been pork chops. I could never tell the difference. Nawnie was in the kitchen cooking dinner and watching "Oprah." I'll speak to her later. I closed her squeaky door as far as I could and I carefully reclined on her unmade bed and contemplated. *Should I take a shower? Should I not?* Make a decision, Dana. No more picking off flower petals to make my decisions now. I am a teenage woman. No more "Eenie, Meenie, Miney,

Mo's." *Am I or am I not going to take a shower? That is the question.* I will. I will wash all the sperm, or whatever this jelly stuff is off of me.

After the hot shower, I felt a little better but not much. I slipped on my extra large Brazilian t-shirt, sat back on Nawnie's bed, peeled apart her purple floral drapes and looked through the square part of the bars in her window. I sought to find God moving in and out of the clear, blue sky.

"Father, I promise I won't ever do this again. Please forgive me God. I'm sorry, please don't let me be pregnant. Please don' let Nawnie's fingers itch for me. Let it stop itching. And please don't let Mommy find out that I crossed over. Please. I love you, thank you. A men."

I'm glad my homework was done. Where's Mommy? She's probably hanging out with Shirley and Cherie. I'm tired. I need some rest. No more Georgie, porgie, puddin', pie. It's over. Everything. Forget about you never know a person until you live with them. I believe you never know a person until you've slept with them.

16
sheltering-deaths

Whew! My period came today. I jumped up and down, punched my stomach, did cartwheels in the grass so that the sperm wouldn't meet my egg, I even douched but ultimately I prayed. It turned out that Nawnie's fingers wasn't itching for me, it was itching for Auntie Geneva. Thank God! She's six months pregnant and she's wilding out. Nawnie tells me all the time, not to worry about her, it's just her hormones. Hormones my ass! How dare she wake me up 5:30 in the morning just to clean both of the bathrooms! My cousins and I instantly became her slaves. Troy was ordered to sweep the entire hallway, Jason was to dust and wash loads of clothes, folded and packed them in the shopping carts. Deshawn had the kitchen and the refrigerator and freezer. Donell scrubbed the bathroom tiles and mopped the entire floors.

Well, I know this move is going to be somethin' interesting. A new place, new faces, new guys and new experience. The longest we've ever lived anywhere was in Queens with Daddy-James. That was for six long abusive years. We lived from house to tenement to projects and now the shelter. Family members (and I ain't mentioning no names) have often said that Defrager was not a sufficient provider for her children. They said she partied too much and we didn't get enough stability. I believe Mommy did a great job with us. She made sure we said our grace before every meal and our prayers before bedtime. I kind of dig Mommy's spontaneous personality. I think it made it easier for us to adapt to different environments and situations. We learned the law of detachment early.

The time had come and Nawnie cried. She pleaded with Mommy in her sweetest way to let us stay with her. Her point of having us stay with her was so that we didn't have to resort to some homeless shelter. Mommy reassured her over and over again that we would be okay. Donell and I spent time joking with our cousins, soothing their feelings of missing us, until it was time for us to leave. We left early that Saturday afternoon. Bags and bags of clothes and books were heavy but lighter than those burdens.

We, Mommy, Donell and I, were back to being one again. We are a tight knit team. We kept close and watchful of our belongings in the shelter area. We left one shelter in the Bronx on the Grand Concourse for another one in Manhattan. Mommy had to go through humiliating paperwork with unprofessional office workers who played their radios loud when their supervisors weren't around. This shelter had a different feel, down to the smell and its vibrations, but each place had a similar sound at night. At night, I could hear the cries of babies. Their cries gave me some sort of consolation. It made me feel, for some reason, that everything would be okay, that God was somewhere around us, because God protects babies and fools. Having babies in a place like this is sad but at the same time comforting. It felt like music to a lonely, depressing, quietness.

Every week, Mommy would go to the office to find out about any vacant apartments. It was always the same ol' story,

"Ms. Strong, we have to transfer you to the main branch. They have the information for you over there. But first you have to sign your name on this waiting list and fill out the rest of these forms."

"But, I'm already on the waiting list! I've been on the waiting list for two years now! What exactly are y'all doing around here besides playing music all day?"

We kept our clothes and bed area clean. It was word of mouth that the head security does room check once a week, and depending on how clean we kept our sleeping area, they are supposed to speed up the process of moving us into our apartment. But don't bet your life on that. All of our valuables were kept locked in a locker. We received three cot beds, which we sprayed down bleach and Lysol disinfectant, then covered it with plastic from any bed-bugs. We combined our three cots into a king size bed. Mommy hung two of her canvas paintings over our bed. She said those paintings were to help us visualize our dreams and our new home. One picture was of a marijuana plant sitting on a windowsill with a woman holding a broom smiling inside of her loft apartment sweeping. Her walls were the colors of soft orange. Mommy said this painting symbolized "freedom and happiness" to her. The other picture was a stage facing an audience of thousands of people with their fists in the air. She said that painting symbolized "liberation" to her.

We kept quiet, stayed close and clear of those who were lost in the system. The lost ones had no knowledge of self and they were the type of people who were addicted to pain, drugs and drama. They were the murderers who slaughtered their dreams and depended on the system to take care of their families.

Mommy kept in touch with Nawnie to find out who called or what mail came in for her. It was mostly mail for me. Absentee cards, absentee calls week after week. I stayed committed to punishment for weeks throughout the summer. Not one of my apologetic letters softened Mommy into releasing me. I should've never lied about cutting classes. Mommy detests liars. She told me I was a lousy liar. Couldn't even lie right just like my father, that's why she's not with him now.

Summer school was my only outlet. School lets out at noon but I told Mommy it was let out at 1 pm. I hated lying to her but I really needed some airtime. Being that I was not allowed to go outside, I would go down the hall to the recreational center that was located inside the shelter. That was fine with me 'cause the recreational center was the hang out spot for all the cuties. The shelter we were living in used to be a public vocational school. It was settled on the strangest location. Not on a corner or the center of the block but it was settled right in the middle of projects downtown in Manhattan. The trees were healthy and green. The grass wasn't broken. The playground was visibly colorful and the elevators were clean. What made these projects decent was seeing old Chinese and white people walking around and sitting on benches, feeding pigeons and squirrels. They even had windows in their bathrooms.

I've been calling Sherman, and every time his baby's mother picked up, I hung up the phone, wishing I had the talent to disguise my voice into one of his homeboy's deep tones. If she was a nicer person maybe I would ask for him. I would even consider not pursuing him.

Coincidentally, the day my punishment was over was the day Sherman called.

"What's up Dana?"

"Sherman?"

"Long time no hear. Your grandmoms said you moved and she gave me your number. Is it okay for me to call?"

"Yeah. Wow, I thought I'll never hear from you again."

"Nah, that ain't me. You may not believe this but I been missin' you.”

"I've been missing you too. Every time I call, some mean girl picks up. Was she your girl, Elaine?"

"Elaine? Hell no, she ain't my girl. That was probably my baby's mom. We not gettin' along tho'. You got a pen? I want you to take down my beeper number."

"Hold on." I ran into the recreational center and snatched a pen from a cutie's back pocket.

"Okay, go ahead." I wrote his number on top of my lifelines.

"Sherman, are you sure I can page you? I don't want no problems, now."

"You cool, you cool. Me and my girl broke up. What chu' doin' tonight?"

"Nothin'."

"So let's hook up. Maybe I could come over and see you?"

"Uh, no!"

"Why? What? You livin' with a man now?" He teasingly asked.

"No, no, I don't have a man. Just my mom's is strict, you know. I'd rather go to your place."

"You cool with that?"

Yes."

"So meet me on the corner in front of Wendy's at Union Square. I'll see you at six sweetness?"

It was confirmed. I slowly hung up the phone and couldn't believe what I just heard come out of Sherman's mouth. He called me his sweetness? He has a ride now? What kind? Oh my God! It's two o'clock. I have to look good. I hummed my favorite tunes. My red Reeboks, dungaree mini skirt and Mommy's denim tank top should look good. Thank God Mommy touched up my hair the other day, now I can flip-curl my shoulder length hair. I mustn't forget perfume. I'll wear Joanne's obsession perfume when she leaves to go to the bathroom. She won't miss a couple of inches. It pays sometimes to have a room-mate.

I'm not educated on cars, but I have to give it to Sherman. He pulled up in a hot onyx Audi. A glossy, black exterior with leather tan interior. His sunroof was open. I felt like a queen posing on his right. I barely looked at him. He looked too beautiful, driving with a tooth-pick in the side of his mouth. His facial hairs were all cleaned cut and his skin so clear and flawless. Lips slightly glossed from his pineapple lip balm. If I'm not careful, I could love to fall in love with his romance. He defines the word fine. Everything happened fast like his driving; 88 mph. Babyface's "Tender Lover" album blasted though his speakers.

"Sherman, I can't stay out too late. I have to be back by 9:30."

"Curfews, curfews, curfews. Don't worry, shorty, I'll bring you back by 9."

He parked his car in the parking lot across the street from Forest projects. His building looked fucked up. I thought Nawnie's building was bad. Those demon queens weren't lying when they said I shouldn't fuck with a nigga from Forest projects. But Sherman is so fuckin' fine! He was nearly touching perfection.

We took a shower. Sherman's physique was muscular but lean. He's about 6'1, 195 pounds. Popping veins flowed through every angle of his body under the cascading water. Unlike George, Sherman's body was developed manly and mature. His bronze chest hairs made a fuzzy stream down his six-pack with his deep wet sand complexion. He is truly a man, my Mr. Sandman. He even had stretch marks on his butt. Once we stepped out of the shower, he wrapped me in a clean white towel, picked me up over his shoulder and gently placed me on his bed. I hid my body underneath his tan covers.

He massaged my back with his body and then my front. My dam broke, when he slithered his tongue upside the roof of my mouth. Then he kissed the neck of my hand, followed with a gentle peck on my lips to a well calculated kiss. Sort of like an improvisational dance. He had the timing down to the turn and the dip. His kisses made me moan.

"Have you done this before?" He asked.

"Once."

"Once? Did you enjoy it?"

"No, not at all."

"Are you afraid?"

"A little." Forgive me for that lie. I'm terrified.

"Don't be, Baby, I got you. I won't hurt you. I'ma take my time and make love to you. I want to make you feel good." Sherman stretched both my hands above my head and pressed his mouth on my rib cage. He rose up to turn his tape over. "Do Me Baby" by Melissa Morgan played on. I surrender to his cologne with soft kisses coating my neck and earlobes. Slight pinches on my nipples. Firm squeezes on my thighs.

"Let me feel you. I wanna feel you."

Feel The Fire," played. Go on Stephanie! Sing it!

I fell in love with Sherman the moment Prince started singing "*Slow love*".

"Turn it up." I said. Sherman got up and turned up the volume.

"*Love's in your eyes…Eyes never lie…don't rush the feeling… you've got me reeling…The man on the moon is smiling, for he knows what we're dreaming of…Tonight is the night for makin' slow love…Slow Love…*"

After touching heaven, Sherman kissed my tears and smiled looking down on my face.

"What are you smiling for?"

"Why are you so serious?"

"That's just me."

"Put down the wall. I'm smiling at you cause you're beautiful."

I blushed.

"What are *you* smiling for?" He threw back at me.

"That was a sweet compliment," I said.

"That wasn't a compliment, that was the truth." I buried my face in his chest.

"I want you to be my girl."

"What about her?"

"What about her? I said I want you to be my girl."

"I went through drama after that jam." He apologized for not telling me about his situation. He joked around with me, kissed me and we resumed to creating more love.

"I don't want no other nigga in this."

"And I don't want no other bitch on this."

"It's all yours, Dana. This is all who's?"

"Mines." I responded.

"What's my name."

"Moet. Moet."

"Let's say it together." He whispered again softly in my ear. "This is my jewelry. Let's sign my name. M…O…E…and T." Sherman's nickname was carved in the cavity of my womb. Then he wrote in script emphasizing the T. Those T's confused me. Those T's brought tears to my eyes. I cried not because it hurt but because I was in ecstasy! The feeling everyone has been going ga-ga for, had finally touched me.

Sherman grunted and I held onto him tighter.

"You okay? How do you feel?"

"Complete," I stated.

"You know you my boo now right?" I nodded my head. I still couldn't make out his smile. "I want you to know somethin'. I don't get down like this, goin' up in girls raw-dawg. I only did that with my baby mother. Word up. I don't want to hear about anybody being in this."

Everything Sherman rapped about, I believed. I forced myself to believe he was in an unhappy relationship with his baby's mother. I wanted to believe he was going back to school next semester as soon as he save enough money from selling. I wanted to believe Sherman was different from all the other drug dealers. I believed he was special like me. He then rolled over to his side and lit up his spliff.

"You don't smoke, do you?"

"No."

"Good, don't start." The aroma from his smoke scented his room with a mixture of a lusty incense. I began to dress my complete body. He watched me apply my cherry lip gloss while he took his fourth pull. His tongue glazed over his lips while watching me dress. Third round came. We climaxed together.

"So what's up, Miss Beautiful? When you comin' back to see me again?"

"Whenever you want me to."

He laughed, "Call me tomorrow."

Sherman said he was too high to drive me home. Thank God, 'cause I didn't want him to know that I lived in a homeless shelter.

"Do you have money?"

"Of course. I ain't no broke chick!" Forgive me God for the lie.

It was too late for me to use my school's train pass. The cops were at Jackson Avenue train station. I barely made a dollar for train fare. On the train ride, through Harlem, I was busy thinking up a lie Mommy would buy. That's hard 'cause Mommy is a picky shopper. She inspects everything. My coochie itched. I moved around in my seat and tried to act like I was tying my sneaker laces. I should've washed up before I left Sherman's house. The train doors opened and I saw Daddy-James walking across the platform. I stood up and was about to call his name but the door closed and everybody looked at me. So I sat back down and thought about him.

He still had that agile physique from those Saturday afternoons of walking three miles along the back roads of Far Rockaway and when it was real nice outside, we'd walk the boardwalk. His words of wisdom bit my ears when he continually rode in "Appreciate this" and "Be grateful for that." I cannot let go of the beatings Donell and I had to endure every Sunday because he had his bad come down. I didn't want to remember how frightened I was six days a week when it was time to do homework check. Over and over and over again, I edited and checked to see if my homework was correct and then I hoped he forget to check it. Never did he forget homework check. Sometimes I wonder, if Mommy had stuck it out with him for five more years, would I have been an honor roll student? Would I have gotten skipped to college by now? Or would I have achieved all of the above combined with nervousness, an unhappy, and bounded spirit never to discover any of my dancing talents or some of the knowledge I have of myself.

I just made it in for curfew. The shelter's curfew was at 12:00 a.m. If you came in after midnight, then you're locked out until the doors open back up again at 7 a.m. The light was dim because our roomate Joanne was asleep. Donell was sitting on our bed, drawing when I walked in.

"Why you drawing in the dark?" He jumped up. "Where's Mommy?"

"You know you're in trouble, Dana. You was supposed to have been here over two and half hours ago. We have to meet Mommy in Queens. I have good news and bad news."

"Wait a minute, why do we have to go all the way to Queens to meet up with Mommy?"

"I'll tell you in a minute. Pick one, good news or bad news."

"Bad news."

"Daddy-James passed away."

"What? Daddy-James?"

"Yup."

"That's crazy. I just saw him at the 59th street train station!"

"Maybe you saw a look alike."

"Maybe I saw his spirit?" I said.

"Maybe you did."

"Damn and I was about to call him out."

"Why didn't you?"

"The doors closed in my face."

"That's some spooky shit, right there."

"Yeah. So tell me the good news."

"Auntie Geneva had twins."

"What? Twins? Identical?"

"No, fraternal. Boys."

"Yes!" I sang. "I'm still Miss Special. I'm still the only girl! Ha! Ha!"

"You stupid, Dana." Donell smirked.

"When did Daddy-James pass?"

"This is going to sound crazy."

"Tell me."

"They don't know exactly when he died. All they know is he died in the apartment. You remember Dee next door? She started complaining to management about the foul odor. Then other people in the building started reporting it. When the police broke down the door, they found him on the toilet decomposed."

"What?!"

"They said his heart bursted inside his chest from taking speed with cocaine and you know he had a bad heart to begin with."

"Oh my God." I tried to imagine what he must've looked like or how he must've felt when his heart bursted inside his chest. The thought made me cringe.

It brought me back to when I was a nine-year-old girl and he came home from the hospital one Wednesday afternoon. I was home alone. I forgot where Donell was. He told me the doctor told him they would have to operate on his heart. His heart wasn't doing too well. He was so afraid that he hugged me. I hugged him back because I understood what being scared felt like. That was my first time witnessing an adult show fear like a child.

Donell gathered his belongings. "Come on, we have to go all the way to Jamaica, Queens to meet up with Mommy and Grandma Jimmy."

"I need five minutes to wash up real quick."

"What you been doin' girl? Fuckin'?"

"Sherman."

"Word? You finally got him?"

"Yup. You know how long I've been waitin'."

"Dana, we gotta leave. Hurry up. Five minutes," he warned, "If you're not ready in five minutes, I'm leaving."

Ahhhh! The wash relieved my itch. I ran down three blocks and caught up with Donell. This was a long train ride to Queens without any cuties for Donell to look at. I wasn't hungry for any, Sherman completed me. We killed time by rhyming and talking.

If you're in hell, I'll put you in heaven
This power of mine is the kind to wine & dine
Just you and I listening to the ice tingling
No words involved my eyes are jingling
It's how I use it on you lover, your feeling drunk
Even though you're sober
I'm not the best but I excel
Make you undress call out my name
Darcel...

"Donell, I feel kind of responsible for Daddy-James' death."

He chuckled. "Dana, what are you talking about?"

"Remember when Daddy used to beat us every Sunday?"

"Yeah. I could never forget that shit."

"Well, I used to pray to God to please kill him."

"Word?" He laughed. "Don't feel responsible. Remember Daddy-James had a bad heart to begin with ever since the Vietnam War?"

"Yeah and look at the war he did on me. Look at my eyes."

"What's wrong with them?"

I looked up.

"Oh I see." Donell said. "The bottom of your whites look like brown tears."

"It was those fuckin' cigarettes he smoked!"

Donell nonchalantly said, "He smoked around me and the whites around my eyes didn't turn. You're being paranoid."

"No, I'm not! Did Daddy-James have you stand up for three hours straight while talking and blowing cigarette smoke all up in your face?"

"No."

"That shit is torture. Especially for a little child, Donell. Let me tell you, on school nights, when you was sleeping, he used to make me stand up like a fuckin' soldier, talking my ears to death."

"Talking about what?"

"What else! Vietnam! And if I blinked, he'd slapped me silly."

"What? That shit is crazy! Why would he smoke cigarettes in your face and then slap you for blinking?"

"Paranoia, 'cause his ass was high off of weed. He used to say I looked like I was rolling my eyes at him."

"That's plain silly and stupid and I don't care if he can hear me, where ever you are. I remember when I got an ass whipping for hanging my clothes in the closet the wrong way."

"Donell, I have to give it to you, you was a good brother."

"Was?"

"You had my back. You took my beatings."

"Yeah, you owe me a few." He said.

"Remember I used to ask you to help me straighten up my room before Daddy-James inspected it?"

"Do I? Every Sunday you run in my room looking like you're about to cry, beggin'. 'Donell, could you please look at my room.'" He made me laugh.

"You know what bugs me out till this day?"

"What?"

"Remember the grace Daddy-James taught us?"

"Oh yeah!" I remember.

"Where did that grace come from? He claimed we were Muslim but we never been to the mosque, we never wore the garbs and you know I asked my Muslim friend Omar, what *'Ahalla Wah Tee A Lay*" meant and he told me that shit meant 'nothing.' "

"Oh shit. He misled us?"

"Well look at it like this, Daddy-James is dead, gone, cat-put. He doesn't have a chance to redeem himself. You may not want to hear this but Dana, we have to forgive him."

"Forgive him my ass. Ass still sore from those whippin's."

"All I'm suggesting is we have to try to find the good in him. The good in what he did for us, so we can forgive him."

"Why? Hell no! I hope he rots in hell! I don't want to forgive him!"

"Dana, don't say that. Remember what Mommy taught us about evolving to our God-like selves. We can't harbor bitter thoughts on people. That shit'll rotten up our insides and anchor Daddy-James from passage. We have to try and find something good in him so we could set him free. What were some of the good things he did?"

"Okay, let's see what needle we can find in the haystack besides the one he stuck in Mommy's arm."

"Oh damn, Dana. That's real cold..." We chilled for a minute then he continued, "I remember the good pepper steak he used to cook. He was a slow cook but it used to be worth the wait. He was an excellent cook."

"Look beyond his good cooking. Didn't he care about us and made sure we were fed everyday?"

I reluctantly agreed. Donell did his best to help me think positive about Daddy-James. It helped somewhat. I did not forget the times he used to kiss me on the mouth when I was nine years old in the bathroom. I thank God that was the farthest he went. Donell grew angry after hearing this. We sat in silence and wished Daddy-James luck on his passage. Donell said,

"I hope Mommy doesn't get mad at us."

I sighed, "I feel the same way."

"Let's walk in this church and let go of all the messed up things he did to us and forgive him for his short-comings."

"Cool."

Through Daddy-James imperfections, I've learned to not treat people good or bad, young or old the way he treated us. In all goodness, I'm glad we fled from him. And I'm glad to see that Mommy was strong enough to know that we could do bad all by ourselves. No matter how many times he called and begged us to come back and give him another chance, Mommy stood her ground.

When we arrived at the Jesus is Lord Church, Mommy was too busy talking to Pastor/ Grandma Jimmy to notice how late we were. Grandma Jimmy said,

"James always talked about y'all. How much he loved y'all n' all and how he missed Defrager." Grandma Jimmy believed her son died not of a bursted heart but of a broken heart, spiritually speaking. I wouldn't be surprised if she blamed Mommy for his injury.

It's been about seven years since we've seen Grandma Jimmy and she aged terribly rapid. About seven years ago, she couldn't have been any more than 50 years-old, looking so young and vibrant. Now as I stand before her, she must have gained 20 years on her life! Her weight came down ungracefully in the saddest places. Her once plump cheekbones were now hardened by lack of fatty cells. As fragile as she appeared, I was afraid if I hugged her she would disintegrate. Grandma Jimmy resembled a very, slow cooked turkey, with skin so tender that it could slip off of her bones. Her neck sagged like the skin of a turkey's neck. Constant clicks of her nervous jaws sounded like the Turkey footsteps. What happened to her life? What happened in her life these past seven years? Did she get sick? She spoke to me as if I was still nine, as if time did not pass between us. Grandma Jimmy apparently wasn't aware of my growth. I think she was too old to see the change in me. Maybe it's good for her not to see the new, woman in me. It'll probably shock her into a stroke.

I pretended as if I didn't notice her shaken hands or her frail body or her graceless face. I forced myself to laugh at her redundant, ole played out southern jokes. She laughed at her own jokes. My cheek muscles burned from smiling too hard. She then took out her handkerchief and wiped the whites on the sides of her mouth. She slowly opened her change purse and looked in. She handed me and Donell...a dollar.

"Y'all go on and buy something nice with it. Ice cream, whatever your little heart desires." Donell and I just looked at each other and almost cracked up in front of her. Grandma Jimmy clicked her false teeth and smacked her lips, then slowly turned to Mommy. I excused myself and went into the bathroom. After I peed, I scratched down there, again! Shit was killing me! I know I washed myself real good. Why am I still itching?

Daddy-James' funeral was small and short. I knew Mommy was a little buzzed off of a joint. I don't mind weed. Weed doesn't make you look unattractive like dope. Daddy-James's funeral was sad because for one, his casket was closed and two, his poor cadaver was packed in a beige, cheap, thin, un shalacked wooden box that I could've hammered together myself. I guess it came from his veterans benefits. But really, Karma is a bitch.

Mommy asked me to change my name back to Daddy-James' last name so that I could collect his social security and government checks, but I refused to. I didn't want his last name or his money. She understood why and she didn't pressure me about it either.

"Dana, how do you feel about us moving back into that apartment?"

"I think it's kind of spooky but hey there ain't nothin' like having our own. Did you ask Donell?"

"Yeah, he said he didn't mind either or. So why don't we do this. We should take all of our clothes and things back to Nawnie's house until we get ready to move back into the apartment."

"Ah, Mommy! I don't want to go back there. I don't want to see everybody again."

Donell overheard us and interjected, "Swallow your pride, Dana. We'll only be there no more than two weeks."

"Thank you, Donell." Mommy reminded, "We have to support each other, we're a family here."

"Okay, okay. But why do we have to wait so long to move in?" I asked. They looked at me like I was crazy.

"Do you think anybody's going to clean his remainders?" Mommy asked.

"I thought housing would do all of that." I said.

"Are you paying housin' to clean up all that blood n' stuff?" Donell sarcastically asked.

"Donell, don't start on your sister. I told y'all no fighting, right? After we leave here, I'ma call Nawnie and let her know what's going on."

We left the shelter and brought all of our belongings back to Nawnie's house. Everybody except for Berlinda was so happy to see us. Mommy reassured Nawnie that we would be moving into our own place in two weeks. I caught Berlinda giving Nawnie an unbelieving look. I was stationed at Nawnie's house while Mommy and Donell went to air out the smell of death in the apartment. Mommy felt I was too sensitive to go with them. She knew my spirit would not be able to handle the low vibrations in the apartment.

When Donell and Mommy returned, Mommy couldn't sit still for nothing. It was like she was re-living her teenage life. She went back outdoors, hanging with her friends Shirley and Cherie. I told Mommy that I resented her for leaving me and Donell stressed out, over at Nawnie's house, while she relieved herself at Shirley's house. She understood and decided to take us along with her. Besides, my school's location wasn't too far from Shirley's house. Yes! Fun, excitement, no more stress and no more responsibilities.

17
idle working

Shirley Clare lives further up on the high hills of the Bronx where there are tall, abundantly healthy trees and botanicals. If you walk toward the end of her block and look at New Jersey, a beautiful sunset would come into view. I love natural elements, natural places and natural people. When I grow up, I want to live on the countryside. But how am I going to get to that point? What will I be when I grow up? Hmmmm…I don't know. A dancer? A writer? I don't know. I'm sure if I keep asking God what I will be, the answer will come some day.

Shirley is the mother of four kids. Three of them are from different boyfriends. I've been noticing how all four of Shirley's children suffer the same issue. They always quarrel about whose father is a better man than whose. They don't realize that not only are they hurting each other but they're hurting everyone around them. The one who suffers the most is Towonna. She is always the one left crying in the end. She told me she resents her father for not being there for her. She's gets upset and asks why could he make time for his other two children (her half-sisters)and not make time for her. She resents her mother for making poor decisions with a low beat man like her dad.

Lately, Donell and I have been hanging around Towonna and Brian. I hope their bad habits doesn't rub off on us. Brian is on the verge of dropping out of junior high and Towonna has been held over twice. She is still in junior high. Living in a house like Shirley's, without stability could knock a kid off balance and focus.

Donell and I sat right in front of the TV watching Shirley's silly behavior. Wayne has me by three years and he thinks he's so grown. He sits around in his stuffy room watching porno tapes (his hobby) after work. Shirley's eldest child, Sheila, has her own life, cramped up in her own room. She has her mini refrigerator, a cable box she doesn't pay for because her wires are attached to her neighbors' and her own phone line with a lock on it. She said she and her man are getting their own apartment before she has the baby.

"Ma! Would you please stop it! God, I hate this house! We need food! What are they gonna eat? They're our guests ya know. This is so embarrassing!" yelled Towonna. Shirley's eyes swayed with her speech.

"Go in the room and ask Wayne to let me borrow $5."

"Wayne! Wayne!" Towonna banged on his door. "Ma wanna borrow $5 so we can eat." Towonna's patience was already on E.

Wayne yelled back from behind his door, "What happened to her check?"

Towonna's voice pitched. "I dunno! Ain't no food here and we all are hungry." No response. "Come on, Wayne, you know if I was old enough to work, I'd be workin' right now."

"Yo' ass'll be stealing right now."

"Wayne, we got company here! That's not how you're supposed to treat guests. Give Ma five dollars please?"

"Y'all are the ones who got company! Not me!" Wayne yelled back.

"Wayne, please let Ma borrow five dollars so we could get somethin' to eat."

"Hell no! I ain't givin' nobody my money. I work hard to save my money and I ain't supportin' nobody's fucked up habits!"

Towonna punched his door and walked away.

Donell and I sat quietly watching "The A-Team." Our eyes watched Mr. T jammer his lips while our ears listened to Shirley amuse herself with Absolut vodka. Fuzzy pink slippers sat beside her thighs. With a cigarette hanging out the right side of her mouth, glassy eyes staring at us, Shirley started making confessions about how pissed off her children were at her and why. She repeatedly said to us, "'Cause my ass fucked up…I'm a picker, fucker-upper…a picker, fucker-upper, ha! Ha!…I fucked up." She spiraled herself up from the floor, holding onto the belt of her paisley, royal blue silk robe. She barely held her balance while trying to put her Aretha Franklin album on her record player. Shirley was having a hard time. It must've been like trying to put a dry thread through a needle. Her body rocked back and forth and around with her head tilted to the side, still holding up that cigarette with her lips.

Shirley slowly pulled the lint off from the needle and damn near scratched the album trying to play her song. Saliva made a line down her mouth. She sang loudly,

"Say a little prayer for you. Forever and ever!" And then she laughed at herself. God blessed Shirley with a beautiful set of straight, ivory teeth. Music and vodka lifted her cheeks, reminiscing of her yester-years of singing on stage with the Delfonics. They pulled her on the stage. A wonderful experience in her past. She wasn't as lucky as Tina Turner to continue her singing career. At least she had an experience and a memory.

Curtains and sheets hung in absent doorways due to the many fights that occurred in her apartment. Only three doors swung in her four-bedroom apartment. One door for the bathroom, one in Wayne's room and one in the entrance door. Healthy spider and rubber plants held their own beauty and fame on the stage of her windowsill. If Shirley spoke to no one else, it was her abundant plants she spoke to and loved as if they were kittens. I thought it was sad how Shirley's children disrespected her but I believe they know not to go too far before she snaps and black out on them. Shirley would not think twice about stabbing a second time. She damn near killed Towonna's father for whatever reason I don't know. He was in the hospital for a minute. The Clare family with whom Mommy involved herself and loved unconditionally is a very intelligent and musically talented family but they are stifled financially. All of the adults who either helped pay rent at Shirley's or freeloaded, all had drinking and drug problems. Their occupational duties consisted of running numbers and playing lotto. Everyone wanted to be lucky. When they won patches of money, they would spend it up like sick fools who only had 24 hours to live. Time was not important to them.

On lucky days, I could smell the perfumes from flowers throughout Shirley's apartment. Mr. Robert would stick a flower in my hair, stick food in the fridge, stick four spoons in four bowls of ice cream for Towonna, Donell, Brian and I.

Everyday was like a vacation to Hollywood on Shirley's location. Drama. Cuts! Ambulance lights! Action! A bone fractured…

Towonna tapped me on the shoulder, and whispered in my ear, in her husky voice.

"Come wit me to tha store."

"I have to ask my mother."

She pulled my wrist. "I asked her already. She said you could come."

"Where is she?"

"She went back out."

"Donell, I'll be back. I'm going to the store."

"I'm leaving in a few. I'm going to hook up with this girl I met yes-terday."

"Okay, so if Mommy asks where you're at, what should I tell her?"

"Tell her I'll be back around twelve." Donell said.

Towonna turned around to her mother, "Ma, I'll be back."

"Huh? Where ya goin'?" She spoke in monotone. She was out of breath from all that singing and shouting. Her whole circumference smelled like Absolute Vodka.

"Out." Towonna answered.

"Out. Out where-ah?"

"Out, Ma! To tha store, I'll be back."

"Bitch, don't be talking to me like I'm annoying you! My ass was annoyed with your stinky ass for 48 muthafuckin' hours. Where the fuck are ya' goin'?! 'Scuse me Dana." I nodded.

"I just said, to the store, Ma!"

"UhhO," she belched. " 'Scuse me."

Before we opened the door to leave, her brother, Wayne stuck his afro-head out his door. His metal fan blew his masculine, oniony per-spiration out his door. He was a mixture of black and Puerto Rican. Kind of cute but not my type. His hair was slightly curly but overall, an Afro. A shape up wouldn't hurt around the kitchens. He had a nice bare and tight chest but what fucked it up was the cigarette parked behind his earlobe. His teeth could be a little whiter too.

"Y'all goin' to the store?"

"Why?" Towonna asked.

"Here. Get me four chicken wings with pork fried rice and a Tropical Fantasy. Y'all can get somethin' 'cause I don't want your stu-pid ass stealin' nothin'." Wayne took out a twenty from his stringy Gucci wallet. "Don't want to find your ass in a precinct."

"Shut up, Wayne! With no brain."

"I should entrust my money with Dana because of thieves." He said.

"Shut up! Ain't nobody going to steal nuthin'!" She snatched the twenty-dollar bill.

"Yeah right, I know your ass is addicted to that shit. Cleptofuckin'maniac!" He laughed as we headed down the staircase and he shouted, "Oh yeah, and get me a pack of Salem Lights 100's!"

Towonna and I raced down six flights of stairs by three's. I won of course. I opened the broken lock on the exit door. Outside equals freedom. Freedom to be whoever the hell I wanna be! Besides, nobody around here knows who I am anyway. I tucked my buttoned down white and blue Gap polka dot shirt inside my blue Levi jeans. I tighten my belt two more notches tighter to reveal my sexy figure. I licked my finger wet to wipe off Towonna's sneaker print on the back of my two-week old red Reeboks. As we walked down the block, we passed different brands of boys. I kept my jacket halfway open so the guys could see everything. It's about forty degrees outside but I didn't care. Some of the cuties on her block were aspiring athletes and others were street rough necks. I prefered to talk to the flawless pretty boys. They're more pleasurable to look at.

"Yo, Towonna, who dat?" A corner dude asked.

"My cousin."

"What's her name?"

"Ask her yourself!" Towonna was getting aggravated with all the guys on the block using her as their middleman to talk to me.

She wore Wayne's old faded black Lee jeans. Towonna's small ass cheeks imprinted two gray circles below her pockets. She wore an oversized yellow and black striped Gap shirt. Her white Olympics were kept up with the help of a toothbrush, soap, and bleach. Then White-Out was applied on the creases near her toes. A scissor would have been perfect in trimming off the loose strings hanging from her Louie Vuitton bookbag.

You talking about cold! It started to feel brick outside! The high winds made it impossible to walk around with my jacket open. Fuck that. I zippered up my coat and we hurried in the direction of Tito's grocery store. On the way, Towonna was being careless with stepping on the lines and cracks in the ground. Her mother drank wine eight times and she broke her mother's back twelve times. Before I could push the door open into Jose's grocery store, she pulled my arm back.

"What?" I said.

"My moms is back on credit. I don't wanna hear his mouth. We're going to Associate's."

I don't know how Towonna did it, but girl stuffed eggs, bacon, a whole chicken, canned milk, butter, and Kool-Aid mix into her LV bag. Then purchased some cookies and ice cream, Wayne's Salem Lights 100's and one liter of Tropical Fantasy. She pocketed the $5 and spent the rest of Wayne's money on Chinese food. That girl is crazy talented.

We saw her brother Brian looking fresh walking up the block with a shorty. His new Jordan's were dope. Where did he get them? He told us that Big Jeff is having a get-together tonight. Everybody is going to be there. Who's Big Jeff? I hope he's cute.

Towonna and I went back to her house to freshened up before going to Big Jeff's. Shirley was snoring on the couch. I lifted the needle off the record player and put the covers over her. I went into the bathroom, where Towonna was spraying some of Shirley's opium perfume on. We both stood in the mirror. She let me get ahead of her because I was slightly shorter than her. I wet my ponytail and brought down my baby hairs. She did the same. I put mascara on my eyelashes and eyebrows. Towonna put lipstick on her lips.

"Wanna put some on?" She offered.

"I'll get in trouble."

"How, Dana? Just put a little on."

"What color does it say?"

"It's Really Red."

"I don't know, Tee."

"Let me put it on for you and if you don't like it, take it off." My nose smelled her fingers. She was real close up on me, lining my lips. I wanted to laugh.

"You look pretty, girl? Look." She said.

She was right. I felt like a beautiful princess when everyone in Big Jeff's room looked at me. A beautiful red light shone in a corner. Anita baker's album played in his tape deck. After Towonna introduced me to Big Jeff, he introduced me to everyone in his room as 'his pretty girl.' He was so lucky to be cute 'cause if he wasn't, he would've gotten dissed.

There were eight girls and ten guys in the room. Those who couldn't find a partner had to leave, meaning Big Jeff kicked them out. Big Jeff was so cute. A football head, tightly curled eyelashes, beautiful, strong teeth and a small, attractive nose. I was loving his leadership attitude and his strong physique. Everybody started dancing and doing the latest dances like "The Rooftop" or "The Basketball". Big Jeff started freaking a new dance I had never seen before. It looked funky when he did it with confidence. He said he learned the dance from his school, Lehman College. It was called "The Rudy". Nice 'n Smooth had us all doing the James Brown moves with our feet. Big Jeff and I connected in a special way.

"Jeff, why don't you put on some Janet Jackson?" I asked.

"Yo', y'all wanna hear Janet?" Answers were unanimous. He played "When I Think of You." I sort of impersonated her and everybody parted to give me space, like Moses parted the sea. My moves lit up eyes and shocked Towonna. A proud grin crossed her face. Jeff was open off of me. I received and politely accepted their powerful compliments.

Then Anita Baker brought me "Joy!" Everything became quiet. There were a few giggles in corners of the room.

Sherman was getting the big payback for negligence. Out of sight, out of mind. Everybody started kissing and making out. I liked the wonderful sounds Jeff's kisses made. They turned me on. Then "Funny How Time Flies When You're Having Fun" came on and people started sliding to comfortable positions on the floor.

Towonna is a bright girl. She and Eric sat on the floor to secure the door in case his moms tried to come in. Jeff and I could not stop kissing. It felt so good. We whispered conversations between kisses.

"So... Dana... How old are you?"

"How old are you?"

"I asked you first."

I giggled and we kissed some more... "I'm sweet 16."

"I'm 18." His eyes circled my face. "You're so pretty."

"Thank you." *What a kisser.*

All the things that were going on in Shirley's house were dramatic and interesting but I'm getting tired of it all. I'm ready to move into the apartment already. Thank you Daddy-James for not taking Mommy's name off the lease. That's the best thing you could've done for us. You didn't give up hope and I'll forgive you one day at a time. Sometimes it's good to never give up hope. Had he given up hope, we would've still been sitting up in those crazy shelters waitin' for an apartment. Fuck those shelters! Shoot! That's right. 'Cause, God had a plan for us. Best believe that.

18
the master's plan

God had a special plan for Mommy. On Thursday around four o'clock, Nawnie and Mommy walked in solemnly from the hospital. Mommy startled everybody by suddenly bursting into tears.

"The doctor told me I have six months to live. I don't want to die! I'm not ready to diiiiie!" She hysterically cried. Everybody hugged Mommy, including Berlinda.

This moment for me was real crucial. At this point, I needed to continue writing in my journals on a daily basis. I pray my worst enemy does not experience what Mommy is going through.

It literally took five and a half weeks for the odor to leave that apartment. Nawnie made sure everyone pitched in to help us make our move successful. Nawnie and I put bags of clothes and food into two shopping carts and rode the train all the way to Far Rockaway, Queens. The ride took us about an hour and a half. Mr. Washington was supposed to had brought his truck to take us there, but he never came through. Nawnie was right, never depend or put expectations on people 'cause you'll set yourself up for disappointment. So everybody did their share of helping out. The move took two days.

"If y'all need to come back, don't hesitate. Mommy's door is always open for y'all. Y'all hear?" Nawnie told us.

"Yes, Ma." Mommy said. We all hugged each other. Boy did it feel good to finally say goodbye to dependency.

Donell and I decided to keep our same rooms. I circled my room and I thought back to how it used to look bigger. But hey, at this point I wouldn't care if my room were the size of the bathroom, I just thank God for giving me my own room back. I sat and bounced on my old twin bed. Looking around, noticing how Daddy-James hasn't touched a thing in my room. I smelled my sheets and the rose oil scent was buried quietly under dust particules. My unkept Barbie dolls were still sitting on top of my closet and window sill. Hmm, let me see if the prize is still in my hiding place. I lifted the mattress. My baby was still there where I left it. My sweet little diary. I'll read the first page and I'll read the rest tonight in bed. Wow! I'm surprised I filled half the book.

Dear Diary,
My name is Dana Strong and I am eight years old. I am in the third grade. My school is P.S. 105. Today is April the 14th. Mommy and Daddy are sleeping in the living room and Donell is playing with his GI-Joe men. I have a boyfriend in school. His name is Sharleek and I have a boyfriend in Texas named Darwin. I love Darwin a lot. My cat's name is Jamella. I love her too.

Dear Diary,
Today is Sunday the second day Darwin has been here. All day yesterday Darwin and I were holding hands everywhere we went. My friends got mad at us because Darwin picked out a flower for me from Miss Carter's garden and didn't pick anything for them. We're going out with each other now. Me and Darwin tap kissed and humped in the elevator…It felt good.

I got my room back. God is good and God bless you Daddy-James. May you rest in peace. Thank you.

This past month, Mommy's been fairly healthy, just a lot of coughing though. This disease is so ugly and unpredictable. It's like today she may feel well enough to go outside and play a game of handball or even paint a complete portrait and then tomorrow she may not have the strength to even feed herself. Like when I walked in from school today, the house smelled like ammonia and pine. Furniture rearranged, windows halfway open, fresh ocean breeze blowing through n' all. Sunrays warmed every plant sitting in the window. Music blasted with dancing high spirits in the air. I heard the twinkling melodies of Mommy's silver bracelets call me. I went into the kitchen.

"Hi Mommy."
She came strolling toward me singing,

"Oh don't talk about my Father,
God is my friend (Yes he is my friend)
He made this world for us to live in

And he forgive all our sins
And all he ask of us."
She touched my chin while
dancing her body language.
"Is we give each other love. (Oh yeah)
Love your mother, love your Father,
Love your sister, love your brother, your brother!
Ah, don't go and talk about my Father,
God is my friend."

She tempted me to dance with her. I did.

"This was me and your father's song. We used to always sing this song to each other."

"Mommy, I wanna ask you something." She listened. "If Rudy were to come back to you right now and ask you to be with him and start all over again, would you take him back?"

She smiled softly and said, "Yes." I smiled too.

"You would? You still love him like that?"

"I never stopped. He will always be in my heart. He was my first love."

"Wow, that's real good to know…And Mommy how are you feeling?

"Why? You want me to go with you somewhere?"

"Do you feel like coming with me to the beach?"

"You wanna catch the sunset?"

"Yeah," she thought about it for a second. I added, "it's not that cold outside. I wanna catch the sun before it sets. It should be dawning in a half of an hour."

"I hear you. Okay. Now before we go, I want you to take a look at your room."

"Mommy, I straightened it up before I went to school."

"Look at it, again." She smiled.

"You cleaned it up?"

"Look at it."

I opened my door halfway and gasped. The picture of Mommy and I doing the snake from my fourteenth birthday was sketched and painted on a canvas that took up half of my wall. She posed her snake from the left behind me and I posed my snake from the right. Together we formed an 8. Turn it to the side and you got infinity. All sorts of abstract designs of beautiful colors and sparkling stars glittered from my walls. Dim track lights put a soft and cozy feel to the room. A new red (one of my favorite colors) rug covered my floor near my bed. Rose-colored drapes hung from my window. My bed was nicely made with five pillows of red, orange, yellow, green and purple. On the ceiling sparkled different fonts and sizes of Dana Makieba painted in sky blue and white glitter.

"Oh, Mommy. Thank you, thank you, thank you. You're so beautiful." I landed a triple kiss on her smiling cheeks.

"Just keep it up, Dana."

"I promise."

"I saw something behind your bed that I didn't like." She touched my chin, "I know you're almost a woman now and I'm glad you're being responsible but I want you next time (that's if there would be one) is to think about your hygiene and respect this household."

Oh no, I hope it's not what I think she's talking about.

"I should've told you this when I saw the change in you."

"What change?"

"The way you've been walking lately. Your behaviors are new."

"What do you mean? Am I switching hard now?"

"No, it's not that, Dana. You crossed over. I can't explain it, but it's something about your spirit that has changed. Dana, I wish you could've waited until you got married. I can't get too mad at you 'cause, shit, I had y'all when I was 16 and 18. But damn, learn from my mistakes."

I looked down at the floor.

"The reason why I'm saying all of this to you because I saw a used condom on the floor behind your bed. Now you know that ain't cool, Dana. Don't let me see anymore of that shit layin' around this house. You hear me? Let him take you to a hotel or something'. No motel. A hotel."

"Okay." I wanted to sink inside the floor and hide in between the cracks.

"I'm sorry, Mommy."

"Dana, I forgive you. If you wanna talk about it later we can, okay?" I looked around again and redirected the energy.

"I like the way you have my name written all over the walls in different styles."

"Did I ever tell you what name I was going to name you at first?"

"No."

"Yetunde Monique."

"Yetunde Monique? Wow, I like it. Why did you change it?"

"Your Aunt Denise, you know, your father's sister gave you the name Dana Makieba. I thought it was nicer. It kind of fit you. Come and look at Donell's room."

I opened his door.

"No, you didn't, Mommy! No you didn't! Where did all this energy come from?"

"God gave it to me. I feel if I got it now, I might as well use it up before I lose it."

"Mommy, Donell's going to love it!"

"You think so?"

"I know so."

She had positioned a desk in the far right corner of his room with all of his baseball cards neatly stacked on it. Mommy had all of Donell's historical books on top of shelves that she nailed up by herself. She painted hundreds of figures of people on his wall. It looked like I was standing in the middle of Yankee stadium. He already had brown carpet on his floor so she hooked it up with a bright green rug.

"How did you make the carpet look like a baseball field?"

"I bought a big green rug and I cut it."

"Genius. You know you're the best when it comes to creation."

"You mean innovation."

"Okay, give it up for Defrager Strong!" She smiled at my cute humor.

"I'm going food shopping tomorrow so whatever you want from the supermarket add on to the list. The list is on top of the kitchen counter. What do you want to eat tonight? Ooh, my song is on!" She ran toward the living room, turned up the volume and started singing.

"And when I get this feeling
I need sexual healing. Sexual. Healing
It's good for me, makes a me feel so fine...."

"Pizza!" I shouted. Today me and Mommy will watch the sunset together. She opened the closet door and put on her navy blue pea coat.

"It's not that cold outside. It's like 58 degrees."

"Dana, you know my condition. I'm more susceptible to catching colds than you are."

"That's right, I'm sorry, I forgot."

Mommy went into the bathroom while I waited for her on my lovely bed. I love my room and I love you, Mommy. Dana Makieba sparkled all over my walls in beautiful baby blues. I carefully sat on my bed trying not to wrinkle the spread. Wow, I would've been a Yetunde Monique. Yetunde Monique....

"You're ready?" She asked.

As we walked on the boardwalk, she locked her arms through mine. The ocean's breeze blew ripples in my rainbow tie-dye lappa. If I stared at the sun, it would blind my eyes with swirling yellows and dark oranges.

"Mommy, are you okay?"

"Yeah, I just need to slow down a little." We cut our pace in half. Mommy was out of breath so we walked slower. AIDS added 50 years to Mommy's life.

"Mommy, I ask God all the time, why this had to happen to us?" She didn't say anything. "You know sometimes I get angry at the government, and the drug dealers for selling those drugs to you. I get angry and I hate your friend Lil Tina who first introduced you to drugs and then I get angry at the people who started drugs period but more so the government for allowing drugs to come into this country."

"Dana." She called my name ever so calmly. "Don't hate them, I was the one who fell into the traps of temptation. I'm the one to blame for indulgence. And Mommy is so sorry for putting you and Donell through this. Mommy's sorry for putting this burden on y'all." I nodded my head. I forgive her and I have to accept the things I can not change and be grateful for the fact that Mommy is here with me right now.

Mommy and I held hands and I helped her get over the hump of rocks. The waves' clashes roared like thunder as the dusk winds crashed the water against the rocks. I untied my lappa and draped it over Mommy's head and then wrapped it around her neck. We sat near the edge of the rocks, but not too close to the roaring waves. Our eyes caught the yellow and darkening orange sun.

I inhaled the thick, salty air and stared at the half sun. Oh God. Thank you for this. Thank you for giving Mommy the strength to come with me and appreciate your glorious creation. Please stay with us. Please take care of us. Please take care of Mommy. I love her so much, God. The sky's color is so beautiful. Amen.

I turned to her and said, "Thank you, Mommy, for coming with me."

"Dana, if I had the strength, Baby, I'd be here everyday with you."

Quickly, I turned to hug her. But she inched her chin back to get a good look at my face.

"Dana, you cryin'?" I said nothing. "Come here." She held me tighter and smiled. "You're still sensitive. That's my, Baby. Come on. Let's go get some pizza."

19
remainders of black holes
at the end of a rainbow

I have an addiction. I'm addicted to blowing bubbles. I found a new way to blow bubbles from a wand. I hold the wand in front of a fan and let the wind blow through the wand. Then bubbles suddenly appear in the form of light bulbs. It looks like electricity is flowing out of the wand. I hold the bubble wand and watch each color organize itself. It's always the same beautiful patterns of red, orange, yellow, green, indigo, and purple. But then once the colors are done organizing themselves, black and gray oily holes push the rainbow out of the way and then pop goes the bubble. Well, everyone and everything definitely has an expiration date, at least on the physical plane.

Six months quickly turned into three years for Mommy. That goes to show anybody how much doctors know. All praise due to God!

I'm eighteen years old and I've grown strong emotionally and mentally. I'm trying to gain self-control. I have to work on my discipline. I quit my job at Ben and Jerry's last week. I started working there about a month ago, shortly after I broke up with Sherman. The job was a nice distraction but I couldn't take my manager's treatment. His eyes, his mouth, his stinkin' fat ass. He wanted me to do everything. I had to be a scooper, a server, work the cash register, clean up after closing and mop the floors and to top it off, lock up! That fat old bastard tried to take advantage of my kindness and my youth. I quit 'cause I wasn't raised to be nobody's slave and I'll be damned if I'm going to age prematurely over a damn business I don't share ownership in.

I should've graduated last year but this school bit is not for me, either. I don't have time to kiss my guidance counselor's ass. It's not that I hate school, I hate what the teachers are teaching me. I hate having to deal with immature, spoiled students who're still living with their parents and all they're thinking about is their grades and college. The girls in school are spreading rumors about me being bi-sexual. Whatever, they don't understand moi. They're so much lesser than ignorant. Maybe it's because of the way I am built. My body has grown thick and strong like a brick house and I'm not afraid to play basketball or climb a tree. Even though I am careful not to break a nail. Maybe the girls are afraid of their own sexuality, maybe it's me they secretly want.

Why go to school when I damn near have my own apartment? Mommy is hardly ever home anyway. I always keeps money in my pocket 'cause my three sugar daddies won't have it no other way. It's been a good year now that I've been holding down the apartment while Mommy's been in and out of the hospital. Mommy spends most of her time over at Nawnie's house because Nawnie lives closer to Mt. Sinai Hospital than we do.

I feel like I'm fooling myself attending school when my heart really isn't in it. I'm a B average student. But still my heart isn't in it, I'm just going so Mommy doesn't get stressed out over me. I'm better off self-teaching. If it were up to me, I'd rather hang out at the library or the American museum of natural history.

After I left school, I took the 6 train to 103rd Street to see Mommy in the hospital. Mommy gave me her photo identification card to pick up some money from the check cashing place. The hospital's policy did not allow patients to leave the hospital without a dismissal form. I imitated Defrager's serious facial expression at the check cashing spot. I wore her tinted sunshades. Each time the clerk eyeballed me, I pretended I was looking for something down in my purse.

"Sign here," She said staring all in my face. I forged Mommy's signature. She compared our handwriting and then our faces.

"This isn't you. It's probably your sister. But this is not you."

"Excuse me?"

"This is not you!" She clarified.

"What do you mean not me? Yes it is me." I kept Defrager's serious face up to par and didn't dare remove her sun glasses and quickly signed the check. The clerk handed me the money and as I walked out, I was ready to shit in my panties.

"It's not you!" She shouted again. I ran.

When I returned to the hospital with the money, Mommy already had her budgeting pad sitting on her neatly made craftmatic bed. Mommy was sitting upright, on top of Mt. Sinai's crocheted, sky blue quilt. The pad sat between her spread apart legs. She made me responsible for making sure the rent was paid. I wish Donell was the one who had to handle the food shopping and deal with the embarrassment of buying food with food stamps. He wouldn't care about it no way. I pocketed the money and held onto Donell's money for him in case I saw him tonight.

It's been two months since Mommy began asking me where did my periods go? She reminded me again that this is the second month my period has been "irregular." It'll come, I think, well I hope. I hope I'm not pregnant 'cause if I am, it's probably Renee's. If I am, I'm getting rid of it, quick, fast and in a hurry. I refuse to have a baby by a dude I don't love, especially if he's broke. I know this can't be Sherman's baby. I don't think he can have any more kids 'cause he's been bustin' up in me for the past three years and I never came up pregnant once. Thank God I didn't, 'cause my ass would've been a single parent visiting him up in Sing-Sing for the rest of his life. A drug dealer seems to always end up in the grave or in a cage.

I have to go to the clinic and get a check-up. If I get rated, it better not be PG. When I decide to get pregnant, it must be by a man who's intelligent with a warm heart and good conscience. He has to have a healthy relationship with both of his parents, if they're still around. I need a man, no, I want a man who will respect me enough to not even think of breaking my jaw. It's a shame that I allowed Sherman to go that far with me. I tell you one thing, he's the last muthafucka that will ever lay a hand on me.

Love is a crazy emotion. But then again love is really what you make it. Honor love. True love. Like really what is love? All I know is love means that three letter word.

Mommy held on to her life for her two kids. She battled with pneumonia, tuberculosis, skin breakouts, losing her vision, fatigue and her loss of appetite. Her pride and weight loss constantly fluctuated. Her anemia, her meningitis, her coughs and her self-esteem came and went. I know Mommy's a pure warrior because she proved to those soulless doctors that she could extend six months of her life into three years. The new ADT drug that's out is helping somewhat, but I believe it's a mind over matter thing.

There was a night nurse who used to work on Mommy's floor. She was compassionate toward Mommy. She was a kind person. I believe she had a clear understanding of how precious life is, especially to a mother and her children. She was cool enough to let me spend nights over with Mommy even though it was against the hospital's policy. Sometimes Donell would spend nights with Mommy too.

As I lay my head on her bosom, her heartbeat reminded me of when I used to live back in her palace. Nostalgia, oh God! How I wish we could start all over again. *Mommy why didn't you take heed to what I told you when I was nine?* Well, no sense in trying to change what already has happened. The question is what are we going to do about it, right now in this moment...Maybe all of this was destined to be...I wonder what is the lesson that needs to be learned here?

"Dana, what have you been doin' lately?"

"Going to school and practicing my dance steps."

"Dana, listen. Whatever you're doin' you're doin' too much of it. Damn, Donell sees me more than you do. What's going on Dana? Are there any boyfriends in the picture?"

I sort of laughed, "No Mommy. I'm sorry if you feel neglected. I'll come and visit you more often."

I'm glad I was there to help ease her agonizing pain because I'm sure the nurses wouldn't do it. I massaged her temples until she fell asleep. She always complimented my "healing hands. Halfway through the night, I changed the towels that covered her pillows 'cause it would be soaking sweat. The whole night through I slept lightly, in case Mommy needed me.

As Mommy came closer to her due date, she began forgetting who people were and certain objects. She was passing through the next plane. It bugged me out when she lost memory of her brothers and her sisters. It was weird that at times she couldn't even tell you who she was. I didn't believe her at first 'cause she liked to joke about a lot of things. But when I looked deeper into her eyes and saw that she was serious, that scared me and made me want to be more consistent in writing and recording things in my journal. It was ironic that she remembered Nawnie, Donell and I. Maybe it was because we were the ones who loved her the most? Maybe she was seeing things the same way a child or an infant would.

She also lost weight in the weirdest way. Some of the other AIDS patients looked like skeletons to me. Their cheeks hallowed in, their fingers resembled spider's legs and their eyes bulged with intensity. Mommy slimmed down and lost the muscles in her lovely legs. Instead she developed love handles, a round tummy and bloated facial cheeks.

I guess it came from the medication and the vitamins the nurses were intravenously giving her. Mommy's complexion grew dark and muddy and her hair grew long yet thin. Being that she wasn't pressing clothes anymore at the cleaners, her hands softened up and her nails grew long and pretty. It was like all of her rough edges shed themselves off and was renewed. Parts of Mommy metamorphosized into an orchid and other parts of her stung me like thorns from a rose stem.

The next few days, Nawnie and I went to visit her. Mommy taped her get well and birthday cards onto the sea green wall. The curtain to her roommate's side was open. She must've gone home. Mommy's space was nice and clean. Her bed was made and she sat on the windowsill with the I.V. stuck in her arm. There were also pictures of Cindy Crawford wearing a button down white shirt taped onto her wall. Me, Nawnie, Donell, Naomi Campbell and Salt 'N' Pepa filled a section on the wall.

"Hi, Ma! Hi Dana!" She jumped up.

"Sit down. Relax," Nawnie said as she went to hug Mommy. I hugged Mommy too and kissed her lips.

"How you feelin' Baby?" Nawnie asked.

"I'm feelin' better. I'm not in that much pain. I just wanna get outta here. I want to go outside."

"Let the doctor take care of what he needs to do with you, Baby. Don't be so much in a hurry to go outside. Ain't nothing out there but trouble."

"But Ma, it's boring up here. I'm tired of looking out this window watching everybody walk back and forth. I want to smell some outside air."

"Stick your head out the window." Mommy laughed. "You will get to go outside sooner than you think. Be patient. Let the doctor finish running tests on you. Okay. Do you need anything?"

"Just cigarettes."

Nawnie dipped in her change purse and gave me the money.

"Dana, did you remember to bring me my clothes?" I handed over her bag of clothes. Mommy started rummaging through her clothes.

"Dana, I hope you ain't cut up none of my stuff."

I laughed. "No, Mommy."

"Why would my Miss Special cut up your clothes?"

"Ma, you don't know Dana. You know she cut up all three pairs of my jeans and sewned them into skirts! She polished my white Reeboks black, and cut up my tee shirts into half tee's. But you know what? She won't dare cut up her own stuff!"

"I do cut up my things, Mommy." I defended.

"Yeah, right," she retorted.

"But Mommy, c'mon you can't front. Don't the clothes look nice?"

"If you had a sewing machine, yeah, it would look a lot more professional. I keep tellin' her, Ma, to make her stitches smaller. But she don't listen."

"Well, I'll teach her how to make those stitches smaller okay? That's my Miss Special." I smiled back at Nawnie.

Mommy always find a problem and Nawnie always chalk it up with solutions. Mommy detested the hospital and she made it clear and sound to the entire staff. That's my mother, never concealing the truth. She never believed in suffering in silence. She said, 'she might as well be called the walking dead.' Nawnie changed the subject.

"How's your nice neighbor, baby? Did she go home?"

"No, Ma. She passed away." Mommy sadly said.

"Oh baby, I'm so sorry. When?"

"Saturday. She was up all night moaning the night before. I heard her praying and asking God to please release her and he did…Ma, I'm tired of all this too. I'm tired of getting stuck all day with needles! The doctors tell me they have to run tests for this and run tests for that, like I'm some kind of guinea pig! I just wanna go home, Ma."

"Okay, alright now. Are you in a cage?" asked Nawnie.

"No, but it feels like I'm in one. Being hooked up to all these I.V.'s like I'm NOT A," she raised her voice, "HUMAN BEING! I mean I can't even go across the street and sit in Central Park."

"Why?" I asked.

Mommy's eyes shifted from side to side and then she shook her arm with the I.V.'s. at me.

"I'm sorry, Mommy." My nose squeeked from holding in my laugh.

"You ain't sorry, Dana. Ma, she is always laughing at me." Mommy transformed into a 10-year-old girl.

"No, Nawnie, I'm laughing at her facial expressions." I explained, "Mommy, I'm not laughing at you, I'm laughing with you."

"Do you see me laughing?"

Nawnie interjected, "Better her laughing than crying, right? When you were her age, nothin' made you laugh. I don't know a teenager who was a grouchy as you were." Mommy remembered and laughed. Nawnie perked Mommy up by smoothing some of her old-fashioned, syrupy humor on us and caressing her hand.

Nawnie turned to me and smiled proudly.

"Look at that beautiful smile, that's my Miss Special."

"You spoil her too much, Ma."

"So what? I spoil all of my kids." They both paused and smiled on me.

"What?" I asked.

"Nothin'. We're just looking at you," Mommy said.

I swung my upper torso and arms halfway around like a child.

"Tell her." Nawnie said to Mommy.

"Dana, you know I'm proud of you, right?"

"You are?" My eyebrows rose. "Why Mommy? My grades are below average."

"I know but that's not all of who you are. If you were focused and interested in what your teachers were teaching you, I know you would get all A's. You've had all A's before. I see beyond grades, Dana, I see you. I'm proud of *you* for being *you*."

"Thank you, Mommy. I love you." We hugged.

"I love you too, Baby."

Nawnie was happy. She labeled me as the mother and Mommy as the daughter.

Troop's "Spread my Wings" was the song I've been listening to on the regular. I've been keeping the apartment clean, trying not to think about the pain Mommy constantly goes through. In between my not thinking about it, I cry and pray endlessly. Weeks, days and nights I cried and prayed for God to please take Mommy out. Take her out of her misery. Mommy wasn't comfortable anymore in her shell. Her days were filled with so much pain and agony. Why was she holding on? Why hold on to the suffering? Let it go, just let yourself go, Mommy. I watched my energetic, danceaholic, high-spirited mother go through an incredible transformation.

It was the day before Martin Luther King Junior's birthday, in the year 1991. I was at the hospital with my hand on her back. Only one person was allowed in her room at a time. Nawnie and Donell waited in the hallway. She was rocking back and forth in her hospital gown, staring past the wallpaper, looking up at God, coughing up red phlegm. It scared me. She wasn't in her right state of mind. She was sort of in between worlds. Her aura glowed luminously and then she turned into a child. Her eyes seemed prettier today. Dreamier like. They were the color of pure, brown sugar crystals, and when she looked up she nodded her head like an obedient 2-year-old. Then she started rocking back and forth again and she looked through me, inside of me, still holding on to what life she had left. She was ready to go. Her eyes had a calm, shiny look in them. Peaceful eyes. She communicated with me verbally and telepathically.

She spoke, "Dana, I'm proud of you and Donell. I want you two to take care of each other and Nawnie."

"Yes, Mommy."

"I love you, Baby." And she turned to throw up. I reached over for the paper towels but the cleansing process was already on the floor. I patted and then circled my hand on the middle of her back. Time stood with us.... I love you....It stood still for some moments.

"Call...Nawnie...in...here." She was still rocking back and forth.

This was a moment of transition for all four of us. I sensed Mommy wouldn't it make through the night. Donell and I stood near the slightly open door.

"Ma, I don't want to stay in here. I don't wanna die in the hospital! I want to be in your bed, like Barbara was in hers, Ma. It's not peaceful up in here."

"It's gonna be alright, Baby. Mommy will be right here with you, okay, Baby?" Nawnie was searching for the right thing to say.

Mommy saw me and asked if I was coming back tomorrow.

"Yes, Mommy, I'll be back tomorrow," I said through the cracked door.

"Okay." She was in her own mind state. She became pure and innocent like a child of God.

"Mommy, be strong, okay? Remember what I told you about the playground? I'll meet you there later?"

"Okay. Okay."

"I love you, Mommy," Donell and I simultaneously said. She started mumbling to herself and waited to face God. The nurse rolled Mommy upstairs to the Intensive Care Unit. We kissed her goodbye.

The next day, I couldn't go to the hospital to see her in the state she was in. That afternoon Nawnie called the house and told me and Donell that Mommy was in a coma and the doctors had her on a respirator. Those doctors were preventing my mother from transportation. I sensed that Mommy understood my reasons for not coming back.

Donell and I sat on Nawnie's bed looking and feeling powerless. I mean what was there for me to do in that cold and sterile hospital? Watch her lay in a coma? Mommy was on her own on this journey and she didn't need any of our sorrows and sympathies to hold her back from peace. What she needed was our support, blessings and loving farewells. Donell and I laid down on Nawnie's bed in silence, waiting for Mommy to surrender. Less than a half of an hour later, she surrendered her fear of detaching from this crazy world. All of those who guided her and loved her throughout her lifetime, welcomed her aboard. She took her first step and fell, like a baby, trying to adjust. But Defrager neither look down nor back. After realizing her renewed form, without pain, she focused straight ahead with faith, determination and purpose, and she took off like a cheetah! Ahhhh freedom! She found peace and love.

Auntie Berlinda, Geneva, Leniece, Uncle Junior and Uncle Jerry had paid their last visit to their sister Defrager. Queen Defrager. This was too much for me and Donell to handle, to see or to swallow. We didn't want to see our strong, warrior mother in a coma hooked up to a damn respirator. It's bad enough we had to imagine it. Donell and I laid in silence, I guess waiting for Nawnie to call us, to pronounce that Mommy was...

"Donell, you and I know what Mommy died from, okay? As far as other people are concerned, she died from lung cancer."

20
my best friend

As I neared the parlor, the hums of the cars and the laughing children running behind me did not distract me. I was wrapped in my own world of emotions. I counted three steps and slowly opened the thick shiny oak door. Very soft and consoling music filled the huge and immaculately furnished room. I heard sniffles and whispers. Mumbles and soft and suppressed cries. Mr. Switton, the funeral director, sheltered my hand inside of his soft and warm hands. He looked at my eyes, barely looking in, conveying the monotonous sympathetic words that I failed to listen to.

I felt nothing but wet kisses on my cheek. The piano was playing but no one was playing it. Tissue passed on from different hands and rotated the room. The place was jam packed with Southerners, harlemites, and South Bronx folk. Everyone's hurt was identical to mine. We all loved Defrager. She brought people together. If you knew Defrager, you were considered cool peoples. If she liked you, that meant you was a real person. Mommy always kept it real with people.

The genuine love she had for people was very interesting. Her love was not an in between love. Not an iffy love. It was an either or kind of love. Either you loved Defrager or you didn't. In my opinion she only radiated, strong love. Anyone who didn't love her, probably didn't love him or herself. I'm not saying this because she is my mother, I am speaking from all honesty and I'm sharing what many have witnessed also. She was definitely a special woman.

My eyes froze on the floor. I knew the casket was open by the sudden reaction of everyone. I did not lift my eyes. Someone respectfully walked to the casket. Cries hummed deep songs, someone fainted, others stormed out of the room in disbelief and my mother's childhood friends, Naomi and Shirley, buried their heads in their boyfriends' chests. Towonna walked up to me and Donell and hugged us.

My eyes swiftly gazed over and then bit-by-bit, I lowered my gaze onto her profile. My eyes did not move from her face. Mommy was sick for a while, so this was the day I had been preparing for. The day I was promised. She was now out of her misery. No more cab fare to go back and forth to Mt. Sinai Hospital. No more hearing her painful moans and coughs in the middle of the night.

Cousin Dora is here? She stood up pissy drunk and she still dressed like a fox. The last time I saw her I was 5 years old. I remember spending weekends at her house. Cousin Dora stood up facing Donell and I and shouted, "The children! Oh my God, the children!" Berlinda and Geneva busted out laughing from behind me. As I turned around, a brownish, handsome man caught my attention. He sat across from me and Donell. He smiled just like Donell. His eyes were youthful and deeply set in like beautiful, shiny black buttons. His beautiful heavy eyebrows resembled mine. Rudy! My beautiful father. *Wow, Mommy you had good taste!* My father's beauty, I would say is very magnetic and majestic like mine. Well, vice-versa. He looked happy to see us but sad to have lost his first love. Rudy and his wife kissed me and Donell on the forehead. His kiss made forgiving him a whole lot easier. Our eyes connected when he looked into mine. My blood, my love, my distant father.

"Listen, Baby, you two are welcome to live with us. Y'all are my family, you know that right? Ya got brothers and a sister that love ya. Anything you need, we're here for the both of you. Ya hear?"

"Thank you, Rudy." We said. But no thanks. I need to move forward and be an adult now, not backwards and be your child again. What are we going to do, pick up from where you left us at, 5 and 6? I'm a woman now. I need independence to grow and privacy to fuck whoever I please.

I looked up at the casket and Troy took it real hard. He kept kissing Mommy's face and telling her she was his favorite aunt. He kept telling her he loved her and he's going to miss her. He cried out over and over,

"Why? Why? Why is everybody dying?" Troy's cry sounded like laughter, that's how hurt he was. It seemed like Troy failed to accept Mommy's passing. I think he forgot what she taught us. She used to build with all of us in the kitchen. All of my cousins and some of our neighbors in the building, would be sitting at the kitchen table, some on the washing machine, on the counter, or leaning against the windowsill. One of the things I remember she strongly expressed to us was understanding the meaning of life and death. She would grab onto the skin of her arm and pull it and say to us, "This ain't nothing but flesh. This is only flesh. Take care of this but know that this flesh here is just a shell, it's temporary. It came from this earth and it will go right back to this earth. It belongs to this planet. Now your soul has more substance. Your soul is what will take you there. Your soul has longevity, Baby...." Her skillful lessons always perked us up and showed us a different perspective on life.

This was not the right time nor place to remind Troy about the knowledge she passed on to us. He was way too emotional and caught up on the surface. Troy didn't know how to let go and accept Mommy's death. He didn't understand yet that life and death were like breathing in and breathing out. They're inseparable & unavoidable. Troy kept kissing her face. I prefer to kiss Mommy's spirit.

Donell and I stood up and the whispers turned silent. We viewed the body or her "shell" as Defrager would put it. *Why did they have to dress her in some pink grandma looking gown? And why that old fashioned wig, and what happened to...QUIET DOWN WITH THE CRITICISMS.* I rubbed the front of her stiff hand and whispered over her body,

"See you in the playground, Mommy. I love you. Goodbye physically."

After Donell was seated, I turned around and took the sheet of paper from out of my jacket pocket and unfolded it. I stepped to the podium and spoke into the microphone.

"Good mourning, everyone," I somberly said.

"Good morning." They responded.

"Um, I didn't plan to come up here and speak. I wrote this just now and I would like to read it, if you all don't mind." My eyes graced almost every sad soul in the funeral parlor. Everyone was very receptive.

"Can y'all hear me?"

"Yes," they responded.

"Okay...*My best friend.*

My best friend has journeyed away from me. Defrager and I had what I would call the ideal mother and daughter relationship. She was the type of mother who wouldn't even think of kickin' her kids out of the house. To her that was pure cruelty. She would put her trust in God and give us our space to breathe. But then again she did a great job at raising Donell and I by herself with the support of her dearest mother, "Geneva Turner" and family.

Defrager did not earn a college degree nor did she finish high school. She never learned how to drive a car or how to balance a checkbook. And so what. Her not having a degree, or a drivers liscense, did not take away her wisdom and insight or her powerful character. She was very wise for her age, at the same time youthful. Her spirit was too pure for her flesh. Mommy was a pure human. In its rawest form. She knew how to treat people with respect. Her love had no fears. If she loved you, you knew it was real."

Clapping!!! Someone shouted, "Hallelujah! Amen! Tell it like it is!" Came out my people's mouths. I continued,

"Defrager gave birth to Donell at sixteen and me at eighteen and it is ironic that she left me at eighteen. I guess this was the plan. God's plan. I pray that her journey is safe and peaceful. No more pain. Lots of sunshine, lots of rain to purify and cleanse and heal and to grow stronger. Ms. Defrager Strong may you rest in peace. we love you eternally."

I walked toward the exit door and many hands touched my shoulder in consolation. Nawnie and Donell got up and walked with me. I was escorted to the limousine and I sat there silently, meditating while they went back in. There was a knock on the limousine window. It was Rudy. I opened the door and he sat down next to me.

"Baby, are you okay?" His beautiful eyes showed a lot of hurt and concern.

"No."

"Come here." He opened his arms to me and enveloped me.

"Rudy, if you didn't leave her, none of this would have happened. She wouldn't have died!"

"Dana, I didn't leave your mother, she left me. You don't know how much I cried for her to come back to me."

I remembered but I wanted to be difficult.

"Rudy, what ever happened between y'all? Why didn't my mother take you back?"

"I'm gonna be honest with you Dana. You deserve that much." He sighed. "When my mother sent me upstate for me to have a better life because I was messing up in school and so forth, I messed around on your moms. I wind up having a son three years younger than you. Your mother did not forgive me or take me back. I hurt her baby, but I didn't mean to."

"I understand things happen Rudy but you could've still been here for me and Donell. It feels like it's too late now. We're much older."

"Dana, baby it's never too late. One thing you gotta remember is that I was young. Do you know how old I was when we conceived Donell?"

"No. It doesn't matter."

"Yes it does. I lied to your mother and told her I was 16, because if I told her my real age, she wouldn't have gave me play."

I didn't remove my eyes from the window. Nothing interesting was going on but cars breezing back and forth.

"Dana, I was fourteen years old. Look at me. Will you stop being so difficult. Just like your mother." We were silent for a good five seconds. We couldn't hold it in. We laughed. I decided to open up.

"Rudy, you *was* young."

"And dumb." He chuckled to himself. "Dana, I want to do the right thing and start on a clean slate with y'all. I know I missed out on you and Donell's childhood but I don't think it's too late for us to get to know each other all over again. Baby, I hope you believe me when I tell you I never stopped loving you and Donell. I need you to please forgive me. Would you forgive me?" I nodded slightly. He looked up, "Defrager, you did an excellent job on our children. Defrager, baby I still love you, always will. Rest in peace, baby. Please forgive me..." He repeated himself a few times, mumbling.

"Rudy, she forgives you." He looked at me. "She wants you to shut up and enjoy your time with us."

He smiled, "Okay."

"I know that you never stopped loving us. And I understand you were young. I love you too Rudy. I would like to one day call you Daddy but you have to earn that title."

He laughed, "I got patience, Baby. I will always love you and Donell. Don't you ever forget that." We cried together. Donell opened the car door and sat in. Rudy wrapped his other arm around Donell and said,

"My first son. Rudy's sorry I haven't been here for you my son. I was telling your sister, that I want us to clean the slate and try this again. Lord knows I loved your mother, man she used to put me through some shit. No doubt, she was a challenge and I have to give it to her she was an excellent mother. I am so proud of y'all." We simultaneously thanked him. He kissed and cried and hugged us.

Practically all day and all night, I heard apologies that irritated me like a juicy mosquito bite and for the next few weeks it went on and on. Donell and I felt close again because there was no longer any room to argue and fight to win Mommy over. We were faced with each other so we basically had to "take care of each other" and have each other's back.

"Dana, do you think Mommy's mad at us for not coming back to see her in the hospital?"

"Nah, Mommy wanted us to stay here. She was just talking out of fear. Mommy's strong."

"Yeah."

"Trust me, wherever she is, it's better than this place, I tell you."

"But you told her we was coming back, Dana. We didn't even say our last goodbye."

"Donell, please! I don't mean to sound insensitive but trust me, Mommy understands. This isn't our last goodbye, Mommy is still here…" Donell looked at me like I was crazy with tears welling up in his eyes.

"Why are you lookin' at me like that for?"

"You look and sound just like Mommy." His teardrops fell.

"Donell, please. You're scaring me. We gotta stay strong." I wanted to hug him but I'm not ready to get all sentimental like that with my brother. I have to be strong right now.

Before he could break down, he left. I did all my breaking down when Mommy was here suffering in misery over that genocidal disease. *I thank you, Father, for removing her from misery. Thank you.* I won't ever forget those nights of rubbing cream on her face, arms and back from the bumps she developed. Going back and forth to the pharmacy to get her prescriptions filled and carrying cases of Ensure milk. Taking cabs to Mount Sinai hospital when her blood count got really low. Rubbing her temples when the meningitis pain kicked in, catching her when she fainted, patting her back over the pail when she couldn't hold down her food. Holding her hand when her stomach was in pain from diarrhea. Her laughs, her humor and her Heavenly love stays here with me, eternally. Mommy, I miss you.

"I need some air, I'll be back in two hours." Donell took it hard.

It felt weird that my brother gave me a time as to when he was coming back, like I was taking Mommy's place or something. Donell went out for a walk and as I sat in the chair, in Nawnie's bedroom, I thought I finally have the freedom I had always wanted. I guess I thought I was ready for this big step, but I'm not. I'm scared. Staring up at the ceiling trying to swallow these tears, I coached myself. *Come on, Dana. You've got to be strong. Be the woman you are and utilize everything Mommy taught you.*

Oh God, you know, right? You know...our love was respectfully on a high plane. Our relationship was limitless and our love was unconditional. And the world feared she was crazy 'cause she didn't follow any man-made programs and their silly rules. She only followed universal law. She was perfect to me, perfectly normal. I know most of my friends coveted our relationship. I saw their jealous glares and evil eyes. Mommy and I used to walk down the block, holding hands. People couldn't take it. Our bond and her youthful appearance always kept people guessing. I knew it was coming! Our love was beyond the "norm," it was ethereal. It was too good to be true.

Now who can I really, I mean really trust in this hour? I feel, I feel so incomplete. I have no one I can share my secrets with, no one I can confide in. No advisor, no one to hold me at night when my haunting dreams visit me. No one to kiss goodbye, no one to wipe my tears when I cry. Between each pause, between each comma, I ignored the delicate voice interjecting, *YOU HAVE GOD. YOU HAVE YOU. YOU HAVE GOD. YOU HAVE GOD. YOU HAVE YOU, YOU, YOU.*

The words flew from my mouth, "I got me."

Maudlin Auntie Leniece entered the room crying as usual. She put on more weight but she carried it beautifully. Her make-up was sitting pretty. She sat with her ankles crossed with feminity and her voice soothed the air like a disk jockey from the quiet storm.

"Tonka Baby, the speech you gave today touched my soul. Everyone was impressed by what you said. Sweetheart, you brought out what we all wanted to say." I responded with a weary smile. She sniffed. "I'm gonna miss my sister you know?....But you know what? She's in God's bosom right now. That means she's everywhere, Baby. Her spirit is not limited inside of her body, she's throughout this universe, she's timeless, she could be anywhere at anytime honey. Timeless." She sniffed and grabbed some tissue from out of her pocketbook and dotted away the mascara and foundation that dissolved in her tears.

"Oh! You look just like your mother. Come here, Baby. You okay?" She hugged me while leaving her Clinique perfume on my person.

"Yes."

"If you need anything, I don't care what it is, you let me know. You need any money?"

"No, thank you, Auntie Leniece."

"Well, take this. Go get a manicure and pedicure. Here get a facial too. Pamper yourself, Honey. She would want you to." I could see Mommy rolling her eyes right now, smirking and shaking her head. Auntie Leniece continued, "You know she's watching us right now?" She dramatically smiled. "Let me ask you a question. Tonka, do you think your mother is dead, Baby?"

"You mean did she pass away?"

"Im-hm."

"Yes, physically."

"Remember this, Tonka. Your mother can never die as long as we keep her name alive. Remember that every time Defrager's name is spoken from out our mouths, we keep her spirit alive. You know that in the beginning, it was the word? And words have power. So be careful in how you use them. Always be impeccable with your word. Never say she's dead. Death is a cruel, cruel word. I like to think of my sister as passing on and not away. You know what I'm sayin'? I like to see it as Defrager passed on to the next stage or level in her life."

"Yes. That sounds about right. I like to look at it from that view. Thank you for that, Auntie Leniece." That was refreshing to hear. Was Auntie Leniece just trying to console us or did she believe what she was saying was right? Does it matter?

In this house, I could find no place for peace except for the bathroom, our office. I locked myself in and leaned against the door facing the mirror. I found something on me. There was something in me, inside me. I could not put my finger on it but something inside of me had changed. Maybe my aura has changed.

Father,

I would like to say thank you for giving us our moments together before she passed on. I mean you could've taken her without giving me a warning. When Mommy was suffering, my grief was great. I believe she is at peace because I feel peace right now, in this moment. I thank you dear lord for giving us precious times together to prepare for this day.

Amen.

21
freedom

Well, my glow is gone. I aborted the baby a week after Mommy's funeral. It wasn't my time, I wasn't in love with Renee,' and I hope the good Lord understands and forgives me. The counselor at the clinic got on me big time. I'm going to start using condoms. Time passed me by to the point of no returning to high school. It's been nine months. I mean I could go back but I'm not trying to be no super-senior. I guess I dropped out. At this point in my life, I'm in love with weed. Weed is my husband. Weed is my therapy. I smoke weed everyday and my house comes alive with mad company. Kenisha, my old high school bathroom friend, Tanisha a.k.a. "Tee," my neighbor home-girl, Tamika, and Tanya come over on the regular. Donell's clean, drug-free friends, Lee, Jamel, Billy and their girlfriends hang out in Donell's room. They like to build on history and politics. My friends come over to dance. I entertain and we sing in my room. Usually we combine our money together to buy a dime bag of trees. If we have enough money, then we put in for a forty-ounce of O.E. or St. Dies (St. Ides) and snacks for the munchies. Doritos, onion and garlic Wise potato chips, Linden chocolate chip cookies, Sunny Doodles, king-size Snickers and Double-Mint gum.

Kenisha is a cigarette smoker, so sometimes if we're out of weed, I share a cigarette with her and get a head rush. Every night is like a party and my neighbors are so cool 'cause they don't complain about the music being played too loud at 3:30 in the morning. They know what's up 'cause I play good music. When I smoke my trees and play my music, I like to put on my strobe light and dance my troubles away. My girls and I dance for different reasons. Some for broken-hearts, others for financial problems, or stress at school. Whatever issue it is, we dance it away. Dancing is also our therapy. Dancing is our way of using our high constructively and creatively. My house is like a place to just let go of troubles and free up stress. We like to dance to Lalah Hathaway, Troop, A Tribe Called Quest, Mint Condition, and Prince. Sometimes if we don't feel up to dancing, we may all harmonize and sing hymns from Take 6 or Bebe and Cece Winans.

One thing I can say is I am truly blessed to not have to go through the stress-related problems my girlfriends go through with their menopausal mothers. They have to go through getting kicked out the house and all types of emotional family drama. But then again, even if Mommy were here (physically), I still wouldn't have to go through it, 'cause Mommy was a real cool and understanding mom. She was not like a lot of my girlfriends' mothers, who came across as self-righteous and when their daughters find out certain truths about the wrong they do, they can't handle it and want to kick their daughters out the house. It's like, 'Wake up already mothers! Your daughters are growing up into women. They're going to speak their minds, so respect that. Don't try to control them and silence them. That shit is played out. Parents must befriend 'change' and reject 'bad-fear'. I believe daughters really want to respect their mothers but it's their mothers who can't keep their hearts open. I wish I could tell my girlfriends' moms this but they'll be quick to tell me off and tell me to mind my own business. I just have to pray that my girlfriends outgrow and forgive their mother's menopausal hang-ups and pray that their mothers learn how to accept change and grow.

Donell doesn't smoke, so when my friends and I smoke, I have to close my bedroom door. I use a damp towel to block the air passages from creeping under my door, and I keep my windows open. It's just out of respect for Donell.

We all jumped back when Donell opened my door without knocking. He smelled the vapors. Tee dropped the blunt behind her foot.

"Are y'all smokin' that shit again?"

"No." Everyone giggled.

"Look at y'all. This ain't funny, where's it at?"

"I don't have it." I tried to imitate my sober self. Everyone looked at Kenisha. She noticed and was too high and paranoid to speak so she held up her cigarette.

"Yeah right. That's not all y'all were smokin'. I can smell that reefer all the way in my room. Don't let me catch y'all smokin' that shit. If I catch y'all, I'm throwin' that bullshit down the toilet where it belongs. Think I'm playin'."

We all caught the giggles after he slammed my bedroom door. The three T-trio was ready to go to the store and they invited Kenisha and

I to a house party. We decided to stay in the house. After the T-trio left, Kenisha and I giggled like two little girls hiding in a closet. Kenisha closed my door and dipped her slim hands into her gap pants pockets and pulled out a phat bag of trees. I snatched it and smelled the herb. We smiled.

"You slick bitch."

"And you know this." She was proud of herself.

"You're crazy. C'mon, let's roll it up."

After about the fifth pull, we started drifting. Kenisha kept gibbering about nothing and I ignored her and kept dancing. Intro had me spinning. I sang to Troop (thinking about Mommy) while Chucki Booker *Turned* me *Away* from singing. Shanice Wilson questioned my dancing abilities. Then Bob Marley *Stirred It Up*. Kenisha went into the bathroom and it seemed as though she was taking a year to do whatever she had to do in there. It shouldn't take a half an hour to use the bathroom. Bathing is different.

I knocked a few times. "Kenisha, open up the door," I demanded.

When she opened the door, her eyes were red. Something about her eyes looked really weird. I saw deep down into the dungeon of her soul. It didn't look too good.

"What's the matter? Why you look so shook?"

"Dana, yo' I'm bugging out. I can't leave your bathroom."

"What's the matter with you!? Look, you've been tryin' to fuck up my high all night acting stupid and talking to yourself."

"Seriously, look at this shit." She pointed at the top rim of the bathroom doorway and whispered. "This big ass, fuckin' roach won't let me pass. Every time I step forward, it looks like its finnin' to jump on me."

"Yeah, you are really bugging out. No more weed for you. Can't you just kill it, Ken."

Kenisha didn't have the courage to kill the roach. She told me to listen to him. She said she was able to hear the roach talking. I grabbed her hand and pulled her out the bathroom.

"Kenisha!" I shrieked under my whisper. I didn't want Donell to hear me and then find out I was high. "Where's that fuckin' roach?"

She shook her head, wiggled her shoulders and stomped her feet, simultaneously. I laughed.

"Yo, Dee that ain't funny. All jokes aside, I believe that roach was talking to me."

"Yeah, aight. Keep in mind, Kenisha, that you're very high. Hallucinating, perhaps?" I pressed rewind and then play. "Girl, you done interrupted my song."

"On the real, Dana, that roach told me your mother died in here." My heart jumped. I pressed stop. "What?"

"Seriously."

"What else were you smokin'?"

"Dee, for real did anybody die in here? 'Cause I can't spend the night here if somebody really died up in here."

"Hell no! Don't be silly. You sound delirious. Did you eat?"

"I had a Snickers earlier."

"Yeah, that could be it. Donell fried some chicken, and I made some broccoli and rice. It's on top of the stove. Make yourself a plate."

"I must be really bugging out. A roach talking to me." She laughed to herself as she walked toward the kitchen.

"Kenisha! Your shirt! Shake it off!" She wiggled her body like electricity shot through her. That nasty muthafucka quickly ran toward my closet but it wasn't faster than me. How dare he have the audacity to try and spook my business like that! Roaches ain't nothin' but crawling, snitchin' demons,

Get it right you snitchin' fuck. It was Daddy-James who died in here, not my mother, you bastard! I stomped the hell out of that roach with my Timberlands.

Donell must be out of his mind to be knocking on my door at 7 o'clock in the morning. "Dana wake up. We have to go to face to face. We're late." Kenisha pulled the comforter over her face.

"Reschedule."

"I already rescheduled. If we don't go today for this one-shot-deal, our rent won't get paid and we'll get evicted."

"Don't worry about it, I'll have the rent money by the end of this week."

"Dana, wake up. Are you sure?"

"Don't worry, I've got a plan. I'll tell you about it later."

"Okay, just don't do nothin' hazardous now."

I sucked my teeth. "Come on now, you know my steez."

"You need to get up earlier. Sleepin' all late in the day. I can't find my keys. Come 'n lock the door."

"Damn, Donell, can't you be a little bit more responsible?"

"Look who's talking?" He closed the door laughing on his way down the staircase to work at his new messenger job.

I can't believe my sugar daddy John reneged on me. Maybe the Western Union was closed. Nah, I doubt that. My sugar daddies never ditch me like that. They're man enough to say "no" if they don't have any money. Well, I don't have the time to focus on John. I need to find a way to get some steady money independently and fast.

I'm 20 years old with a great body made for dancing. If I don't make any money before next week we're getting evicted, Lord. I know one thing. If Defrager were here, the idea of this type of occupation I'm considering, would not dare cross my mind. I have to write a letter to God in my journal. Maybe it'll bring me some clarity.

September 13, 1993

Peace and Blessings,

Father, where will I be five years from now? how can I get out of the projects? Lord, I'm getting no younger and I don't plan to cheat men out of their money for the rest of my life. I cannot bear to leave this earth with a trail of brokenhearted souls behind me. I'm 20 years old now and all I have is a G.E.D . No achievement awards and no college degree. All I hold right now is the hearts and souls of men who would wash the panties I'd wear.
The only income I have coming in right now is public assistance and mommy's social security checks, and I tell you, I'm not proud of it. I've read that if you're not focused and if you have nothing to stand or live for in this world, then you're bound to fall for anything that'll come your way. God, I've been thinking about dancing for a while now and I feel that I can really use the money. I've been told that the exotic dancing industry is equivalent to selling drugs. It's fast money and you're bound to lose your soul and self-respect. I know myself well enough not to throw away and disrespect my precious soul. I don't see this business as a career. It's just a means for me to get from point A to point B. Put some money in the bank and pay off these beggar bill collectors. Then I'll get out.
Everybody I told is opposed to my decision. I don't see it as a big deal. It's not like I'm not going to save any money. Father, I am aware that I will be opening the door to lust, jealousy and Satan's desires. Whatever might happen to me, I ask of you to please keep an eye on me and please have Mommy guard my back, for my soul belongs to only you.
Love,
Dana
Amen.

22
baby

I just got off the phone with one of my playmates. Devon agreed to hook me up with one of his female friends who happened to be a bouncer. I don't know if nice is the word, but she was cool enough to help me get started in the business.

That autumn evening, we linked up in White Plains, N.Y. I waited by the token booth for her. Her appearance surprised me when she approached me.

"Are you Dana?"

"Yes. You're the bouncer?"

"Yeah, Paula. Nice to meet you." We shook hands. Her grip was firm and she was pretty small for a bouncer.

"Please take no offense, but I expected you to be tall and amazon like."

"Nah, it's okay. Everybody thinks that. People think a bouncer is supposed to be big and husky, ya know?"

"Yeah."

"Would you believe me if I told you that I'm a black belt in all styles and forms of T'ai Chi Kwon Do."

"Say word."

"Word."

"Girl, I'm scared of you, but I like your vibration."

"I'm feelin' yours too."

She hailed a dollar cab and we rode for about a good seven minutes.

"Okay, we're almost there." Paula seemed to be in deep thought.

"Are you okay? You look preoccupied. Is tonight the wrong night?" I asked.

"No, no don't worry yourself, girl. Tonight is a good night. Weekends are good. I'm just hoping that I'm doin' the right thing by takin' you here. You don't know how many beautiful women I've watched drown in this shit. All this prostitution and drugs. They be thinking they're escaping one problem and here they find themselves in a deeper one. It takes a strong person to make it in and get out."

"If there's one thing I got, it's inner strength. I'm new at this, but I'm adaptable. All I need is for you to school me on what to look out for. The ropes."

"You sure you wanna do this? It takes more than strength to get in this business, ya know what I'm sayin'? It takes street smarts too."

"I hear you, but I have no choice at this point. I got bills to pay and a deadline to meet. Let's see what it looks like inside first."

"When we get in, Ima show you around and hook you up with a few people I know. Don't expect these girls to put you on 'cause they lookin' at you as competition. Everybody is tryin' to make a dollar up in here. I'm gonna be honest wit chu'. This place ain't like what you see on TV. All that no touchin' innocent shit, let me tell you, girl, it's raw up in here. I'm talkin' 'bout a hustle and a half, that's if you don't play your cards right. Know what I mean?" she winked. "You got yo' pushers, yo' playas, yo' pleasers, the hookers, all types of shit up in here, girl. Be smart and play your shit close, and watch your back." Paula pulled out a double mint.

"Want a piece?"

"Thank you."

"Always keep your breath smelling good especially if you smoke or drink."

"Thanks. Is it true what I hear about girls getting raped and killed in this business?"

"Wait a minute, where you from again?"

"The Bronx."

"Oh shit, really! I'm from the Bronx too. What part? I'm from Forest." she said.

"Word? My ex used to live in Forest. I'm from J.A."

"Okay, okay, I know where that's at. That's where those jams used to be, right?"

"Yup."

"DJ Jerry was the shit."

"He's my uncle."

"Oh shit. This is a small world, girl! But you don't even sound like you from the Bronx. . . before we forget. To answer your question about getting raped or killed, it depends on what type of lifestyle you live. You know what I'm sayin'? It also depends on what kind of person you are. Like if you do your set and mind your business, and try to live honestly, I think you'll be aight."

"I don't understand what you mean by do my set?"

"What I mean is. Okay…The owner, we call him Nes. Nes would pay you anywhere from like 10 to 30 dollars for every set you do. Some girls have a closer relationship with him, so he may pay them a little bit more than $30 if you know what I mean." Paula's chinky eyes narrowed. "There's usually two girls he would book at a time. One girl dances on stage for a half an hour and then you dance for the other half an hour. Back and forth until closing. Now the extra money you make comes from tips, lap dances, private dances, however else you choose to make your money, but that's your business. You followin' me?"

"I don't follow, but I'm getting what you're sayin'."

"I like that attitude. Don't lose it."

She made me feel a little confident but I was still nervous. I felt like vomiting up whatever was floating around in my stomach. Could I handle having strangers touch or even look and lust at my body? My temple? I just want to go back home. Can't. Eviction equals living back at Nawnie's house.

Who's gonna pay the bills? Certainly not Donell and welfare can kiss my muthafuckin' ass. I refuse to get back on that shit. I'm sick 'n tired of those face-to-face appointments and all of that guttural bullshit that goes along with it.

We pulled up in front of the spot. Cars double parked. Paula tipped the dollar cab driver three dollars. The exterior part of the club was painted all black and it had paintings of pink and brown women posing seductively in skimpy bikinis. "Fool's Paradise" was written in big, pink, bubble graffiti letters with clouds floating in and out of the words. Benzies, Jaguars, and a couple of Bentleys parked and double-parked in front of the club. Paula stepped up and buzzed the bell. My body followed my mind and stood behind Paula. She pointed at the security camera in the top right corner of the doorway.

"See, we have security here, so you don't have to worry about cops tryin' to blow up our spot. But you know what, you'll be surprised to find out how many cops be up in here on the regular trickin'."

"Word?"

"Don't be fooled."

She banged her knuckles on the door. I concentrated harder on trying to look calm instead of being calm.

"Dana, it's okay. Try to relax, don't be so tense." A hefty male bouncer opened the door and frisked Paula and I. The music was blasting. After he frisked me, he turned to Paula and said,

"She must be a fresh fish." Paula smirked and shook her head,

"You crazy, Dezul."

My quiver and the powerful bass that made the speakers quiver from the music was reciprocal. As we walked away from Dezul, I neared Paula's ear.

"How did he know I was new? Was it because I'm a new face?"

"No, it ain't your face. Plenty of new faces come in and outta here. He can tell by your demeanor. Your aura. But I think it was more your body language that gave it away." She smiled.

"My body language? How so?"

"Your hands, your brow, the forced smile on your face. If you want me to nitpick, I'll take a rain check. This ain't the place for that, no offense."

"None taken."

"I can tell you this much, Dana, if you don't learn nuthin' from this business, you'll learn how to read body language."

Damn, the club was big! Graffiti art covered the walls, flashing red lights bounced off of oily skins, asses hung out exposed. It was too much for me to deal with. I sensed a weird kind of freedom in this place. The high-class dancers had fifty and hundred dollar bills skirting around their g-strings. Lust, music and hunger for love made the air too thick to think morally. I turned to my left and a barmaid was wearing this red satin bra and tight blue Guess jeans with her hair freshly done in a doobie.

"Don't look too hard, Sindy likes girls. I mean that's if you go that way."

"What? Hell no! I was just admiring her bra."

"Ain't nothin' wrong with liking girls, honey. If that's your preference, then people just gotta accept it."

"No, don't even go there, Paula! I don't lick carpets!"

"Okay, okay take it easy, Dee. I was just sayin', in here, it's highly accepted. Trust me, if you down with it, you cool and if not, you're still cool."

"Well, I'm not down with it."

"Cool."

So many girls passed me by with ice lighting up their necks, wrists, earlobes and fingers. Jewelry showed a sign of their body's worth.

Cubic zirconium chains wrapped their tiny waists, hoops hung from their navels and a little sparkle on their nose. I felt naked although I was clothed. I felt the contagious need to clothe my wrists, neck, fingers, ankles, tummy and nose with ice.

Paula interrupted my plans and pointed to her right and shouted over Luke's Too Live Crew "Do Do Brown" song.

"This stage over here is only for auditions and beginners." The stage was covered with a bright red carpet. Racing white lights tracked around the stage. A girl looking about eighteen danced on the stage with her cheap-department-store-looking g-string. I watched her while she sang along to the music, smiling, trying to convince herself that she was having a wonderful time doing the right thing up there. She danced offbeat sometimes and a bit too fast for the music most of the time. Right there she gave away her amateurism. I made comparisons and glanced over at the professional stage. Those professional dancers took their time when they moved. They moved with certainty. It was amazing to see how they shook their asses like it was Jell-O gelatin, on time to the up-tempo beat.

The men were watching miss Amateur with pity. They tipped her a few singles for trying. The music changed and amateur-girl squatted outwardly to pick up the rest of her singles.

"Do you wanna audition now or do you wanna wait till later on tonight for the larger crowd to come?" Paula asked.

"I can wait. I still need to learn more."

A woman dressed in black platform Barbie doll heels came running out the dressing room like Jackee' from 227. She had a long rip in the middle of her red-hot unitar dress, revealing half of her caramel colored nipples and navel ring. She hurried with her boobs bouncing up and down. It was ten minutes after eight. Time was money and money was her time she'd done wasted. Her big, black curly weave reached just above her creamy plump 36DD breasts. Her body stood tight and firm like those superhero women while she briefly spoke to an anxious customer. Her glossy lipstick imitated the color of a cocktail cherry. Her person was covered with diamond links, diamond body glitter, diamond earrings, everything diamonds. Diamond watch, diamond anklet and a diamond waist chain. A pure attention getter. When she spoke, you could barely see her teeth because she moved her full lips in a puckering way. I could see why all the men gravitated to her. Every movement she made, made sense. Pure sense-uality, from lick-ing her lips to batting her lashes. Diamonds moved her hands like a magician, smooth so that the eye can catch every twinkle of shine her bracelets and diamond rings made. She switched her hips toward us, looking unaffected by the compliments shown in my eyes. She was numb and unaware of her beauty (probably tired of it). She walked up to Paula and they kissed on the cheek. I was the only one who smiled when introduced.

"Diamonds, Dana, Dana, Diamonds," Paula said.

"Hi." She turned back to Paula, "Paula baby. I have three tricks tonight and I need you to have my back. I'll pay you good, sweetie." I was surprised to hear that her voice did not match her image. She sounded just like Lil' Tina! This sexy, glamour girl's voice rubbed me like sandpaper.

"How much are they payin' you?" Diamonds kept looking back at the stage. Her attention was on the slender girl picking up the remainder of her tips off the stage.

"They payin' me good, baby. I'm sorry about last time, they were some real fuck-ups. Trust me honey, I got you!" she promised as she hurried away. The girl waited for Diamonds to get on the stage so she could step off. "I gotta get up there!" Diamonds shouted walking away.

"We'll talk after your set!" Paula shouted back.

Diamonds nodded her head and climbed onto the 6-foot stage. She paused and posed on her knees, shook her ass up and down, in and out and paused, swung her hair around toward her audience and paused, smiled a wide and kiddish smile. She opened her mouth and waved her tongue slowly, revealing a diamond stud on her tongue. Instantly a crowd of dollar bills were flapping around the stage. Sindy, the barmaid handed her a clean glass. Diamonds opened her legs and inserted the drinking glass into her womb. Men began putting dollar bills into the glass. Once her glass was full, she slowly pushed it out into her pocketbook. She then crossed her legs around the pole, crawled up like a caterpillar and swung her body around the pole, sliding down like a snake. Diamonds stood up and grabbed the spike of her heel and straightened her leg upward ballerina style while wiggling her ass.

Paula turned to me,

"Close your mouth, Dana. Here's a word of advice. Do not stay in this business past thirty."

"I don't plan to but why would you say that?"

"Let me tell you girl, I remember Diamonds used to get paid five G's a head. That girl was too valuable for these tricks. You know what brought her down?"

"What?"

"Drugs."

"Drugs? She's on drugs?" I was astonished.

"Yup, all that money went to waste 'cause now she ain't got nuthin' to show for it. Do somethin' wit yo' money. Invest, go to school, do somethin'."

"No doubt. Well, I think she really looks good."

"She looks good but she used to look better than nat. Could you imagine?"

"Wow, nope."

"She's tired, Dana. Diamonds is real tired. I don't ever remember Diamonds to be doing sets like this. She was too, I mean literally, too busy to be doin' sets. Would you believe almost every man in here done had her?"

I looked around. There had to have been over 100 men in the place.

"No." I couldn't believe it.

"Yeah, I mean she still get tricks but she's definitely not as dope as she used to be."

"Paula isn't sex expected. Isn't it all about sex and money? Aren't the men and women here just for that?"

"Yes and no. It's not what you do, it's how and who you do it with. Girl, don't just be fuckin' anybody. Men are just like women, if not worse. They will talk and gossip 'bout who had you and what you did to them and how much they paid for it. I believe you can make money without selling your body. It's all about having good game. Come on." I followed her to the entrance of the dressing room.

"Okay, this is the dressing room." Four rectangular mirrors, very smoky, loud and nude. Girls sprayed impulse body spray from their manicured toes to their private little folds.

A dancer shouted,

"Shit, I'm tired of these new hoes puttin' they oily fuckin' asses on the poles! I'ma tell Nes he need ta put those hoes on the floor. They not even professional about how they do they shit! How you gon' let these tricks rub on your pussy with they dirty ass money? That's why Nes wants us to wear g-strings. Hello? They makin' business bad for us. They fuckin' shit up! Shit, I've been in this business for 15 years and Nes never let shit like this go on!"

"Berlin, do you know if he saw what they were doing?" Another dancer asked while lining her lips.

"Hell nah! That bitch wouldn't be shakin' her ass up in here this long if he did!" Berlin took three more sips of her Moet champagne. "That shit pisses me the fuck off! I'm tryin to make some muthafuckin' paper and bitches like... Paula!" Berlin stood up with her champagne glass in one hand and her Moet in the other. "Paula! I'm glad you here, girl. I need you to tell Nes to stop lettin' these amateur hoes on our stage! Let them dance on the amateur stage where they belong!"

"What happened now B.?"

"These new hoes don't know a muthafuckin' thang 'bout swingin' on no poles and they fuckin' up our money. I'm not tryna break my neck slippin' off of no poles! Shit! You know Berlin gotsta stay paid. Know-what-I'm-sayin'? I'm a high paid bitch!" She had a smooth cocoa brown complexion with a wide forehead.

"Okay, I'll let him know."

"Let him know that all his girls are not happy!" Then her attention went to a very, thick, big-boned, full lip woman walking in. "Hey Ebone,' you got some stuff for me?"

Paula turned to me. "Anyways, this is where you change your clothes. Don't get caught up into these girls' web. Sometimes they act just like children."

From a distance Berlin looked radiant but up close she wore heavy mascara on her eyelashes or perhaps she wore false eyelashes. Her gloves hid her arms. Foundation filled and smoothed the craters in her skin. Berlin reminded me of Billie Holiday, she was a 90's version.

"Let's get outta here." Paula pointed toward the seven lap dancing tables near the bar, that weren't occupied.

"The minimum price here is $5 between four and five minutes. Most songs last about that long. Most of the girls don't like to sit on men's laps unless they're buying the girls a drink."

"Why?"

"They say it's too much work to be grinding on a man's lap while he's just sittin' there doin' nuthin. If he insists on sitting, charge him $10 for five minutes or whatever you feel you're worth but be reasonable. So over there is where most of the girls give guys stand-dances. A lot of the girls met their tricks through stand-dancing. Some girls get too lazy to shake their asses, and they turn to prostitution. But you know the easy way ain't always the best way."

To my right side, I noticed a man leaning against a wall with a lady dancing on him, she looked bored. She wore jean shorts cut in g-string style, rubbing and grinding her plump ass on his crotch. I tried not to look but I couldn't help myself. They were out in the open and she looked oblivious to what he was doing to her body. She just kept chewing her gum real fast. The man was getting off on cheap thrills. His hands cupped her breasts while pinching her nipples and then his hands slid down and remained on her hips.

A pretty petite, light-skinned girl wearing a sexy, pink fish net negligee walked out of the dressing room and caught the eye of that same man. And it looked like I must have caught her eye. The DJ spun a new song and the man handed Ms. Boredom a $20 bill, left her and went to follow the pretty girl in pink.

"Paula," I said, "that guy just gave her a $20 bill and walked off."

"She probably danced with him for about fifteen to twenty minutes"

"I'm nervous. All jokes aside, I don't want beef with none of these girls up in here. This girl just gave me the evil eye."

"Which one?" The club was getting packed. As the night wore on, more girls began to fill the lap-dancing section.

"The one with the Halle Berry cut," I said.

"Where?"

I pointed my brownie and said, "The light-skinned girl over there in the pink."

"Oh, Sunshine? Please. She wasn't eyein' you like that, she's a sweetie. If anything Sunshine was checkin' for you."

"What kind of checkin'?"

Paula spoke slowly and then looked inside me. "You know what I mean."

"You mean, gay checkin' for me?"

"Mmhmm. I told you, there's a lot of 'em floatin' around here. No time for nervousness hon', only time you got right now, is to make that money."

"I hear you." I heard her but my heart wasn't tryin' to listen to that.

A misunderstanding was at the front door and Paula left to see what was going on. Paula's words echoed inside of me. It didn't feel right though. Her words straight-arrowed me with a harsh and honest point. The point is back, I better shake my ass and make some money tonight or I'll be living back at Nawnie's. Her words hurt because they were cold and loveless. While sitting at the bar, I observed and learned the different techniques the featured dancers on stage used to keep the men's money flowing. Some jiggled their asses promptly to the drumbeat, others did splits, some wrapped their legs behind their necks. I'll find my way in this crazy maze. I stood up and went inside the dressing room and sat down to gather my thoughts.

"You new here?" A southern speaking belle asked.

I hesitated, "Yeah."

"Don't be scurred. I was scurred the first night I danced but after you start making that money, girl, please." She was lining her lips with her Mac Vino lip liner.

"What's your name pretty?" Her accent consoled me.

"You can call me Dee."

"I'm Sassy." She sprayed her Il Bacio all over her long legs and beautiful body.

"It's nice to meet you." I said.

"Same here. Want a piece?"

"Oh, no, I already have gum. Thanks. Sassy?"

"Mmhm." Her pager beeped. She pressed the button to her pager, huffed and rolled her eyes.

"How long have you been doing this?" I asked.

"For about four years now. Next year, I'll be graduating college with my B.A. This money is helping me pay my tuition. Plus I got 60 G's saved up in the bank. I'm trying to buy a house."

"Wow that's good."

"Yeah. There's people out there waitin' for me, girl, I'll talk to you later. Oh and good luck, sugar."

"Thanks." Sassy gave me inspiration as she switched her perfect peach ass in her short white latex skirt.

Tag-ups and love poems of girls in love with each other and "has-been tricks" names were written all over the lockers. Business cards were taped to the walls. Taxi numbers, hotel numbers were available to us. We even had the convenience of "flower, trees or weed service". Only a pager number was available.

Slow and uncoordinated footsteps came dragging into the dressing room. I sat still and waited. A middle-age woman with a bookbag on her back walked in.

"Hi." she said. She looked so sad and tired.

"Hi." I sat quietly in front of the mirror. She changed her clothes, slipped foot cushions inside her thigh-high spike boots, powdered her face, poured alcohol into her baby wipes and wiped her coochie and buttocks with the cloth. Then she sprayed impulse body spray all over herself. She lit up a Camel cigarette and blew smoke while minding her own business. She said not one word to me as she dragged her feet out the dressing room.

I couldn't stop thinking about Sassy and how well put together she was. She's tall, young and well sculptured with the smoothest pecan complexion. God has blessed her with an ironing board stomach, a small and tight waistline, and a brain. When I go home, I'm going to do some sit-ups and stared at myself in the mirror.

I have to get out there and dance. I need some money for fare to get home tonight. I'm scared but I have to go out there and flirt. A man cute enough to get my pager number pulled me by the waist and asked for a dance. I flirted my body and grinded my ass on him as if I was in a reggae dance hall. He liked me and our chemistry. After his money ran low, I went to the dressing room to get dressed. First, I counted my earnings and had the same smirk on my face as Troy. $35, 40, 41,42,43,44, 45, 55, 65 dollars ain't so bad for my first try and for the first half hour. In fact, this was pretty easy.

Dude I was dancing with offered to drive me home but I had to decline. I took a dollar cab to the train station and bought a ten-pack of token. As I rode the train, I thought about coming back tomorrow. *Twenty dollars for twenty minutes? I'm coming back.* That was my chain of thought on the train ride back home to Queens. Money stayed on my mind. I thought about how I could buy a car, pay off my bills without struggling with dead end jobs and then end my welfare situation. I could afford the clothes I've always wanted and furnish my apartment.

I calculated how much money I would make in one night. For every hour, I would make around a hundred dollars, if the night is good. Five hundred a night sounds sweet.

I'm going to change my name to Baby. When my sugar-daddy give me money, I'm going to invest in a costume and buy myself a nice black wig in a bob style, two lingerie outfits and black high-heeled shoes. I need a lock for my locker, baby wipes, baby oil and Impulse! body spray.

After I completed my fifty sit-ups, I looked in the mirror of my bedroom and practiced dancing. I tried jiggling my ass like the girls I saw on stage. No jiggle. My butt is too tight.

"Just like my damn money." Sighing to myself.

23
tiresome

I've been two years deep in this tired ass industry. It's time for me to get out! I've stayed longer than I had anticipated. It's all one big trap. You get a taste of the fast money, you make plans, you need more money to meet your plans. And what happens? Nothing in this world is for free. If you want more money, then you might have to sell parts of your soul for it. The whole process is draining and tiresome. I like me and I don't want to give up the beautiful parts of my authentic self.

I'm fortunate to have just made it in to being one of the dancers to witness the classic dancing from the pioneers. Recently, there has been too many teenagers coming into this business, more so for the wrong reasons. These young ladies done lowered the bar and their self-respect. The old school dancers were all tense 'n shit because what used to be the minimum $150 to give head (which ain't nothing) has now shot down to 20 fuckin' dollars. I don't have a problem with that 'cause I don't give head. But I pity those who feel they have to settle.

I have to say, the old school dancers danced with class. When money is slow, sometimes they sit in the dressing room, get high and reminisce and laugh about how back in the day, dancing took them a long ways. Topless dancing back then paid their rent, their car notes and doctor's note, phone bills and the whole shebangyang. But now? Forget about it. To get that same coverage, you're better off doing escort services.

This industry has gotten congested with these teenagers who probably come from group homes, broken families or orphanages. They don't know a damn thing about value of self, responsibility and sacrifice and it's sad. They're just dancing for extra pocket money so they could buy clothes to floss at the clubs. These young ladies done screwed it up for the hardworking, long-time investors who mastered the art of sensual dancing. Basically, they've cheapen the industry.

I think instead of the pioneers getting upset with the teenagers and detaching themselves or looking down on them, the pioneers should have taken the time to teach them the way and used their young bodies to make a profit, like a Madame. Even though it's equally wrong but I think it's healthier than holding onto jealousy. These old scholars should have known that nothing stays the same, everything goes through tests and changes. So, one must always keep their sneakers on in case you may have to run. Ultimately, it's commonsense to know that physical youth could last for no more than 30 years. Considering this industry, you'll be lucky if you can preserve your youth by the time you reach 40.

A lot of the girls left Fool's Paradise and turned right into the escorting business. They appear to be in love with their job and told me I could make triple of what I'm making at Fool's Paradise. Sounds tempting but I'm just fine with dancing and dealing cocaine. I tell you one thing, I'd rather sell cocaine than to sell my ass. My coochie is too quality to put a price tag on it. But all jokes aside, I'm ready to just end all of this lust and fantasy shit and move on with real life. I want to share my energy, talents and substance with a higher part of the universe. These horny, carnal losers are sadly caught up into this fantasy bullshit. It's disrespectful and spiritually and mentally degrading. Too much fantasy will bring out the insanity in a person. Believe me, I've seen it happen many times.

I'm sort of in between worlds right now. Yes, I'm annoyed with these raggedy ass cheap, chicken-headed hoes but at the same time, they're not a threat to me or my salary. Dana knows how to hustle her money. But that's not why I need to get up outta here. These clubs and bars are filled with too much smoke and slime, and congested sex-funk. All of this affects my skin, my lungs and my spirit. My face is not as smooth as it used to be. I have to stay on top of myself cause nobody else will. If I relied on my clients' opinions about my appearance, I would look just like everybody else in here. My clients don't seem to care about these little bumps on my face or on my asscheeks. The way they see things is, 'as long as your titties are sittin' up and that ass is still fat then it's all good.' They don't care.

I am not safe working under these hazardous conditions and what makes it worse is there are no health benefits, no social security, no pension and no type of stability. Ain't nothing guaranteed here, only change. A big change happened when Fool's Paradise closed down because Nes lost his lease. Such a dickhead, he wasn't focused. Nes was too busy fuckin' around with them dancers, losing his head. I kept firmly in my head that I have to have my own back no matter what. I opened up a bank account so for every dollar, every tip I made would go straight into my account. I'm ain't playin'.

I have clientele that I have known for about a short year. They think we have some kind of long-term relationship. I see my occupation as a tenure job without the contracts. My clients and I meet up at no other place but Fool's Paradise, I don't play that. That's just about as far as my part of this business goes. I'm not with that one-on-one hotel bit, it's too dangerous. That's how the late Diamonds got murdered, going in and out of hotels without a bodyguard. She was found dead in a hotel closet with her own panties wrapped around her pretty neck. Not one diamond on her body was found. It only takes one time. I don't care how many years I've known a trick, I will never trust him, unblindfolded.

A trick is just a treat. There are no honor amongst thieves. And if you want to keep a client, you never fuck him. Just like you never suppose to fuck your sugar-daddies. Thank God I don't have to worry about my bills getting paid cause of my many fans who come to see me every Thursday and Friday with their checks cashed. And if I don't feel up to dancing, say for about a week or two, I'll still be alright cause I've got my sugar daddies as my back-up.

The downside to this ride is I know all of this will have to come to an end one day. There's going to be a time when I'm going to have to earn my money by using my brain and not mens' emotions. I look forward to the day when I'll autograph my beautiful books and receive phat movie deals.

Yeah, that sounds sweet. When I get paid through my writings, I'll say goodbye to my grindings.

Most of the dancers wasn't prepared for the big change. They didn't keep their sneakers on in case they had to run. So when Nes lost his lease, they all scattered through out the boroughs. Some dancers migrated to the dirty south, others like myself stayed. I kept in touch with my clients on what club I would entertain in next.

The girls cried but I could care less about Fool's Paradise. I got whatever I needed from there. Besides, I didn't like the way things were set up in Nes' spot anyway. You know, amateurs over here, professionals over there. Regular hoein' dancers in the back dressing room with the lockers and folded chairs. Featured and professional dancers in the elegant dressing room with the starlit mirrors, sittin' pretty on comfortable sofa-beds with a bouncer to protect their belongings. Nes separated "the good dancers" from "the all-right dancers." The "good ones" were put on a pedestal, inciting envy and jealousy in "the all-right" dancers. What saddened me the most about the whole psychology was these dancers could not see below the surface. They eagerly sold their souls for a slice of Satan's pie. Too many girls aimed to be a featured dancer or pin-up-poster girl in Black Tail magazine. Black Tail magazine?! It was their dream to be in Hustler or Playboy but not many made it past the front door. I always kept in the back of my head, *This job is not set-up for a long term career. My goals are broad and wide.*

I put my old high school friend Kenisha on 'cause she needed to make some immediate money. She said she had to stop transporting weed, for whatever reason, I don't know. I sat her to the side and explained how crazy this industry is and to be careful cause money sometimes makes ya do some crazy things. Her eyes weren't right there with mine. They were anxious.

"These are the rules.

1) Don't fuck the tricks,

2) Don't talk to nobody. The ones who talk the most are the ones you have to watch out for, and

3) Invest in yourself and open up a savings account. That's the best thing a dancer could do for herself."

"Okay, but, Dana, I mean, Baby, when you say don't fuck the tricks, are you saying that even if the owner of this club was to proposition me, should I turn him down too?" Kenisha asked with an egotistical grin in her eyes.

"I don't know about that, Ken. All I did was lay down the rules for you, it's up to you to determine what's right for you. You know what I'm sayin'? I've been here for over two years and I can smile and say, I've got a clear conscience. In my opinion, I don't think you should do it but it's up to you." Couldn't say I didn't warn her.

"I hear you Dee. Trust me, I'm smart. I'm going to make sure he pays me first." Well, I see she made up her mind.

"Now, Kenisha," I squared my eyes with hers, "Are you sure you want to do this?"

"Come on, Dana," she whispered, "Fuckin' the owner is no different from me fucking Gin. The only difference is I'm just getting paid for it."

"Well, Kenisha, Gin is your man and you're not his prostitute. You're a grown woman. You know I can't tell you what to do but I will tell you what'll be good for you in the long run."

"And what is that?"

"Don't get all defensive…" I had to smile, cause I made it inside of her conscience.

"I'm not defensive," she denied.

"Okay. Okay. I, personally think you shouldn't have sex for money 'cause it'll catch up to you one…"

Kenisha interrupted me. "Well, that's your opinion, Dana."

"And this is your temple." I pointed my finger at her heart. My voice grew stronger than hers. Then I added, "Just remember that each time you pocket that paper before you get fucked, just know that you are lowering the value of your womb. And each time that hungry man or (woman) scraps you out, just know their spirit is poisoning your soul."

"Girl, I don't wanna hear that talk! I'm trying to make some money."

"Okay, I just wanted to clear my conscience. I want you to know that when the shit hits your heart, I don't want you to blame nobody but yourself for the choice you're about to make. I just wanted to put that bug in your ear."

"Yeah, Dana. Look, I'll see you at 3:30," she agitatedly said.

"Be safe." She didn't respond and I changed into my clothes.

This dancing industry is so fast paced that if you're not grounded, it can swipe you off your feet and have your soul debited from your spiritual account. *I pray she'll be alright, please.*

I don't dance every day like most dancers. I try to balance the fantasy with the reality. Dancing everyday will drain the living blood out of you. It will dry you up, draw circles around your eyes, and give your emotions an anesthetic. This type of anesthesia doesn't wear off until you totally detach yourself from the industry. Before my eyes, I watched so many beautiful girls lose themselves. Too many lost their special glow. The glow of innocence, life, and vitality. The drugs, the smoke, the disrespect they had to endure broke down their spirits. It became a mess when I see that naturally beautiful woman, now masking heavy make-up all over her face. A mask to hide not just her damaged skin conditions but to hide her deep down sorrows or her addictions to cocaine.

A lot of the young ladies need to get some sleep instead of chasing that money. They don't even realize they're just like bats. Their skin is dull and it's hungry for sunlight. They should at least try to take

Vitamin D. I would say two out of 10 dancers actually take vitamins. It bugged me out to have known a dancer named Lisa who is about 21-years-old and she's a virgin. I shake my head on that because she is on coke but she has never had sex before.

I guess being in a place like this is hard to stay sober. Basically, everybody is fucked up. I don't do heavy stuff like coke. I'm content with my greens. One thing I won't do is smoke trees on the job, it'll interfere with my money. After that one experience of when I smoked weed on the job, I was so paranoid. Anybody could've taken advantage of me but one of the dancers, Carmella, calmed me down. We sat safely in the dressing room. She kept joking with me and making me laugh until my high came down. Thank you Carmella. I love you Lord for that girl. Trees are only for special and intimate occasions. That's probably one of the reasons why I make the most money everywhere I go because I stay focused.

An older head named Tippin' put me on to this other underground spot. Tippin' is 6'2" shapely, strong and very intimidating. Her complexion is like that of a butter croissant. I like Tippin' cause she keeps it real. I respect her for who she is and what she is doing this for. She told me she's dancing to put her 20-year-old daughter through college. She can't wait until her baby graduates and buys her a house. Money was slow at the Flamingo bar. Tippin' turned to me and said,

"Baby, these girls up in here think they too good to go ta The Sheeps 'cause there's a lot of Dominicans and Puerto Ricans up in there. But I think they could use some black love up in that spot. You-know-what-I'm-sayin?" She flipped her hand over and I gave her a pound.

"How's the money in there?" I asked.

"The money's not as fast as it was up in Ness's, but those singles add up quick. I'm tired of this fuckin' place, I'm 'bout to bounce. You wanna come?"

"Yeah, I'll check it out." I don't take this industry seriously anyway, so whatever's whatever. Anything that'll help pay my bills, more power.

Tippin' and I were the first two from Fool's Paradise to start going to The Sheeps. It took a month before familiar faces found our trail. I'm not gonna lie, I was happy to see the girls from Fool's Paradise trickling through The Sheeps' doors. The Sheeps was set up differently from Fool's Paradise. It had a very down low-to-earthy setting. The "professional dancers" received the same treatment as the "regular dancers." Either they had to deal with it or leave. Working at the Sheeps meant starting all over again from the bottom up. There were no big names, no featured dancers to put on pretty pedestals. Every dancer had to earn it with the new crowd of men. The men here didn't care about a dancers' reputation, she had to show and prove it in The Sheeps. In here, there was no Nes to watch our backs. We had to watch our own backs and unite. The Sheeps was a raw yet safe and free place to be in. If that makes any sense.

Fuck topless. The men out there wanted raunchy, naked, striptease dancing. I'm not the raunchy type, but whatever I do, I'm sure as hell original and creative about it.

Word of mouth got around that The Sheeps was the shit. More girls came flocking through its doors. It felt like a little family reunion. Dancers are so different from the ordinary straight-lined girls who secretly fantasize about being a dancer. To be a part of a dancer's world, one must be prepared for risk, inner-courage and inner-strength.

In a dancer's nakedness, they hold nothing inside and if a dancer keeps anything to herself, it is called mystery. A dancer keeps a state of awareness with her environment. What brought out the realness in these sisters is the fact that we have a certain kind of freedom. We have the kind of freedom to be organic and unprofessional. We don't have to deal with the pressures of conforming, or have to worry about what society thinks a lady should be. We just be and bring out our best attributes. You know what I'm sayin? There are very little restrictions going on in the underground world of The Sheeps. You got some jealousy in here but that's those fake, low self-esteem, loud barkin' hoes. It's all relative, you get jealousy everywhere you go. The real love comes from the real money makin' sisters.

What keeps us grounded in our vanities? The psychological and spiritual pain we all share. We are all in the same boat. Fishing, hooking on our costumes and g-string as bait to hook a shark for dinner.

I was surprised to see the bouncers from Fool's Paradise securing The Sheeps doors. It was refreshing to see Dezul but he could quit playing so much with me. He flirts too much. He needs to slow down on me and focus on the baby he's about to have with Sassy. How in the hell did Sassy get sucked into this dead-end underground world? But then again, college will do it to you, if you're not consuming your education carefully and correctly. And that's how life is. Sometimes we stop to take a breather, wherever we are in our lives or whenever we get tired. Everyone at some point or another gets caught up into the strangest situations and then one day, even if it's too late, we wake up and see the light. So I have to always be conscious of my judgments on people because even I do some silly shit. I see it as getting webbed into a dream but, sooner or later, we'll all wake up out of it. And when we come out of it, be thankful for coming out and pray you're a lot stronger and wiser than you were when you first got in. One shouldn't blame others or get angry at ourselves for making ridiculous choices. Just don't turn those mistakes into habits. It's all about growing through experiences and understanding that these are phases. Because at the end of the day, it's all lessons that needs to be learned. It's all about becoming wiser and passing up the knowledge to the youth so we can evolve as human beings.

As I walked through the crowded bar of men from ages 21 to 92, standing around, I peeked in the back of the bar to see how business was going. A few girls were stand dancing in the dark. I noticed a bright blue sequenced bikini in a corner. Of course, it was Miss Latoya Jackson's twin, S'fine. S'fine is about 93 pounds and her breasts probably weighs about 10 pounds each. How does she balance her breasts and the high heels she wears? God has blessed this girl with a strikingly beautiful face. I like the way she carried herself despite whatever else she did. But there is a true saying, It is not what you do, it's how you do it. And whatever you do, be the best at it.

Two girls sharing a booth were squatting to give proper blow jobs. Three others were rubbing their behinds on the men's exposed penises. Their hand pocket flashlights swung back and forth halfway around their thighs. It made the floor look like a homemade disco. The hand pocket flashlights were to check for counterfeit bills. Sometimes if I'm lucky, I would find careless money on the floor. One time I found $70.

Cigarette fumes and Impulse body spray misted up each of the nine dark rooms. Open condom wrappers were flung carelessly out on the open floor. Sticky soiled rubbers rested worn out in the dents of corners. Spilled semen crawled down the walls leaving traces of hurried hand-jobs.

Middle-aged Dominican mommies crawled the bar and steered clear of the matchbooks, ashtrays, plastic cups, pitchers and Heineken beer bottles. Their asses got touched on, squeezed on, slapped on and kissed on, licked on and pasted on with dollar bills, while they paraded down the bar holding empty smiles.

When I stepped into the homespun dressing room, I always spoke to the girls. I'm very careful of the cocaine users. They carry bad attitudes.

"Hey y'all. How ya doin?" I say.

"Ain't no money up in here, Baby." The Cokeheads always got something negative to say.

"Really? Damn." Ain't no money up in here for y'all. Shit my money's waiting for me. But I won't let them know because it's none of their damn business. Candy, Staxx, Plenny and Toy, sat on the long leather cushioned couch. That was their get high spot. They sat like pigeons huddled together snorting over their white bread. Poor Sandy, the owner's mutt had to guard the door, inhaling every toxic thing that passed her way.

Star was standing in front of the mirror shaking her ass, warming up her adorable petite body. She probably weigh about 90 cents. She wore piercings in her nose, tongue, clitoris, ears, eyebrow and nipples. When Star danced, she appeared as that little innocent daughter, batting her big and round eyes to her sugar-daddies. In the dressing room, you can forget about it. Star is just like her name. Just a hot ball of gas. She cussed too much like she had something to prove.

July stepped out of the bathroom in her hot orange bikini. July's body fits her name. She kept her hair in mushroom style and her body absolutely flawless. When I say flawless I mean a *Sports Illustrated* non-computer generated body. She is very careful with how she takes care of her body. I observed July as she sat down to softly oil her elbows and ankles, then wrists and shoulders.

"What's up Baby?" She softly asked.

"Chillin'. What's up with you, July?"

"Nothin', just trying to get rid of this nigga." July took her time sealing her elbows.

"I hear you. He's still on your back, huh?"

"Is he? Girl, this place is the only place that would help take my mind off of him." We laughed and she resumed to oiling her ankles.

"What's up everybody!" Shouted the dancer entering, stepping over Sandy.

"Hey, Flo," Everyone said.

Flo walked into the dressing room with her white mink jacket fitting perfectly around her small waistline. She can dress her ass off with her tan leather pants and her high-heeled white boots. Flo is just Flo. She seldom smiles only if there is a purpose behind it. She's like a second cousin who's into her own thing. I have great respect for Flo. She is a sister I will never forget. She's not an eye-catcher in terms of looks but her body is. Her body is definitely made to dance. I love to watch Flo dance. She doesn't show face at all. All the attention is on how she wiggles her beautiful brown legs and ass. Flo doesn't need to smile, her tips are well earned from her performances.

I see a distinctive beauty in these dancers. Whatever they mama gave them, they make the best out of it and shake it. Even the not-so-striking ones have made themselves attractive by enhancing every good feature they have and downplaying their weak points. What I find amazing about the dancers is their name harmonizes with their personalities. I love these sisters 'cause they're naked about their thoughts. Most of the time we stick together. I guess because it is us vs. the tricks.

As I changed into my sexy, red mermaid dress, girls' eyes admired, wanted to nurture and darted lust all over my reddish-butter brown-skinned body. I paid them no mind. The girls are harmless. It's the carnal men out there that I have to watch out for. The couches and the benches were covered with duffel bags and buttocks. S'fine walked in to change from her blue sequence bikini into her red, sequenced dress. She stood next to me.

"It's now 10 and I've been here since 8:30. I've made $600 without tricking," she confidently boasted.

"You go girl," I said. Shit, I just got here and I have eight men already waiting for me. That's one thing I don't do is boast to other women about my financial accomplishments. I don't like to incite jealousy. See, I'm secure within myself and my relationships when it comes to the men I work with. Most of the girls are not in touch like that. They're only in touch with the money and cruelty and hate they have toward men. Money is in their hearts, all the while they keep it close to their bosom in their bras.

I started to glide out of the dressing room, leaving Candy, Toy, Plenny, and Staxx huddled in their corner, complaining about how cheap the tricks in here were. Just before I could push open the door, Plenny stopped me.

"Baby. Let me ask you a question. You trick?"

"No."

Staxx interjected. "I swear I saw you over there in that corner trickin'." Her jaws moved from side to side, I guess from the cocaine reaction.

"You mean giving hand jobs? I sometimes do that." (that's if I'm horny).

"Hmmphh," Plenny said. "Ain't nobody innocent up in here."

Tippin' came steppin' out of the bathroom.

"Who said that? Y'all talking to Baby? Y'all bitches need to stop that shit. Y'all better recognize that Baby is cool peoples. Don't y'all try to player hate on her!"

"Ain't nobody playa hatin' on Baby. We just wanted to know if she needed clientele," defended Staxx.

"She gets clientele. Betta believe that shit. Right Baby?" I shrugged my shoulders and slightly blushed. She turned back to them, "We all cool and all, and we get high together but don't fuck wit Baby. She like my daughta. She minds her own fuckin' beeiznis. If y'all hoes wanna fuck wit somebody, try fuckin' wit me." She pointed. "Shit, my ass took two muthafuckin' bullets." She pointed, "One in my rib and one in my muthafuckin hip. That girl, Baby, looked out for me, big time. And so what if she duz trick? That's her fuckin' beeiznis. Don't be scrutinizing Baby. Bitches need to stop that jealousy and envy bull-shit. That's why people can't make no fuckin' money up in here 'cause bitches be complainin' and scheming all the fuckin' time."

They rolled their eyes. Tippin' didn't care. She made sure she had the last word. I looked toward them and lip synced, "Sorry." But they asked for it.

Tippin' didn't play. Don't try that trivial talk around her. She'll put you in your place quick. Tippin' is like the Godmother to all of us.

Shortly after the incident, I would say about 50 girls began to fill the dressing room. Some were getting dressed to leave and find another club, and others changed into more interesting outfits. I adjusted my strawberry blonde wig that laid over my right eye. I slipped on my long red gloves and smoothed out my red Jessica Rabbit mermaid dress. Men go crazy whenever I wear this dress! Then the dressing room grew crowded with unfamiliar faces. New whores, oh shit! Elaine? What the hell is she doing up in here? She sat down and changed into her shimmer pink dress and g-string. Her body was still fabulous and she still did not have any titties. I'm sure she'll make her share of money though. I covered more of my face with the wig and headed toward the door. She pat my thigh,

"Dana?"

Shit!!

"Elaine?" I pretended to be surprised. We embraced ever so slightly. "What are you doin' up in here?" I asked.

"The same reason you're up in here, tryin' to get piz-aid, girl." We shared a tense laugh. She still spoke feminine using those 'S' sounds.

"I hear you."

"Is it good tonight?"

"It's okay," I said in modesty.

"Dana, I want to say, I'm sorry about what happened years ago. You know I was so blind to that stupid ass Moet."

"Who wasn't? We all were, including India. I just thank God I didn't get pregnant by him."

"Mmm, word up."

"But yeah, It's okay, I hold no grudges on my end."

"That's cool." Elaine said.

"How is the Sugah Sweet Crew doin'?"

"We broke up five years ago."

"Why?"

"People started dropping out one by one."

"How's Sahidah?"

"Her mom's moved her down south because her mouth was getting her into too much trouble."

"That's a shame." I commented.

"It is…"

"So you're new here?"

"Yeah," she sighed. She looked sort of tired but I trusted Elaine could look nicer on better days.

"How long have you been dancing?" I asked.

"About a year now. And you?"

"Two long honey. Two long years."

She laughed. "How's your Moms doin'? I heard she was sick."

"You didn't hear?"

"Hear what?"

"She passed on."

She liked to cry. "Oh, Dana. My God! She was the healthiest person I knew. she was so athletic. What?! I can't believe this. I'm so sorry to hear this. What did she pass away from?"

"I'd rather not talk about it right now." I thought about it. "Lung cancer."

"How long has it been?"

"About four years now."

"Damn time be flying. I'm so sorry to hear this. Are you okay?"

"Yeah, I'm fine. She's in a better place, you know."

"I ain't gonna front. Even though it seemed as though I didn't like her, on the D.L., I always admired her. Your moms was so dope and I respected her for how she carried herself, you know? She did a great job raisin' you and your brother. God bless her, Mami."

"Give thanks. I'ma talk to you later. I have to do my set. Oh and good luck."

"Thanks."

She whispered, "Dana?"

"Baby," I corrected.

"I go by Sher," she said.

It's time for me to get up out this business. The Sheeps is growing too popular. I'm seeing one too many familiar faces popping up around here. My reputation needs protection.

24
the art exhibit

"Hey Baby." An anxious man called. "Are you going on stage?"

I nodded my head and I walked pass the lustful dark room and almost bumped into Candy. She was bent over like the number seven, taking in her trick's quick thrusts. My attention was drawn to Hollywood. She was very captivating. Her eyes were so full of cheer. If I were to guess her zodiac sign, I would say she fit the characteristics of a Sagittarius. Hollywood danced and shook her tight little ass on the stage. Her complexion was reddish-cocoa. On her lower back was a tattoo that spelled her name in capitol letters. I have to admit she's definitely a foxy chick. All the men and all the dancers were magnetized to HOLLYWOOD's charisma. She shook her little ass like it was a strobe-wave. The men went crazy over her. I could never do that. I'm too shy to stand up and just shake my bootie, much less shake it all up in men faces. Raunchy stuff like that is not my forte'. Hollywood crawled the bar counter to collect her tips. Every slap she received on her ass made me cringe. She's so beyond beautiful. After she climbed down the counter, she kissed me on the cheek.

"Make that money, sexy Baby." I honored her compliment.

DJ Spark smiled at me as I smoothly glided onto the stage. I ignored the hands that curiously felt my lycra & spandex, red mermaid dress. DJ Spark knew my cue. He changed the tempo of the bootie songs that Hollywood liked, to a laid-back 70's soul classic. My intro was The Isley Brothers "For the Love of you" Part 1. Part 2, "Sensuality" brought out the best in my performance and the best in my audience. Before I put on my show, I liked to turn off the yellow lights and leave on the red ones. Something about red lights seriously puts me in a sensuous mood. I'm too nervous to swing around poles. I can't do what the other girls do, so I do what I know and do best, and that is swaying my hips in slow rotations of eights and zeroes. Some would call it a Marilyn Monroe style by the way I tease everyone with my smile and innocent flirtations, but I call it *Baby's* style.

I used my shyness in a sublime way. I cannot face my audience, so

I face them through the mirror behind me. I enjoyed dancing for them as well as receiving the tips. Through the fingerprinted mirror, I get real naughty. I lean to my left and open my legs while everyone lean towards the right. They followed me through the mirror. My viewers were captivated and anxious to see what my big or little fuzz looked like. I must've been doing something right if I had Flo and Hollywood tipping to the right too. Everyone loved my flirtatious dance! I magnetized a broad and attentive crowd. Those at the bar placed their drinks on top of the counter because they preferred my taste. When DJ Spark spun the slow jams on Black Street's "Joy," my audience liked to melt.

Brina, the barmaid and other times a side dancer, smiled and tipped me one of my favorite drinks, a virgin Toasted Almond. She's one of the coolest girls up in here.

I was reeling in those dollars boy! More men flat left Star's show, located in the front, for Baby's show on the smaller stage in the back of the club. I even spotted Elaine in the audience smiling and admiring my art show. There was some ignorant and drunken man by the stage shouting,

"Take it all off, Babe! Eh yo' Bebe! Is you one of Bebe kids!? Ha! Ha! Ha!" He laughed to himself, by himself. "I'll pay you more than all these niggas up in this bitch!" He pulled out a knot. I didn't care to look at the face of his bills or his ugly and sloppy face. For the rest of the night his ego, arrogance and his lousy money was put on punishment. I simply ignored him.

Unlike the other dancers, I discriminate. Most dancers usually remove their garments first and then collect their tips but I don't work that way. I remain clothed until I receive a sufficient amount of money that is worth me stripping off each garment. It also depends on how much fun we all are having too. My audience and I have to have a good chemistry going. If there is no chemistry between us, then there is no *Baby Show*.

I danced in and out to the beats and softly caressed my ass with my hands. I cupped my D-cups, hypnotized the men with my cattish eyes. They all couldn't help but to digest my aura. In the "ugly and sloppy man's" intoxicated state, he threw his bills on my stage and I threw that shit right back at him. Everyone laughed at him. He cursed me and I gave him the middle finger, stroking my genital with it. I can get nasty and ugly too.

My regular customer Terence gestured how he would love to make sweet and slow love to me. All I have to do is give him one chance. As I looked down on my audience from the stage, I witnessed their hungry hearts. Unfortunately, I don't think this is a place for love where pure love is born. *But then again whose to say?* They kissed my hands and toes and those who were farther away blew kisses. I caught them and rubbed their kisses on my heart. Everyone remained still, watching Baby's spirited, expressive dances.

In between DJ Sparks cutting up the record, a young man shouted, "You're a work of art, Baby!" They caressed my ego oh so softly. It was I who picked and chose whom I wanted to take tips from. The men waved their bills eagerly, in hopes I would take their money. This work field turn into a playground. Men turned to boys and made fun by turning dollar bills into airplanes. Some tried to aim it at my coochie. DJ Sparks played the perfect song, "Sweet, Sticky Thing." I turned this striptease hell into a game in heaven. We all gambled. Men flew the airplane straight toward my coochie and if I caught it with my knees then the thrower received a luscious, sweet smelling Egyptian musk hug with my cleavage all up in his face.

DJ Sparks ended my set with Biggie Smalls' "The Unbelievable." When I got off the stage, money was in my hands, in my cleavage, wrapped around my shoe belts, skirting my g-string, and ring dollars around my fingers, styled by my viewers. Many waited by the gate to ask *Baby* for a dance. Talk about ego and confidence. But I'm smart enough to know that this is all superficial and temporary. Dancing with me was like an honor to these guys. My client, Terence and I hardly danced. We only caressed and whispered the sweetest somethings into each other's ear.

"Oh, Baby, I couldn't wait to get a dance from you. You know I've been waiting here for over an hour?"

"Really? I'm so sorry, baby."

"It's okay, you're a busy girl, excuse me, a busy woman. I know you got other people waiting for you, so here. See what we can get outta this."

Terence placed three $50 bills in my hand along with a little gift bag. I turned on my flashlight and pulled two satin red and white g-strings from out of the Gucci handbag. I kissed him on his beautiful cheekbone.

"Thank you, my love."

"Your smile is so beautiful," he said. We hugged. He then whispered in my ear,

"I love the way your oils smell." I massaged his shoulder blades and lower back. My warm voice kept his money flowing.

Across from us, Candy was still bent over, taking in harsh thrusts. "Look man, you gotta bring on the tips! That's 11 songs too long!" She panted.

"Well, if you stop talkin' so much, maybe a nigga could get off!"

"Get your impotent dick outta me, nigga!" Shit got real ugly in their space. One thing a whore should never do is insult a trick's ego, pride and joystick. I couldn't believe when Dude punched Candy in the rib. Three shadowed bouncers came rushing in on the frustrated trick and kicked him out. On his way out, he made threats of killing Candy.

Terence and I shook our heads in shame and sympathy for Candy but was glad that it wasn't us.

"He must really hate himself to have to punch a lady like that," I said.

"I agree with you on that…Well, on a lighter note, I have to tell you, you were so fine up there, Baby? I don't know anybody who could put on a show like you."

"Thank you."

"You believe in God?"

"No doubt."

"Yeah, I believe you. The way you had everybody in here, in love wit chu', it had to have been God. You know what? I never asked you this before but I always wanted to know something."

"And that is?"

"Where did you get that name Baby? I mean you're far from a baby, you're a woman."

"Let me tell you, Terence. You can look at it in many different ways. I will always be my Mama's Baby. I can be your sweet Baby and if you feel my skin, it's as soft as…"

He placed his palms on my rose hips and commented, "You're as soft as rose petals."

Our hands skated upon each other's. "Damn, your hands are like silk! You need to send them to a donor, we're talkin' fine fabric here!" I put my head down and laughed. "I see something great in you that this place lacks, *Baby.*"

"And that is?"

"I'm just going on with all this flattery stuff, right?" he laughed.

"Go ahead, it's getting you somewhere."

"Oooh, I like that." He continued, "I see an innocence in you. That's what I get from your name, Baby. Innocence."

"Mmmm. It sounds contradictory. But then again I don't internalize any of this. I learn from it because I know all of this is nothing but illusions and warped fantasies."

"So are you sayin' that you're an illusion? Someone's warped fantasy?"

"I'm just as real as the next dancer, it's just that I enjoy having fun with my audience. I mean, my illusions are honest. See in this place, I exist only as a fantasy to y'all. The closest anybody's going to get to me is through a dance. No more or less. I don't cross any lines."

"Mmm, I believe you. I mean if you did cross any lines, I would've heard about it by now."

A tall man standing beside us was receiving a lap-dance from Sunshine. He raised his eyebrows and frowned his mouth at me then reached over and sat a $20 tip between my plump cleavage.

"I'm gonna wait for you right here till y'all done."

"Well, you gon' be waitin' a long time, brother," said Terence.

"I bet she's worth the wait." He said.

"That, she is. You besta get on line like everybody else," said Terence pointing toward the bar.

A man at the bar shouted, "Don't even think about standing here. The line is back there."

Terence whispered sweet confirmations in my ear of how special I was. There were girls dancing in the dark room along with me. They had their minds set on money for their next hit. They looked as if they didn't care about who was squeezing or smacking their ass or sucking on their breasts. Their mind was in this moment. These girls had nothing to live for, for they were the slaughterers of their goals. There were no boundaries when it came to how they made their money. You only had a handful of classic dancers up in The Sheeps. The rest were sleezy, uncreative, untalented dancers. They just gave the men whatever they were looking for or whatever they wanted. They didn't know about teaching and inspiring the hearts and spirits of these men.

I took one more fellow before I took my 15-minute break. Seth seemed more interested in what was in my head than my body. That was cool, but he still had to pay me $10 every five minutes. Seth's conversation was refreshing. We drank some Orgasms. He showed me a picture of his wife. Then he asked me what did I think of her. I gave him some suggestions and advice on his beautiful and loving wife. I noticed too many men come to places like this, primarily in search of love, a fantasy or to just get their egos stroked.

"Seth, I can understand your addictions to places like this but look at how lucky, well not lucky, but look at how blessed you are to have a beautiful, strong black woman in your life, in your corner. I mean I'm not the one to judge, but by looking at her picture, it tells me that you've got a rare and special woman right here." Seth listened and nodded his head at my accuracy. "Let me tell you, I see a lot of different men up in here and I see a lot of the same faces. One day I want to meet a man, a decent man, who is not interested in places like this."

"I wish you luck on that, sis. You just might find what you are looking for."

"Seth, be good to your woman and put more faith into your relationship," I pleaded, "Ain't nothing really in here. This place isn't for you. I could be just like some of these greedy hoes and gas you up, possess you and prey on your weakness to secure your money. But that's not me. That shit requires too much energy and karma. I know you really don't want to be here. You want to be home with this lovely woman. I can see it written all in your eyes, and you know I'm right."

He smiled and lowered his gaze.

"You are. And you're very beautiful. I don't know why you're in a place like this. But hey, Baby, I know you have bills to pay. Baby, I know you have to go, but I just want to say to you, thank you. You're a beautiful woman. You know that God is going to bless you, someday," and with that he stood up. "I'm takin' my ass home and I'm going to make sweet love to my woman."

"Don't think of me when you're doing it either." We laughed.

"Wow, you're cool people. This may sound cheesy but as long as I am breathing I won't ever forget you. Just by this conversation, you gave me hope and faith in my relationship. Thank you."

"Thank God." All praises unto you Father, thank you. Seth tipped me an extra twenty and left.

Sometimes I enjoy sitting in the backyard with my friend/masseuse Michael. He's always giggling just like Auntie Berlinda. Before I headed toward the backyard, I made a quick detour to the bathroom. A new cleaning lady was back there.

"How are you doin'?" I asked as I washed my hands. She nodded and handed me a paper towel.

"Thank you," I said.

"You're welcome." She sat there looking at my high, Patricia Fields' platform heels. Are you a dancer too?"

"Yes." I'm wondering what's wrong with this lady? She must be new in her job field.

"Oh, Mami. You all are so beautiful. You don't have to do this." She cried out softly.

"Well, I got bills to pay."

"I understand but please, you don't need to do this to yourself. Your body is your temple. There is another way out of this, sister. Oh God, Am I offending ju?"

"No, it's okay. I'm listening." I got a closer look at her, and her face was flawless.

Her face had the same luminous glow like Mommy. She looked like a blend of Latino mixed with Native American. This woman's sympathetic vibe overwhelmed me. Her eyes held a glare in them that I could not read. I didn't see any pain in her eyes, only peace. I figured she must see something in me, something happening in me, that I can not see in myself. Maybe she feels the same feelings I felt when I was 9 years old for Mommy. I was pure and clear and I was able to see destruction happening to Mommy when she could not see it in herself. What will this woman tell me that I don't already know? *I have to do some soul searching and find in myself that this woman sees before it kills me.*

"When I see this, it brings me to tears, my love." she said. "I was lead here by my Father. I've never did this in my life. Miss, I don't know you, but I feel like I do, from somewhere. A past life perhaps." Her stare held my eyes with hers. "Please, I just ask of you to, please find your way out of here and don't look back. It's slowly killing your spirit."

"What do you mean? I'm sayin' I don't do drugs. I just dance to pay my bills."

"Mami, you are not put here on this earth for exotic dancing, you are one of us." She pointed her finger, sharply at the floor, "You don't belong here. Your spirit cannot thrive and grow here, in a place like this."

"So what am I supposed to do? Get evicted? I got to pay these bills!"

"Only God will show you the way, if you listen, more." I paused and thought, she was right. "Why are you telling me this? You don't even know me. You think you do but you don't."

"I know a pure heart when I see it. *I KNOW MY PEOPLE.*"

I nervously laughed at her confident words, "Where are you from?"

"Nevaeh."

"Never heard of it." I said.

"It's a small town, not too far from here."

"Oh. Well Miss, I don't understand how there's hundreds of girls up in here and decided to pick on me. Why do people do that to me? I'm always the one, they want to chastise, tease, or discipline. There's a hundred girls you could spread this message to. Why me?" She took my hand and I felt her warmth and her love. A love I haven't felt in a long time since 1991.

"Why you?" She smiled while closing her eyes. "Love, your spirit is chosen. You are not lost, you are still searching for the way." She read my heart as if it was transparent. I nodded.

"There aren't many of your types around today. You know, pure hearted folks. A lot of them crossed over to the other side to meet God's speed." She shook her head and smiled, "Lord, you sent me a unique one." She looked down from the ceiling and asked again, "Please, Mami walk away and don't look back. You are not alone, you will be guided."

"Okay, I'll stop. I wasn't planning on staying in this business, anyway."

"God bless you, Mami. God will help. God is with you. Believe him, trust him."

I exited the bathroom and started bugging over the power this simple and humble woman possessed. I recorded our encounter for evening daydreams in my memory for my journal. I opened the backdoor to the backyard and saw "Michael the masseuse" sitting down. He started giggling once he saw me.

"Hey baby, how's my baby's feet doing?"

"Terrible." I pouted like a child. "What's so funny, Michael?" I sucked my teeth. "Are you high?"

"Yeah, man, I got some good ganja, you want some?"

"Not on the job. A little later."

"Okay, come sit here. Listen," he lowered his voice, "a very close friend of mine. He's my boy is feeling you big time. He got triple G's he could spend on you. He told me you were the one."

"One for what?"

"For him. He expressed to me how he loves the way you perform and he wants to take you to the islands for a weekend trip. This weekend if you're available. Are you interested?"

"First of all, He doesn't even know me. Shit, I don't even know him."

"That's my dog, Baby. He want to get to know you. And trust me, you will like him."

"Number one, I don't deal with men from places I work. Number two," My eyes looked into his, "Michael, you know..."

He interrupted, "I know. I know you don't trick. There is no price tag on your body and your heart. You don't make love for money but for meaning. I got you girl. I know your whole steeze. I told him that already and he has no intentions of being a trick."

"And he still want to take me to the islands?"

"Yes. Your show impressed him."

"You said, he has triple g's. Is he rich?"

"Nah, he got a little somethin' somethin'. Put it like this, my boy comes from money."

"So whats he doin' in here?"

"I brought him here. He's from out of town."

"Where from?"

Michael laughed, "You ask him. And Baby, you know, he's never been to a strip joint before."

"You serious?!"

"Dead ass." He started laughing. "Funny thing about it is, all the girls here want him. They're offering free lap dances and shit, and he's turnin' them down left and right. He got his eye on this one dancer and that's you." Michael looked in me and smiled.

"What does he look like?"

Michael pointed. I damn near choked.

"So what are we talkin' Mike? Is he married? Any children? Is he from here?"

"Never married, no children and Brooklyn native." He was dressed so fresh and so clean. He looked like those 5 cent carmel candies. He looked sort of like a J-Crew model. I'm surprised that I didn't see his face from the stage. His face showed an innocence that I found hard to believe. Those eyes and eyebrows looked bright and dreamy-like. I watched his mannerisms and how his elbows posed close to his waist. I observed his mannerisms while Michael bragged to me about where he got his weed. I caught a glimpse of him laughing with Hollywood. I know if Hollywood is taking her time out to chat with a man, he must be worth her time and he must be cool in some way.

He stood there baby-brown and confident in a smooth and reserved way. From a distance, he looked sort of nerdy but interestingly confident in a sexy way. I have to see if his heart is light enough for me to consider going on a vacation with him.

"Michael, how long have you two been friends?"

"For about fifteen years. Our fathers were frat brothers at Howard University. Baby, I'm telling you when he watched you on that stage, you did something to him. He did not move from his spot."

"You think he's star-struck?"

"It's deeper than that. He ain't the star-struck type. Shit, he's like a star himself. Mad talented." He paused. "Oh I almost forgot. Yo', he kept telling me that you have pure, creative energy. I love my boy but he can be a little up in the clouds sometimes." I found that comment to be quite impressive.

"The good thing about it is, he travels alot. He said, he has to take you out of here so you can utilize that energy properly. He said he wants to be the one to provide you an outlet."

Michael turned away from me, "Sup man."

"What's up. That woman Hollywood is a crazy sister." He turned his attention toward me and took off his hat. Beautiful, shiny waves, I yearned to touch with my fingers. Michael introduced us.

"Baby, Jamie, Jamie this is Baby."

"Nice to meet you, Jamie." He stood there very confident, and unbelievably calm. He stood 6'1, nice square shoulders with a lean build. His entire constitution was magnetizing. I could tell by looking at Jamie's expression, he was attracted to me too.

"Well, I'll be inside." I didn't quite react to Michael. He caught the hint and so he walked away smiling. "If you don't see me inside, I'll be out front, man."

He gave Jamie a pound.

"You can have a seat." I offered. He sat beside me and the scent of his cologne said 'abundantly true'.

He spoke to me. "When I was watching you on stage, I was telling my man, Mike about you. About how special and powerful your light is." Our eyes connected in such a way. I felt comfortable with looking in them.

"What did Michael say?"

"He said he knew this. I hope you're aware of your power." He said.

"A little." Jamie couldn't be no more than 27 years old. His skin glowed nicely.

"I was watching you, up on the stage and I was thinking to myself, you should be up in higher places than this."

"Higher places like what?"

"A woman like you belong in the Hamptons living your life. I can see you working on something with more substance than this."

"You want to take me there?"

"Only if you really, really want to go."

"Yes." I replied.

"Under one condition. Nah, I don't like conditions. Okay, under one rule, if I show you the way, give you a taste, you have to promise me that you will not hang on to my coat tail, or be in my shadow."

"What do you mean by that?"

"I'll show you the way but you have to promise me you will grow to be independent."

"Okay, I promise I will grow to be independent."

"So you're going to allow me the opportunity to take you to a place that mirrors your beauty?"

"Wow." I said, "You sure have a way with words. Are you a poet?"

"Sometimes. I told Mike where I wanted to take you. I told him I wanted to take you on a weekend trip, this weekend. And you know what he told me?" I shook my head, blushing all the while. "Mike told me you would never go away with me in my wildest dreams. But see, I'm a man who believes in all the impossibilities."

"But you don't even know me like that and vice-versa."

"Trust can go a long ways, Baby. It starts with you telling me *your* name."

I faked seriousness, "Baby." I stared into his eyes and we got caught up into the feeling of falling in love.

"Your real name."

"Dana."

"Dana." He looked away and up. "Beautiful. Dana what?"

"Dana Makieba Strong." He extended his hand.

"Jamie Ali McLaren." We shook. He added, "Dana, I'm going to be honest with you. I am attracted to you in everyway. Don't get me wrong, you've got a beautiful body but for some reason I can't move my eyes from here." He swayed his hand over my eyes without touching them. He made me smile. The feeling was reciprocal. I told him, 'it was a blessing that he felt that way about me.' He smiled back with a youthful and clean smile. Teeth glistenin'.

"I don't usually do this spontaneity stuff, but for some reason I think it would be cool if you could come with me to Hawaii."

"I don't know." I moaned.

He smiled. I've never been touched by a smile like his except for Michael Jackson back when he was thirty-four years old.

"Give me time to consider it."

"Sure, no problem. But in the midst of you considering this vacation, could we correspond?"

"Yes. One question, does it have to be Hawaii?" I asked.

"Did you have another place in mind?"

"I would like to experience Jamaica."

"Really? Why Jamaica?"

"No real reason. I know Jamaica is Bob Marley's birth place. I don't know, I just want to absorb the culture for some odd reason."

"If Jamaica is where you want to go, then Jamaica it is. I definitely want us to talk. I want you to know that this vacation is a present for you. It'll be a healing experience for you . I don't want you to think that I'm out here trying to sex you or deceive you or anything."

"Jamie, if I felt any of those ways, trust me I would not be sitting here talking to you."

He smiled again. We smiled together. "If you let me," he said, "I would like to get to know you deeper than this. You intrigue me. Is there anything you enjoy doing other than dancing?"

"Yes. I enjoy writing and cycling. Believe it or not, I'm getting tired of this industry. It's time for me to move on to bigger dreams. You know what I'm saying?" He was very attentive. I continued, "People don't know this but I have plans for my future. This dancing is not my only life. There's books I have to write, degrees I have to get, a man I have to love, children I have to birth, you know what I'm saying?"

"I feel you."

"There is more to this world than The Sheeps. I refuse to let the

Sheeps squeeze the life outta me the way it did with some of these women in here."

My impatient clients started filling the room to give me the hint that they wanted my time. One of them interrupted our conversation.

"Well," Jamie said, "It's my cue to leave. You're working and I took up too much of your time. I have to go anyway. I want you to really think about this trip. Here is something for your time." He scribbled an amount on the check. "We've got one day before Friday." He didn't look up from the booklet until he ripped the page off.

"Take it. Business is business, right." It was strange how I felt hesitant in taking the check. I already saw him as a friend. I didn't want him to leave, I wanted us to finish talking. Everyone was looking at us.

"I gave you a check because I want you to put it into your savings account." I didn't look at the check, I just put it into my wallet.

"Have you ever been out of the country?" He asked.

"No."

"It's a beautiful thing. The experience opens your mind to different things, you know?"

"Yeah." I'll think about it, Jamie." It would've been a natural reaction to hug him, but I extended my hand and said, "It was a pleasure meeting you. And thank you for everything."

He didn't shake my hand, instead he kissed them and said,

"It was special to have met you, Dana." He placed his business card in my palm and confidently walked away to meet up with Michael. Nice walk.

A half of an hour went by and I was ready to go home and meditate on my feelings about going to Jamaica with Jamie. But I had to stick to my promise, and that was giving private dances to my clients who had been waiting practically all night for me. As soon as my watch displayed 2:30, I went into the dressing room to gather my belongings. Candy was on the phone with a cab company. She signaled to me that she wanted to talk to me privately in the bathroom before she left. After she hung up the phone, she opened the bathroom door.

"Baby, come here, I want to talk to you." Candy leaned against the wooden bathroom door and handed me $40. I looked around for the cleaning lady, she was gone. So I dug in my purse for a $40 bottle of her favorite. Candy's a fly Harlem girl who sports a neat, jet black doobie hairstyle. She keeps an emerald stub in her cute nose. Butterscotch is the color of her entire body and she's shaped like a vase, small at the top and wide at the bottom. She's dope. When she spoke her voice squeaked and when she smiled both her top and bottom teeth showed.

Someone knocked on the door. "Candy open the door, it's Tippin'!"

Candy whispered to me, "No, don't open the door." Tippin' knocked harder. Then Candy shouted, "Tippin' give me a minute, I'm on the toilet!"

"So! Open the door, Candy." Candy looked at me. Tippin' knocked harder.

"Baby, you in there? Open the door."

"I have to, Candy." I said. She looked away. I unlocked the door.

"What's up, Tippin'?" Tippin' stared at Candy, shaking her head in shame.

"Baby, did Candy buy any coke from you?" I uncomfortably smiled.

"Not yet, why."

"Baby, I know you have to make your money but please don't sell it to her. She's pregnant."

"No more said." I refunded Candy her $40. I had to kill the devil. Tippin' and Candy walked out the bathroom. I can't do this shit anymore.

Someone in the dressing room screamed. The bouncers yelled,

"It's a raid!" Police men slammed open the doors and randomly collected girls. The cops handcuffs clicked Mahogany, Tippin', July, Staxx, Candy, S'fine, and Star's wrists. I flushed all the bottles down the toilet. Focus, Dee, focus. I pulled out my duffle bag from under the couch, quietly got dressed and I paced my way pass the hysteria. I passed the flashlights, the police, and my anxious fans. The strangest thing, was no one saw me. I hopped into Candy's Lincoln cab. *This is all you Father. Thank you for walking me through this. I closed the cab door.*

"You came just in time, I was just about to leave. It looks like a raid is going on in there." Said the driver. Red, yellow and white lights flashed in the side view and rear-view mirrors.

"Yeah, it is." I thought about Jamie and figured he must've left a long time ago. My eyes kept forward. If I turned around I might turn into a pillar of salt. I also thought about that woman from Nevaeh.

"Where we going?"

"Far Rockaway, Queens."

"It's $45." I handed him $60.

"Keep the change."

"Thanks. God bless."

"Thank you and God bless. Sir, would you wake me once we're over the Cross Bay Bridge?"

"Sure, no problem."

I leaned back and sighed. I knew this would be coming. *Too much fantasy turns into insanity.* The Sheeps was too overcrowded to begin with and then the prostitution that was going on in there was only an addition to the congestion. It is now time for me to surrender this crazy business. This is God showing me a sign to get back on the right path and do the right thing, if I want to end up happy.

Thank God I got home safely. I dropped my duffel bag on the floor, ripped off that hot ass wig and fell on my bed. Whew! I'm reeking of bar liquor and cigarettes but I am too exhausted to take a shower. Besides my bed sheets are three days old anyway. I'll change them tomorrow. Oh, how I thank you, Father, for having my back in this craziness. Thank you for your protection and for this roof over my head. I'm so tired. I have to write in my journal about what happened this evening, then I could rest peacefully. Tomorrow I have to take my little cousins to the movies. I don't want to renege on them. Please give me strength and energy tomorrow. Thank you. I'ma just stare at the ceiling and wait for sleep to rescue me.

I looked around the room and then the walls began to expand and stretch and take form into Carnegie Hall. Blue lights shone on beautiful black heads. People started filling reserved seats. Beautiful black people dressed in white, looked like sophisticated angels. I sniffed and sniffed again. Egyptian Musk oil lingered somewhere in the air. But where? Silver bracelets jingled from twists of wrists and lifts of Christals kissed full black lips. To my left, I saw a brother playing the shit out of a tenor saxophone. As I got a closer look, oh my Lord. John Coltrane. Tonight is the night! The trumpet player's high pitched note startled me and then a blue light shone on his person. To my surprise there was Miles Davis on the right of the stage. Everyone clapped while bracelets jingled. I could feel love enveloping me with sweet smells of Egyptian Musk. All the stage lights lit up in blue, all kinds of blues; Royal blue, navy blue, sky blue, torquiose blue, and indigo blue. Miles Davis is playing a beautiful song from "Some Kind of Blue." He is playing "Blue in Green". Everyone clapped while the scent of Frankicense and Myrrh floated pass my view. I flag the smoke so I could see the show.

A woman appeared before me.

"*Anybody sitting here?*" Her voice sounded very familiar.

"No." I said getting a closer look at her face. I gasped, "Mommy?"

"*Hi Baby.*" She smiled. I reach out to hug her. We embraced.

"Oh my God! What are you doing here?"

"*No, the question is what are you doin' here? You're not even born yet. Girl, Did you know that you're way ahead of your time?*"

"I am? Wait a minute, I thought you were supposed to be dead in the ground."

"*My body is in the ground, not me. I dug myself out. Do you remember what my sister Leniece told you?*"

"That's right. You can never die." I looked at her once again,

"Oh Mommy, you look so good. What have you been up to?" Her spaghetti strap, long white lace dress kissed the back of her heels. I looked at the creases of her arms and they looked just as smooth as the way she made her entry.

"*I've been busy, Baby. I'm still healing myself. I'm now working professionally on my silkscreen. And you know, I only deal with people who are about something. You know, people who are constantly growing. I stopped hanging out with Shirley, and, Dana I want you to know, just because you don't see much of me, doesn't mean I'm not with you. I'm always here with you even in spirit. I know you are busy doing your thing, but don't lose sight of your incarnation objective. I'm working on big projects, Dana, so I want you to do the right thing. I want to help you prosper.*"

"Okay. Oh God! I can't believe how good you look and you look so happy! How can I be as happy as you, Mommy? I miss you so much. When can I come and visit you?" I reached out to hug her.

"*I am at the bus stop on the ave of Lee. Catch the 12:20 bus to…*"

"Huh?" Blue lights dimmed. Mommy's white, lace dress took form to the light inside of the white, lace lampshade that Donell turned on.

"Dana," He shook me again, "Lee is waiting for me at the bus stop on the ave. It's 12:20. I need to borrow a twenty."

"Here." He took the $20.

"Thanks, sis."

Damn, a fuckin' dream.

25
=7= *love*

Happiness was written all over Mommy's face. I want that. I long for that kind of happiness. The peacefulness and love that radiated all over her skin, the glow on her face and the sunshine all up in her soul. Do I have to die to experience that kind of joy and light and happiness?

Let me get up and count my earnings from last night. Mmm, three hundred, three-fifty, four-fifty, five, seven hundred. Damn, so many singles. Let me see how much Jamie's check is for. Oh my God! I dropped it on the floor and then I took a look at it from afar while adjusting my vision. I definitely read it correctly. Nine hundred, ninety-nine dollars and ninety-nine cents? I called him and asked him,

"Jamie, what kind of joke is this? I don't like to make assumptions but it looks like you purposely wanted to make me a penny short from a thousand dollars. Why?"

He laughed slow and very sexy,

"You would have to put in a penny for your thoughts."

That was rather corny but then again it was cute enough to make me blush. I analyzed his business card, Jamie S. President of A&R. Epic Records.

My goodness, he pretty much has his life together. I'm hoping he would accept the parts of me that still needed developing and healing. I still have some more work to do on myself. I'm working on clearing the scars Sherman put on my heart.

One day I hope to end up with a decent, beautiful, smart, black man. Maybe get married and have children, like five of them. I hope to someday become a successful writer and dancer and be able to walk down the street without being harassed. Now that's a good life. To be able to do what one planned to do and succeed in the craft yet attain peace on earth. No stalkers, a decent private life but ultimately receive respect from people. Now that's the life. Traveling is what's up. And if I look at this situation through positive eyes, I can say, "What a blessing! I am so blessed to be open to receiving love." I felt it in my heart that this trip to Jamaica would be an uplifting experience for me. *It is time to change my life around. Time to reinvent Self. Before I receive this beautiful man, I need to get my shit together. I have to find my own happiness inside me so that I won't depend on him for it. I want to be able to bring something to the table.*

Dana Makieba Strong. My companion will accept me for who I am and love me more than I could love myself. No, that's backwards. My companion will love me just as much as I love myself. I can't believe I still believe in my beautiful brothers after going through so much shit with them.

NOTICE: To all my black men, hope still dwells inside me. You have hurt me and I have done the same to you and sometimes I feel like giving up on y'all. But I won't. I need y'all. I love y'all. Yes, there are sisters like me who are loyal and still love y'all.

Jamie called and after talking to him for three hours, I have made up my mind to go with him. It was the way he spoke, the words he used, and how he thought. Our chemistry was on point. I found it comfortably strange to want to keep him in my life. Something about him was so true and pure. I can sniff out a gamer but Jamie was no gamer, I would say he's a tamer no blamer. He can tame the grey spots in my personality without judging me. That right there made me trust him even more.

Jamie and I made a plan. I didn't feel comfortable letting him pay for both of our tickets so we agreed to go dutch. He pay for the tickets and I pay for the room and board. I left all of our information with Donell just in case anything should happen to us. We were set to leave for 7:45 tomorrow mornin. He's going to pick me up. We will be staying in Negril, Jamaica for seven days and six nights. Talking about excited? I feel scared but it's a good scared. I can hear Mommy telling me to 'go ahead and experience change'. Maybe this new place would give me ideas, insight and inspire me to start writing my first novel.

'The Sheeps?' He told me, he didn't frequent strip bars, he was just hanging out with his old buddy Michael. He said, he found it flattering that many dancers offered to give him free private dances but he had to respectfully decline. I figured he might have a girlfriend. He told me it wasn't that, he just didn't feel comfortable getting down like that with women who didn't care to know who he was. Having lap-dances or private dances with women he did not know wasn't his idea of having a good time. He told me, 'My parents taught me, early in life, that a man's body is just as precious as a womans'. We must protect and value the fact that our bodies are our temple.' That was something new to me, I never heard anything like that coming from a black man's mouth. Jamie was on some other shit. He said,

"With me knowing this, why would I want to get down and mix with lower body people. I ain't tryin' to be all preachy or nothin' but I'd rather go in that cave to uplift these women and enlightenment them than to go down there and join them and call myself having a good time and I know they are really not. They just need money.' He stared into my eyes and I felt his sincerity.

"So why did you want to get down in the cave and mix with me, since I was in a lower body environment." I asked.

"You were that diamond in the mine."

Jamie has traveled with his father through out the world. He seems a little spoiled but I can see he is trying to not take everything for granted. He told me he was a Muslim for thirteen years and through his religion he learned discipline which was good but the down side to his development, he found himself passing judgments on people who were not Muslim. He felt his religion was better than other religions. Through awareness, he realized that he wasn't growing and he took a hiatus from Islam. He began to recognize that it was religion that kept him separated and out of touch with his peoples. Religion is set up to box people inside of a whole lot of guilt. That shit ain't natural. Then he put two and two together and added that if he were still a Muslim, four whatever reason, our paths would not have crossed.

Jamie shared a lot of his past and present experiences with me. He poured light and knowledge into my mind and stirred my emotions until he concocted something like a love potion that was too soon for me to drink. I read the potion.

'WARNING! NOT FOR FALLING IN LOVE ONLY FOR STANDING IN LOVE.'

Dear God, if Jamie is you, please show me a sign now. As soon as I closed my eyes, I felt something like a sprinkle of water touch my lips and in a split second of me opening my eyes and breathing in, I smelled the scent of fresh pollen grace my nose. Just like that I sneezed.

Thank you dear Lord. All praises are unto you.

26
might be trippin'

I can't sleep. I'll take a nice milk, chamomile and honey bath and then I'll shave my legs.

I pray that this trip will be beneficial in every way for us. I pray we will arrive there safely and back. I can't believe I am going to fly to another country with a man I just met the day before yesterday! Can't front though, the energy between us is truly kinetic. This is weird but at the same time I trust myself. I trust God. Besides I'm bored with living my life too safely. It's time to take wise chances.

As I reflect on my meeting Jamie in the Sheeps (which is very rare)I must say, that meeting him was no coincidence. Nothing is coincidence or chance. Everything has a solid reason and purpose behind it. Thank you for sending Jamie. He's one of your angels.

The phone rang. I just spoke to Jamie and he told me he's in the car right now on his way to the airport. Shit! It's 6:45 and I only got an hours' worth of sleep. The car will be here in five minutes. Am I ready for this trip? Whew, yes. I'm wearing my beige khaki pants, my black pointed pumps and a black V-neck silk top. My hair is pulled back in a neat ponytail. I am natural this morning. I smell good like almond oil mixed with cocoa butter. I love me. I love my hair, I love my eyebrows, I love my eyes, I love my nose, I love my teeth, I love my ears. I love my skin, I love this beautiful pimple on my cheek. I am proud of me for trusting in you God. If only I can hear your voice Mommy. The car's horn made me jump.

On the way to the airport, the sun rose quickly like fire in the sky. Strong winds blew while seagulls balanced themselves still in the air. The driver pulled up to Delta airlines. I spotted Jamie waving at me with his bright and beautiful smile. His colors were neutral and earthy greens. Our hug felt natural for some reason and boy it felt so good.

"Good morning, Dana. How are you feeling?"

"Beautiful."

"And you're lookin' beautiful."

We walked through baggage claim together and boarded the plane in first class. I am very impressed with Jamie's disposition. I saw two beautiful, brown-skin Jamaican flight attendants. He kissed my forehead in front of them. Jamie and I ate breakfast and then we napped. The flight was a smooth one. The pilot said it was 89 degrees now." As we landed on the grounds of Jamaica, instantly I felt the difference. I smelled the difference in the air. The air felt thicker and it smelled cleaner. The skies were filled with abundant clouds. Tropical, warm winds blew trees that sat on top of pregnant lands. Jamie took my hand like it been his for seven years and I didn't mind. A sweaty van driver took us to our destination which was about 2 and half hours away. The driver's seat was the right side of the vehicle which I found to be quite weird. That confirmed to me that I was definitely out of the United States.

We drove through the village market and saw indigenous people selling fruits, vegetables, nuts and live meat under their tents. I like this place because there were no traffic lights. There were only stop signs that read "Give Way." I saw chickens running across the streets, goats and even donkeys too. Some people didn't wear shoes, others didn't wear shirts and it was all right. It was all good.

I turned toward Jamie, "Have you ever been here?"

"Yeah," his smile looked reminiscent, "My close friend has a vacation house in Negril. He went away to Europe and he's coming back by the end of next month. You don't know how glad I was when you said you wanted to go to Jamaica."

"Why?"

"Because this place here is one of my favorite spots to vacation. I thought of Hawaii because there is this particular place in Maui, I never been to before." Jamie's cologne teased me. He smelled so fresh, so natural, mmm. The driver made a turn off the road, onto the beach into a pink and green beach house. The more I looked at Jamie, the more his beauty intensified. The way his eyes moved when he was in thought, the way he communicated with the driver and the way he communicated with me made potential for loving him unconditional. We would do well together. We sat so comfortable with each other that the driver thought we were husband and wife. When we told him that we were just friends, the driver blessed us and told us we look very happy together. We unloaded the bags and Jamie stood at the door looking for the right key.

"Is this a rental or what they call a villa?"

"No, this is his vacation spot."

"Does he mind we're here? Does he know that we're here?"

"Dana it's okay. I spoke to him already. He said we could use it but don't abuse it." I laughed.

"I want you to meet him one day. He's in Europe working on some project dealing with architecture."

"That's good he trusts you with his space."

"Yeah. His father and my father are real tight. Michael's his brother. When you told me you wanted to go to Jamaica, I thought it was the perfect opportunity to come here since he's out of town."

We walked into a complete wooden spacious house that spelled tons of money. Beautiful wood carvings shaped closet doors and paisley designs carved wooden ceilings. African portraits roamed freely on the walls and beautiful exotic plants rested peacefully on floors with the suns' rays shining from the glass ceiling. This earthy home felt like the warmth of chamomile-honey tea with a pinch of cinnamon to fill my belly on a cold, snowy, winter, Sunday morning. I followed Jamie into a spacious lime-green kitchen. Wine bottles decorated the walls. I watched him open the windows and the back door. The deck was filled with beautiful, colorful wild flowers. Seagulls flew and called from above. A few feet away in the backyard was a moving shore. I opened the bathroom door and bright white shone in my eyes. A big, hallow tub sat in the center of the white tiled room. What a life to live! Imagine living a life like this. Me, being an author, living in this beautiful beach house on the land of Negril Jamaica, writing abundantly healthy novels.

A violet and yellow butterfly flew threw the window and back out onto the deck. Under the sink sat a silky, shining spider web with a slender, spider chillin' in the center of it's being. I heard Jamie drop utensils.

"Jamie are you okay?"

"Yeah." He was okay.

"The energy feels good in here." I said.

"It does."

I walked around and found a nice picture of a happy, bald-headed black man smiling with great, ivory teeth. *It must be Michael's dad.*

"Jaime, what's his name?"

"Stanley."

He looks like a Stanley. I went into the kitchen. The kitchen smelled like peppers, plantains and cinnamon spices all mixed together. Jamie started writing.

"What are you doin'?"

"Making a list of what foods we need to buy."

"Can you cook?" I asked.

"My ass off." We both laughed.

He closed the refrigerator and added honey onto the list,

"Something told me to go and pick up some fruits from the market. It's okay, we'll get a cab. Come here." We embraced. I felt my heart jump over its beats. "How are you feelin'?"

I feel at peace, I feel special, I feel beautiful, I feel like I'm in love with you.

"I feel good. And you?" I asked.

"Blessed." We almost kissed but we stopped ourselves. "So." He exhaled, "What do you want to do today? It's a quarter to one."

"Let's unpack, and relax for a little while. I would like to go to the beach a little later and watch the sunset."

"Sounds good. Are you hungry."

"A little. I have a taste for some jerk chicken."

"Me too. I want some curry chicken."

We unpacked and I grew tired. Jamie made up the king-size bed. I relaxed on it and felt so damn comfortable. Jamie burnt some Sage and then Frankincense and Myrrh incense. He put Gil Scot Heron's CD in the CD player. The vibration in the house rose high like Heaven. The oceans' warm breeze blew ripples through white see-through curtains.

"I can see you're tired so I'm going to run out and get some food for us. I'll be back like in an hour, okay?" Jamie bent down and kissed my forehead twice.

"I'm glad you came down here with me. You are one bold, brave and special woman."

"Jamie, I am only a mirror of what you see." With that, Jamie took in my lips with his and I could've cried from his pure tenderness. His tongue tasted so sweet. That was the right spot. Jamie…made me throb. I wish we knew each other longer. I would love for us to make love but it would only have to be at the right time, and in divine light. First, we need to finish dating. *Ahh! I have to write in my journal.*

I was awaken by the scent of fresh flowers laid across the pillow. I heard rummaging of paper bags in the kitchen. I sat up in bed and picked up the bouquet and couldn't resist sniffing them.

"I picked them from the backyard." Jamie said.

"Really? They're beautiful. How thoughtful of you, Jamie. Thank you. You don't know how much I love flowers. I'm almost flower obsessed."

He laughed.

"You know, God is good." I said.

"All the time, all the time. How are you feeling? Did you get enough rest?"

"Yes. I feel much better."

"Good. C'mon, let's dance." I hesitated at first but then I couldn't resist spinning myself around his finger. Then we did the hustle, laughing together doing the bump. *If only, if only you could read my mind, Jamie that I am standing in love with you.*

Jamie and I walked and talked on the white sand. We learned alot about each other and where we stand today and what was our purpose here on earth. I felt real comfortable with his comforting touch and non-judgmental attitude. He was the first person I told of what Mommy passed away from. I cried hard over Mommy. I didn't realize how much I had missed her. Jamie wiped my tears with his beautiful, blue handkerchief. He told me he empathizes with my grief and he would be here for me. We walked to a restaurant on the beach and I ordered a jerk chicken dinner and he ordered an escovitch fish dinner and a curry chicken for later. His manly hands held mine as we said grace together. We fell in love with the food. The chicken tasted unbelievably fresh! I must say very different from America's steriod, infected antibiotic chickens.

He felt comfortable with me to express his feelings about how he cared about me and that he wanted me to stop dancing. I told him I had already planned to stop dancing for it was slowing me down from attaining my goals. Yes, the money is good for now, but it's really my writing that has longevity.

"I knew you had it in you, Dana. Although, we had just met each other a couple of days ago, I feel comfortable enough to tell you that I am very proud of you."

"Thank you so much. Why do I feel like we've been friends for a long while?" He agreed. "You know, I haven't heard that since my mother was alive, 'I'm proud of you.' And I feel comfortable telling you that, I care for you."

We healed through gentle kisses wrapped in tender tropical breezes. In between sips of Pina Coloda, my sugar waltz flooded a pool all over my private property. Oh, how I wanted him to just dive in and swim deep up into the abyss of my heart. Instead, we went back to the beach house and fell asleep holding each other.

DANA WAKE UP.

"Huh? What time is it?" I looked at the clock and it was 5:45 in the morning.

I WANT YOU TO GET UP AND TAKE A WALK ON THE BEACH WITH ME.

"Yes, Lord."

JAMIE IS STILL ASLEEP, DON'T WAKE HIM. LET HIM REST.

"Okay, I'll leave a note for him." *YOU'LL RETURN IN 2 HOURS.*

I covered Jamie with the sheet and took the walk on the beach. Soon the sun became one with the stars in the sky. Earth's music began with the beauty of the ocean waves clashing and relaxing on the shore over and over again. The seagulls used their voices to communicate with the universe mixed with a chorus of crickets. I touched the water with my toes, and inched myself in until my knees were hiding inside. Curious, tiny, colorful fish swam around my legs.

DANA, WALK OVER THERE.

The green on the trees' aroma filled my lungs with healing oxygen. With each step, I cracked small branches under my feet. I heard drums play from a distance. I followed the sound up a hill, pass the rocks and trees. I stepped over, ducked and weaved in and out of gigantic, bamboo leaves. What a beautiful planet earth is. 'Please dear God protect me from snakes'. I walked faster, following the sound of Djembe drums. There, I found a group of men and women and some children singing and playing music to different rhythms. They wore colorful elekes around their necks and white cloth covering their heads. Incense smoke swayed like a genie upward to the heavens. Flutes played, Ishake's rattled, cow bells rang, powerful drumbeats and hypnotic chants invited me into the circle. My eyes connected with everyone else's and some form of telepathic communication took place.

Just then the rhythm of the drumbeat changed. The music slowed down and a Priestess began to chant a beautiful song. The chant was contagious and catchy. I began to chant along with them while snapping my fingers. The snapping of my fingers was my musical instrument. I lowered my voice because I had the strongest urge to listen to their beautiful voices. This chant's melody was slow moving and erotic. Ahhhh!

It sounded just like food for my ancestral spirit. I walked inside the circle, stopping and listening to every voice that sang from out of their mouths. I loved the sounds that came out of the second soprano. She sang with great passion. Her voice was sensual and strong with a tint of pain all intertwined together. Involuntarily, my eyelids kissed and vibrated about. My ears grew hungrier for Song. Song moved my hips and twirled my wrists. It rolled my shoulders around and around and arched my spine. Chant was moving all up and down my body in one spiral line. Then I snapped my fingers double time. The muscles in my cheeks began to quiver, I could not speak.

Everyone in the circle expressed love to Oshun. Their harmonious voices swayed my body sensually. I inhaled deeply and exhaled twice as long. The Djembe drumbeats, the flute, the cowbells, all the music and the beautiful chants intoxicated my spirit. I didn't know what was happening to me, but that flute became my lover. I kept flute near my side. Flute made me dance, it made me flutter, it made me spin and it made me cry. A feminine energy led me away from the musical sounds to a nearby pond. She held my waist so that I didn't fall and she dressed me up.

The chants opened my heart while my eyes remained closed. The life inside their voices made this deity inside of me hungry for more song. A China Musk scented woman, fed me, sweet, raw honey. I drank sweet champagne, or was it rum? I ate meaty mangos and wet and juicy strawberries while holding an orchid to my nose. The smell of Cuban cigars made me crave for a drag and I couldn't resist taking a pull from that good ganja. In time, my body grew tired and so did the chorus. A high Priest offered Oshun her chair. I sat. The music quieted down to a stop. Moist leaves, cigars smoke and incense mixed with a quiet anxiousness clouded the air. The Priest kneeled on one knee and lit my cigar. I heard the Priest ask the deity Oshun a question, and she answered back. Oshun wanted all the little girls and little boys to sit beside her. I heard the children hurry beside me. All I know is, the message I sent to them wasn't coming from my own mind. It was Oshun talking from inside of me. I heard words come out of my mouth but it wasn't my voice. I could barely talk, I heard myself whispering. I don't remember any of the wisdom I shared. When my eyes gave way, Oshun exited me. I looked around and everyone looked thankful and content. Then the deity Oshun entered a Priestess.

She laughed, danced, sang, smoked, drank, licked honey and rejoiced. She was very professional, very talkative and humorous. She liked to party. She made everyone laugh at her jokes. After Oshun left the Priestess, she sat down in a yoga position to stop her energy from being depleted.

I received a hug from the entire class and everyone was surprised that I experienced my first trance. I heard some of the teenagers speak amongst themselves while I wiped the baby powder off of my face with the lappa they clothed me with. I walked to the nearby pond to wet the material and knelt down. I saw my reflection. I observed rose petals in my hair, red lipstick on my lips, green and yellow elekes around my neck. What a sexy, green and yellow 2-piece dress they styled me in. I placed the pretty orchid on the right side of my hair and washed the rest of the powder from around my chin and neck. *Wow, this deity went all out with her femininity.* I removed the copper and brass bracelets from my wrists, and the rings from my fingers and the elekes from my neck and placed them back onto the Oshun shrine.

"Yeah, dat was deep, mon." I heard a voice say as I was preparing to leave.

"No mon', deep not the word. Dat right dere was special, mon. Dat womon de mon', she's gifted wit the transmission of energy, mon'. The gods got plans for her, mon."

Priest Zion gave me three hugs on each side of me.

"So how ya feel now daughta?"

"Different but I feel good. I feel renewed," I said.

"This is why you have ta keep coming back, mon."

"Okay, I'll think about it." We hugged again and I felt as though he healed me.

"Make sure you do dat you know, because you really need to get back in touch wit the ancestors you know, the spirit, you know. An really talk to Self."

"Yes. And thank you." Ashe! Ashe!

27
a fiction novel

By Dana Makieba Strong

Chapter 1 Seeing Through The Wool

Darcel wondered how will she act when she sees Karil again. It's been almost a year since they had seen each other. She spoke to herself, "don't act, just be. Go with the flow. Don't forgive him, don't forgive him, don't forgive him." She reaffirmed to herself. "He used you! Remember he dissed you for that bitch, Brigette!"

For the 5th time, Darcel checked her appearance in her full-length mirror before meeting Karil. She turned around to see if her panties were lined correctly. She powdered the shine off of her nose and forehead then hurried into the bathroom. Grabbed the potpourri spray and ran through her apartment for the third time spraying. Then she opened the windows so the air could blend the potpourri scent naturally throughout the house. The sun was calming down and the winds were stirring cool. Pretty soon the green on the trees will turn yin colors and spin themselves away to the pavement. The car's horn beeped again. She scanned her entertainment room quickly to see if everything was in its proper place.

Karil sat in the Dayton Lincoln cab waiting for Darcel to come downstairs. His eyes connected through the car window with hers. She comfortably stared back into his mysterious eyes. He opened the car door and stood in a pose. They began to walk toward each other. They shared similar smiles. He embraced her and she inhaled his Tunisia and Myrrh Muslim oil. Then she opened her eyes to get a good look at him.

"It's good to see you." Darcel said. "You look great."

"Yeah." He sighed. He grabbed her waist and said, "You're lookin' greater."

She massaged his muscular arms. "Let's get inside, there are too many satellites." She pulled him by the arm.

"You mean satellite dishes?" He followed.

"No, I mean people around here are nosy as hell."

"Oh." He sped up.

As they entered her apartment, located on 76th street and 1st Avenue, Karil inhaled the flower essences. He didn't want to sit; he stood looking at her 10-foot high windows and her beautiful plants.

"Maybe you should close the windows. It's feeling cool in here. Should I remove my shoes?" He asked.

"Yeah." He neatly placed his gray Prada shoes against the wall by the door.

"I miss it here." Karil said looking around.

Darcel stood saying nothing. She used that silent moment to close the other two windows.

Flowered plants hung from all seven of her windows. Oak and cherry wood framed pictures of Darcel and her dance class, replaced the romantic pictures she and Karil took in Puerto Plata and Brazil.

"It still feels great in here. That's one of the things I liked about you, is you know how to put good energy into your home. Warm vibrations."

"Thank you." What does he want? She thought. Darcel excused herself and went into the bathroom to unwrap her indigo Gele'. Darcel reaffirmed to herself, 'He's trying to creep his way back into my heart. Don't fall! Be strong!'

"Are you still at the florist shop?" He asked.

"No. I found a job teaching modern dance." He followed her voice halfway to the bathroom.

"That's what's up. I'm glad you're utilizing your talent. You know I stopped by the florist shop last week and Rosa didn't even tell me you left."

"She wasn't supposed to." Darcel thought again, "I was too upset with you."

She removed her Gele' and sprinkled some water to loosen up her matted hair. She massaged her head and suddenly her kinks loosened and curled up. When she walked out, Karil paused and stared at Darcel with drop jaw. She stood there giggling, waiting for his compliment.

"You cut your dreads?" He flatly said.

"It was time for change." She felt like she needed to explain.

"I can't believe you cut off your dreads? Why?"

"Karil, I carried my locks around my neck, shoulders and back for 7 long years. It was time. My girlfriend, Pam started my locks, and she is so mad at me now. But I don't care, cause it was I who had to carry the weight around my head, not her."

"No doubt. But wow, your locks were so long and beautiful. And now as I look at you I can see more of you." She did not sit down until he was finished exploring her new look. "I can see your features now. Your face, your neck and...you don't look so bad."

"I know. Thank you."

"You're still the same. Miss Vain."

"Correction, Miss Confident."

"You go, girl."

Karil walked through her kitchen, passed her dining room, and made a left to the entertainment room. He stopped in front of her broad collection of CD's. He scanned through the alphabetized CD collection and picked out a CD to play. Darcel slipped her manicured feet from out of her dance slippers and relaxed herself onto her leather, brown couch. She grinned at his clean white Kenneth Cole tank top tucked comfortably inside of his black Dolce and Gabbana jeans. His chest sat upright and firm. Two of his nipples pierced through his tank top.

"Are you still in the gym?" Darcel asked.

"6 days a week."

"I could tell."

'Still a fly guy. Hasn't changed a bit.' She thought to herself. Darcel's ankles circled around, as she watched Karil stand in his sexy pose opening the CD case.

"So what's new Karil?"

"Just working hard on new projects."

"Any love in your life?"

"Any love in yours?" He questioned back.

"Inconsistent love," She facetiously said. "If you know who I'm talking about."

"Huh?" (if you can huh, you can hear.)

"Did you bring any trees?" she changed the subject.

"Indeed my Queen." He pulled out the Skyy album cover, laid it across his lap and began to clean the weed. He chewed a seed.

"Karil, I've always wanted to ask you this."

"What." He looked at her attentively, adjusting to her new look.

"Why do you always eat the seeds?"

"I don't know. That was something my father used to do, so I just kind of picked up the habit from him."

"Oh. What does it taste like?"

"It tastes sweet. That's the secret to telling the difference between what's good weed and wack weed. This is good weed. This seed has a sweet taste to it. And I only found one. Bad weed has a lot of dry seeds in them."

Karil rolled the blunt on the album cover and licked it to a seal.

"Here." He handed her the blunt to spark.

"What kind of weed is this?" she asked, lighting the stove.

"Hydro."

"Mmm." She sparked the blunt. They took a moment to inhale and exhale the green vapors. He opened the CD player and placed the disk in.

"What are you about to play?"

"You'll see." Smiled Karil.

Darcel took in another pull and said, "Damn…This shit is good. Yeah, you got hooked up big time with the good green."

Karil pressed play. She stared somewhere in concentration, listening and waiting for the music. "Oh shit. Sly." She said in calm surprise. "You're the best, Karil!"

Darcel stretched her chest up and her arms out to him like a swept away dancer. Karil received her. He danced with her and held her lean body close to his warm and strong body. And together they sang,

"You got me smiling, again."

"Look at you," he said, as he pulled her chin up to get a good look. "And that pretty smile." He kissed her forehead and then tilted himself and kissed her full moist lips. Karil draped Darcel in his love and kissed her soft cheekbone. She almost suffocated from his overwhelming passion.

"Wait…Wait…" She said surfacing herself, "I need to get something to drink." Girl came back sipping on wine. Karil suddenly laughed.

"What's so funny?"

"You are."

"Why would you say that?"

"You're just funny. I thought you were going to bring out some

juice or water and you came out with a glass of wine. You are funny."
She laughed with his perception.

"Here." She handed him the empty glass. He steadied the glass
while she poured the wine in. He taste tested it by circling the wine in
the glass, smelled the wine and then tasted it.

"This is good. What kind of wine is it?"

"Rodney Strong Merlot. Let's make a toast."

"To you." He said. They sipped and resumed to dancing in deep-
down kissing. Glasses were placed on the floor inside wine puddles.

Darcel danced and spun herself around Karil's finger. Then he
placed his hands onto her hips and thighs. She began to grind her
cute-little-o'l-juicy-ass on his stiffness. Her C size magnets attracted
Karil's palms to cup them. Without much attention, clothes melted to
the floor. Undergarments and straps barely hung on to attractive body
parts.

He inserted his finger to see what he was getting back into. His
penis harden through his exploration. Her warm tightness pleased and
excited him at the same time. Her scent was mild, sweet and edible. He
licked his fingers and kissed her earlobes and spoke in.

"You're so wet." The two couldn't believe her extreme wetness.
Darcel's wetness aroused them. She began to moan softly. Her respon-
siveness drew Karil to kneel and deeply kiss and lick her love. In each
kiss, with each lick on her minor lips, Karil gained power from her
essence. After she came, she grew weak like a man. Karil kissed her
body up north. Darcel gathered all of her strength to turn her face to
break away his suction. An unsuccessful hickie. He began to kiss her
on the mouth. She smelled her mild, sweet scent on his mouth and
couldn't resist the interesting flavor. They kissed wildly.

Karil could not break his desire to kiss her soft and moist lips. His
expressive, strong beautiful hands magnetized Darcel to helplessly surrender all of her armor. 'Fuck it, you only live once,' she thought. She
kissed and stroked his head a few times. Her open mouth, with hot
breath, came dripping down some warm salivary juices all over Karil's
sweet and sensitive head. He instantly switched places with Darcel.
She held his vulnerability in the back of her throat, just sucking, devour-
ing his sensitivity. Then she chilled and pleasured his head between
her big, warm and supple breasts.

The two shared themselves, intertwining. Karil licked Darcel's
smooth, long legs and then he entered her palace while gripping onto

her ankles. She cried in bliss.

"Stop. Please."

"Why?" he did not like interruptions.

"I'm cuming."

"Go ahead, baby." He jumped out of her and sucked her clitoris and then resumed sex. Karil couldn't stop himself from pumping in her wet and warm walls and tasting her again and pumping again and tasting her again. Darcel reached orgasm after orgasm, et cetera after et cetera. Karil brought full pleasure onto her red chakra point. Faster and faster he pumped his iron inside of Darcel's wet muscles.

"Oh Karil! You're...so...big...and...juuuicy. Oh God! Oh Yes! That's it. You've hit it right there!" In the heat of the passion, she screamed out "Aah...fuck me!"

"I love you, damn." Karil told her for the first time. She gasped his love inside of her walls. "I love you. I love you. I love you. I love you."

"You're going to make me..." He was ready to let go. She changed position to doggy-style. Her walls tightened and waited for Karil's food.

"Wait, please. I'm about to come too. Please wait for me Karil, baby." She begged.

Karil had consideration for Darcel's needs. The best way for him to hold back his ejaculation was to concentrate on the eczema rash that was on the back of his children mother's ass. It was the sounds Darcel made with her strong kegels that interrupted his concentration.

"I've gotta come now, baby." He warned.

"That's not my name."

"Darcel....Darcel..." He grunted. "Darcel".

"Oh Karil!" She cried back, squeezing her legs and arms around him.

"Where do you want me to go?"

"In me."

"Can't do that."

"On my face." He hopped on her stomach and coated all of his vitamins and nutrients all over Darcel's face. She masked his semen onto her skin, leveled herself up and swayed her sexy hips into the kitchen. She quickly began blending fruits together from the blender and handed Karil a tipping glass full of a fruit concoction.

"Thank you, babydoll. What's this?" He asked in limp weariness.

"A natural protein drink. Strawberries, spirulina, vanilla Rice Dream, vitamin E, C, and D and raw honey. Giving you back everything you lost."

"Why, thank you for caring so-." He looked up at her face. "What tha fuck is that on your face?"

"You." She calmly laughed.

"You are crazy." He laughed.

"You're just as crazy as I am 'cause you're still sitting here with me."

After he finished the beverage, Darcel kissed his forehead. He fell fast asleep. She grabbed the cordless phone off of its cradle, closed the bathroom door and called Pocahontas.

"Hello?!" Poka yelled.

Darcel whispered in screaming excitement. "Poka, we did it, girl!"

"Y'all did it? Hold on, I got to hear this. Let me turn this thing down." She lowered the volume on her radio and pulled her long hair to the side to connect ear to phone.

"Okay."

"You got time to talk?" Darcel asked.

"Yeah, whatssup?"

"Girl, I don't even know where to begin."

"Anywhere." Poka was impatient.

Darcel sighed a long pause.....

"Come on girl! I don't have all year."

"Okay. You're ready?"

"Stop playin' Go ahead."

She blurted out. "He told me he loved me."

"What? Karil told you he loved you?"

"Yup, I can't believe it. He said it when we were making love."

"One question. Did he say it before or after."

"...During."

"Ahh shit!"

"Why do you say that?" Darcel continued in her excitement. "Girl his love is so intoxicating. His sausage is so fucking delicious! Whenever I think about him, my clitoris jumps."

Poka laughed. "You're crazy girl." she continued. "But seriously, he must really love you." Poka said in a daze.

"Why do you think that?" Darcel grew hungrier for Poka's wisdom.

"'Cause if he tells you he loves you before sex, he's just sayin' that just to get some ass. Now if homeboy tells you after, then he really meant it. Now if he says it during..." Poka thought about it for a second. "It's a possibility that it could just be pillow talk, so he can keep getting some more."

"But why would he wanna pillow talk me? He knew me for what, almost 3 years?"

"Wait, what position were y'all in when he said it? Tell me his exact words." Poka started analyzing. Darcel's twinkling eyes stared behind the sea-shelled wallpaper in her bathroom.

"He was laying down, and I was riding him with my back facing him and he said, 'I love you, damn'."

"I don't know girl. That's hard to decipher. He probably meant it." She optimistically summed.

Poka added. "Or he could've been talking about how much 'he loves your sex.'" She sucked her teeth in and said, "I don't know. This is hurtin' my brain. Well, how did you feel about it?"

"Umm, I was stunned. I was open. I kept telling him over and over that I loved him."

"Never do that again. Once a man hears those three words come out your mouth, he knows he got your coochie on lock."

"Damn! Then I fucked up!"

"Calm down. You didn't fuck up. You was basically expressing yourself like most of us women do. See shit would be different if he put a ring on your finger, then yeah you could tell him how much you love him all you want but not while he's courting you."

"Okay. Well, as I think back on how he told me he loved me, he sounded sincere. I mean this is the first time Karil ever told me something deep like that."

"Question is, why all of a sudden he's telling you, he loves you now?"

"I don't know."

"Be careful Cells. Just take whatever he says lightly."

"Thank you Poka."

"Hold on." Poka clicked over and came back. "Cells, let me hit you back, Cory's on the other line."

"Stay afloat sister. Stay Afloat. Don't let yourself drown in his love."

"No doubt."

"I'm a talk to you later."

"One."

"One."

Darcel grabbed the down comforter and before covering Karil with the comforter, she couldn't help but stare at one of God's most beautiful and unique designs that laid across her couch. She watched Karil's chest rise and fall. The soft hairs on his beautiful, chest glistened with sweat. She had to bend down and kiss his beautiful feet. Darcel imagined Karil being her man, all to herself. She inhaled his Muslim oil and snuggled behind him holding on to his body. She began to meditate and wonder if he really meant what he said about Brigette. Does he still love Brigette? I mean she does have his kids, maybe he should.

"Karil?" Darcel called softly. He didn't answer.

"Karil." She lightly tapped his nose with her finger.

"Huh?"

"Sweetheart, I'm sorry to awake you like this. I need to talk."

He turned over and gave Darcel his full attention while blinking his pink eyes.

Darcel could not stop blushing. "Okay. I'm trying to formulate my words. Are you still with Brigette?"

"No. I told you already we broke up a long time ago."

"Okay. I want to know if you still love her."

"I care about her."

"Karil, then where do we go from here?"

"Where ever you wanna take us."

"I want you to be my man."

Karil smiled on her as if she was a five-year-old child. "You're so cute and bold…we have to have a serious talk about that when I wake up."

Darcel wondered if he just told her what she wanted to hear. 'Only time will tell, she thought.

The next morning Karil did her a favor by over sleeping until noon. She spent the morning preparing breakfast. Karil woke up to (2) eggs over easy, (1) Belgium waffle, (3) free range Italian turkey sausage, Oat crisp toast and a large glass of freshly juiced oranges.

"Thank you baby. Breakfast was delicious." Karil's cell phone rang constantly. He spoke in tones like it was a business call. He spent about a good 20 minutes on the phone.

"Karil, I want us to finish talking about that." Darcel said with arms crossed in front of her heart.

"Darcel, listen, I'm so sorry but this is not the time for me to talk about that right now. I have to go down to the office. Some fucked up shit just happened." He coated her face with quick and hurried kisses.

"So, I'll call you later?" He said exiting her door.

"If you want. I can call you." She said to his back.

She watched Karil get into the Dayton Lincoln cab. She waited for the cue to wave goodbye but he looked straight ahead, pointing while being driven away. Suddenly, Darcel felt empty. She felt her presence was long forgotten about as soon as Karil got into the cab.

"Oh God, please help me. I need strength. Am I being used, Lord? Help me, please. Was Karil being honest about Brigette? Please reveal the truth, Father/Mother. A men."

Darcel removed her down comforter from off of the couch. She carried the comforter hugging and inhaling Karil's scent. She placed the comforter back onto her bed and laid wrapped in it, like a burrito. She could not stop replaying last night over and over in her mind. She enjoyed thinking of Karil's formation. She inhaled his fragrance in her down comforter deeply while paying attention to her body. She felt the slackness in her walls but Darcel was in no hurry to do kegels instead she made love to herself and fell into a light sleep.

The phone rang and she sat up, wiped the saliva from her cheek and pressed the talk button.

"Yeah."

"Hello?"

"What's up, Poka."

"This is not Poka."

"Oh sorry, who's calling?"

"Brigette."

Time told. Prayers had been answered.

"Brigette? Oh. How did you get my number?" Darcel asked in bewilderness.

"I pressed redial on my phone. This was the last call Karil made last night. Is Karil there?"

"No...He just..." Brigette interrupted.

"Wait, who am I talking to?"

"This is Darcel."

"Okay. So he was at your place. Did he spend the night there?"

"Umm, yeah."

"What?"

"The only reason why I'm telling you this, is because I'm realizing he lied to me, big time."

"About what?"

"He told me that he was no longer with you."

"He did?"

Silence interfered for a few seconds.

"That muthafucka!" Brigette said to herself. "Something told me to press redial and I'm glad I did."

Darcel listened.

"You can never fully trust a man! No, I'll give him the benefit of the doubt. He didn't sleep with you, did he?"

"I'm sorry about this." Darcel said.

"No it's alright. Thank you for telling me. Y'all did it huh?"

"Yeah."

"With or without protection."

"both."

Brigette's nerves scattered throughout her body.

"That Bastard! What did he tell you about me?"

"He told me that you and him weren't together anymore and that he cares about you because you are the mother of his children."

"What? We've been together for five years!" Exclaimed Brigette. She then calmed herself and asked. "How long have y'all known each other?"

"Well, we've been messing around, off and on for about 3 years."

"Three years?"

"Yup. And he tells me he loves me and that you know, his phone will get turned on and that he and I are meant to be together. He even spent nights here. His friends Kamau, Eli, Devon and Kito's been here too."

"Kamau has been to your house? He's like an uncle to the family. Did Karil ever take you out or spend any money on you?"

"No. That's the chief reason why I can't be with him. I told him I couldn't be with him because I have needs too. I need to be wined and dined. I'm not gonna lie, no disrespect but I do love him. He told me that you came from the ghetto and he feels like you can't relate to some of the things he go through. He said I have a lot more in common with him because of the similarities in our backgrounds and upbringing."

"I can't believe he dragged my name in the dirt to make himself look squeaky clean. Nobody walking this fucking earth is perfect. You know what I'm saying?"

"Yeah."

Brigette sniffed a few times, "I gave natural home births to his children and breastfed them. Wash his funky underwears, and I'm holding shit down for this family and he goes behind my back and talk about *me* like a bitch to a total stranger!"

"Well, I've known him for 3 years."

"Yeah, and you knew about me for three years, and you still hung around him. Desperate women are just as bad as these horny men."

"I'm not desperate, he told me that you and him weren't together."

"That's not *thee truth*. That was *a truth*. When we would get into our arguments, it was you who's house he would spend nights at." She concluded.

"After 3 years, I find it hard to believe you're now finding out about your quote on quote good man. Y'all must've argued a lot because for a minute I thought he and I was going somewhere."

"Let me tell you something. I'm different from these other unintelligent, desperate bitches. I respect a man's space. I don't pry into people's private business, like insecure average hoes."

"So pressing redial is not an exception?"

"No, intuition is. All I know is that Karil loves me and his kids. But I tell you one thing, that muthafucka couldn't stay two days away from me and his kids if his ass wanted to. Darcel, I know you don't have any kids yet but you should try and have empathy for me. Karil has a family that he takes care of and he loves very much."

"Well, Brigette it takes two to tango. He told me that you proposed to him and he couldn't accept it because he was still in love with me."

"What?!" Brigette exclaimed.

"He told me that you're always in your own world with the kids and that you don't really see him for who he is. He said that you are not the woman he wants to be married to. He said you and him are not compatible."

"I can't hear anymore of this...the devil's a liar! You know what! You can have the muthafucka all to yourself. I want no parts in this mess." Click.

Darcel knew she couldn't take back what she revealed to Brigette.

An apology wouldn't hurt though. She *69 Brigette but the number was blocked. Darcel thought about how much Brigette sounded just like Karil. 'Maybe that is what happens when you're with someone for so many years. You start to sound alike.'

Brigette cried a deep, deep cry while Darcel was relieved to have brought light to Brigette's heart. So now Darcel can move on with her life because Karil is definitely not man enough to be truthful with her. *A man who lies is a mouse.*

Brigette haven't cried a deep cry since she was a little girl. She hugged her children and didn't know whether she was going or coming. She took deep breaths and laid toys out on the floor in the kids' room. She squat down to face her son.

"Karil, baby. Can you do Mommy a favor?"

"Huh?"

She corrected him. "It's yes, Mommy."

"Yes, Mommy."

"I need you to go into your room and play quietly with your sister, okay?"

"Okay." Four-year-old Karil Jr. answered.

"Mommy will be in her room for a moment. We're going to Uncle Wray's house, later?" Tears were welling up in her eyes.

"Yea!" Karil Jr. jumped up and down. "We're going to Uncle Wray's house and we're going to Disney World! And I'm going to meet Mickey Mouse!"

"Yes, baby. I want you and your sister to play quietly okay?"

"Okay, Mommy."

Brigette prayed, cried, and howled in her pillow. She left an urgent numeric message on Karil's voice mail. He called back immediately.

"What happened baby?"

"Who are you, Karil?"

"Huh?"

"If you can huh, you can hear. What world is truer to you? Mines or Darcel's."

"What are you talking about?"

"Darcel told me almost everything. I couldn't hear anymore. Karil…" Brigette's sorrow drowned her speech. Brigette listened to the fear in Karil's voice.

"Baby, it's you and the kids who are truer to me."

"I can't believe you betrayed me! You told a stranger about my business, Karil?! Some lonely and desperate whore! How dare you?! Karil, you fucked her? So you're in love with her, that's why you didn't marry me? So she's going to be a Mrs. Darcel Black?"

"No…I don't want to marry nobody but you. You're going to be Mrs. Black. I didn't marry you because I wasn't ready.." She interrupted.

"You know what? I don't even care anymore. I'm not giving you a choice to decide who you want. I'm making my choice right now." Her mumbles soon turned into shouting. She mumbled clearly, "Telling people about me, dragging my name in the fucking dirt like the crack of your ass don't stink! All this time you've been riding my back for your success while I've been holding this damn family down! Well I tell you what, you ride all the hoe's backs and see how far your ass'll get in your successful, happy life."

"Baby, please…"

"Don't 'baby please' me! You kept me in the fucking dark with everything?! Played me. That was my fault for giving your ass too much freedom and trust. Nigga, I've been good to your ass, loyal and faithful and you were out there fucking around on me with another fuckin' girl who you claim to be much more compatible with? You are so weak and wack. A true fuckin' loser."

"I want only you Brigette, please. Please let me explain myself…" Brigette interrupted.

"Ah, ah. No muthafucka. I love life. I want to live to see my great-grand kids. I'm not trying to catch A.I.D.S. I'm up here thinking I'm in a fuckin' monogamous relationship with you and I'm in the same boat as all these other lonely, single women. I've got to protect myself baby. It's a shame I can't even enjoy a raw dick with my own damn man! If you want the kids, you can have 'em. I can't believe you deceived me after all these years."

"I'm coming home, so we can talk. "

"No, really it's okay 'cause, If I see your face, I just may kill it." Click.

Brigette gathered the travel bags and all the clothes. She left all of the family portraits behind for Karil to keep.

Life was now serious for Karil. His family was his inspiration, motivation, his foundation and his life. Darcel meant nothing to him in this moment. She was just an interesting piece of wet and tight good pussy. He knew that if he lost Brigette, he'll lose himself. The Dayton car service waited at the red light. It's fifteen minutes before rush hour. Karil prayed for traffic and all the lights to agree with him. They were unanimous. Seconds was not fast enough for him. The car paused at a red light about a block and a half away from his house. Karil ran out of the car without shutting the door. His chauffeur understood and pulled up and waited in front of his house.

Karil was already in the house, calling out "Brigette! Brigette!" Their family pictures that hung through out the living room were all smattered all over the floor. Karil stepped over broken glass, and broken in half roses. He called out the kids' name. He heard a musical playing in his daughters' room.

"Please God, let everyone be okay." He stepped on broken pieces of glass. Karil disappointed his Brigette so bad that he was this close to taking his own life. 'Are they alive? Did she break out and leave the kids here?'

Karil's mind raced. He knocked but no one answered. He opened the door and his children's clothes were scattered all over the floor along with some toys they left behind. Karil fell to the floor and cried like a bitch. He wished he could blame everybody, he wished it was all Satan's fault. But Karil could only blame the person in his stupid, weak, ass body. 'Where could she have gone?' God whispered in his ear. Karil ran to the phone and pressed redial. Busy signal. 5 seconds later he pressed redial again. The phone rang,

"Thank you for calling John F. Kennedy airport, where America greets the world."

Karil hung up the phone and ran to the car.

"Abdul, take me to JFK airport."

"Do you know what airline you're going to?"

"Oh shit, no. Just drive, we're looking for a red Land Rover."

God asked Karil and Karil didn't have to think about it. "I truly am ready to marry Brigette, I love her."

Traffic was getting heavy around the airport. Karil told Abdul to stop the car and wait for him. He ran toward the parking lots to find her red Land Rover. He stood looking around but couldn't help overhearing two little girls singing a rhyme and clapping hands.

"Miss Mary Mack, Mack, Mack." As the two little girls continued to sing he heard the words in his head go:

"Miss Brigette Black, Black, Black

All dressed in tack, tack, tack
With golden lovin, lovin, lovin
Like warm butter muffins, muffins, muffins
She asked her uncle, uncle, uncle
For 15 cents, cents, cents
To see the elephant, elephant, elephant
Jump over the fence, fence, fence
He jumped so high, high, high
He reached the sky, sky, sky
But Brigette never came back, back, back
Till the Fourth of July, lie, liar
Karil's soul is on fire, fire, fire.

Brigette never returned for Karil's second chance. He wasn't lucky, like most men.

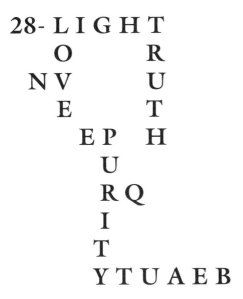

Whew! I completed my first chapter to *Seeing Through the Wool*. Thank you Lord for allowing me to finally meet my potential. Jamie and I didn't want to depart at the airport. We didn't want to separate. We did a lot of talking in Jamaica. He gave me a lot of insight, helped me write an outline and a business plan on getting on with my career and out of the projects.

After the car trunk slammed, and the driver disappeared, I looked toward my building. Stillness. Still the intercom is broken, still the grass is uneven, still there is broken glass in the hallways, the elevator is broken, and piss on the steps. I unlocked my door to a still house with the TV still on. I opened the windows and let the breeze circulate. Donell was in his room sitting on his futon playing some game on the Play Station.

"What's up, Donell?"

"What's up?" He stayed focused on his game. "How was the trip?"

"Beyond beautiful. I heard God's voice as clear as day."

"Word? What'd he sound like?"

"Like. Like, I can't imitate God's voice. It's a voice I remember I used to hear all the time when I was two. And you know what's even better?"

"What?" Donell's eyes was glued to the TV.

"I touched Heaven. You would not believe this but I went through a spiritual awakening. I was taken by a divine deity."

"How?"

"It was early in the morning and I heard God tell me to get up and go for a walk. I walked up the hills and heard Djembe drums playing. That shit sounded hot."

"You went by yourself?"

"Yup. 'Cause Jamie was asleep."

"You are one bold bitch. Look at you all tanned. So how do you feel? Did you bring me anything back?"

"Yup, a chapter."

"You started your book! That's good, yo!" I like when Donell is happy for me.

"Donell, I have some news for you."

"Good or bad?"

"Good for us."

"Okay, go ahead."

"Jamie and I had a long talk and he helped me write out a serious plan so that I could move ahead in my life instead of staying here in this rut."

"Sounds positive."

I took in a deep breath. "Donell. Jamie, hooked me up with a real job starting next week."

"Doing what?"

"Writing for this new hip-hop magazine."

"Say word."

"Word."

"Oh shit! That's dope."

"And...I'm moving into a one bedroom apartment brownstone up in Cobble Hills, Brooklyn."

"Brook-Nam?!" Donell was cheezing. "Well sis, here's some news for you. I won't be staying here for too long either."

"Really?"

"Because Marcia wants to rent her basement out to me."

"Word? Her house is beautiful."

"Yeah, it is but eventually, I want to own my own house. You-know-what-I'm- sayin? I'm ain't trying to fall into her trap. A brother gotsta be free."

"I hear you."

"So Jamie hooked you up with a crib and a job? That's whats up....and no strings attached? Right?"

"None, besides the ones I want attached."

"How old is he?"

"27"

"That's what's up. I got to meet the brother."

"You know that. And all jokes aside, if things get fucked up between you and Marcia, my door is always open."

"Thanks sis. You know I'll be alright. I'm a man and I will find my own way. You know you should tell Nawnie about this. She'll be so proud. And I'ma remind you of what Mommy used to tell us, 'Whatever situation you get yourself into, make the best out of it. Always, do your best.' "

"Thank you. I was thinking about letting Nawnie stay with me for a while too. She's getting too old to be by herself, you know?"

"Yeah. That sounds good. So how much is your rent? Do you know what the apartment looks like?"

"Jamie described it to me as a nice and cozy spot. Tall windows and ceilings. And guess how much I will be getting paid for writing?"

"How much?"

"Two dollars a word."

"Dude must got a lot of power to put you on like this."

I handed him "Chapter 1, Seeing Through the Wool." Donell's expression showed genuine happiness. I could tell he was proud of his sister.

"Dana, I'm proud of you." We hugged. I opened the door to my room and Donell began to read.

I looked around my room and stared at the walls Mommy painted. I fell on the bed and stared at the ceiling. What a virtue patience is. If there is something a person wants, she has to work hard at it, endure all the bullshit until she obtains it. All praises unto you the Indefinable Essence. I thank you for having my back throughout my journeys and thank you for continuing to. You have never failed me, forever I shall remain faithful unto you. All glory be unto you. All of the wealth and riches you shower upon me will go back to my peoples, my communities and to the AIDS research foundations. I promise I will never forget from whence I came.

I love you, eternally.
One Love,

Dana Makeiba Strong

About the Author

Darcel Turner was born in the Bronx, New York and also raised in Queens. Darcel attended Long Island University, The College of New Rochelle and Medgar Evers College in New York. She has worked with The Fourth National Black Writer's Conference and has danced on internationally known stages such as Harlem's Apollo Theater. Darcel's voice can be heard on the hip hop artist, Talib Kweli's *Reflection Eternal* CD "For Women" song. God, music, dancing and prayer inspire her to write. Darcel is also inspired by the talents of authors such as: Zora Neale Hurston, J. California Cooper, Paulo Coehlo and Kahlil Gibran. She is currently at work on her second novel. Darcel resides in Brooklyn, New York with her son Amani and daughter Diani.

For book readings or signings with Darcel Turner contact: **nitewriter28@aol.com.**